THE MO�ON
IS
BACKWARDS

THE MOON IS BACKWARDS

A NOVEL

JUSTINE STRAND DE OLIVEIRA

ISBN: 979-8-9858254-0-4 (Paperback)

The Moon Is Backwards is a work of fiction. All incidents and dialogue, and all characters with the exception of some well-known historical figures, are products of the author's imagination and are not to be construed as real. Where real-life historical persons appear, the situations, incidents, and dialogues concerning those persons are entirely fictional and are not intended to depict actual events or to change the entirely fictional nature of the work. In all other respects, any resemblance to persons living or dead is entirely coincidental.

Front cover image © Shutterstock.com
Book design by theBookDesigners

Printed in the United States of America

First printing edition 2022

Luar Livros
401 The Greens Circle
Raleigh, North Carolina 27606

www.justinestrand.com

For Judite

PROLOGUE

2022

Life makes sense in retrospect. In the day to day living of it events seem random, people and places like pieces of a jigsaw puzzle thrown on a table, and I had no idea where to begin to sort them out. It's only with the passage of years that I see how one thing led to another, how bad things made it possible for good things to happen later. Tragedies may have been foretold but happiness was always unexpected. I have no regrets because all of it made me the woman I am today.

The days and years that brought me here are tantalizing bits of color and sound that flit away if I try to focus my mind's eye on them too sharply. The evening sun bathes the veranda in golden light and I'm soothed by the sound of the waves, the rustling of palm fronds, the scent of jasmine. A light wind riffles the turquoise water of the swimming pool, the gardeners bustling about to finish their work before darkness descends. The distant roar of a jet climbing after taking off from the airport pulls my attention to the sky as it ascends to curve above the sparkling ocean before turning on its path south, its destination no doubt Rio or São Paulo. How I longed as a child to go to Rio, a place of magic to my young mind.

The leather-covered box on my lap is scuffed from years of handling. I can never remember everything that's inside so it's a surprise every time. I remove the lid and put it on the table beside me. First the postcards, tied in a bundle with ribbon. They were so vivid when I bought them but they have faded like old movies, like memory itself. The candy-colored beach-front hotels of Miami Beach, the Christ the Redeemer statue with his arms outstretched above Rio de Janeiro. The vast high plains in the interior of Brazil with the skeletons of the first ministry buildings marching toward the future, images in black and white that don't capture the blood, sweat and tears that made the construction of Brasília possible in just three years.

Family photos in black and white: a stiffly formal portrait of my mother and father on their wedding day, my father in a dark suit instead of his usual white linen, and my mother wearing a lace-collared dress and a serious expression with a smile hiding behind it. A picture of children seated in the parlor of my childhood home; I am a young teenager and there are only eleven of us so it must have been taken in the early 1950s. My vivid smile gives no indication of the weight on those young shoulders. We thought we were wealthy because we had a well with good water and enough food to share with poor migrants heading south to find work in the big cities far from the drought-stricken Northeast of Brazil. Looking back, I recall the lack of indoor plumbing and the doilies covering the threadbare arms of the sofa, the pots and pans battered from so much use. We had everything we needed, but I longed for things that seemed just beyond my reach, things I couldn't yet imagine.

Then there's an old Toddy can, Toddy being the cocoa powder we put in milk when I was a child. I open the lid, releasing the aroma of chocolate. How is its scent so powerful after all these years? I unroll the papers inside, many written in a child's illegible scrawl, instructions for recipes I would later know by heart. Small notebooks with bound pages and carefully written words and definitions in English and Portuguese.

The photo of me as a young woman wearing a crisp white jacket and a look that's all business despite the joyful grin. Another photo of me looking a little shy in what today would be a demure bikini, standing at the edge of a pool of emerald water with a waterfall cascading in the background. Why is it that when we're young we don't think we're beautiful, and when we realize how beautiful we were, we're old and it's too late. This makes me laugh out loud.

I linger over the most precious snapshots of all, lost in the memories of love that changed me forever. The vitality of youth and seeming invincibility, inconsequential day-to-day moments captured forever. I have only a few photos but the pictures in my mind are indelible. Great love is worth everything, even when it breaks your heart.

The dog-eared brown envelope gives me pause, as it contains reminders of the nightmare that Brazil became after the exuberant inauguration of the new capital of Brasília in 1960. I had an unshakeable belief in the bright future of Brazil and the inevitability of order and progress, like it says on the flag. But things spiralled out of control and the military deposed the president and took over the country in 1964, a dictatorship that would last until 1985. Clippings of newspaper reports of protests: Bloody Friday in 1968 where several people were killed, later that year a march of 100,00 that brought on greater repression, and finally in 1984 more than a million people filling the streets outside São Paulo demanding direct elections. Those were dangerous times, though I held out hope as long as I could that things weren't as bad as they seemed. Eventually the people prevailed, thanks to many brave individuals who gave their lives, often without anyone remarking their passing. To think I was in the center of all that for a time.

A happier folder contains restaurant menus with handwritten notes on them, clippings of articles about food trends and restaurant reviews, business cards, hand-written thank-you notes, dried flowers pressed in waxed paper.

Through dark times and happy ones, I held close to my heart the words of my mentor when I told her my next life step frightened me: "This thing is scary. And you will do it. And when the next thing is scary, you can look back on how much you have done even though you were scared, and forge ahead. As they say, faith in God and your foot on the accelerator!"

"Grandma Eva, Grandma Eva! Come sing 'Happy Birthday'!" My great granddaughter appears in front of me, bubbling over with excitement and reaching for my hand. I put the box of memories aside and rise to follow her into the house, saying a silent prayer of thanks for all this life has given me.

PART I

1945

September 10, Monday

It is the rainy time. The river is full, wide enough to need a boat to cross. It rushes noisily over the boulders, carrying my heart with it. I want to jump and giggle. There is the rock-earth-rain smell as steam rises from the riverbanks. Everything is green. I am riding a bicycle, rolling along and laughing. The sun is high and there are no clouds. I don't have a bicycle. I don't know how to ride a bicycle. Up! My heart is full. I am flying, low above the water, twisting and turning. Birdsong mixes with the music of the water, chattering, chirping, whistling. Down. Down, burrowing under the covers. The birds are calling me.

"Eva, wake up! Get your brother! Cacilda will be here soon with the milk."

I slip my feet into my alpargatas and shuffle over to Samuel's crib. He is standing up holding the rails, bouncing up and down. "Come here, little guy. You're wet, let's change you. You will have to give up your crib before long because the new baby will be here soon." He clutches at my hair as I pick him up. I pull off his soaked diaper and put him down on the bed. He wiggles his legs and blows spit bubbles as I change him.

I pick up Samuel and we head for the kitchen. I love carrying him around. He is my big live doll and I love to squeeze and kiss him. Sometimes my heart is so full of love I can't stand it and I have to pinch his cheeks and the love is so strong he cries from the pinching and Mamãe scolds me. I love that baby milk smell when I nuzzle his neck and get a whiff of its sweetness. Samuel no longer gets mamar because Mamãe needs to keep up her strength to make milk for the new baby.

Cacilda is in the kitchen, stirring the milk over the wood fire to purify it.

"Oi, Cacilda! All good?"

Cacilda grins at me. "All good, Eva."

Cacilda is not much older than me, but she doesn't know how old she is. I am almost eight, maybe she is eleven or thirteen. Her family lives in a mud house with no windows, all one room. She works for Mamãe helping around the house and yard, for a bit of money and good meals. She doesn't go to school. Her daddy doesn't believe girls should go to school.

I go to school. My Papai believes everyone should read and write and do arithmetic. He has a good job with the post office now because he taught himself to read. He became a real gentleman on his own. Now that he reads and does math he rides the horse with the mail from Natal to Recife and all the biggest villages in between. He has been gone for two weeks and is due back tomorrow. My new sister (I want her to be a girl!) is expected in three weeks.

The café is ready. Bread, fresh cheese, cassava cake, butter, fruit jellies and steamed yams are laid on the table. Daniel stumbles into the kitchen rubbing his eyes. He likes to sleep and is annoyed until he gets used to being awake. He is seven and we go to school together every day.

Then comes Ana, she is five, and Paulo, he is almost four. They sit at the table and I pour them hot milk and add cocoa powder. I stir to cool it off before they drink it. They reach for bread and ask for butter and jelly.

"Children, not just bread and sweet. Cacilda, Eva, give them some yam." Yam is put on a plate for each, smashed and with butter. Everyone eats. Mamãe says that quiet time when everyone is eating makes her feel happy. She sits next to Samuel and picks up a small spoon to feed him. She stops for a few seconds, looking down at the floor. She looks up and takes a breath.

"Eva, my angel, feed this to Samuel, would you?" She sits back in her chair and closes her eyes.

"Mamãe, do you want me to fix you a plate?"

"No, querida, I'll eat in a bit. I just need to rest for a minute."

We finish eating and I help Cacilda clean up the dishes. She prods the fire and adjusts a big iron pot full of bones, the stub ends of carrot, and onion peel; Mamãe wastes nothing. I love the smell of the broth as it gets stronger. Papai says Mamãe could make soup from rocks and it would taste delicious.

Cacilda and I go outdoors to do our morning chores. She pumps water from the well and I put out food scraps for the pigs and check around the yard for eggs. The chickens like to be clever and hide them where I can't find them. I can't resist a mango that just fell. It is September, near the end of the mango time.

"Eva! It's almost time to leave for school! Look at you, covered in mango! Wash up and bring me a comb to fix your hair. Teacher will not be happy if you are late."

I wash my face and arms at the pump, rinsing my mouth and wiping my eyes and nose. I run inside, get the comb and sit down on the floor in front of Mamãe's chair. She combs my hair and braids it. I love to have my hair combed. There is little time so I have to have one big braid. My hair is getting very long. Pastor says girls should not cut their hair. Mamãe's hair is past her waist. Mamãe ties the end of the braid with a cloth. Daniel is waiting, lolling about while I get ready.

"Blessing, Mamãe!" Both Daniel and I ask for her blessing.

"God bless you, my daughter. God bless you, my son. Study well!"

Daniel and I walk up the dirt road toward the center of town. The sun is high and it is already hot though it's only seven. Dust swirls and clings to our shoes. We walk past the bridge. The River Picuí is just a trickle. We are lucky we have a well with sweet water. Many people are leaving the sertão to try to find work in the cities of the south. Papai told me their animals die for lack of water and food. He says with no food, and no work, they walk south looking for a better life.

Daniel and I pass the big church in the central square. The spire is so tall I think its cross can touch heaven. Our church is very humble and it has no spire or cross because Papai says that is vanity. We must fear God. A fancy church is like trying to be God, which man cannot be, Papai says.

We enter the schoolyard. Teacher is calling the children into the classroom as we arrive. We take our places on benches. There are sixteen of us, all different ages. As teacher enters, we all rise. The Brazilian flag and a map are on the wall, and we face them. We place our hands on our hearts and sing the national anthem, the younger children just humming because the words are hard. To the side of the map of Brazil there is a map of our state, Paraíba. Paraíba is the pointy part of Brazil that sticks the farthest out in the ocean, closest to Africa, although not that close.

We add and subtract, the older children carrying numbers, the younger ones working with easier sums. Older children do times tables. Then we recite a poem we have learned:

"My land has palm trees, where the thrush sings . . . "

Teacher hands out books and tells us to turn to page 15. I turn the pages, my heart beginning to pound. We have read some of the story already. Teacher asks a student to begin reading at the top of the page. She begins to read aloud. I am listening but I'm also trying to find the words she is using. The letters dance on the page. I want to read them, but they are a mystery I cannot solve.

"Very good, Maria. Eva, you may read next."

The moment I dread. I cannot do it. I cannot read. I begin to tell a story that would make sense: what could happen next.

"Eva! I did not ask you to make up a story, I asked you to read." Her hands are clenched, her knuckles on the desk. I can smell the café on her breath as she leans over me.

"Well? What do you have to say for yourself? I am losing my patience. Every day the same thing. You are eight years old and smart enough to read. You are just rebellious, eh? Well, not today! Go sit outside on the veranda."

I hold back the tears until I am outside. I want to cry like when you are so sad the water squirts from your eyes. But I won't. I gulp back the tears and my chest hurts from the effort. I want to read so badly. My eyes just don't work. Papai taught himself to read when he was already grown. Why can't I learn how? Tears sneak out of my eyes and down my cheeks. My face feels hot. I can't breathe.

I sit on the bench outside the classroom, looking at the wall, painted blue to as tall as the top of my head, then white above. The floor has been mopped clean but small dusty footprints walk into the classroom. I want to think of anything to distract me, to not think about teacher. Time crawls by. I can hear the children answering teacher. Then finally the shuffling of benches as everyone gets ready to go home.

Teacher comes outside as the other children leave the schoolyard. Daniel stands in the doorway, looking embarrassed. I wish I could melt into the floor.

"Eva, I am very disappointed in you. I have done everything I can but you still refuse to read. Tell your father and mother I will be asking them to come see me. You may go home now."

Daniel and I walk back home.

"Eva don't be upset. You will read soon, I know you will."

I choke back more tears and put one foot ahead of the other until we are back home. Lunch is being laid on the table. Mamãe says to wash our hands. We quickly wash up and come back to the table and bow our heads.

"Our Lord, we are grateful for this bread, for our lives. Bless this food to our bodies. Bless our home and all those we love. In Jesus' name, Amen."

We all murmur Amen and lift our faces to our plates. Mamãe looks over at me.

"Eva! What is wrong? You have been crying! What happened?"

I start gulping and breathing fast.

"Mamãe, the teacher was angry I could not read. I try, Mamãe, but I just can't!" I look down at my feet.

"Eva, you are a clever girl and I know you can do well in school. Please stop worrying for now and eat your lunch, and we will talk afterwards. Good?"

"Yes, Mamãe, thank you." I slowly start eating my lunch.

After lunch we wash the dishes and clean the floor. The younger children lie down in the hammocks on the veranda to take a nap. Mamãe watches Cacilda and me sweep and mop, holding the lower part of her big tummy and closing her eyes.

"Don't worry, Mamãe, we will take care of it. You sit and rest."

When the kitchen is clean, Cacilda lies down on the floor with her face toward the wall and goes to sleep. She likes to sleep on the floor. I sit down next to Mamãe.

"Eva, I love you so much. You are a smart, very good girl and we will work together to help you learn to read. I think your head is different somehow, but it does not mean you aren't smart."

She takes my face in her hands and looks into my eyes. Her

hands are warm and soft and she brushes a stray hair away from my face. She kisses my forehead and hugs me.

"Oi in the house!" The clapping of someone outside the front gate announces their arrival. We go to the front door and there is a man in ragged clothing, with two little girls hiding behind his legs. My mother greets them.

"How are you, sir, and your children? Are you from this area? Where are you headed?"

"We come from north of here. We have been on the road for some days. I hope to find work in the big city."

"Sir, have you had lunch already? Please come in, let us fix you some plates."

"Senhora, we are most grateful. It is very kind of you."

Mamãe tells me to wake up Cacilda, and we set about preparing meals for the strangers. They want to sit outside the front gate to eat but Mamãe insists they come into the yard and sit in the shade of the mango tree. The two girls are small and thin but their tummies are large. Their hair is light red and wispy. They watch me silently with their big dark eyes. When Cacilda brings the plates, their father tells them to say thank you, which they say quietly, their voices scratchy. They begin to eat slowly, looking all around while they eat. They gulp water. Their father chews his food slowly, watching the girls. They finish their food. Mamãe tells them to rest a while.

"Thank you, Senhora. May God bless you for your kindness. We hope to go on a little more before darkness comes."

We take their plates, and now they are out the gate and walking south again, disappearing down the dusty road. I look up at Mamãe.

"Mamãe, you always feed people who come to our gate. You give them plates and treat them like fancy people."

"Jesus said, what you do for your least brothers and sisters you do for me. These are our brothers and sisters in Christ."

The other kids are up and playing in the backyard. The sun is slanting towards evening in the soft gold of early spring. Cacilda and I are busy caring for the animals in the backyard, taking the clothes off the line and stacking them to iron tomorrow, and baking cake for tomorrow. Cacilda says goodnight and goes home.

We have our evening snack and café, and it is time for the younger children to go to bed. I tuck them in so Mamãe can rest. Papai will be here tomorrow; I know Mamãe is anxious for him to return.

I go into the living room and Mamãe doesn't notice me standing in the doorway. She is clutching her tummy with her eyes closed, panting.

"Mamãe! Are you all right?"

Her eyes open quickly and she looks around, her breathing slowing.

"Eva, go to Cacilda's house and ask her father to ride to Dona Severina's to ask her to please come. The baby is coming!"

"Oh, Mamãe! Will you be all right? I'm worried!"

"Go, Eva, and don't worry. This baby just wants to be a little early for his birthday!"

It is full dark now. I take the lamp and hurry my steps to Cacilda's house. I put the lamp down and clap several times.

"Oi in the house! It's Eva! My mother needs your help!"

Cacilda's father gets on his horse and rides quickly in the direction of Dona Severina. I run home as fast as I can with the lamp swinging and flickering.

Mamãe is on her bed, propped up on several pillows. Her face is pale and she is sweating. I know what to do from when Samuel and Paulo were born. Stoking the coals, I add wood to the stove. I put filtered water in a large pot to boil. I get up on a chair and bring down the basket with fresh linens. Things are almost ready when Dona Severina arrives.

"Eva, my child! You are a marvel. I know how much your mother appreciates how clever and helpful you are. Run next door and tell Dona Helena I need her help."

I run next door to alert Dona Helena, and rush back. Dona Severina is organizing things in the kitchen.

"I want to help you take care of Mamãe."

"No, querida, it will be many hours. It is late. Your mother will need a lot of help tomorrow. Dona Helena will help me. Sleep with the angels and I will come get you to meet your new sister or brother in the morning."

With that, she kisses the top of my head and pats me and turns toward Mamãe's bedroom. I can hear the women murmuring and bustling about as I drift off to sleep.

I am dreaming again about the rainy time. So much water in the river, the smell of the rain. The sunlight on the water, the birds and their songs mixing in my dreams as I burrow down into the covers. Someone is softly calling me.

"Eva, Eva, wake up! Come ask your mother for her blessing!"

I sink down into the dream and my covers again.

"Eva! Wake up!"

But I don't wake up. The voice mixes with my dreams and I go on sleeping.

September 11, Tuesday,

EARLY MORNING DARKNE*ss*

A baby's cry wakes me up. My new sister is here! I toss back the covers and hurry to Mamãe's bedroom. Dona Severina stands at the door.

"I want to see Mamãe! And my new sister!"

"Your Mamãe is resting, she can't be disturbed. Your new brother is going to sleep for a bit too."

"A brother? I wanted a sister! I want to see Mamãe!"

Dona Severina seems tired and she's so quiet. My tummy feels funny. I can feel the tears streaming down my cheeks. I want to see Mamãe! But I go back down the dark hallway to my room and get back into bed. The other children are sleeping; the rhythm of their breathing calms me, and I fall asleep.

I wake again though it is still dark. I slip quietly down the hallway and peek into Mamãe's dark bedroom. No one is there, but it smells funny. I go to the kitchen, also empty. I look out the door to the backyard, where light is flickering in the storage building. I hear voices, praying. The voices become louder as I approach the doorway. The lamplight flickers; soft murmurs of women crying. I am afraid to pass through the door to what lies beyond. What are they crying about?

I slip into the building. None of the women notice me in the shadows. There are four of them washing something on a table, wringing rags into a basin.

I can't breathe. My tummy hurts. A baby cries! In the corner, another woman picks up a baby and gives it mamar. Where is Mamãe? What are these women doing?

"José will be home soon. We must have her ready."

A wail bubbles up from my chest. No! Where is Mamãe?

Dona Severina turns from her work and sees me hiding by the doorway.

"Eva! How long have you been there?"

I am unable to stop the sobs, every breath is painful, I feel cold.

"Where is Mamãe?"

"She is resting with the angels, Eva. She has gone to be with the Lord."

"No! Lying! No! She is fine, she is resting!"

"Eva, she worked very hard to bring your brother into the world. But it was too much for her. Your father will be home in a few hours. We must prepare your Mamãe for him."

"Where is my brother?"

"Dona Maria is holding him. She still has milk from her baby, to make your new brother healthy and strong."

I run over to Dona Maria, sitting in the corner. The baby is mamando: holding fast to her breast. My tears stream down on the baby's soft head. He looks perfect. My heart is confused, filled with love and sadness. Maybe I am still asleep. Maybe it's a bad dream. The way things are in a dream, where you know it can't be real. But I am cold, the chanting voices, the prayers, the women washing something on the table. Mamãe.

Dona Severina says the other children must not be told. Papai will be home this morning and he must know first. Cacilda arrives and we get the children fed and send them out to play. I tell Daniel we will not go to school today.

"Why, Eva? Where is Mamãe?"

"She is resting with our new brother. Hush, drink your milk."

"I want to see Mamãe! I want to see my brother!"

"Soon, Daniel. Dona Severina is with them. Go outside and play with the other kids."

It still seems like a dream. My tummy hurts. I can't eat. The children are running around the yard and acting silly. Dona

Severina is with the other women in Mamãe's bedroom. They are cleaning things up. The floor and wall are covered with blood. Dona Maria took the baby with her to her house, she has to feed her kids. She will give my new brother mamar when he needs it.

"Hello, hello, I'm home!"

Papai is here. Dona Severina comes from the bedroom and rushes to the door, meeting Papai before he enters the gate. He stops, doesn't move. She walks up to him and quietly tells him something. Papai wails and drops to his knees in the dust. He throws his head back and cries big sobs. I have never seen Papai cry before.

"Oh God, mercy! How could you take her from me?"

He drops his head and weeps, holding his face in his hands. The sun beats down. It should be raining, raining hard. The sky should be crying. How can people be doing normal things, like nothing happened? People in the street move away, going around Papai. Dona Severina tries to console him but he keeps crying.

Time passes. Papai is weeping, on his knees in the street. Dona Severina stands there, praying quietly. Papai gets to his feet and walks through the gate.

"I want to see her." He turns to Dona Severina and she leads him into the house and out the kitchen door to the backyard. I watch from the doorway as he enters the storage building. He is there a long time. Papai appears in the doorway, wiping tears from his eyes and gasping for breath.

"Eva, gather the children in the living room. I must talk with them. Send Cacilda home. Dona Severina, please stay with her. I will come talk with you soon."

Dona Severina nods, and goes past me to the storage building. I go to gather the children and tell Cacilda she can go home until tomorrow. Everyone is silent. We kids move into the living room and sit quietly. Papai comes into the room.

"Children, Mamãe has gone to be with the Lord. She is in the place of eternal peace. Your new brother is healthy, thank God. We must go on. Mamãe would have wanted us to. Now let us pray."

The kids are starting to cry, trying to talk and ask questions, but Papai just looks at everyone and we bow our heads.

"Heavenly Father, be with us at this time of sadness. Lift up our hearts to praise You as Mamãe rests with You in the place of beauty and joy forever. Give us the strength to go on with our lives to the glory of God. In Jesus' name, Amen."

"Amen."

All of us are crying. How can there be so much sadness? We were happy yesterday. How will we go on? Papai is right to ask the Lord to help us be strong. I don't see how I can be. I did not say goodbye to her. I did not tell her how much I love her. I did not wake up when Dona Severina called me.

"Eva, please come to the backyard with me."

I follow Papai into the bright sunlight. He leads me to sit under the mango tree.

"Eva, I need you to be strong. You are the oldest and I need you to take care of the other children. I must continue to go to work, and you will have to miss school for a while."

"Yes, Papai. I will do my best."

He nods and walks to the storage building. He and Dona Severina talk quietly.

Dona Severina gestures to me. "Eva, come here querida. Please go get the neighbors to help me prepare your mother. Your father is going to get the coffin and arrange for the burial tomorrow."

I do as I am told, stumbling as I go to the neighbor ladies and ask them to come. They hug me and smooth my hair, saying sweet things.

The sun bends to the horizon as the day draws to an end. I watch from the door of the storage building as they dress Mamãe. She is lying on large pieces of cloth, and when they have made her ready, they use the bands of fabric to lift her up and place her in the coffin. Neighbor men have arrived and they lift the coffin and take it to the living room.

Women are busy in the kitchen, preparing café and serving the food people bring as they arrive. People pay their respects to Papai and to me; the other children are in bed. The preacher comes and joins the group, offering prayers. I am so tired I fall asleep sitting. But I won't go to bed. I will stay with Mamãe until she must be taken and put in the ground.

September 12, Wednesday

Mamãe has gone to be with the Lord. She has left this vale of tears for a better place, walking on the banks of the river with Jesus in heaven. We are going to the church today to pray for her soul and commit her body to the ground. I must get the children ready. They don't understand and keep asking for Mamãe. I don't understand how she can be gone. But I must be joyful that she is with the Lord.

Everything is different. I am sad but I can't cry because I have to take care of the children. Cacilda has come today but she seems lost; without Mamãe to guide us we do our best but the house is a mess. We have food because neighbors bring meals to us. My new baby brother has no name yet. I want to see him but he is with Dona Maria, who is caring for him and giving him mamar.

Papai walks back and forth in the yard looking up at the sky, praying. He must cry at night when we can't see him, because his eyes are puffy and red. He has not gone to work because we are at home with Mamãe and will take her to church and to the cemetery today.

Dona Severina comes to speak again with Papai; I hide and listen but can't hear everything she says. She is talking about blood: everything was fine, then blood, couldn't be stopped. Mamãe didn't suffer, she was gone quickly. My baby brother was born healthy before the blood came and Mamãe died. Papai hangs his head down while she talks to him.

Cacilda and Dona Severina and I get the children washed and dressed in their finest Sunday clothes and nice shoes. They are all very quiet and do as they are told without complaining and playing around like they usually do. Papai comes out of his bedroom wearing a dark suit. I have never seen Papai wear a dark suit, only in the picture of him and Mamãe on their wedding day on the wall in the living room.

The men from church have come to take Mamãe for the service. Papai won't preach today, Pastor Jônatas will be doing the service. Papai gathers us together and we go out the front door and into the street, following the men as they carry Mamãe's coffin through the streets to the church. People come out of their houses and join the procession, dressed in their Sunday best, walking silently.

We arrive at our church. We enter behind the pallbearers and they place the coffin in front of the altar. We sit together in the front. Everyone files in and sits in the pews. The church is so full that people have to stand in the back. Pastor Jônatas begins with a prayer then he begins to preach. He talks about Mamãe: that she was a good Christian, she loved the Lord, she loved her husband and her family, she was upright in the ways of the Lord, she cared for the poor. People murmur in agreement. He talks about something in the Bible and how good Christians go to be with the Lord. I can't really pay attention to what he is saying, and I look up at the rafters and try not to think about Mamãe being gone forever.

Everyone rises to sing a hymn, their voices filling the little church. A small band plays as people sing. The preaching, the prayers, the singing all blur together with my tears. Then the service is over and we walk into the bright sunshine as the men carry Mamãe to the cemetery next to the church. My eyes are frozen on the dark hole in the ground as the coffin is lowered. Papai throws the first dirt deep in the hole and there are more prayers.

Everyone goes back to the church, this time to the social hall, where huge amounts of food are laid out. The band is playing hymns and people get plates and fill them with food, everyone talking as they eat. I am not hungry but some ladies fix me a plate. I sit at the end of the table with my brothers and sisters as everyone is talking. Three women are talking about Papai.

"He may be crying, but he has a hole in his handkerchief."

"Yes, he is looking around, definitely."

"He can't possibly get by with all those children, what will he do otherwise?"

I can take care of the children, I am old enough. I know what to do. Mamãe taught me a lot about cooking. I will not cry anymore. I will take care of everyone, so that Papai can work and Daniel can go to school. And I will take care of the new baby as soon as he can take a bottle. I will show them.

1946

January 7, Monday

Spring turns to summer, the days pass. It is January, so Daniel goes back to school and I stay home to take care of the younger children. Cacilda comes every morning. Neighbor ladies come with food.

Papai puts on his white linen suit and goes to work every day. I get up early and make café for him with fruit and bread and fry him some cheese, and sometimes I make him tapioca like Mamãe taught me.

Papai is going to be staying at the post office in Picuí: they are giving him a permanent job so he doesn't have to ride the horse and deliver the mail. He worked very hard to learn numbers and counting money and now God has blessed him with this new job.

My new baby brother is named João. He is still with Dona Maria because he needs mamar, and making bottles is too hard for me with four other children to take care of. We walk to Dona Maria's house every few days to visit. She has lots of children but she feeds us cookies or rice and beans. Baby João is quiet and calm, always looking around at all the commotion with those blue eyes, eyes like Papai. I hold him and kiss him and I try not to cry.

We are six children with no mother. Samuel is two, happy and laughing most of the time. Paulo is three. Ana is five and she will go to school next year. Daniel is seven, very serious, helps me around the house when he comes home from school, does his homework. I am eight years old but I know a lot about taking care of the house and kids.

Things were a mess at first because caring for the chickens and pigs and tending the garden and making food and cleaning are very hard, but I have learned how to take care of everything. I get up early and go to sleep when all the children are in bed. Sometimes one of them will cry in the night and I hug and kiss them until they go back to sleep.

We go to church on Wednesday and Sunday. Papai preaches sometimes. I am obedient and follow the ways of the Lord. I must wear long sleeves. I must not cut my hair—it is down past my shoulders. I braid it to keep it out of my face while I work around the house. I pray with the children before we eat, before we leave the house for a walk to Dona Maria's, before bedtime. We ask for peace for Mamãe in heaven. We ask for strength and health so that we may serve the Lord.

It is not our will that decides what happens in our lives, it is the will of the Lord. When I work with Cacilda and the neighbor ladies to plan for our Sunday dinner, I can't say we will have a nice dinner, I say, we will have a nice dinner if God wishes it. And I cannot be proud of Daniel doing well in school, I must say, thanks be to God Daniel is doing well in school. And I cannot say it was wrong for God to take Mamãe, I must say that she is with the Lord and walking beside the river in heaven.

The days are hot, without a bit of rain. Sometimes there are little puffs of cloud in the distance, but they are just pretty and bring no rain. We have a well but we must be careful not to use too much water. Just enough for the animals, just enough to keep the garden growing, just enough to be clean. To wash clothes, we use the same water with a little soap and don't waste it: we pour it on the garden. When I was little everyone would wash clothes on the banks of the creek, but the creek is only a trickle now.

People pass through town walking toward the cities in the south, because there is drought where they come from. Parents with children and men by themselves looking for a better life. They stop outside our door and clap, "Oi in the house!" I don't answer them because I can't let them in and feed them like Mamãe did; we can't let strangers know we are children alone. I wish I could help them. The children look so tired and hungry. I say a prayer for them.

January 20, Sunday

It is full summer. The sun beats down on Picuí and the dust is everywhere. It sneaks inside the house when I have just cleaned and mopped the floors. It settles on the windowsills. I cover everything in the kitchen with dish-towels to keep the dust off. The flies are sneaky too, they buzz around and get inside when I am not looking. I always have a dish-towel over my shoulder, ready to swat a fly if she gets into the house.

Today we will have lunch at church after the service. Cacilda helped me make a maracujá pudding so we have something to take for the meal; it's easy to make and delicious. The children line up by the front door and I make sure they all look nice before we head up the road behind Papai.

The main church in town is big and grand, but ours is a simple building that is painted blue. We have lunch in the church after service on special days. Papai is a respected deacon; he was there at the beginning and helped build the church.

I'm not sure how many families are in the church, but they fill the hall. The church has one large room in front and a social room in the back, with a kitchen and long tables for eating. The older church sisters organize things and keep everyone in order for social times. It's not Christian to talk about other people in unkind ways, but I pay attention and listen as the women talk mean or laugh about people sometimes. I'm just a kid so they don't notice me paying attention.

"Sister You-know-who, she is having a time with her daughter."

"Yes, what a disgrace!"

"To think a girl from a good Christian family would sneak off with a man in broad daylight! How old is she, anyway?"

"I'm not sure, maybe fourteen?"

"Her mother must be so ashamed. Has she got her under control now?"

"Yes, I heard the girl is kept at home under lock and key. And I hear the guy left town—or maybe the father took the law into his own hands, I wouldn't blame him."

"One thing is for sure, that guy is gone. But a girl like that, if she'll do it with one, she'll do it with another."

"Mercy!"

The sisters busy themselves with putting the food out and everyone lines up and fills their plates, talking and laughing. The food smells delicious and it's making me hungry. I sit the children at a table and make them plates. Baked chicken, rice and beans, a slice of tomato. I can't eat until the children are settled, mashing their rice and beans and cutting the chicken into small pieces so they can eat by themselves. Samuel tries to eat with a spoon but he's so hungry he gives up and uses his hands. He isn't smiling, just busily chewing and looking around, but I know he is happy. Eating together without talking is a happy time.

March 5, Shrove Tuesday

It is March and we haven't had any rain since Christmas. It is not so hot but the dust is still everywhere. I wish it would rain hard and make that smell when the rain hits the dirt and everything gets clean and sparkly. I miss Mamãe but I don't have time to think about her because the children need me. João is six months old so he is home now, and I feed him bottles and soft food. The neighbor ladies come by every day, and Cacilda helps like always.

They are celebrating Carnaval in the streets by the main plaza, with music and costumes and dancing. School and work are closed so Daniel and Papai are home for a few days. Picuí is a small town so we don't have a fancy Carnaval. They say the Carnaval in the capital, Rio, is very grand, with costumes and parades like something from a fairy tale. I don't know anyone who has been to Rio because it is very far away, a beautiful city by the ocean with buildings dropped down between humps of mountains.

We do not celebrate Carnaval. Papai says the celebrations are far from the ways of the Lord. Worshipping a golden calf, like it says in the Bible. We can hear the music in the street. I would like to see but I am obedient. Children come to the gate wearing rough cloth bags over their heads with holes cut for eyes, carrying big sacks, begging for money and sweets. They make little growling noises to pretend they are monsters. I just wave them away.

I am happy Papai can rest for a few days. He sits outside under the mango tree and stares at nothing. I take him juice and some cookies I made.

March 6, Ash Wednesday

All the children are in bed and my chores are done, Cacilda has gone home for the night. Papai is sitting out on the back veranda by himself. I peek out the kitchen door and he's sitting quietly, looking up at the sky. He doesn't seem to be crying or praying.

"Papai, can I get you something? Some maracujá juice will help you sleep."

He turns to look at me, surprised, and I see his mind was somewhere else. "Oh, Eva. Come sit next to me, my daughter."

I sit down on the bench and look up at the moon, a glowing crescent nearing the horizon.

"Eva, is the moon rising or setting?"

"Setting, Papai. Because that direction is west."

"Yes, very good. What phase is the moon?"

"I don't know, Papai."

"Here is how to know. Raise your hands like this, and see that you can hold the round part of the moon in your left hand. The moon is getting bigger, waxing. The moon grows until it's full, then gets smaller until the round part fits in your right hand, the waning moon. Then it's dark, the new moon. And the cycle repeats every month."

"This moon is in my left hand, so waxing."

"That's exactly it, Eva."

I keep my left hand up against the sky, imagining that pearly slice cool against my palm, committing to memory what Papai just taught me. We sit in silence for a long time, then I get up and go to bed. Papai is still sitting outside when I turn out the lights.

March 23, Saturday

It is Saturday morning so Papai does not have to go to work. I am up early anyway, preparing a bottle for João and getting breakfast ready. Papai comes into the kitchen and I turn to greet him. He is wearing a dark suit.

"Papai . . ."

"Eva, I will be gone this morning, but I will be back by twelve. I need you to bathe the children and dress them in their Sunday best. Make sure the living room is presentable. I will be bringing someone to the house and I want everyone on their best behavior."

"But Papai . . ."

"That's all, Eva. Just make sure to have everything ready."

"Papai, don't you want café? I can make you tapioca with coconut. Or with cheese? Sit for a little while and eat, Papai."

"Thank you, my daughter, but I must be going."

He puts on his hat and goes out the door.

Something is making my tummy feel funny. I can't think well, but I must. The bottle! It will be too hot for João. I run to the kitchen and take the bottle off the stove. João begins to cry. I run to his crib and change his diaper, blowing bubbles on his tummy to make him laugh. I pick him up and kiss him and squeeze him too hard and he squawks a little. Holding João on my hip, I go to the children's rooms to wake them.

"Everyone up, get up! Papai has said we have to get dressed up for a visitor!"

"Eva, who is coming?" Daniel rubs his sleepy eyes and squints at me.

"Daniel, I don't know. He didn't say. But it must be serious because he is very dressed up this morning in church clothes. We have to bathe and dress for church."

"Are we going to church? It's Saturday!" Ana protests.

"I'm not sure, Papai didn't say. Everyone up! Make your beds! Daniel, get Ana and Paulo washed up. I'll lay out their clothes. I'll get Samuel and João washed and dressed."

My heart pounds as I feed João his bottle, sitting Samuel at the table with some bread and fruit pieces. No time to make juice. Cacilda arrives just in time to help with the babies while I run around and dust the living room, swatting the cushions on the couch and adjusting the crocheted pieces on the arms of the chairs. I open the shutters to let the sunlight in.

I have to get ready too. The children are quietly washing up outside at the pump, and I join them. They look at me with big eyes but don't say anything. I wash up and comb my hair, fighting to get the tangles out and tie it back with my Sunday ribbon.

Back inside, I dress quickly and Cacilda helps me get everyone ready. No one fights me like they usually do; they sit quietly as I pull the comb through their hair and help them put on their church clothes and nice shoes.

"Cacilda, we had better put together a nice café for the guest! Help me! What shall we do?"

"I will slice some cheese. And we can make toast with the leftover bread." Cacilda puts the cheese on the counter and begins to cut careful slices.

I stoke the fire to warm the oven, putting the bread on the counter to slice and butter before toasting.

"Daniel and Ana, go to the yard and get a papaya and any other fruit that looks nice. Bring me a few bananas, yellow, no brown spots."

"Yes, Eva."

Ana follows Daniel out to the yard. I get the special cafezinho cups out of the hutch, and the small silver spoons from the drawer. João is in his crib and cooing; thank goodness he isn't unhappy and crying. Samuel is playing on the kitchen floor with some pot lids I gave him. He might get a little dirty but I can't worry about that now. Paulo is sitting quietly at the table watching us work.

The café is ready to make, I just have to boil the water. Cacilda and I put everything nicely on a tray and cover it with a cloth. Time to gather the children in the living room: it's almost time for Papai to arrive with the guest. Cacilda will stay outside the kitchen door in case I need her to help with anything when the guest arrives.

We children sit on the small chairs in the living room with our hands in our laps, leaving the couch and nice chair for Papai and the guest to sit on. None of us speaks. The clock on the sideboard ticks, ticks, ticks. My tummy still feels funny. I hope Papai will be satisfied with how we children are dressed, and the café Cacilda and I prepared. We sit and wait and the clock ticks.

The front door opens slowly. Papai walks in carrying two suitcases, which he sets down beside the door. He takes off his hat and hangs it up. His left arm reaches out to the guest. She is a young girl with curly black hair and dark eyes squinting after being outside in the sunlight. She has soft, rosy cheeks and her lips are closed in a tight line. Her flowered dress is tight against her tummy and chest. She looks around at all of us children, then looks at Papai.

"Come in, come in, Amara! I want you to meet the children!"

The young girl steps hesitantly into the room, her eyes darting about. Papai puts his arm around her shoulders.

"Children, Amara and I were married this morning. You must respect her and show how we are grateful to God that she is now part of our family!"

I can't breathe. My chest hurts. I can't see, everything is black. I want to vomit. But the clock ticks, ticks, ticks and somehow I start breathing again. I look at Papai but he is looking only at the girl, helping her to sit on the nice chair.

"Eva, bring us some café!"

I can't speak, I just walk to the kitchen, somehow. I put my head out the door and whisper to Cacilda to come help me.

"Eva, what is it?"

"Just boil the water and make café."

"Who is the guest?"

"Not now! Please just make the café and then go home, go out the back way."

"But Eva . . ."

"Not now!"

The café is ready and I bring the tray into the living room. My hands are shaking and my legs feel soft and loose. I move slowly and carefully and put the tray down on the small table by the couch and chair. Papai looks at me and raises his eyebrows, so I begin to pour the café. The young girl speaks.

"No, no, I don't want nothing."

"But dear . . ." Papai begins.

"I just want to take a nap. I'm tired. Where is my room?"

"Of course, querida, let me show you. Eva, bring the suitcases to my room."

I stumble after them, carrying one suitcase at a time because they are heavy. The young girl lies down on Papai and Mamãe's bed and rests her head on a pillow. She curls up and turns her back to us, and Papai covers her with a blanket.

"Eva, close the shutters so she can sleep."

I reach to the window, pull the shutters and latch them closed. The young girl begins to snore.

My feet walk me around the house, tidying and cleaning without thinking. Papai is sitting in the living room reading the Bible, but I keep my eyes down to the floor. I can't look at him.

I send the children to play outside and I stay in the kitchen with baby João. I put him on a blanket on the floor and he is happy. It feels like a bad dream where everything is crazy but you know it's a dream because it doesn't make sense.

My face feels hot. I go out by the side of the house and try to throw up but there's nothing in my tummy.

"Eva, are you all right?" Daniel has come up next to me.

"I'm fine, Daniel, don't worry."

"Eva, I need to talk with you. I don't understand why Papai brought that girl home!"

Daniel and I go sit under the mango tree. I want to cry but I can't, it will upset the children and I don't think I have any more tears left. I just feel tired. And very sad.

"Eva, what is going on? Who is that girl?"

"Daniel, you heard Papai. He married her. She is our stepmother now. She married Papai, so she is our Madrasta."

"But she is just a kid, she's not much older than us, is she?"

"I don't know, Daniel, maybe she's older than she looks."

"Do we have to call her Mamãe?"

"I will never call her Mamãe. She is not our Mamãe. I will call her Senhora."

We sit there for a while without talking. I feel so lost but I must try to act normal for the children. What will happen now? How will we live with this new Madrasta? I don't understand how Papai could do this. He married without a wedding. And just brings this Madrasta home, like that is a normal thing? I may be a kid, but I know it's not.

"Eva, come inside please!"

Papai is calling from the kitchen doorway. He has changed back to his linen pants and a shirt. I walk into the kitchen.

"Eva, please put some lunch on the table. Can you do that for me?"

"Of course, Papai."

There are beans in a pot on the stove and I stoke the fire to warm them. I put oil in another pot once the fire is hot, and some onion and garlic pieces, and stir them until they smell good, then add rice and stir it all around. Then comes water, which bubbles up. Stir, lid on pot, put to back of stove for low fire.

I go out to the storage room where the carne de sol is hanging, and remove the cloth covering that keeps the bugs off the dried meat. I use the big knife to slice off a piece. Mamãe never let me use this knife, she said I wasn't old enough. I take the meat back to the kitchen, holding the knife very carefully. I rinse the meat with filtered water to remove the salt. Then I slice the meat as thin as I can without cutting myself. Then meat into pan, pan into oven.

Out to the yard again for vegetables. I pick tomatoes and peppers, and slice them, along with slices of white onion, for a salad. My slices are not pretty like Mamãe would make. Filtered water in the pitcher. Set the table.

"Children, wash up for lunch!" I call to them from the kitchen doorway.

Daniel looks up. "Yes, Eva, I'll get them ready."

I pick up João from his blanket.

"Papai, lunch is ready. I need to change João's diaper and wash us up to eat."

"Very good, Eva. Thank you. I will wake Amara."

Papai goes into the darkened bedroom and I hear muffled talking. I change João's diaper and wash his little hands outside at the pump and wash my hands and face, holding João on my hip.

Inside, the children are all seated quietly at the table, their big eyes looking toward me. Papai comes into the kitchen with Amara, his arm around her shoulders.

"Querida, have a seat. Eva has made us lunch."

She looks over at me, squinting again, and looks around at all the children. Papai pulls out a chair for her and she sits down. Papai sits at the head of the table and we all bow our heads. I sneak a look at the Madrasta and she turns towards me but bows her head as Papai begins to pray.

"Lord, we thank thee for our family and for this food we are about to receive to nourish our bodies. Teach us to be ever grateful for the gifts we receive from thee, in Jesus' name, Amen."

Everyone murmurs Amen.

Food is passed, and I help the children take just a little meat, cutting it into small pieces and telling them to chew well. I mash the rice and beans for Samuel and João. I pour water for everyone. The Madrasta just looks at me. No one speaks.

The Madrasta begins to eat, slowly at first, then hungrily putting forkfuls of rice and beans in her mouth. She slices a big piece of carne de sol and chews and chews, swallowing with water. She must not like my raggedy salad because she doesn't put any on her plate. The children watch her with their mouths open a little but look down at their plates when she looks over at them.

No one says anything while eating lunch, but this is not a happy time of eating and not talking. I don't feel hungry but I eat a little bit, and make sure the children eat enough. When everyone is finished, I pick up the dishes and put them on the counter. I put water on to boil for café.

"Papai, may I be dismissed from the table?" Daniel says. When Papai nods yes, he runs outside with Ana and Paulo.

"Wash your hands and faces and rinse your mouths!" I call after them.

I put the café on the table, with the nice cafezinho cups and little silver spoons from this morning. It seems such a long time ago, waiting for a guest to arrive with Papai. Madrasta breaks the silence.

"Is there a sweet?"

Papai was staring at the wall, and he sort of wakes up when she speaks.

"Eva, what do we have to offer for dessert?" He looks at me and raises his eyebrows a little bit.

"Only fruit, Papai."

I bring the plate of cut fruit from this morning and place it on the table, removing the dish-cloth. A few gnats buzz around it.

"No, I don't want that," says Madrasta.

Papai stands, pulls the chair out for her, and they move to the living room. I put the dishes in the big metal bowl and take them out to the pump to wash them up. The sun beats down. I wish it would rain.

March 24, Sunday

It is Sunday, the day of the Lord. I wake up early and get café ready, get the children ready, and get dressed myself. Everyone is seated around the table when Papai and Madrasta come into the kitchen. She is wearing a dark blue dress with a white lace collar and black shoes. Her hair is pulled back and bumped up a little on the sides by her forehead, with the rest pinned back in a bun. Her black hair is very curly and there are wisps around her face; her face is puffy and her cheeks are red. Papai is wearing his white linen suit.

"Good morning, children, today is the day of the Lord."

"Blessing, Papai."

"God bless you, my children."

He sits at the head of the table and everyone bows their heads.

"Oh Lord, bless the food we are about to receive, Amen."

Everyone murmurs Amen. I made cajú juice and there is café, bread and butter, and cut fruit on a plate. No one speaks, and the children aren't eating much. I don't fuss at them. After we eat I take the dishes outside in the metal bowl and put water on them, but I will clean up later. We gather in the living room and go out the gate, walking to the church.

When we arrive at the church, there are people gathered outside talking as they always do. Several look up, and everyone stops talking. I see them sneaking glances at each other out of the sides of their eyes, but they look down at the dirt and say nothing. We all walk in together and sit in our usual pew. Pastor comes over and greets Papai and nods to Madrasta. The sermon goes on forever, more forever than usual, but finally we are out the church door and walking again, a dust cloud following our group as we head home.

Everyone changes from their church clothes. I think I will have to make lunch again today, because Madrasta hasn't come in the kitchen except to eat. She stays in the bedroom most of the time. She doesn't say much. After lunch I am tidying up and putting João down for a nap, when I pass the big bedroom. The door is open just a little bit and I hear her crying, the kind of crying that isn't noisy but you hear the little gasps for air, and sniffling. I listen for a little while.

"Eva! Let's get lunch going please!" Papai is looking at me from the doorway to the living room.

"Yes, Papai."

"Let's slaughter a capon for a nice lunch. Cacilda is here, she knows how."

"Yes, Papai."

Cacilda is sitting down outside the kitchen door, cutting green beans. She looks up at me and smiles a little bit, but she is also frowning.

"Oi, Eva. All good?"

"I'm fine, Cacilda, thank you. Papai wants us to prepare a capon for dinner. I don't know how to kill them. Can you?"

"Sure, Eva. But I can't do with my just two hands, you gotta help me."

I don't like killing animals for food, but it must be done. So I take a breath and sit down next to Cacilda on the bench. We sit without talking while she finishes trimming the green beans. I like the crunch and the smell when you cut them; when I think of green, that is a smell I think of.

Cacilda brings a metal basin, knife and a bowl and we go to the chicken house, where three capons sit fat and lazy in their coop. They aren't hard to catch like chickens, and they aren't mean like roosters, which they were until Papai did the little cut to make them capons. Cacilda grabs one with her big hands.

"Okay, Eva, get ready with the bowl. We need to save the blood."

Cacilda holds the capon by the neck, and trims some of the feathers away. She makes a quick, deep cut and I put the bowl underneath to catch the blood. The bird doesn't struggle; this is better than how some people snap the neck and then you have to watch the animal run around the yard suffering until it dies.

Cacilda carries the bird in the basin, I carry the bowl of blood and the knife. I boil water and we put the bird in the water and pluck the feathers. We work silently until the bird is cleaned and ready to roast. We will boil the blood with herbs to serve with the capon.

Dinner is very nice when it's ready, Cacilda and I did a good job. Roast capon, rice with blood gravy, red beans, green beans, and sliced tomato, lettuce and onion. Cacilda eats outside and afterward Cacilda and I wash up.

I sit outside the kitchen door when everything is cleaned up and everyone is resting. Cacilda lies down in the hammock to rest. Papai is in the living room reading the Bible. The children are playing quietly. The day is heading toward sundown, the light golden behind the trees. Everything is peaceful. I can breathe a little bit. Maybe things will be all right. Different, not what I wanted, but all right.

March 25, Monday

Today is Monday, and Papai goes to work. How can it be just two days since everything changed? It seems like years ago that I was sad missing Mamãe but happy taking care of the children, like I am their mom now. That was before I heard of a guest coming to visit, who turned out not to be a guest, who turned out to be the Madrasta. If I were older I would travel to Rio and get a job. Maybe I will go to Rio, the beautiful city by the ocean, the capital. Many people go there or to São Paulo to find work. If I were all grown up . . .

"Girl, come here!" Madrasta calls me.

"Yes, Senhora?"

"I need my room cleaned. Bring whatever you need and get to work."

I get up from the table and gather the broom, dustpan, water with soap, mop, rags. I pass through the living room where Madrasta is sitting on the couch reading a shiny magazine with curled edges. She tosses it on the couch beside her.

"Well, what are you waiting for?"

"Yes, Senhora, I will make it nice and clean for you."

She picks up the magazine and turns the pages, ignoring me.

When I open the door of the bedroom, I almost cry out. The room is a jumble with sheets and blankets and pillows all tossed around, but the bed, dresser and side table are covered with the most beautiful things I have ever seen. Large dolls with silken hair and eyes that look real, seated as pretty as you please and looking around. One is resting happily on the middle of the bed, looking out the window. I put down my cleaning tools and move toward her. What does she feel like? I sit on the edge of the bed and stare at her. I reach out and pick her up.

"You are beautiful, what is your name?"

She doesn't answer, but her eyes blink! Those blue eyes blink at me, and her blonde hair is shiny and smooth to the touch, with curls on the ends. It feels like real hair, only nicer. She is wearing a red plaid dress with a black velvet collar, white stockings with lace at the tops, and shiny black shoes with a little strap across the foot. I smooth her dress and stroke her hair.

"I wish you were my baby! I want to squeeze and hug you just like a real baby!"

I close my eyes and hug her to my chest.

A cracking noise and pain in my head, then again a hard cracking noise, both ears ringing, pain, sparks behind my eyes.

"What do you think you're doing? Are these yours? Did I say you could play with them? How dare you!"

Madrasta yanks the doll out of my hands.

"Get up! You were spozed to clean the room, not play with my dolls!"

"I'm sorry, Senhora! I won't do it again!" Hot tears are running down my face. My head pounds. My ears ring.

"I am in charge here. You will obey me and do as I say. When I tell you to clean the room, you clean the room. And never touch my dolls. Ever!"

I pull my head down and shrink away from her. She hit me! My head is a jumble now. I scooch over toward the wall, wiping my tears with the edge of my skirt.

"I'll have to clean my own room, I don't want you touching my things. You are a very naughty little girl!"

I'm sobbing and I can't stop, trying to catch my breath. My ears are still ringing. My head hurts.

"Now get up and go to the kitchen and get to work! And I better not have any more trouble from you today, do you hear?"

"Yes, Senhora." I run to the kitchen as fast as I can.

Somehow I get through the day and put lunch on the table. Papai comes home for lunch like he always does on workdays. I keep my eyes looking down at the table and Papai doesn't say anything to me. The children are very quiet. Madrasta is chattering on and on to Papai, about the weather and too bad there's no rain, and how is work. More than I have heard her say since she got here. I can't look at her. When lunch is over, Cacilda and I begin to clean things up in the kitchen. Papai turns to me.

"Eva, it is time for you to go back to school. Studying is very important, and all my children will be educated. I will talk with teacher today and plan for you to begin school next Monday."

"Yes, Papai."

I want to go to school but I am scared of when teacher asks me to read and I can't. I want to, but I can't. It's like the letters are all under water, shining and moving. They won't stand still to let me read them, as hard as I try.

April 1, Monday

My first day back to school is hot and sunny with no clouds. I am glad to get out of the house. Madrasta doesn't talk to me, and I try to forget what she did. For a few days I thought she might say sorry, but she hasn't. Daniel and I get ready and walk through the dusty streets to school. I am glad to see my friends; the girls gather around me and ask how I'm doing. We have a little time to play outside before class begins.

We go inside when teacher calls us. Teacher has given me a new seat right at the front of the class. I wish I could sit in the back like I used to. We rise at teacher's signal and face the Brazilian flag, hands over our hearts. We sing:

> On the banks of the placid river Ipiranga
> The resounding cry of a heroic people
> And brilliant beams from the sun of liberty
> Shone brilliant in the skies of our land

The anthem always gives me goosebumps and makes me feel proud. The words are hard to sing but we children learn them and sing them every day in school. I love the green and yellow of the flag, with a bright blue earth in the center sprinkled with white stars. I think we have the most beautiful national anthem and flag in the world. We learn in school that Brazil is a modern country with a bright future.

Teacher tells us to be seated. I am worried she will call on me to read, but she doesn't today, and I am happy when Daniel and I walk home.

The weeks pass, and teacher doesn't ask me to read out loud. When she asks us to read silently, I try but I have to pretend. The end of the year and final exams are getting closer. Once the

43

exams are done, we are on vacation for the winter. I love the winter celebration Festa Junina, and our family celebrates with everyone because the church allows it.

June 6, Thursday

The day of exams is here. It is not so hot now that winter is here, and a thin cover of high clouds blocks the sun. Daniel and I walk to school without talking. He is always serious and studies very hard. I am good with numbers but reading and writing are just a mystery to me.

We enter the school yard and line up outside the classroom with the other children. When teacher opens the door we file in and stand next to our desks. Hands over hearts, we face the flag and sing the anthem. Teacher tells us to be seated. I bow my head and say a prayer: Please Lord, help me to do well in the exam. Please make the letters hold still on the paper so I can read them. I promise I'll be good. Please help me. Amen.

Teacher puts the papers face down on our desks; we can't turn them over until she tells us to. She gives the signal and there is a rustling noise as everyone turns the pages over. Some of the kids shuffle the papers to look at everything but I just start on the first page, which is numbers. I can do this. Add, subtract, multiply, divide, fractions. Three pages and I know I can get a good grade. Then I turn to page four.

Words. A story and questions. The letters dance on the page and tease me. I sneak a look at teacher who is walking between the rows of desks with her hands clasped behind her back, watching everyone working and making sure their eyes don't stray. I want to look out the window, but I won't look away from my paper and get in trouble. I pretend to read, and then write a few words I know how to write and pretend to answer the questions.

My tummy hurts and my head feels hot. The clock on the wall goes tick, tick, tick. I keep my eyes down and pretend to work. Finally the teacher calls time.

"Put down your pencils and turn your papers over so I may collect them."

She goes down the rows, picking up papers and stacking them in her arms. She goes to her desk in the back of the room to put down the exams, then returns to stand in the front of the class.

"Children, this year we have something new to evaluate your progress in school. We will be calling you one by one to Senhora Rocha's office where you will be given a passage to read to her out loud. Please sit quietly until your name is called."

One of my friends is called and goes out the door. She is gone for about ten minutes and returns, smiling. Maybe it won't be so bad. Maybe I will be able to read it. Other students return from the office, pick up their things and leave for home.

"Eva!"

I can hardly get up from my desk, but my feet take me to Senhora Rocha's office door.

"Eva, come in. Have a seat there."

She hands me a piece of paper with print on it.

"Eva, I want you to read as far as you can down the page. When it becomes too difficult, just let me know and you will stop there."

She has a paper with a ruler on it; I guess she follows along the same thing the student is reading. I look at the letters, the words shimmering and disappearing like the heat in the distance on the road outside of town.

"You may begin, Eva."

I try to read a few words that I know, like *the*, and *you*. But I can't put them together in a sentence. And I can't read it, there's no use in pretending. I try not to cry but I can't stop the tears. I look up at Senhora Rocha.

"Eva, what's wrong? It's not so difficult, you don't have to read all of it! We just want to know how you are doing with your reading."

"Senhora, I can't read it. I want to, but I can't."

Tears are coming in big sobs now and I try to catch my breath.

"Eva, I know it's hard when you're nervous. Why don't you take a moment to compose yourself and try again?"

"It's no use, Senhora. I can't read. Something is wrong with my eyes. I really want to, but I just can't!"

She stares at me a long time, while I try to catch my breath. She isn't mean like teacher, she just looks puzzled and worried.

"Very well, Eva. I will review with teacher and we will look at your written exam. We will then speak with your father about your progress and what comes next. You may gather your things and go home."

"Thank you, Senhora. I'm sorry, I'm really sorry."

She nods kindly and I go back to the classroom. Daniel is waiting outside.

"Eva, what happened? Are you all right? Did you do all right on your exam?"

"I can't read, Daniel. I am good with numbers but I just can't read. I am going to be in trouble with Papai."

"Eva don't worry. It will be all right."

We walk home slowly, not talking. My tears have dried on my face. I look down at the dust swirling around our shoes as we walk.

June 16, Sunday

Several days pass and no word from teacher, so maybe I won't get in trouble. Maybe I can just go back to school after winter vacation and start again. We are all seated at the table after lunch on Sunday, and Papai says he has an announcement.

"My dear Amara is going to have a baby!"

We children sit and say nothing. Madrasta looks at Papai with a little frown. Her face is getting rounder, and she looks more chubby, it's true. But she doesn't take care of the babies now: I do that with Cacilda. How will she take care of a baby of her own?

Madrasta is doing a little more in the house since I've gone back to school, but mainly just bossing Cacilda. She doesn't seem to know how to cook anything, but she watches me and Cacilda and sometimes asks us questions. She always lets us wash up, though. Cacilda and I do all the house cleaning. Daniel and Ana are helping more, too.

I try to stay out of Madrasta's way and not do anything to make her angry. She doesn't ask me to clean her bedroom anymore, just gives me the sheets to wash once a week. I don't look in Papai's bedroom ever, I'm afraid she will give me a good one if she catches me looking at her dolls.

June 19, Wednesday

Papai comes home for lunch with a serious look on his face. He looks at me but doesn't say anything, just goes out to the pump to wash his hands. We eat our lunch in silence, and I get up to clear the dishes. I put them in the metal basin to take out to the pump to wash. Papai tells the children to go outside to wash up and play until they are called to come inside.

"Eva, please stay here with us."

Papai is seated at the head of the table with Madrasta to his right. He points for me to sit at the opposite end. I sit down and wait.

Papai clears his throat. "Eva, I had a visit at the post office from Senhora Rocha. She is very concerned about your progress in school."

I just stare at him without speaking. I can't breathe.

"She says you can't read at all. She says you do very well with numbers, but you are not reading, not even what a child in the first year can do. Is that true, Eva?"

I try to clear the frog out of my throat. My voice is raspy.

"Yes, Papai. It's true." It feels hard to say it out loud.

"What do you think is the problem? I know reading is hard because I learned when I was already a young man. But you are a very bright girl, a very good girl, thanks be to God."

"Papai, I want to read, I really do. But the letters won't be still on the page to let me read them."

"Eva, I'm not sure what that means, but I have a plan for you. When school starts in August, you will have a private tutor. I will engage Senhor Julio from the church. He is a very learned man and he will work with you individually to help you learn to read."

I look up at Papai. Senhor Julio is an old man who speaks in a very fancy way. He seems very odd and he scares me. But I want to read and write so I will do anything. And it isn't until August, so I won't worry about it now.

"Yes, Papai, thank you, Papai."

"Now run outside and clean up, and then you can play with the other children."

After Papai goes back to work Madrasta calls to me and tells me to come back into the kitchen.

"Kneel! Face the wall."

"What? Why, Senhora?"

"Just do what I say!" She pushes me down to my knees.

"You are a very bad little girl. Your father does so much for you, but all you do is make him worry. You wasted your time in school this year and now your father has to hire a tutor with money we don't have. What do you got to say for yourself?"

"Senhora, I try, I do! I want to read, I do! But I can't! The letters won't hold still for me to read them!"

She yanks me by my hair and slams my head into the wall. I push back against her but she slams my head again. I can't breathe, everything is black except for flashes of lightning. I am going to die!

And again, *slam*, can't breathe, please God make her stop; my hands are on the floor and I'm gasping for air as she yanks my head up again. She slaps me on the side of the head with her other hand then lets me go, wiping her hands on her dress.

"When school starts again, you're gonna study like you're spozed to. And if you don't, you're gonna get it. You understand me?"

"Yes, Senhora." I'm gasping for breath but I don't cry because I'm afraid that will make her hurt me again.

"And never tell your father about our little talks. If you do, it'll be very bad for you."

She turns and leaves me in the kitchen, my ears ringing, breathing gulps of air and crying without making any noise.

June 24, Monday, Dia de São João

Festa Junina is my favorite time of the year, when we are on winter break from school and everyone in town celebrates together. The children all dress up like people from the country with pretend raggedy clothes and straw hats. At night there are bonfires in the square, and good food and hot drinks. There is music and dancing. The celebrations go on for the whole month of June.

Mamãe always sewed us kids special costumes: for me and Ana, cute dresses in flowers or polkadots, with layers of flounces and lace and ribbons. She bought the cloth right after Christmas and we got to pick our favorites. For the boys, she took a pair of each of their old trousers and sewed on patches in bright colors. Ana and I would put on our Festa Junina dresses and tie our hair in high ponytails on the sides of our heads and paint freckles on our faces with pencil. We weren't allowed to use lipstick but sometimes we could color our mouths with beet juice so it was almost like lipstick. We painted mustaches and little beards on the boys' chins. Mamãe would ask us to stand in front of her and turn around so she could see how nice we looked.

This year I did my best to make our costumes, after I asked Madrasta, and she said she doesn't know how to sew. Ana is wearing my dress from last year, and I can sew enough by hand with a needle and thread so I added some ribbons and things to one of my dresses using pieces from Mamãe's sewing box. Opening the box, I think of Mamãe and want to cry, but I also feel her love and feel happy. We are part of Festa Junina this year!

Madrasta says she is tired and doesn't want to go, so I put Samuel and João to bed early. Samuel whines at me a little as I put him down to sleep.

"Eva, I want to go! I'm big enough!"

"Shhhh, next year, querido. Let's say your prayers so you can sleep."

"But I'm free!" He holds out four fingers and pushes his lower lip out.

"Samuel, you are almost three. You're still two. I promise you can go next year."

After prayers I kiss him and tuck him in to bed, patting him for a few minutes until he's sleepy. We wait for it to get dark and Daniel, Ana, Paulo and I walk over to the main square. The sky is bright with stars but no moon.

I point at the sky. "Look, where is the moon?"

Ana is staring at the sky. "There is no moon."

I smile to myself. "Ana, even when the moon is gone, when she is dark, she is still there. She's just hiding."

We can see the light of the fire before we get to the square, sparks going up into the sky, and we hear the music of the accordion. As we come around the corner and into the square we see the bonfire is as wide as a house, with stacks of logs as tall as a roof.

There is music from the accordion, tinkling from the triangle, and the big zabumba drum and people singing. Couples are dancing forró in circles with groups of people, their feet moving quickly as they twist and turn. Their faces are bright in the firelight, smiling and laughing. Our church does not approve of dancing, but watching people dance makes me happy even if I can't dance myself. Daniel and Paulo walk around the square to see everything.

People are putting sweet potatoes into the base of the fire and we will eat them with manteiga de leite, liquid butter from a bottle. There is canjica, too, big white corn pudding with condensed milk and the delicious smell of cinnamon. That smell is winter to me, and Festa Junina. There are little corn cakes, coconut candy and hard candy made with peanuts. My favorite sweet is paçoca, little chunks of smooth peanut paste—I hold them in my mouth until they melt, it's better than chewing them and lasts longer. Some grown-ups drink spiced wine and hot cachaça and sometimes act silly or start to argue with each other as the night goes on. No one from our church drinks alcohol.

Daniel and Paulo come running, asking for coins so they can play the fishing game. For one centavo they give you a fishing pole and you try to catch a prize in the pretend fishing hole. Daniel lets Paulo go first; we are giggling but Paulo looks very serious. He hooks a small carved wooden bull and he is so happy! Daniel has to spend two centavos because the first time he doesn't catch a prize. Then he gets a tiny wooden andorinha, the swallow that flies at night. He gives it to me.

"This is for you, Eva."

I give him a hug but don't kiss him because he would be embarrassed.

Next we go to the ring toss, laughing as we try to get the ring to land over the little pole. It's harder than it looks! They let the younger children stand closer so they have a chance to win. We don't get any prizes this time, but we laugh a lot.

After we eat sweet potato and canjica and walk around the square many times watching everything and talking with our neighbors, I tell the children it's time to go home. They complain a little, but we walk home together, laughing and talking.

When we get back, there's a bonfire in the street outside our house. Papai built it for Madrasta, who is sitting in a chair outside the gate watching the flames. She looks tired and stays quiet most of the time. Her tummy is getting bigger and sometimes I watch her when she doesn't know I'm looking, when she frowns and makes that tight line with her mouth.

June 30, Sunday

We have a big lunch at the church today, with all the church sisters bringing dishes. Cacilda helps me bake two chickens to take as our family's dish. This time I kill one of the chickens with Cacilda helping. I don't like it but I want to help the animal not suffer. We cut the chickens into pieces and roast them with chunks of cassava.

Our family walks together carrying our food to the church. When we arrive I take the clay pot to the social hall and help the women set things up. There are so many delicious dishes, it makes my mouth water just looking at them. Some of the older sisters are the very best cooks and everyone shuffles in line looking at their dishes and hoping there will be some left when they get to the front and make their plate.

Everyone wants to eat Dona Francisca's food, no matter what she brings for a feast day. Her dishes are always tasty, with just the right amount of salt and spice and the meat and vegetables cooked perfectly. Today her dish is baião de dois, a casserole with rice, black eyed peas, fresh cheese, and carne de charque, another kind of dried meat. But the way Dona Francisca makes it, the meat is soft and tender, not chewy. She also makes all kinds of delicious sweets and desserts, and today she brings torta de limão, a lime tart with a white layer on top that looks like a hard crust but is light as air when you eat it, with little slices of candied lime on top.

After everyone has finished eating I help the sisters clean up. Madrasta sits fanning herself; her face is red even though it's winter and not hot. The sisters tell her to rest in the chapel where it's cooler; they will take care of cleaning up and I will help. The children go outside to play Festa Junina games, and it's just me and the sisters in the social hall tidying up.

"Dona Francisca, I love your cooking. I wish I could cook like you!"

"Goodness, child, I just make simple food of the sertão, nothing fancy. But thank you, dear."

"I really do, Dona Francisca! Would you teach me? I could help you in the kitchen and learn. I promise I wouldn't be any trouble!"

"Are you serious, Eva? You really want to learn to cook sertão food?"

"Yes, Dona Francisca, I really do."

"Your mother was such a good cook, and a true Christian, rest her soul. I know how much you must miss her."

"Papai says the Lord works in mysterious ways. I try to be a good girl and take care of my brothers and sisters now that Mamãe is not with us."

"You are a good girl, Eva. Listen, if your father will allow you to come to my house on Tuesdays, you can work with me in the kitchen. I don't know that I can teach you much, but you would be most welcome."

"Oh thank you, Dona Francisca! I will ask Papai! Thank you!"

So many things I wish I had learned from Mamãe while she was here with us. Papai really likes good food and I think he must miss Mamãe's cooking. I do my best but it's not like the dishes Mamãe made for us. Madrasta may be a problem, she always needs me at home to help in the house. And I will start school again soon. But Madrasta always wants something sweet, so if I tell I will learn to make desserts, she may allow me to go.

July 3, Wednesday

For lunch today I make carne de sol, rice and beans and a salad of tomato, lettuce and onion, but today I leave more salt on the meat and fry it fast on the stove so it's very chewy. For dessert, irregular slices of banana with brown spots. After the children leave the table, I begin picking up the dishes and putting them in the metal basin. Papai and Madrasta are at the table having their cafezinho.

"Papai, may I speak?"

"Of course, Eva. What is it?"

"Papai, I want to learn how to cook better. How to make really good dishes. And sweets, I would like to learn how to make really nice desserts."

"Eva, of course that's admirable. But how do you propose to learn these things?"

"Papai, Dona Francisca says she will teach me if I can go to her house and help her in the kitchen on Tuesdays."

Madrasta looks at me. "We need you to do your work here at home. And even more when the baby comes."

"Senhora, I promise I will do all the work I do now. Just one day a week. And I will work hard to learn to make really nice food for us!"

Madrasta doesn't look happy.

"And desserts! I want to make beautiful desserts like the torta de limão, the cake with the puffy white top and pretty slices of lime. So good—it looks like a cloud and melts in your mouth when you eat it. I want to learn how to make that torta. And so many other good things! Please!"

Madrasta and Papai look at each other. After a long silence, Papai speaks.

"Eva, go ahead and clean up the dishes outside. Amara and I will consider your request and talk with you about it later."

Papai calls me to me after the dishes are washed and put away.

"Eva, Amara and I have considered your request, and we will allow you to go to Dona Francisca's every Tuesday morning until school starts again, once I confirm the arrangement with her. We will see how it goes and consider then whether you can continue when school begins."

"Oh Papai, thank you! I will work really hard and still get my chores done here at home, I promise!"

Madrasta speaks. "Don't let me catch you loafing around, or that will be the end of your visits to Dona Francisca, do you hear me?"

"Yes, Senhora. I understand."

July 9, Tuesday

Tuesday comes, and I am so excited to go to Dona Francisca's that I get up extra early and do lots of cleaning before everyone is up. She lives just two blocks away and I skip a little on the way to her house.

"Oi in the house!" I clap outside her gate. Dona Francisca comes to the gate.

"Good morning, child! Please, come in!"

I enter her house and try not to look around like I'm being nosy, though I want to. She calls me into the kitchen.

"What is the first thing you do when you come into the house from outside?"

"I'm not sure, Dona Francisca."

"You wash your hands. Always, the first thing."

"Yes, Senhora." She has a basin with soap on the side, and a pitcher of water. She shows me how to wash my hands carefully so they are really clean.

"Very good, Eva. Now we are ready to think about cooking. I think today you will just help me with cutting vegetables; have you used a big kitchen knife before?"

"I know to be careful. Mamãe didn't let me use the big knife but now I have to because I am doing the cooking."

"Are you doing all the cooking for your family, Eva?"

I think carefully before I answer because it's probably not a good thing for me to be doing all the cooking.

"Well, my Madrasta cooks some things too. And Cacilda is there every day helping; she is older than me."

"That's fine, Eva. Let's be sure you can handle the knife."

She shows me how to use a knife so I can control it and not cut myself. Then how to cut onions into small chunks and really teeny pieces. My right hand holds the knife and I curl the fingers of my left hand to hold the onion as I cut it. The pieces are pretty and all the same size. This is fun!

"Eva, you must always respect the knife. If you don't pay attention, that is when you get hurt."

"Yes, Dona Francisca."

She teaches me how to cut different vegetables, onion, pepper, carrots. And to keep the stems and the seeds and cut around them; that way the vegetables stay fresh longer. She gives me a bowl with chopped vegetables that I can use to make a nice rice for lunch. It seems like just a few minutes pass and it's time for me to go home.

"Eva, you have done very well today. You are a quick learner, very bright. I will talk to your father about sending some meat and other ingredients next week so we can make lunch."

"Yes, Dona Francisca. Thank you so much. I love to cook!"

July 23, Tuesday

I come very early bringing carne de sol to make lunch for my family. Dona Francisca teaches me how to make dried meat soft by soaking it in milk after rinsing the salt off. The salt keeps the meat from going bad, but it has to be brought back to life, she says, and milk does that. Then we smash garlic cloves in a mortar with salt and herbs to make a paste that we rub on the meat, then let it sit for a while before we cook it. That is how she makes her meat so soft and tasty.

We now make a main dish and a dessert every Tuesday. Dona Francisca is a widow and only needs one serving, so we put some aside for her lunch and I take my big pot home where I just have to make rice and warm up beans and slice tomato and onion. Madrasta is always excited to see what sweet I bring home.

Dona Francisca asks if I want to write down how to make the dishes, but I tell her I am good at remembering, and I am, but I'm embarrassed for her to see that I can't write very well. When I get home I write the recipes down on pages that I keep in a can that used to hold Toddy cocoa powder; I love the chocolate smell when I open the can and put in a new recipe.

Tuesday is my favorite day of the week. I am learning so much about cooking from Dona Francisca, but about other things too. She has beautiful paintings on her walls, drapes on the windows with big green jungle leaves, and lamps on tables by the sofa. Most people just have a picture of Jesus and a light bulb in the ceiling. I love her house, and I want to ask her about so many things but I've been too shy. Today I can't stand it and I ask her a question.

"Dona Francisca, how did you learn all the things you know about cooking?"

She laughs. "Oh my goodness! Just like you, I suppose. I wanted to learn and I found someone to teach me. In my case it was our cook when I was growing up in Rio. She was a Baiana, and she made all the typical dishes of Salvador and Northeast Brazil. From there I just learned from cooks whenever I could. The thing about cooking is it has a beginning but it has no end. You always learn new things."

"Yes, I want to keep learning about cooking my whole life. And I want to go to Rio."

"Perhaps you will, child. Perhaps you will."

August 5, Monday

August comes too quickly and I must go back to school. I also have to go to the private tutor every Monday. Senhor Julio lives near the church, and I have to go there by myself after school so he can help me learn to read. Today is my first day. I still get to go to Dona Francisca's once a week, and I will now go on Saturday, but only if I have all my homework and chores done by Friday night. I will work hard all week to be sure I can cook on Saturday.

Daniel and I walk to school. Senhora Rocha is at the front gate greeting everyone on this first day back. I'm happy to see all my friends and talk about Festa Junina. Teacher makes me sit in the front of the class like before, but she doesn't seem quite as mean. She doesn't make me read aloud today. After school, Daniel walks home and I go in the opposite direction to Senhor Julio's house.

"Oi in the house!"

Senhor Julio comes to the gate. "You may enter, young lady."

This is another house completely different from anything I've ever seen, dark, with walls covered with books. It smells musty and dust dances in the light coming through the one open window. There is a small table and chair next to the bookcase.

"You may be seated."

I sit on the chair and look down at my hands, folded in my lap.

"Young lady, please give me your undivided attention!" Senhor Julio has a ruler in his hand and raps it on the table.

I look up. "Yes, Senhor Julio!"

"Your father informs me you are unable to read. I have also spoken with Senhora Rocha and she provided me the results of your end-of-year examination. We will begin today with the basics. You must work hard or I cannot be bothered to teach you. Do you understand?"

He glares at me over smudged glasses that sit low on his nose. His eyebrows are long and stick out in all directions. He has hair coming out of his nose and I try not to look. He squints at me and frowns.

"Well, I am awaiting a response!"

"Yes, Senhor Julio."

"Yes *what*?"

"Yes, I do understand."

"Very well, then. Let us begin."

He places a sheet of paper in front of me and tells me to write the alphabet, in both big and small letters. I can do the alphabet, even if my writing isn't pretty. He goes into his kitchen for a few minutes while I draw the letters on the paper.

"Well, have you completed your task?"

I look up from the paper. "I think so, Senhor Julio."

"You have either done it or you have not. Don't equivocate! Show me."

He picks up the paper and sighs a bit. "You will have to do much better than this. Here is another piece of paper; write it again but do it properly."

It is hard but I try to make the letters more pretty and line them up better. He seems to accept this one but doesn't say anything. He hands me a book, the one children use in the first year to begin reading.

"Please read, begin on the first page."

I can do this because I have heard it many times. So I read the story, turning the pages as I look at the pictures. He corrects me a couple of times. Then he asks me to read it silently. I look at the pictures and remember the story, and I know some of the words.

He smacks his palm with the ruler.

"Very well. That is enough for today. Your assignment is to read this book and to write the alphabet as I have instructed you, but do it properly. Bring me a faithfully executed page next Monday."

I'm not sure what that means exactly, but I know I must do my homework.

"Yes, Senhor Julio."

"Very well, then, our session for today is concluded. You may let yourself out."

"Thank you, Senhor Julio." I am glad to get out of the darkness and into the sunshine, hurrying to get home.

September 14, Saturday

I am able to get my chores done and go to Dona Francisca's on Saturdays. I keep up with my schoolwork and go to Senhor Julio's every Monday. I think he is losing his patience with me because I can't read better quickly. He makes me write and gives me a book to read every week. He teaches me to sound out the words, and I can, a little.

Madrasta's tummy is getting very big and her feet are puffy. She started having tummy aches one day and sent me to get Dona Severina, who went with her to the bedroom then said it was a "false alarm" and gave me some herbs to make a tea to calm her down. Madrasta is very tired and rests most of the time, telling me and Cacilda what needs to be done.

It's the day before my birthday. Last year no one noticed my birthday because it was right after Mamãe left us, but this year I want to celebrate my ninth birthday and João turning one year old. Dona Francisca teaches me how to bake a special cake. It is made with carrots and oranges—you would never guess it had carrots in it. We bake it until it is golden, then Dona Francisca teaches me how to make an icing with fresh runny cheese and special sugar that looks like talc. She makes some little sugar flowers for decoration, and we even put some orange flowers from her garden on the top of the cake. They are flowers you can eat, but they taste like pepper so she says they're just for looks on a cake. It is the most beautiful cake I have ever seen! I am so excited to take it home to my family, and they will sing "Happy Birthday" to me and João. I want to skip on the way home but must walk carefully with the lunch and the cake.

Even before I get to the house I hear screaming, which gets louder as I reach the gate.

"Oh, my mother! Help me! I can't stand it! No!" Madrasta is wailing in the bedroom.

Papai is pacing back and forth in the living room but he stops and looks at me.

"Oh, Eva. The baby is coming. Dona Severina is with Amara, and she says it will be hours. Please keep the children occupied."

"Papai, may I serve lunch? And a cake I baked?"

"Yes, but stay in the kitchen or outside."

I take the food and the cake into the kitchen. Cacilda is standing outside the door, her eyes very big.

"Cacilda, let's make a picnic out here for us kids. Help me get the table from the storage building. It's heavy but I think we can move it."

We have to stop and rest a few times but we get the table on to the veranda and cover it with a cloth. We make rice and set the table. I am glad to be busy and I try not to think about anything but lunch. We call the children to wash up.

I go to the door of the living room. "Papai, lunch will be ready soon. Would you like something to eat?"

He looks up at me and waves his hand. "No, Eva, thank you. You go ahead with the children."

"Yes, Papai."

The children sit and we say grace. Everyone is very quiet and I try to get them to chatter a bit to drown out the noise. They are hungry once they get started. João is on my lap and I feed him from my plate, mashing rice and beans. He puts his little hands on my plate and grabs some food.

"You little robber, look at you! You're very hungry."

He giggles and smashes some rice into his mouth. I give him a sip of water. Once everyone is finished, I tell them to sit and wait for a special treat. I put the cake on the table. Cacilda speaks first.

"Eva, is that a cake? It got flowers on it."

"Yes, Cacilda. The flowers are just for show. This cake is for my birthday tomorrow, and because João turned one on Wednesday, but we are going to eat it today."

"Sing 'Happy Birthday'!" The kids start screaming.

"Okay, Daniel, can you start it? I can't, since it's my birthday."

"How old are you today?" asks Paulo.

"Nine years old."

They sing all out of tune, "Happy birthday to you, happy birthday to you . . ."

They make me laugh, and we forget about everything and eat the whole cake by ourselves.

The screaming goes on and on but sometimes things get quieter. I think Madrasta gets tired and falls asleep between pains. We kids are sleeping outside in the hammocks to be away from it. Late in the night I hear a commotion as other neighbor ladies come to help Dona Severina. The kids are all sleeping but I have to see what is happening. The kitchen is dark and I stand in the shadows to see who is here. Two older sisters from the church are in the door to the hallway talking softly but I can hear them.

"Mercy, she has hours to go. She needs to calm down so she has energy to push when the time comes."

"She's so young, she had no idea what it was going to be like."

"She wants her mother to be here, she keeps calling for her."

"Her mother is not speaking to her. Who knows, maybe she will soften up when the baby is here. It will be her first grandchild, after all."

"He's only been married to her since March and that baby is too big to be early."

"I know he needed help with the house and his kids, but this is a very complicated situation. Mercy!"

September 15, Sunday

The sun comes up and the kids are all sleeping peacefully. I listen for sounds. A baby crying! That must be what woke me up. I tiptoe into the kitchen and stand quietly at the door to the living room. I can't hear what the women are saying in the bedroom. The baby stops crying. I hear the front door close. Papai comes in, he must have been walking outside. I step back so he doesn't see me. Dona Severina walks through the hallway door and speaks softly to him.

"It's a girl. It was hard on Amara, but she and the baby are both healthy. The sisters will take turns staying and helping her for the next few days."

"Thank you, Dona Severina." Papai seems very tired.

"Would you like to see them now?"

"Yes, if she is up to it."

"Of course, but just a few minutes. She will need to sleep a lot in the next few days, just waking up to give the baby mamar."

They go through the hallway door and into the bedroom. I hear quiet murmuring and Papai comes out very quickly, holding his forehead. I think he is crying. I want to go to him but I stay hiding in the kitchen.

I go back outside and lie down in the hammock. I can't sleep but I pretend to, in case Papai comes out to check on us. After an hour or so I get up and go into the kitchen to make breakfast for everyone. It's good to be busy as the kids wake up, but my thoughts are jumping around. Everyone sits to eat but I'm not hungry.

September 18, Wednesday

Three days pass and Madrasta only leaves the bedroom to go to the toilet house outside and stays in there a long time when she does. She doesn't speak to anyone, just walks slowly holding her tummy. The sisters from church are in and out of the house taking turns helping, bringing me sheets and rags and diapers to wash and taking food to Madrasta. Papai is going to work as usual. I make him café and he says thank you, but stares out the window and hardly eats anything. He is working long hours these days and comes home for lunch, then doesn't come home until late evening.

After lunch today Papai asks me to go to the bedroom to take a plate to Madrasta. Then he goes to the door, puts on his hat and leaves the house. I stand outside the bedroom door with the food. None of the church sisters are here now.

"Senhora, may I enter? Papai asked me to bring you a plate."

She clears her throat. "Yes, you can come in."

She is sitting up in bed giving the baby mamar. A blanket covers her shoulder and the baby. She looks around for a place for the plate, but she can't hold the baby and eat at the same time.

"Senhora, do you want me to hold the baby while you eat? I'm good at holding little babies, I'll be careful."

She looks around like she doesn't want me to help her, but then takes a deep breath, takes the baby off her chest and hands her to me, wrapped in the blanket. I pick up the baby and hold her to my shoulder, patting her back to burp her. Madrasta puts her legs over the side of the bed and begins to eat from the plate I put on the bedside table. She is very hungry, eating really fast.

"Senhora, may I sit down in the chair?"

"Yeah, sure."

I sit down and put the baby's head back on my elbow, to let her lie across my lap. I almost stop breathing when I see her. She

69

has soft black curly hair, so much of it! And then she opens her eyes and squints at me. Her skin is warm brown and her eyes are as dark as the stones at the edge of the river when there is water.

"Senhora, she is beautiful!"

Madrasta turns to me and her eyes fill with tears. "Do you think so?"

"Oh yes, Senhora. She is so beautiful. What is her name?"

She wipes her eyes and sniffs like she isn't crying. "I don't know yet. Your father will have to decide. I haven't even asked him yet."

I stroke the baby's cheek and she tilts her head toward my hand, opening her little pink mouth. I look up at Madrasta.

"Senhora, Sunday was my birthday. My sister and I have the same birthday."

Madrasta pushes her eyebrows together. She speaks very quietly. "Yes, she is your sister."

September 29, Sunday

My new sister's name is Miriam, and she is two weeks old. Today is Sunday and we are going to dedicate the new baby to the church. When all the kids are ready, I help Madrasta dress Miriam in a long white gown that all the babies in our family have worn, which I washed and ironed carefully yesterday. Our family walks slowly up the street toward the church, Madrasta leaning on Papai's arm. It is almost October and the sun is higher in the sky.

Today Papai does not preach. We all sit down in our usual pew. Papai nods to people as they come in and sit down in their places. He is very quiet and serious, not smiling or talking with anyone. After the service, as people are leaving, I see some of the sisters trying to catch a look at Miriam but pretending they're not. Madrasta keeps her wrapped in her blanket with her face covered. Miriam is quiet and doesn't cry.

We walk home without talking, and Cacilda and I get lunch on the table with Daniel and Ana's help. Madrasta sits at the table with us; the kids talk quietly and Papai looks out the window while he eats. We have cocadas for dessert, chewy sweets made with coconut, canned milk and sugar. It is the first sweet Dona Francisca taught me to make because it is very easy. Madrasta seems happy as she eats and drinks her café.

Miriam lets out a little cry from her crib in the bedroom. I jump up.

"Senhora, don't worry, I will go get her and keep her happy for a few minutes while you finish your cocada."

Madrasta looks at me and nods, then looks over at Papai, but he is still looking out the window. I bring Miriam into the kitchen, bouncing her a little to keep her from crying.

"Senhora, it's nice on the veranda, why don't you sit out there with her? I will bring her to you."

"Yeah, I guess I will." She gets up and walks slowly out the kitchen door.

I get busy cleaning up with Cacilda and the older kids. They are getting to be good helpers, and we go outside to play, and to get some mangos off the tree. Madrasta is sitting with the sun on her face, giving Miriam mamar. I feel happy when everyone is calm and content.

September 30, Monday

Monday comes too soon, with school and Senhor Julio after. I have spent a lot of time trying to read the new book he gave me, but it is a harder one and the letters shimmer on the page, moving around and mocking me. The school day passes quickly and I wish I didn't have to go see Senhor Julio. I know I can't read this book to him and he will be impatient. He uses a lot of big words and sometimes I don't know what the words mean but I know he is not pleased with me.

I enter the gate as he has told me to do and knock on the door.

"You may enter. Be seated and let's begin work immediately."

He never does any nice talk like How are you? How was school? How is your family? Just snap, get to work! He has the ruler in his hand like always. I sit at the table next to the window and get my book and paper out of my school bag. He stands looking down at me through his thick glasses.

"You may open your book to chapter one and read it aloud."

I open the book, looking down but trying to look at Senhor Julio at the same time out of the side of my eye. It's no use: I can't read it. I look up at him and try not to cry.

"Well? What are you waiting for? I have given you an instruction and I expect you to immediately comply whenever I do so!"

"Senhor Julio, I am sorry but I just can't! The letters dance on the page! I try hard and do my homework but it just doesn't work! I don't know why. I'm sorry."

"You will rise and stand by the desk. Wait here and I will return."

He goes into his kitchen and shuffles around, pulling things out of his cupboards and opening tins, clattering around like he is angry. I wonder what he is doing. After a few minutes he comes into the living room with a tin, which he opens. He pours

73

something on the floor next to the desk. When I look down I see they are dried kernels of corn.

"Kneel!"

"What? Senhor Julio, I don't understand!"

"You require punishment to learn to pay attention and to motivate you to do your work when I give you instructions. Kneel!"

I look at him and tears sneak out of my eyes. He picks up his ruler and raps me on the shoulder.

"I told you to kneel!"

I kneel on the corn. The pain in my knees is like fire, then aching and stinging like a wasp. I want to cry and beg him to let me get up but I won't let him see me being a scared girl. He finally lets me get up. The hard kernels stick to my knees, and there is blood where the corn has cut my skin. I feel dizzy and grab the edge of the desk to help me hold still.

"You may go home now, get out of my sight. When you come back next week you had better read me that book as I instructed you. Unless you begin to do some proper work I will tell your father I can't be bothered to teach you."

I look down at my feet and nod. I put my book in my bag and go out the door as fast as I can. My knees are stinging as I walk home.

October 6, Sunday

Sunday is here again. I have tried to study what Senhor Julio told me to read, but I can only catch a few words. I can't read the sentences. After lunch is cleaned up, I sit down in the living room to try again. I begin to think about going to Senhor Julio's tomorrow and begin to cry. Papai walks in the room and sees me.

"Eva, what is wrong? What are you crying about?"

"Papai, please don't make me go back to Senhor Julio. I am doing the homework he gives me but I still can't read and he gets really angry and punishes me."

"He punishes you? Do you mean he speaks harshly?"

"Yes, Papai. But he raps me with his ruler too, and last week he made me kneel on dried corn. It really hurts, Papai!"

"What? Let me see your knees!"

I lift the edge of my skirt and he looks at the bruising and scabs from where the corn cut the skin.

"Eva, I am very sorry."

He goes to the door, puts on his hat and walks out.

Less than an hour later, he walks back through the door and hangs up his hat.

"Eva, I have spoken to Senhor Julio. He will not be punishing you anymore, though he may continue to speak harshly. That corn really hurts, and I am very sorry. I am glad you told me."

"Papai, how do you know it hurts?"

"Because, Eva, they did that to me as a child in school. It did not make me a better student. Now come, let's sit outside and watch the sun set."

He puts his arm around me and we walk out to the veranda.

1947

December 22, Monday

It is Christmas time, and I am ten years old. The year 1947 will be ending soon. I have a new little brother named José, he is two months old. I help Madrasta with all the kids, but I especially like little babies. João turned two in September, and Miriam and I celebrated our birthday together. Miriam is one year old and walking, and she says a lot of words. I love her curly black hair and her dark eyes, and the little shrieky noise she makes when she giggles. Everyone says she is stuck on me, because she won't let me out of her sight without fussing until I pick her up.

José has soft brown hair and those big blue eyes that follow you around. Madrasta gives him mamar in the living room while the kids are running around and Cacilda and I get lunch ready.

"Eva, are you ready to go back to school next month?"

"Yes, Senhora. I am doing better with my reading and writing. I'm slow but I can read better. And I like seeing my friends again."

"That's good, Eva. You know I have to be tough on you, but it is for your own good. I don't like punishing you so I'm glad you are studying well."

"Yes, Senhora."

Madrasta hasn't punished me in more than a year, since her tummy got big with José. I am allowed to go cook with Dona Francisca two days a week. Madrasta cooks more often too.

There has been no rain for months, and the dust is everywhere. We sweep and clean but right away the dust settles in the corners and on the windowsills again. More people pass through Picuí on their way south to the big city to find work.

1948

January 12, Monday

The first day of school is hot and dusty. Daniel, Ana and I walk to school together. Senhora Rocha greets us at the gate. We are early, so I have time to talk with my friends before school begins. My friend Júlia is in the school yard.

"Eva, did you have a nice Christmas?" she asks.

"Yes, Júlia, how about you?"

"Yes, we had family visiting from up north, then they went south by bus."

"We had a quiet time at home, my new brother José is three months old."

"I know you love babies, Eva!"

"Babies and cooking!" We laugh.

"Did you hear about the cinema they are going to have in the main square tonight?"

"Cinema? In the praça?"

"There's some people that travel to towns and bring a movie. They put a big cloth up and everyone can watch! It's going to be late because it has to be really dark."

"Oh, I hadn't heard about that. Will you go?"

"No, I have to be in bed. My father won't let me. It's for adults."

I have to go see what the cinema in the praça is like. I have heard people talk about the movies but we have never had movies in Picuí. I can't imagine what it must be like. I do all my chores and homework and get all the kids into bed a little bit early. Papai and Madrasta are in the living room talking.

"Papai, Senhora, I am going to bed now." Papai looks surprised.

"Eva, it's early. Have you done all your homework, and are you ready for school tomorrow?"

"Yes, Papai, it's all done."

"All right, then, good night. Sleep with the angels."

"Good night, Papai, good night, Senhora."

I close the bedroom door and get into bed with my clothes still on. João and Miriam are breathing softly, so I know they are asleep. I listen for a while to be sure. I almost can't breathe. I get up and open the window as quietly as I can. Out the window, around the corner of the house, to the side gate. The gate is never used and makes a squeaking noise when I open it, and I hold my breath for a few seconds. I close and latch the gate and start walking to the praça.

I keep to the shadows; a couple stumbles, laughing, out of the door to a house and I back up against the wall so they won't see me. People in the streets are walking toward the main square.

There are little lights on strings hanging from the lamp posts around the praça, and tables and chairs have been moved from the café to the center of the square. I squat down in the darkness of the bushes while I look around. A large white cloth is hanging from the gazebo, and people are drinking and talking, some are smoking. When the square is full of people, a man walks in front of the cloth and claps his hands for attention.

"Ladies and gentlemen! We are pleased to present a cinematic extravaganza all the way from Rio de Janeiro and São Paulo! Watch carefully, and at the conclusion of our film we will be offering products for sale. Only the most discerning among you will appreciate the quality and uniqueness of our offerings, designed to improve your health and beauty, and supplies are limited! Without further ado, Cine Espetacular!"

All the lights around the square are switched off. There is another man across from the suspended cloth who has a metal box that he does something to and a flickering light comes out the end. I am close enough to see insects in the light, then I look over to the cloth and there are images of a big city, cars driving and lightning coming out of the top of a building. Then people in fancy clothes, dancing. Then a beautiful woman's face covers the whole cloth and she is painting her lips and patting the tall shiny hair on her head. I could watch it forever, but too quickly the metal box makes a clicking sound and the images turn to spots.

People in the praça are talking and pointing, looking at the cloth and then back at the man with the metal box. Then the other man gets up again and gestures toward some tables and invites everyone to come look. I want to see what it is so badly but I can't let them see a kid out alone at night. And I have to get home! If the babies wake up Papai and Madrasta will find out I'm gone and I'll be in the worst trouble of my life.

I hurry home, hiding in the shadows whenever I hear voices, my heart bumping in my chest. When I get home the house is dark and I open the creaky gate as slowly as I can. Holding my breath, I open my bedroom window just a little and listen. No sound. I open the window some more and pull myself up and in. I sit on the floor under the window for a long time, listening. I close and latch the window and undress in the dark.

I lie awake a long time, listening to be sure no one is awake. And thinking about the big city, about the beautiful woman with shiny hair and painted lips.

PART II

1956

February 20, Monday

The Mendes Mercadinho has almost anything you could want. The shop has hardware, farm tools and animal medicine, dishes and pots and pans, fabric and laces and thread, vegetables and fruits and food in tins. And my sweets and savory salgados. I bake new items for Senhor Mendes every other day. They sell out the first day but I don't have time to bake more often.

The shop faces the main square of Picuí, and this morning the only light in the shop is filtering in from the praça. Antônio Mendes is tight with money, and if he can see well enough to count it he doesn't need electricity. The light is dancing with fine dust as I enter the shop.

"Seu Antônio, bom dia!"

"Bom dia, Eva, all good with you?"

"Yes, thank you, Seu Antônio. I have fresh sweets and salgados for you."

"It's a good thing, because they fly out of the shop. For the last batch, do you want cash?"

"Thank you, but this time I'd like to use store credit. I'm ready to make myself a new dress, and I have my eye on that flowered fabric up there."

He looks up at the top shelf of the fabric section.

"You have very good taste as always, Eva. That is my most expensive bolt, viscose imported from Italy."

"I love the way it drapes, and I have just the style to set it off. Two meters please."

Senhor Mendes takes my tray and hands me back the empty one. He moves the ladder so he can reach the bolt of fabric. He carefully measures and cuts, then calculates the amount on a scrap of wrapping paper and I add enough cash to cover the cost.

"So you are the angel who makes those sweets!"

A deep voice like a panther purring. A man in the shadows where I can't see him well, leaning with one elbow on the counter in the hardware area. I didn't notice him when I came in. Senhor Mendes looks over at him.

"What can I help you with, Luiz?"

"Electrical supplies, as usual. But go ahead and help the young lady, I have a long list."

Senhor Mendes wraps my fabric carefully in paper. I put the package on top of my tray and thank him, then walk out squinting into the sunlight. A shadow blocks the sun and I look up. The man is tall. I cover my eyes with my hand.

"I'm not usually one for sweets, but I can't get enough of those cocadas. The coconut just melts in your mouth."

His voice is like warm molasses in my ears. He turns to face the sun and I turn to look at him. He's young, but his black hair is already going silver. His dark eyes crinkle like a smile, but his mouth is serious, like someone who is keeping a secret.

"Excuse me, Sir, I cannot talk with you in the street like this. We have not been properly introduced."

He laughs delightedly. "Goodness, where are my manners! Luiz Carlos Caetano Lima; it's a pleasure to meet you." He bows his head slightly.

I just stand there staring at him. Thinking.

"And you, Madame, are . . .?"

"Eva."

"Eva who?"

"Just Eva. I have to go." I turn and head toward home, stumbling a little on the cobblestones. He calls after me.

"I hope to see you again soon, Eva! A good afternoon to you!"

My face is hot. As my feet hit the soft dust of the small streets closer to home my thighs start to tingle and zing up through my tummy. I have to stop and lean on a wall to catch my breath. I wait there for a few minutes, clutching my package to my chest. After a long while my breathing slows and I put one foot in front of the other, making my way home.

"Eva, is that you?" Madrasta calls from her bedroom in the newest part of the house.

"Yes, Senhora." I put down my package and tray in the kitchen.

"I got my hands full here, come help me!"

The addition to the house added four bedrooms, very important because the house was bursting at the seams with fourteen of us now. Madrasta is giving mamar to Deborah, who is almost a year old, and Mordecai, two, obviously has a dirty diaper and is lurching around and giggling as he upends things around the room. I scoop him up and change his diaper as he protests.

"What took you so long?"

"Senhora, I wasn't gone that long. I bought some fabric to make a dress, I've been looking at it a while and I wanted to get it before someone else bought it."

"Well, I guess you can buy what you want with the money you make from baking. But I don't know why you need a fancy dress."

"Who said it will be fancy?"

"I know your taste, you'd think you lived in Paris."

"I'd love to live in Paris!"

"Yeah, you think it's funny. But you need to be more realistic about your future."

"What do you mean?"

"Ana is married already, but you are eighteen years old. You can read and write, but just barely. You will live here with us and help with the kids, but your chances of getting married are slim to none at your age. Besides, as the oldest girl you have to take care of us when we are old."

I turn and look at her, and let Mordecai slide down my legs and run off.

"How can you know what God has planned for me?"

She gives me an exasperated look. "Eva, I'm sorry, but you know you won't be allowed to marry outside the church. And the only place you would meet a suitor is at church. And there is no one your age who isn't already spoken for."

"Very well, Senhora. I will keep that in mind. Thank you." I head to the old part of the house, where I share a bedroom with the two other girls, Miriam, who is nine, and Raquel, six.

Just because Madrasta got married at fifteen doesn't mean it is the right thing to do. I was very unhappy to see Ana get married this year, though she waited until she was sixteen. She is very smart and could have gone on in school but she fell for a boy in church and that was the end of that.

Feb 22, Wednesday

I'm impatient to take my next batch of baking to Senhor Mendes's shop. I'm curious to see Luiz again, but I can't let him know that. I slow my steps as I come around the corner to the praça. It turns out the shop is empty, and there is no one hanging around outside.

"Oi, Seu Antônio! How are you this morning?"

"Very well, Eva, thank you. And you?"

"Just fine, thank you. How is business?"

"Not too busy this morning."

"Say, who was that guy who was here on Monday buying electrical supplies? He was very forward . . ."

"Yes, he was, wasn't he? He's all right, though. He just came down from Ceará to work with his brother. Luiz is an electrician, and his brother Chico is a carpenter, maybe you know him?"

I shake my head.

"Well, Chico has work here so Luiz came down to help. There's almost no work anywhere in the Northeast, as you know."

"Mmmm, I see. All right then, that's it! See you on Friday. Thanks!"

February 25, Saturday

It's a Saturday morning, so there is an open-air market in the praça. I don't really have anything to buy but Luiz was not around Mendes's shop yesterday and maybe I will catch a glimpse of him. I put the finishing touches to my new dress and love the way it looks and feels. I made up a story about needing spices, to throw Madrasta off the scent because she's always suspicious.

I grab my shopping satchel and head out the front gate, trying to suppress the bounce in my step, like when I was little and happy and wanted to skip. The praça is busy with lots of booths and people milling about. I slowly wander around, saying hello. I linger at the booth selling peanuts and buy a piece of paçoca, letting the first bite melt in my mouth. I turn to move on to the other booths, and bump straight into Luiz.

"Whoa, watch it there, you'll choke on your paçoca!" He's laughing as he looks down at me. This makes me mad, and I look up at him with a frown.

"I think there could be a question as to who should watch where they're going, actually."

"Well, I suppose that's true, fair enough. But how are you? How is the sweet and salgados business?"

"Very good, thank you."

"I'm glad to hear that. May I offer you a Coca-Cola?"

"I'm sorry, I don't know what that is."

"It's new, from America. A cold drink for a hot day."

"It doesn't have alcohol, does it?"

"Of course not. Try one?"

"All right."

He leads me over to the pharmacy and a big red metal cooler. The bottles are fat and curved and cold to the touch. The worker pops the caps and hands them to us. Luiz tilts his toward me.

"Cheers!"

The liquid is cold and bubbly and tastes like sugar cane juice and spices. I like it a lot.

"You know, this is very good actually."

Luiz laughs. "Yes, a different kind of treat."

We enjoy the cold drinks silently for a few minutes.

"Eva, can we meet in the praça to talk one evening next week? I want to learn more about you."

I think for a minute. "I would like that, Luiz, but there is a problem. My family's church is very strict, and my father is one of the deacons. I'm not allowed to see anyone from outside."

"Well, then, I guess I'll have to join the church! I was raised Catholic but I don't go to mass these days."

"Luiz, I'm not sure you understand. It's a very conservative evangelical church. They are very rigid. It wouldn't be easy for you to just drop in."

"Don't they want more converts? I'll press my brother into service and make him come with me."

"Okay, but I warned you. It's the blue storefront on the other side of town. Morning service tomorrow is 11 a.m. I'll understand if you change your mind."

"I won't. I'll see you tomorrow."

We say goodbye and turn our separate ways. Then he calls after me.

"Oh wait. One more thing. Nice dress. You did wonders with that fabric. Congratulations."

My face gets hot and I just nod and look at my feet as I head home.

Feb 26, Sunday

I'm nervous about church this morning. Luiz probably won't show up, but if he does, what do I do? I don't want my family to know I've been talking with him. But how can I act like I haven't met him? The whole conversation happened too fast yesterday, and later I realized we need to get our story straight. Especially because he is so bold and I'm worried what he will say.

I try on dresses and change them several times. I have to wear a prim dress with long sleeves like the church requires, but I want to look nice just in case Luiz shows up. I definitely can't wear a dress like my new floral one. I settle on a navy dress with a white lace collar.

"Eva, what is taking you so long? Hurry up and help me get these kids ready!" Madrasta sounds flustered, as usual.

"Coming, Senhora!"

We gather everyone together, wipe noses, smooth hair, adjust collars, tie shoelaces. It's like trying to control a herd of wild animals. One gets straightened out and another escapes to go play instead of going to church.

"Ready, everyone?" Papai is holding the front door open. We file out behind him and walk slowly to the church. It's hot today, and I'm feeling it in my navy dress. Sweat trickles down my back. The kids are skipping and jumping and stirring up a dust cloud.

"Kids! Walk calmly, I'm going to be covered with dust by the time we get to the church!"

"So what, Eva? That's just how it is. Is something different about today?" Madrasta's sixth sense is on high alert now; I mentally kick myself and resolve to be quiet.

Pastor is at the front door to the church greeting everyone as usual. I pull the kids together and head for our usual pews, so we can be seated quickly. If Luiz and his brother show up I won't have to react. Pastor speaks to Papai.

"Allow me to introduce our guests, Deacon! Luiz and Francisco are from Ceará and have not yet found a church home here in Picuí."

Luiz and Chico got here early. I don't dare turn around. My whole body feels hot and sweat is pouring inside my dress now. Oh God help me.

"Welcome to our church, gentlemen." My father greets them with a handshake.

Luiz extends his hand. "I am Luiz, and you can call my brother Chico."

Papai is acting like having someone new show up at our church is not an unusual event. I can't remember anyone new who wasn't attached to a church family. But no one seems to think it's strange.

We are seated at the front, so I don't have to look at Luiz, thank goodness. I think I will faint if I see him. The service goes too quickly. I want it to go on and on so I don't have to think about what happens next. But it is over and now the congregation goes into the community hall for coffee and sweets. Maybe Luiz and his brother will leave now. As I move the children to the social hall, I hear Luiz and Chico talking with people and introducing themselves, moving in the same direction. I help get the kids seated and gather sweets and juice for them, keeping my gaze down. So far, so good. I fuss around the kids and start to breathe a little easier.

"Excuse me, Deacon, may we be seated?" No! Luiz is asking to sit with our family!

"Of course, please be at home." My father indicates two chairs across from me. Keep breathing. In, out. In, out. At least he's not talking to me.

"So, you are from Fortaleza?" My father begins small talk with the two of them.

"Juazeiro do Norte, originally. But yes, we lived in the capital for several years because there is more construction work there." Chico replies.

"Juazeiro is a religious center. Are you not Catholics?" Papai goes straight to religion, and I wish I could hide under the table.

Luiz jumps in. "We were raised Catholic but have not practiced the religion in several years."

"Ah, I see. I found God as a young man and was baptized in the evangelical church." Papai will be off on a proselytizing jaunt soon if someone doesn't distract him.

We are spared because Pastor clears his throat to make an announcement.

"Brothers and sisters, I would like to welcome our visitors today. Luiz and Francisco Lima are new in Picuí, having moved here from Ceará. They are seeking the peace of the Lord in a church, and I would like us all to make them feel welcome."

Everyone murmurs and claps a bit, turning to say welcome, clapping them on the back. It's nice, actually. Though the church can be rigid and mandates lots of things that chafe me, it is a true home among brothers and sisters. And many are true Christians, like Mamãe was. Welcoming the stranger as Jesus would.

Thank goodness Luiz doesn't speak to me directly. He and Chico chat with Papai about the construction business and ask Papai about the postal service when they learn he is head of the Picuí office. Luiz draws him out a bit and learns about his days riding the circuit by horse from Natal to Recife. And soon enough, it is time to go. I stay behind to help clean the dishes with a few of the sisters, while Madrasta and Papai take the kids home. Everyone files out of the hall and things are quiet.

"When was the last time we had visitors?" one sister asks the group.

"Remember, we had a family who visited last year?" another sister replies.

"Yes, but they were living with the Silvas, they didn't just pop in out of the blue."

"Yes, that's right. But single young men . . . I can't remember anyone like that visiting before."

"They seemed nice enough."

"Easy on the eye, I'll say that, especially that younger one!"

I keep my head down, washing and rinsing and looking for specks of dirt on the counter.

"Eva, what do you think? Good-looking young men, huh?"

"I didn't notice."

"Well, I think you need your eyes checked. I think you need glasses."

They all cackle uproariously and my face is burning. I take a deep breath and finish tidying up; I hang up my apron and leave by the side door.

"I thought you'd never finish cleaning up!" I almost jump out of my skin. Luiz has been lurking at the side of the church waiting for me.

"Shhhhh!" I hiss at him. "What is wrong with you! If people see me with you I'll be in huge trouble!" I start to rush past him toward the street. He reaches for my wrist, just glancing, not grabbing. Electric shocks run up my arm. I turn and look up at him.

"Eva, don't worry. I just can't stand not talking with you. I promise I'll be respectful and keep things quiet. I plan to come to service for a few weeks before I ask your father if I can begin to see you."

"Why do you want to see me? There are plenty of other fish in the sea."

"None as strong and beautiful as you. You don't know it but you cast a spell on me and I can't resist. I'll wait as long as it takes, do whatever it takes."

I want to cry, but with happiness. I can't speak.

"Eva, may I pursue you? Will you allow me?"

I look into his dark eyes and take a deep breath. "Yes, Luiz. I would like that."

"Go with God, querida. Nothing will keep me from you."

I put my head down and head out to the street, then home.

April 8, Sunday

It's the Sunday after Easter, and Luiz has been to church every week since his first visit. Chico is now staying home with his wife and two small children (it turns out he wasn't single after all) and Luiz comes alone. He mainly talks with Papai and the older brothers in the church, but sometimes chats with me a bit. I've relaxed some about being near him, but it still makes me nervous. We speak briefly in passing at the Mercadinho or in the praça and have had a few secret moments of conversation on side streets. But I still don't want anyone to see us.

As we file into the church hall after the service, Luiz goes up to Papai and speaks quietly with him. Papai listens with a frown on his face and then looks intently into Luiz's eyes. Luiz nods, shakes Papai's hand and goes to get coffee. Papai comes over to the counter where I am helping serve.

"Eva, come here for a moment, would you?"

"Yes, Papai."

We go to the side of the hall, where he speaks quietly to me.

"Luiz has asked to talk with me and I have invited him to lunch. Why don't you go home and let Cacilda know we need to set another place at the table?"

I look up at him, hoping I don't look too guilty.

"I . . . yes, I will, Papai."

I excuse myself and take off my apron, leaving by the side door and heading home, my feet gliding through the dust and over the cobblestones. When I reach home I call out to Cacilda.

"Oi in the house! Is everything ready for lunch?"

"Eva, you're early! Things are not quite ready, you know. What's going on?"

"Never mind about that, and I don't want any questions. We will have a guest so let's set one more place at the table."

"Who, Eva? Who is the guest?"

I give her a withering look and say nothing. She looks down and shuffles off to the kitchen. I go to my room and smooth my hair and pinch my cheeks to make them pink. But they're not pink enough so I slap them a little. I want to bang my head against the wall but have to keep moving so things will be ready. I try not to think about what is going to happen and how things will go. In no time at all, everyone is back from church. Papai has invited Luiz to sit in the parlor. The kids are hiding in the hallway, whispering and snickering. I grab two of the younger boys by the backs of their collars and turn them around and silently wag my finger in their faces with an angry look on my face. They get very quiet and slink away.

Lunch is excruciating. Things are pleasant enough, and the roast capon is delicious. We have orange carrot cake and coffee for dessert. Conversation is very subdued throughout the meal, though. I can hardly eat a thing, but I force myself to eat enough to keep up appearances. When the meal is finished, Papai sends the kids out to play, and asks me to go out in the yard to keep an eye on them. He leads Luiz back to the parlor. Madrasta and Cacilda busy themselves cleaning up in the kitchen. After an eternity, Papai comes out on to the veranda and asks me to come in. He leads me to the parlor. Luiz stands when we enter the room.

"Have a seat, Luiz. I've asked Eva to join us to make her aware of our conversation and our understanding. Eva, please take a seat." He points to a straight-backed chair across the room.

"Luiz, you have said you are serious about seeing Eva, and that your intentions are honorable. And I let you know that she is not to be trifled with, that I will only approve of you seeing her if your intent is marriage. And you have indicated that is your intent."

Luiz looks over at me and nods and looks back at Papai, who continues. "I have made Luiz aware that there can be no marriage outside of our church, and that if after an appropriate amount of time getting to know each other you do indeed resolve to be married, then he must convert through baptism. He states he would do so in that situation. Have I described our conversation accurately, Luiz?"

"Yes, Sir, you have."

"Further, you may not be together without an escort. You may meet on the front or back veranda in the evenings, or you may meet in the praça if your sister Ana can be there. Of course she will sit discreetly on a bench across from you. Do you understand me?"

"Yes, Sir."

"Yes, Papai."

"Well, then, you have my approval under the conditions I have set forth. And I trust you will inform me if you begin to think about more serious plans."

We both murmur agreement. Luiz shakes Papai's hand and bows his head to me, arranging to return Tuesday after dinner. And then he is gone, and my heart and head are doing somersaults. I can be with Luiz! I want to talk with him for hours and learn all about him.

April 10, Tuesday

Two days take forever to pass; I feel impatient and short-tempered, wanting to be with Luiz. I'm excited, nervous, scared and happy all at once. Dinner is over, the dishes are done, and the little kids are put to bed.

"Oi in the house!"

Luiz is at the front gate. I try not to run to let him in. We don't touch when we meet because that wouldn't be proper, but I feel waves of heat coming off our bodies when we get close. We sit on the bench outside the front door. Prying eyes can see through the iron filigree front gate, but I think it's better than the prying ears if we talk on the veranda outside the kitchen.

"Eva, thank you for letting me pursue you. I know it isn't easy, and I know I am a stranger in town, really."

"I'm very happy, Luiz. I really want to learn more about you."

"As do I. Shall I go first? What do you want to know?"

"How you and your brother came to Picuí, of all places. About your work. Growing up, your family, everything."

"Whoa, that's a lot. Where to begin? Well, I grew up in Juazeiro do Norte in the interior of Ceará. It's a small town and there is not a lot of work. My parents died when Chico and I were young, so it was just us, living with our aunt. I followed my brother to the capital, Fortaleza, so I could apprentice with an electrician. My brother, Chico, came to Picuí to build several buildings for a rancher and got me a job here too."

"What will happen when this job is over?"

"I will have to find more work. But this is a big job and it won't be finished for a few more months. What about you?"

"I think you know I'm the oldest of twelve. I will be nineteen this year. I finished school and got my diploma, but for now I am helping here at home and doing baking for the Mercadinho, and

I take orders for cakes for birthdays, and so on."

"What do you feel excited about? What are your dreams?"

I look down at my lap and smile a little. "No one has ever asked me that. I love cooking. I love learning new things. I love to create beautiful things like dresses. I love babies and kids. And you?" I dare to look into his dark eyes as he goes quiet.

"I am passionate about justice and freedom. About every Brazilian having a chance to earn a living, to be happy. And for an end to poverty and misery."

This is deeper than I expected. "Luiz, that is very profound. Are those things even possible?"

"I think J.K. will help make these things possible."

I've heard about the president who took office in January. Juscelino Kubitschek, who everyone calls J.K., is talking about "fifty years of progress in five," and makes us proud of the sentiment on our flag: *Order and Progress.* But I just barely follow politics.

"Luiz, are you involved in politics?"

"Only to vote and to help organize workers. We have been exploited too long by the colonels and the wealthy, who control everything."

We sit without talking for quite a while. I'm proud of Luiz for his high ideals, but I worry about his involvement in the workers' movement. Stirring around in that pot can be dangerous in Brazil. He breaks the silence.

"Eva, you are so beautiful. I want to get lost in your eyes. Are they brown or green?"

"I don't know, Luiz. My mother had green eyes, so I think they're like hers. My mother died when I was eight so I don't remember exactly."

"Eva, I'm so sorry. How did she die?"

"She died when João was born. From bleeding."

"That is very sad. It must have been so hard for you growing up."

I just nod my head and try not to cry. I feel Mamãe is still with me and guiding me, but it hurts to think about how we lost her.

"I've upset you, Eva. I'm sorry. And it's getting to be time for me to go. How about Friday evening? Can you see if Ana can sit with us in the praça?"

"Yes, I'd like that. Plan on 6:30 at the praça; if I'm not there just come here to the house."

We look into each other's eyes for a long moment before he nods and is gone, out the gate and down the street.

April 13, Friday

The sun has just set and I am walking to the praça with Ana. She is full of questions about Luiz but I just shush her. As we come around the corner I see Luiz is early, pacing back and forth.

I grab Ana's elbow. "Go sit on the bench across the praça, and don't be obvious."

Ana sighs and heads across the square. Luiz greets me and we stand and look at each other for a long moment. His shoulders are wide and his sleeves hug the muscles of his upper arms. My head starts to swim a little and I'm glad to sit down.

"How are you, querida?"

"I have no patience to wait days to see you. I wish we could be alone instead of sitting here for everyone to gawk at. And my sister is the main one staring!"

He just laughs. "Shall we have a Coca-Cola?"

He buys one for Ana and she sips it from her bench across the praça. The drink is cold and bubbly and sweet and I calm down a bit.

"How is the building project going?"

"More quickly than I would like. I don't think there will be work here in Picuí after this project is finished."

"What will happen then?"

"I had hoped to wait to tell you this, but there is talk of work on the president's new project, to move the capital from Rio to the interior. They're calling it Brasília."

I had heard on the radio of the president's vision, hacking a new city out of the scrub in the state of Goiás. It sounds impossible.

"J.K. wants to finish building the new capital by 1960, and he has already laid the plans out, with a design by the famous architect Oscar Niemeyer."

I'm holding my breath. "Will you be leaving for good?"

"Chico and I will travel there when this project is finished. From what I hear there is plenty of work."

I can't talk because I know I will cry. I look down at my lap.

"Eva, I wanted more time before I talked to you about this, but I just can't wait. Please forgive me."

He is going to tell me goodbye. I won't be able to keep from crying. I hold my breath. He kneels by the bench and looks up at me.

"Eva, will you marry me?"

Not goodbye . . . *marry me* . . . what? My head is spinning.

"I know it's too quick. I know people will talk. But I have never been so sure of anything in my life. I love you. I want to spend the rest of my life with you. It's all right if you aren't sure, I can wait for your answer. Just please don't say no."

I take his hand in both of mine. His eyes are wet. "Yes, Luiz, yes. I will marry you."

His arms are around me and his mouth is on mine, warm and tasting of Coca-Cola. Footsteps running across the praça as Ana moves to intervene.

We step apart, laughing. Ana stops and looks at us disapprovingly.

"It's all right, Ana. We are going to be married!" I laugh and wipe tears from my eyes. She just shakes her head and moves to a closer bench.

"Eva, I must talk with your father. He would have expected to give his approval before I asked you, so let's pretend, all right?"

"Yes, Luiz. It will be a scandal to get married so quickly but I don't care. And my father can't really say anything about quick marriages."

We head back to the house with Ana close behind. As we enter through the front gate, my father comes to the door. He opens it for us.

"Seu José, may I have a word with you, Sir?"

My father nods and beckons Luiz to enter the parlor. I sit on the bench outside the front door with Ana. It's taking too long, Papai must be giving him a real going-over.

"Eva, will you come in please?" It is Luiz calling me, not Papai. My breath is jagged and my hands are shaking. We all sit.

Papai speaks first. "Eva, Luiz has asked me for your hand in marriage. To be honest, this has been a very quick courtship. But he has told me of his plans for your life together, and because you are a grown young lady I believe you can make your own decisions. Is this what you want?"

"Yes, Papai. I want to marry Luiz."

"Well, then, you have my blessing. May God bless you both."

Luiz takes my hand and squeezes it.

"Luiz is aware that I will not approve a marriage outside the church. For this reason he must be baptized. We will arrange it for a week from Sunday."

And just like that, I am engaged to Luiz. We must plan the wedding quickly, but first, the baptism.

April 22, Sunday

"Glory to God. Let us welcome our candidate, Luiz Carlos Caetano Lima."

My father is doing the introductions. Everyone is gathered behind the church, where a large tank has been filled with water. The Pastor is wearing a loose white linen shirt and stands in the tank next to Luiz, also wearing all-white linen.

"Celebrant Pastor is our pastor, Dr. Aníbal Sousa Martins."

Pastor raises his hands toward the congregation.

"Let us pray. Our dear God and father, we rejoice in you. And today your son Luiz through these waters this morning proclaims his faith. May this experience be one that is never forgotten by him, and let everyone here share this feeling of joy in the Lord."

Luiz clasps his hands together in front of his heart, and Pastor puts his hand on his, and another behind his back, and dips him back into the water. He holds him there a bit longer than usual, and Luiz is lifted back up sputtering and gasping for breath. Everyone applauds and is murmuring prayers.

We all file into the church hall, and there are sweets and salgados and café. Luiz appears in his usual clothes, his hair wet and combed. Everyone congratulates him. He stands next to me and puts his arm around my waist where no one can see.

"I would do anything for you, Eva. Now you know."

His eyes are smiling but his mouth is serious. Like someone keeping a secret.

July 22, Sunday

As I enter the church on Papai's arm, all eyes in the congregation turn to me. Luiz is waiting in front of the pulpit. It is a cool evening, and there are small bouquets of flowers at the ends of the pews, making the church beautiful despite the harsh overhead light. A few rose petals are on the ground in front of me. I'm holding my breath, each step leading me closer to my new life.

Luiz's brother Chico and his wife Sónia are on the groom's side. On the bride's, my oldest brothers Daniel and Paulo, my sister Ana, and my best friend Júlia from school. Miriam stands to one side and takes the bouquet from me so my hands are free. Piano and guitar provide the music. Papai shakes Luiz's hand and hugs me, giving Luiz my hand. We turn to face Pastor.

The Pastor delivers a brief welcome and prayer, and we recite our vows. I want to cry from happiness. Luiz looks deep in my eyes as he recites his vows. Then it is time for the rings. We turn as five-year-old Raquel brings our rings on a pillow. The rings are placed and Pastor offers a prayer and welcomes us to the married world.

"Whom God has brought together let no man separate!" We exit the front of the church to music. Outside, Luiz bends me over backward and kisses me on the lips.

"Luiz, people will see us!"

"Who cares? We're married now!"

"I know but they are still rigid about things like that." My cheeks are hot and I pat my hair and little veil back in place. We walk around to the side door of the church and enter the hall where the reception is laid out. Congratulations and good wishes all around. My heart could burst as I look at Luiz, tall and distinguished in his dark suit.

Dona Francisca gives me a hug of congratulations and several other church ladies step over to greet me. "Eva, what a beautiful dress! I've never seen one like it, where did you get it?"

"Thank you, sister. Three of the sisters gave me fabric and lace, and I did what I could to make a gown."

"Well, that is spectacular. Congratulations. And the cake? Absolutely gorgeous. I know no one but you could confect such a thing."

"I love the details and the sugar flowers," another sister adds.

As the reception winds down, Papai and Madrasta lead us out the front of the church and back home. I don't have to lift my skirts because I didn't have enough fabric to make a long gown. When we get to the house, I go to my room to change and finish packing my suitcase. We will live with Luiz's brother, his wife and two children. Luiz takes the suitcase as I enter the parlor and sets it beside the front door.

"Luiz, may I have a word with Eva please?" It seems strange for Papai to be asking Luiz's permission. Papai leads me out to sit underneath the mango tree.

"Eva, may God bless and keep you and Luiz. I wish you health and happiness and a long life together."

"Thank you, Papai."

"It is hard for me to lose you, but I am gaining a son, as they say. Of all my children, you most remind me of your mother. Your determination, your kindness, your creativity."

I start to cry a little. "Oh, Papai . . ."

"I knew what was happening with Luiz from the beginning."

"What do you mean?"

"Seu Antônio told me after that first day at his shop. I made sure everyone kept an eye on you. And you behaved like a good Christian girl. I am glad you have found happiness. May God be with you."

Papai stands and I throw my arms around him. He hugs me back. I wipe the tears, and we go back into the house.

Chico and his family live on the other side of town. The town taxi is waiting outside.

"Luiz, the taxi? I don't mind walking."

"Not today, Dona Eva. Today we ride in style." The taxi takes a long route, but I'm not looking at the scenery. Luiz's mouth is warm and soft and he kisses me gently, except when we hit potholes and laugh uproariously. I feel like my tummy is bubbling up through my heart. Like an animal in a cartoon movie with its heart going bump, bump, bump out of its chest.

When we arrive home Sónia greets us at the door. She shows us to our room, which is simple and sparkling clean. Luiz sets down my suitcase and shows me around the house: two bedrooms and one indoor bathroom. The parlor is small but neat and the kitchen has enough room for two cooks.

"Do you want café?" Sónia has snacks on the table covered with a cloth.

"Thank you, Sónia, but I couldn't eat a thing. It's been a big day." I lean on Luiz.

"Very well, then. Chico and I are taking the children for a walk into town. We'll be gone for two or three hours. Just make yourself at home, Eva."

"Thank you!"

After they leave I turn and look at Luiz. He reaches for my hand and leads me to our bedroom. All the weeks of waiting tumble away and I throw my arms around him with more force than I mean to. He embraces me and kisses me gently but my lips want more, finding his tongue with mine, wanting to eat him up as a delicious salty-sweet aching grabs me and won't let go. I fumble at his belt, pulling and trying to undo it. His breath is jagged and hot on my neck. Breathing in my scent.

"Whoa, Eva, this is your first time. Let's go easy, I don't want to hurt you."

"Forget that!" I push him back on the bed and jump on him, smelling his neck, kissing his mouth, grabbing at his belt. He gets his clothes off and I toss my fancy dress on the floor, yanking my bra and losing patience with my undies. We roll over and he enters me slowly but the fire is burning so hot that I push, push, push until the stars go out and blackness overtakes me.

"Eva, are you all right?"

Luiz is looking down at me. "Gosh, I fell asleep, just like that." I yawn and stretch like a cat. "I'm starving, let's go have our snacks and I'll make café."

"I'm starving too. I'll make the café, I'm sure you want to take a shower."

"Perfect."

I towel off and put my house dress on. Luiz has cakes and café laid out on the table. We sit and eat without talking, and we are happy.

Friday, August 10

The days pass easily, Luiz and Chico leave early for work and come home after dark. Sónia gives me full rein in the kitchen and writes down recipes as I make them. She asks a lot of smart questions and says everything I make is delicious. I also help Sónia with the kids; Cícera is three and Lorival is nearly two.

Luiz and I go to service on Sundays, and I go to Bible study on Wednesday evenings. I am glad to see my brothers and sisters but Madrasta treats me coldly. She is angry that I'm not there to help any more. I haven't forgotten how she treated me as a child, but I must forgive her. She married too young and punishing a child was the only way she knew to feel in control of her life. I'm just glad she took it out on me and not the other kids.

I love spending every minute I can with Luiz, sitting with him after a meal, drinking café and talking, snuggling in bed with him in the early morning before he goes to work. I love how refined he is in his habits. I don't think I could be married to a sloppy guy. Luiz eats like a true nordestino, lining up food in little rectangles with his knife and carefully putting it on his fork to eat, constantly tidying up the food on his plate. He always eats everything, which makes me worry that I haven't made enough, but if he didn't eat it all I'd think he didn't like it.

I am still making birthday and wedding cakes to order and selling sweets and salgados at the Mendes Mercadinho. Luiz keeps up with all the expenses, so I am able to save. If I keep at it, I know we can buy a house one day.

Luiz and I are alone in the parlor; he is reading a newspaper and I am trying to read a novel. It takes me forever but I am making progress. Being calm and patient helps me to read, and my writing is very pretty now after years of practice. I've always been good with numbers, and I keep an account of every penny we spend and every one we save.

"Eva, I need to tell you what's happening at work."

"Oh? How is the project going?"

"The foreman is cutting the crew because the house and buildings are nearing completion. The main work still to be done is plastering and finishing in the house, so Chico and I aren't really needed. The foreman has kept us on and lets us do other things, but that will come to an end soon. We need to plan for that."

"You and Chico are so skillful and honest and hardworking, I'm sure you can find work here in Picuí or nearby."

"Eva, I'm sorry but that's just not realistic. There is no work. That is why people are all moving south. Chico and I have been talking, and when this job is over we plan to go to help build Brasília. We talked about this, do you remember?"

"Oh, Luiz, I didn't think it would happen so soon! Well, I will come with you to Brasília."

"Eva, that really isn't an option. There are no houses to live in: people live in tents or shacks or outside. And there are hardly any women there, just men. You and Sónia will stay here, and Chico and I will come home when we get time off."

I'm heart-sick to think of being separated from Luiz, even if it's only for a few months. But maybe he is wrong, maybe some work will turn up for them here in Picuí.

September 7, Friday

A couple of weeks ago I woke up in the middle of the night with a fierce pain in my belly. I thought it was my period starting a little early, though I usually don't have bad cramps. My tummy ached and hurt and I felt sweaty, but it was gone by the morning.

My period is now two weeks late. This morning I woke up feeling sick. I went into the backyard and tried to throw up but just had dry heaves. There is no doubt in my mind what is happening. I watched Mamãe and then Madrasta go through this. I'm excited but I'm scared, because I don't want to be here with a new baby without Luiz.

Sónia and I put the finishing touches on the evening snack and the table is ready. The two kids are in bed, and the four of us sit down to enjoy our café at the end of the day. Chico speaks first.

"Well, the foreman made it official today. Two more weeks and the project is complete. Luiz and I will need to find new work."

Luiz jumps in. "We have been talking about the opportunities for skilled workers to help build the new capital. Chico and I will travel there right after this project is over. So we need to plan for that."

The reality of this hits me at the same time as a wave of nausea. The café smells disgusting, but this is too much. I run to the bathroom and throw up. Luiz is right behind me.

"Querida, please don't take it so hard. Everything will be all right. This is a great opportunity for us! Once I get established and find a place for us to live, I will send for you. We just need to be patient. I know you are upset or you wouldn't be vomiting."

I turn to him as I wipe my mouth and face. "Luiz, I'm upset about that. But it's our baby that's making me sick."

His eyes open wide and he grins from ear to ear. "Oh, sweetheart, that is wonderful news! I didn't think it would happen so quickly." He wraps me in his arms.

I bury my face in his chest. "I didn't either, Luiz. It shouldn't be a surprise, but it is to me too."

September 21, Friday

Luiz and Chico had their last day of work today and I hate to think of Luiz leaving. The smell of food makes me sick. I can keep down dry bread, and I take little sips of water to keep from feeling dizzy. Sónia understands and she does all the cooking so I can I rest. I feel better lying on my bed but fresh air outside helps too.

"Dona Eva, we're home!" Luiz comes into the bedroom and bends down to kiss me, brushing my hair back from my face. "I brought you something special to help your tummy. Come join us in the kitchen."

Luis stopped at Senhor Mendes's store and brought me a cold bottle of Coca-Cola, which looks good to me right now. I swallow it in little sips, and it goes down easier as it warms up.

"We have good news!" Sónia and I look up from the table as Chico makes the announcement. "We have jobs already, and they are even paying for us to take an airplane from Recife to Brasília. We just have to take a truck to Recife."

"Oh that is good news, but so soon?" I look at Luiz.

"Querida, this is a great opportunity. The big construction company Severo Villares is taking us on, and they pay very well. President J.K. wants the capital built in three years, so we will be working seven days a week."

"Luiz, can't I come with you?"

"Eva, I don't want to be away from you, but we have to be patient. Workers are living in tents, and the baby will arrive in the spring. You and Sónia will keep each other company here until the city is more established and Chico and I find a place for us all to live."

"But Luiz, how soon will you and Chico leave?" I am trying not to cry.

"Monday, querida. We have the weekend to pack our necessities, and then we get the 'parrot perch' truck—it's a bumpy ride but I'm excited about flying on an airplane!"

September 24, Monday

The weekend passes in a blur of preparing and packing, with Chico and Luiz organizing their tools and Sónia and I making food for their journey and washing and mending their clothes. We are up before dawn making breakfast: they have to be at the praça pick up point before dawn to get the truck. Sónia kisses Chico goodbye and I walk with Luiz and Chico through the dark streets to the praça.

"I will write as often as I can, Eva. You need to take care of yourself and our baby. Next May will be here before we know it."

There is a group of men waiting at the praça with toolbags and small bundles of clothes. Some of them are smoking. I can't speak because I will start crying, and I don't want Luiz to begin the journey with the memory of me sobbing. Luiz and I step aside and he hugs and kisses me. I can feel the heat off his body. I want to smell his neck, to hang on and not let go.

"Luiz, I love you. I am very proud of you with this new job. I will be all right. I will wait for the baby and for us to be together again."

"No more than I love you, Eva. Be well and be patient. I know it will be hard. But I won't delay. This will be a great adventure for us, you'll see."

The truck pulls up in a cloud of diesel smoke. The men all clamber up on to the truck bed, which is covered with a canvas awning. They sit on rough wooden benches and put their belongings underneath them. The first light of day casts a pink glow as the truck lumbers down the road. I don't begin to cry until it pulls around the corner and they are gone.

December 21, Friday

Just a few more days until Christmas, and I'm glad to be busy with all the preparations for the holiday at church and all the orders I need to deliver. Sónia and I have been making soft toys for the kids, a doll for Cícera and a dog for Lorival. We chat and laugh as we work on projects after the kids are in bed. Sónia is like a sister to me now.

I hold the doll out to look at her. "How do you like dolly's hair, Sónia? It's just yarn but I think she looks pretty cute. I'll make little braids and tie them with bows."

"Eva, I think you like dolls more than kids do!" She laughs.

"With all the baking and preparations for the church and at Papai's house, I'll barely get everything done before Christmas."

"You are so sweet, Eva. And everyone wants your cakes and salgados for the holidays."

"Ooh, that feels funny!" I giggle and pat my tummy.

"What does it feel like, Eva? It doesn't hurt, does it?"

"It feels like bubbles, or butterflies. Really odd!"

"Eva, that's the baby moving! You're feeling the baby moving!" Sónia jumps up and hugs me.

"I thought he was supposed to kick, not blow bubbles in my tummy."

This strikes us both really funny. Sónia says, "The baby isn't big enough for you to feel kicks, but you will before long. And how do you know it's a boy?"

"Just a feeling I have. Or maybe it's a wish, I'm not sure."

1957

February 28, Thursday

"Oi in the house!" It's Papai, stopping by on the way home from the post office.

"Papai!" I run to the front gate to let him in. "I didn't know you were coming. Blessing, Papai."

"God bless you, my daughter. I thought you might want this." He holds out an envelope, smiling.

"A letter from Luiz! Oh thank you, Papai."

"I'm sure you'll want to read it right away, so I'll be on my way."

"No, Papai. Come in and have café. Just for a few minutes."

"All right, then."

I stoke the fire and put the kettle on to boil water, and gather some sweets and put them on the table.

"Eva, that baby is getting big. How are you feeling, okay?"

"I'm seven months, Papai. And this baby is very rambunctious." He smiles and drinks his café. We talk about the kids and church and how much we need rain. Papai leaves just as Sónia and the kids arrive from town. The sky is lavender and pink from the dust in the air.

April 30, Tuesday

Dona Severina is an old lady now and she moves slowly, but she is still the best midwife anywhere. She delivered me when I was born and next month, God willing, she will deliver my baby. I visit her at home once a month so she can check on the baby and help me make sure everything is ready when the time comes. Even though I've helped prepare for many births with Madrasta, it's different when it's your own.

"Oi in the house!" I call the greeting and Dona Severina comes to the open door and gestures for me to enter. After she checks my tummy and says the baby's head is at the bottom where it should be, we sit at her kitchen table and she gives me fresh orange juice. She treats me like a princess.

"Eva, is the baby active every day?"

"Oh yes, Dona Severina. He especially likes to jump around when I lie down to sleep."

"Yes, they do that, don't they? The baby is growing well and should be here around the end of next month. Do you have everything ready?"

"Yes, and I'm so anxious to meet him! I wish Luiz could be here but they are working seven days a week to build the new capital. He hoped to come home but he can't be gone that long."

"I know it's hard, Eva, but we will have several sisters from church, and Sónia and Ana will all be there to help too."

"Thank you, Dona Severina."

"Eva, I know your mother would be so proud of you. You are so like her, always caring for others. You are making a wonderful new life for yourself. And this baby will arrive safe and sound, if God wills."

"If God wills, Dona Severina."

May 25, Saturday

When I walked to the market this morning I had some sharp pains that made me catch my breath, and now that I'm home they seem to be more regular. Ana is here with me and the pains are about twenty minutes apart.

"Eva, it's important for you to rest. It will be hours before things really get going."

Ana has two kids already, so she can be the expert even though I'm the older sister. I smile to myself. "Yes, Ana, I know you're right. Thank you for being here."

"Of course, Eva. Sónia and I will be with you the whole time. I sent João from church to let Dona Severina know the baby is getting ready to arrive. He was worried, poor thing—even though he's only twelve he's very protective of his oldest sister."

The pains aren't bad yet, but I know it's still early. I recline on the bed and look around the room. I'm nervous but peaceful. Everything is ready, all the baby clothes clean, folded and put away. Lorival is almost three so his crib is now for the new baby. Fresh sheets, cloths and basins for hot water are all stacked in the kitchen. I close my eyes between pains and let my body relax. Dona Severina will be here soon.

May 26, Sunday

It seems like a dream, just like Mamãe always said. From one day to the next, I am a mother. When I wake up, even before I open my eyes, I think, I have a baby! I feel very tired, but warm all over.

"Ana, where is my baby?"

"Don't worry, Eva, they have just taken him to wash him up a bit. They will bring him right back."

Dona Severina and a church sister enter the bedroom and gently hand him over, all wrapped up and cozy. I hold him to me and kiss his forehead, unswaddling him to count his fingers and toes, watching to see if he will open his eyes.

I announce to the sisters, "His name is Carlos. Luiz and I decided before he left for Brasília because I was sure it would be a son. We didn't even have a name for a girl."

Everyone laughs and says that Carlos is a nice name. Dona Severina is smiling but she looks very tired. "Eva, you gave us a bit of a scare. Carlos is a big boy and tried to be difficult. All glory to God, all is well. He is healthy and strong. And you did excellent work to birth him, many hours of work."

"Yes, Dona Severina—he is a big boy, isn't he? Is that why you were all pushing my legs to my chest, and pushing down below? That was rough, but how wonderful when he jumped right out!"

Dona Severina sighs and smooths my hair. "I thought he might be a big boy, especially because Luiz is a tall man. I'm just glad this baby didn't decide to come late. Thanks be to God, all is well."

September 26, Thursday

The days and nights pass in a blur. I sleep when I can and give Carlos mamar constantly, it seems. I love feeding him, those blue eyes staring into mine as he suckles away hungrily, making little grunting noises.

Carlos can be fussy sometimes and I'm grateful for Sónia. I hate to admit that I can lose my patience when I'm tired, but it's true. Sónia seems to know, and knocks on my bedroom door: "Eva, give me that baby!" She takes him into the backyard and lifts him up among the branches of the tree, and the breeze rustling through the leaves calms him.

Carlos is four months old and I feel bad that Luiz is not here to see him. Luiz's last letter was two weeks ago, and he says they are working non-stop so coming home to Picuí is not possible now. He admires our president, Juscelino Kubitschek, so much, calling him "J.K." like everyone does. He says J.K. is living in a wooden house where they also have all the government meetings, and construction is going day and night to build the Palácio da Alvorada, the presidential residence. Luiz writes that the design is modern and huge, just like the high plains and endless sky where they are creating the capital.

1958

January 28, Tuesday

Carlos is a handful. He is only eight months old, but he's pulling himself up on furniture already. It seems like he is always hungry, and when he whimpers to tell me he wants mamar, I feel a pressure as the milk comes into my breasts; it's the oddest feeling. I'm giving Carlos mashed banana and oatmeal and he likes to play with the food and rub it on his face. He makes me laugh several times a day.

Another Christmas has come and gone without Luiz and Chico. Soon Carlos will be walking and talking and Luiz will have missed it. I can't tell Sónia yet, but I have decided to go to Brasília. I will be disobeying the instructions Luiz sends in every letter, where he says he will come to Picuí as soon as he can and to wait and be patient. But I just can't anymore.

I've made plans and will tell Sónia a couple of days before, otherwise she may send a letter to Chico and it will create a lot of trouble. I have money I've saved from all the years selling cakes, so I will make my way to Recife and take an airplane to Brasília from there. Just thinking about it makes me excited but also a little scared.

J.K. says Brazil must make fifty years of progress in five, and it seems we can achieve the dream of being a modern country. Order and progress, just like it says on the flag. It can't just be men that work for that dream. I want to be a part of it, I want to help build the new capital.

February 23, Sunday

I'm helping Madrasta clean up after lunch, and Papai is sitting under the mango tree in the shade. It is very hot. Once everything is tidy, I take Papai a glass of maracujá juice and sit down next to him.

"Thank you, Eva."

"Papai, I have something to tell you but I hope you can keep it a secret for a few days."

He looks at me and stops drinking his juice.

"Papai, I have decided to go to Brasília to be with Luiz. I have everything organized and planned but it will be a surprise to Luiz. He keeps telling me to be patient but Carlos is nine months old and hasn't even met his father yet."

"Eva, are you sure? I hear it is a very rough place. Everyone living in tents and shacks. It will be difficult for a young mother and baby. Perhaps you should reconsider."

"Papai, I'm sorry but I have made up my mind. I have saved plenty of money so you don't need to worry about that. I leave on Thursday. I know it won't be easy, but I will be careful, I promise."

He looks at me and his eyes are wet. "You are very brave and independent, Eva. Just like your mother. May God bless you and Carlos and keep you safe. And don't forget about us here in Picuí."

"Oh Papai, of course I won't! I'll come by in the evening on Wednesday to let the family know."

I walk home through the dusty streets, holding Carlos on my hip and singing a little song to him.

February 27, Thursday

Sónia walks with me through the dark streets to the town square, where the parrot-perch truck takes on passengers. Papai gave me a little suitcase and I'm not bringing many things, just enough clothes and some food. Carlos buries his head in my neck and looks out of the corner of his eye at the people gathered in the darkness. The first part of our journey is to Campina Grande, still in our state of Paraíba, where we will get a bus to Recife, in the state of Pernambuco. I will have to get a hotel overnight in Recife and go to the airport first thing the next morning.

The truck pulls up and sits idling. I am the only woman boarding. The men seem surprised but they help me up and Sónia hands Carlos to me. Sónia looks sad but bites her lower lip and doesn't cry.

"Eva, go with God! Be safe! Write and tell me how things are going, so I can come too once you make the way."

"Don't worry, Sónia. Thank you for everything. I will miss you and the kids."

I wave goodbye as the driver puts the big truck in gear, and I almost fall over, grabbing on to the bench and holding Carlos tight as the truck heads down the road to the big city.

The men stare at me, but one of the guys finally speaks up.

"This isn't a very nice ride for a lady and a baby. Where are you headed?"

"To Campina Grande, to get a bus to Recife." I don't want to give them too much information: you have to be careful talking to strangers. Especially a bunch of men in a truck. Two of the guys start asking the others for their bundles, and they make a little spot for Carlos and me in the corner next to the cab. I thank them and settle in, holding Carlos close. He pulls at my blouse and I cover him with a cloth and give him mamar, then he sleeps.

It's a bumpy ride over dusty roads, with the truck driver having to constantly downshift to slow to a crawl because there are so many big holes in the road. Changing Carlos's diaper when he needs it is a challenge. Four hours is a long time to be bumping around, and I'm glad I don't have to sit on those hard benches.

Finally we reach Campina Grande, and the truck lets everyone off at the bus station. Carlos is hot and fussy, and I hold him on my hip and carry the suitcase in my other arm. The station is very modern and there is a shiny silver bus with people boarding. I rush to the ticket window.

"Good day, I need a ticket to Recife, please."

"Just one?" The ticket agent looks me up and down.

"Yes, Sir, please."

"All right, that is nine cruzeiros. Boarding now, departs in ten minutes."

I rush to the bathroom and almost don't make it after all that bumping for hours. Carlos is not wet, thank goodness. I wash his face off with water and he giggles as I pour some over his head. I quickly wash my face off too.

"Let's go get that bus, Carlos! We better hurry."

The bus is new and the seats are nice and comfortable. The trip will take about six hours. I put the suitcase on the shelf above our seat, and we settle in as the bus leaves the station. The vista is dusty in all directions, and Carlos and I nod off to sleep.

After a couple of stops at roadside cafés, we finally arrive in Recife. It is already dark, but the bus station is in the city center and I get directions to a modest hotel across from the post office and just up from the river. The reception clerk gives me the eye but says nothing, just hands me the register to fill out.

"Six cruzeiros a night room and breakfast, how many nights?"

"Just tonight, please. I need to go to the airport in the morning. Will there be a taxi available?"

"Shouldn't be a problem. Here is your room key, a towel is on the bed. Bathroom is down the hall to the left."

I'm hungry but too tired to think about going out to find something to eat. We still have fruit, dried sausage and cheese. I eat, give Carlos mamar and some fruit, and we go down the hall to the bathroom and wash up. We are both asleep as soon as we lie down on the bed.

February 28, Friday

The sun begins to brighten the sky before 5:00 and I'm wide awake and hungry. I take Carlos to the bathroom and he sits on the floor while I shower, then I pick him up and shower him too. I put on fresh clothes and organize our things in the suitcase. I take the key to the reception.

"When is breakfast served?"

The clerk looks up at the clock behind him. "The restaurant opens in thirty minutes, down the hall to your right."

"Could I leave my suitcase with you for now? I'd like to go out for a walk until breakfast."

The city is already awake, with cars and buses and horse carts going by on the main street in front of the hotel. I walk down to the river and look up at the post office building across the street. It is imposing and modern, like a big square honeycomb with a clock tower on one side. The sun is already strong as we cross the bridge over a huge river. They say Recife is like Venice in Italy, with so much water when the rest of the Northeast is dry.

"What do you think about that river, Carlos? This big city is very grand, don't you agree?" His big blue eyes take it all in and I hug him a little too hard. "I love you, my boy. We are going to see your father soon." I hold him on my hip so he can look at everything as we walk back to the hotel.

I've never seen anything like the breakfast spread out in the restaurant. The usual café and hot milk, many different fruit juices, breads and sweets, jams, yogurt, ham and cheese slices, and so many kinds of fruit: sliced mangos, pineapple, banana, papaya. I fix Carlos some oats with fruit and yogurt and make myself a huge plate.

At reception the clerk hands me my suitcase and I ask the

bellman to call me a taxi. The driver puts my suitcase in the trunk and Carlos and I sit in the back seat.

"Where to, Madame?"

"The airport, please, Sir."

It's a short ride and the car enters a curving drive lined by royal palm trees and we have arrived. I pay the driver and enter the airport. I walk up to the Loide Aero counter.

"A ticket to Brasília, please."

The girl behind the counter smiles at me; she is dressed in a beautiful suit and her hair is pulled back in a sleek bun secured by a hairnet.

"Yes, Madame. Would you like to check a bag?"

"May I carry it with me on the plane?"

"It is quite secure, Madame, to check the bag. And your hands will be free for the little one." She grins at Carlos and he laughs back.

"That will be fine, thank you."

"One way or round trip?"

"One way, please."

Ticket in hand, Carlos and I head toward the embarkation area. The airport is beautiful and modern, with a colorful mural depicting the history of Recife and the Northeast covering one wall. The huge windows of the waiting area look out on a gleaming silver plane with a stubby nose and four propellers on the wings. All my attention has been focused on getting here but now I can breathe in the excitement of the adventure.

"Carlos, look! What a beautiful airplane!"

"Just you and the baby going to Brasília?" I turn to look at the woman behind me. She coos at Carlos and smiles at me. "What takes you to that dusty construction site? It's unusual for a woman to be traveling alone."

She is dressed in a smart red skirt and jacket and stylish

pumps. I wonder how she can walk in those high shoes. Her dark hair is short and wavy with little flat curls in front of her ears. Her large gold earrings glint in the light.

"I'm going to be with my husband, he is working to build the city."

Her eyebrows jump up and she tilts her head and smiles. "Where will you be staying?"

"I don't know, I will find my husband and then I guess we'll see."

"Well, you are in for quite an adventure, querida!" Her voice is a little husky and her laugh is like tinkling glass.

The loudspeaker breaks into our conversation. "Now boarding for flight 72 to Brasília."

We queue up at the door as they check tickets and people walk to the metal stairs up to the door of the airplane. I try to calm my breathing and hold Carlos close as I climb the stairs. The stewardess greets us and checks my ticket and points toward the back of the plane. The woman in the red suit is getting comfortable in a seat near the door.

The stylish woman speaks to the stewardess. "Aeromoça, let the young lady sit here with me. The plane isn't going to be full, is it?" When the stewardess nods her okay, she pats the seat next to her, by the window. I smile and take the seat with Carlos on my lap. There are little curtains over the windows, and I peek out at the airport and all the workers bustling about with carts of baggage.

"My name is Célia." She extends her hand.

"I am Eva, and this is Carlos."

"Carlos, your mom is taking you on a big adventure! Is this your first time flying, Eva?"

"Yes, Dona Célia. It's exciting but it's a little scary."

The tinkling laugh again. "Oh, don't worry, it will be fun."

"Are you traveling alone too?"

She smiles at me. "Yes, but I fly quite a bit. I work as an assistant to the vice president's wife. Dona Maria Thereza Goulart, have you heard of her?"

I hate to admit I haven't. "I don't follow the news and politics very much. I just know the president is Juscelino Kubitschek, J.K."

A tiny whiff of a sneer crosses her face but is gone in a second. "Oh, looks like we are actually leaving on time for once. You'll need to buckle this belt." She shows me how. The stewardess is opening the curtains as she goes down the aisle in the middle of the plane. There is a low hum and the propellers on the wings are a blur. The captain's voice tells us we are cleared for take-off. The stewardess takes a seat at the front and buckles up as the plane begins to move toward the open fields. The pilot stops the plane for a moment then the engines come to life and the plane lumbers forward, gaining speed, and suddenly we are up in the air. My heart is leaping and I want to giggle as the wing dips down and the plane turns, the bright blue of the ocean below. We climb higher and higher and now everything below is brown.

When we have been flying for a while the stewardess offers us café or juices and serves us a snack on beautiful white china. The back of the seat has a little table that drops down. After we eat, Carlos is fussy and I cover him with my big scarf and give him mamar, and he goes to sleep. I drift off to sleep also. The pilot's voice wakes me, telling us we are about to land in Brasília.

The earth below is red and the plane passes over a long open area with heavy equipment moving around and the metal skeleton of a tall building. As the plane descends steadily toward the ground, I see the concrete runway and the plane lands with a couple of bumps.

The humid heat hits me as I walk out the open door to

descend the stairs. The airport is just one simple building, and we wait as the bags are put on a cart. I retrieve mine and head toward the building.

"Eva, you don't know where you're going, do you? Why don't you ride with me?"

I turn toward Célia with a grateful smile, and she leads me out the other side of the building to a waiting black car. The driver is in a black uniform and cap and takes the suitcases and puts them in the trunk. We sit in the back of the spacious car.

"Driver, this lady doesn't know exactly where to go, she is looking for her husband. A candango, came from the Northeast to build the capital. Where might we take her to find where he is staying?"

The driver looks over his shoulder and asks me, "What kind of work does your husband do?"

"He is an electrician," I reply.

The driver starts the engine and puts the car in gear. "Dona Célia, her spouse will most likely be in the tent encampment they built for the skilled workers, near the north wing. We'll try there first."

Célia settles back in her seat. "Brasília's plan is like a map of an airplane, with a center like the body of the plane, and wings to the north and south. Hopefully we'll get lucky and find where he's staying. What is his name?"

"Luiz Carlos Lima." It feels strange to be riding in a fancy car and getting help from Célia, who is obviously an important person.

The dirt streets are wider than any I have ever seen, and the car glides over them quietly with the windows closed to avoid the dust. After a while we pull off the main street and wind around until a series of tents comes into view.

"Driver, stop here please and go ask."

The driver steps out of the car and calls over a worker dressed in orange coveralls. They talk for a minute and he returns to the car.

"There are several electricians who stay in the fourth tent. We can't be sure right now because everyone is at work. But it is probably this encampment. The worker will show you which tent."

The driver gets my suitcase from the trunk. Célia hands me a small card. "The telephone works some of the time, call me if I can help you. I may have work for you once you get settled a bit. Be careful, querida."

"Dona Célia, I don't know how to thank you. I am so grateful for your help. May God bless you for your kindness."

The driver closes the doors and turns the car around, heading back to the main street. Célia smiles and waves at me as the car pulls away.

The man in orange coveralls reaches for my suitcase and gestures for me to follow him. The tents are lined up in a big area that has been cleared, with stumps of trees and brush pushed up around the edges. I take a deep breath and look around as I follow him. The sky is the biggest I have ever seen, with towering clouds on the horizon that look like they could bring rain.

"Here you are, Senhora. I don't know for sure, but I think the electrical worker guys stay in this one." He opens the flap of the tent and I enter. There are twelve beds lined up, six on each side. There are bundles neatly stashed underneath each bed.

"Senhora, why don't you go ahead and rest on the cot in the back there. I'm sure they won't mind. They should be getting back in a couple of hours."

"Where might I find a place to wash up, and the . . .?"

"Oh, the latrines. There aren't any ladies here but all the guys are working so it should be okay now. Go out the front, then left to the end of the tents. And if you turn right instead and go to the other end, there's the place for cooking."

"Thank you very much." He puts the suitcase by the cot and grins at me as he backs out of the tent.

I open the suitcase and organize my things a bit, then with Carlos on hip I head over to the latrines. There is a wooden counter with a crude sink and mirror and I wash our faces and hands, change Carlos's diaper and try to make my hair look nice. The humidity is making it curl, so it's a struggle. I hear a crack of thunder and look up to see that the clouds have turned black. A huge bolt of lightning splits the sky in the distance and I scoop up Carlos and rush back to the tent.

Just as we get inside, the skies open and a torrential downpour begins. That smell of rain on dirt and the sound of the rain beating on the canvas makes me feel peaceful and happy and I lie down with Carlos for just a minute.

Men's voices pierce my sleep. It is dark now. I sit up and pat my hair into place, stand up and smooth my dress. My heart is pounding as I pick up Carlos and smooth his hair. He rubs his eyes with his little fists and looks around. Two men come into the tent.

"Whoa, what do we have here? Excuse me, Senhora, how did you get here?"

"I . . . I . . . came from Paraíba to be with my husband," I stammer.

"Really! Well, that's a first. Who is your husband? What does he do?"

"His name is Luiz Lima, he works with . . ."

"Eva! My God in heaven! What are you . . .? How did you . . .?" Luiz has entered the tent with a group of men and rushes toward me. At first he stands opposite me, not speaking, looking at me, looking at Carlos. Then he is wrapping me and Carlos in his arms. Kissing me, kissing Carlos's face.

"Luiz, please don't be angry. I couldn't stand to be away from you. And your son is nine months old."

"Eva, I'm not angry, just stunned. How did you do it? Did you travel by yourself?"

"Luiz, I will tell you the whole story later. It was fine. I flew on the airplane."

"Oh, Eva, you are something. And this boy . . . Come here, little guy." Luiz reaches for Carlos, who begins to wail uncontrollably and pushes his face in my neck.

"It's okay, Carlos, this is your Papai." Carlos sobs more slowly and looks at his father out of the corner of his eye. "Here, let Papai hold you." Curiosity takes hold and he lets Luiz take him. Luiz distracts him and soon has him laughing.

Luiz shows me his bed in the middle of the tent, and I move my suitcase there, apologizing to the man whose cot I borrowed, who just grins and shakes his head. Another man comes over to Luiz. He seems to be the foreman as the men look to him when he speaks.

"Luiz, let's have you switch cots so we can put you and your family at the back of the tent. Pablo, let's see if we can give them a little privacy."

Luiz and I head to the cooking area and I make myself useful making café and toast, and we sit with Carlos among the men at one of the long tables and drink café while we stare at each other. I can't believe I'm here. When we get back to the tent, the men have suspended a tarp to create a little room. Our family will spend its first night together in the birthplace of the new capital, the new star in the Brazilian flag.

March 1, Saturday

Luiz works seven days a week; he got up before dawn this morning and kissed me goodbye. I stayed busy today tidying things in our little area of the tent and playing with Carlos. I also walked around the encampment and tried to get a sense of where we are in the new capital. The encampment's cooking area is a rough clay-brick house plastered white, with a metal roof. It's evening and there is a cooling breeze through the open windows. I've made us an evening snack and café. Carlos is sitting on Luiz's lap making bubbling noises.

"Luiz, I saw some women today, so I'm not the only one after all."

Luiz puts down his cup and looks at me. "What were they doing?"

"Just walking around the tents late this afternoon. I said hello but they weren't very friendly."

Luiz is silent for a few moments. "Eva, those women are different. They're not like you."

"What do you mean?"

"Well, they aren't wives and mothers. They are not here with husbands."

"Luiz, I don't understand."

He looks down at his café. "They are here looking for lonely men."

"Lonely men?"

Luiz wipes his brow. "Eva, they are here to make money. I am sorry to talk this way, but men pay those women to have sex with them. I think they're here because yesterday was payday. Eva, this is a rough place. But you'll be fine, just stay away from those women."

March 5, Wednesday

It's still dark outside. I am up early to make breakfast in the cook-house and pack a lunch for Luiz. Carlos is sleeping on some dirty clothes I put on the floor in the corner.

"Eva, you shouldn't fuss about my food. There are people selling food at the work sites."

"Don't be silly, Luiz. I found a place yesterday to buy rice and beans and dried meat and made you a kind of feijoada as a surprise. I don't like you eating street food."

He smiles and nods at me. "Thank you, my sweet and clever Eva. What do you plan to do with your day?"

"I have to wash clothes today. There's not enough water at the cookhouse, so the camp workers tell me I have to walk to the creek. They say it's not too far."

"All right, but please be careful. Be aware of what's going on around you at all times."

"I promise." He kisses me, takes his lunch tin, and I watch him join the other guys who are climbing into the back of a big truck. I wave but he can't see me in the dark.

Carlos wakes up and fusses for mamar. After he is fed and happy I clean up the area and head back to our tent and tie the dirty clothes up into a tight bundle. The sun is just coming up as I head down the hill, Carlos on hip and bundle on head. I've been walking for about fifteen minutes when I hear the sound of rushing water. I round a turn in the path and there is the creek splashing over big rocks. So much water, I love the smell. No one else is here. The sun filters through the big trees that surround the creek.

I arrange a spot for Carlos, though it's a struggle to keep him in one place. I can't let him near the water but he is enchanted by it, reaching out and babbling and making little shouts.

"Mamãe has to wash clothes, Carlos. I need you to stay put."

I have brought a couple of spoons and a lid from a pot and give them to him to play with. Untying the bundle, I begin washing the clothes piece by piece. I bought a bar of washing soap at a little shack that sells supplies. I dip one of Luiz's shirts in the water and soak it, then spread it out on a flat rock at the edge of the water, soaping it good and rubbing to get it clean. Then rinse, wring, rinse again. The water is clean and cool and I rest between each garment and watch the soap make little eddies as it swirls and rushes away down the creek.

It's an all-day job, especially with Carlos wanting to explore and play. I give him mamar and we have a snack and then he sleeps. When all the clothes are washed I bundle them up again and head back to the tents. I rig up a clothesline inside and hang up the clothes.

"There, Carlos. Nice clean clothes, fresh from the creek!" I laugh and Carlos giggles as we roll around on the cot and I sing a little song to him.

Luiz gets home after dark as usual and I can see how tired he is. There is never a day for rest. President J.K. wants fifty years' progress in five, and the workers are determined to make it happen. We go to the cookhouse and I make café and couscous. Several of the other guys sit with us at the table.

"Luiz, how much longer do you think we'll be working on the presidential palace?" One of his coworkers asks.

"Well, the walls are up and they are starting to finish the inside. They want it to be done by June. After that I think they will move us to that big open space where the ministry buildings are going up," Luiz replies.

"I heard the architect Niemeyer and some dignitaries talking last week when they toured the palace. They say that once we finish building the capital we all have to go back to the Northeast. What do you think?"

Luiz is quiet for a moment. "I think we have as much right to live here in the new capital as anyone. And our skills will be needed for other projects. People will move here and the city will grow."

"Yes, but what if they try to force us to leave?"

Luiz clenches his jaw. "The workers must organize. We must demand our rights. Fair pay and a place to live with dignity."

May 26, Monday

Carlos is a year old today and we will celebrate—every night is a work night for the guys building the city. I made a cake and a big pot of café and bought some cola and orange soda. The workers stream into the cookhouse and admire the big cake on the table. Luiz holds Carlos and everyone sings "Happy Birthday" while clapping in time. I cut the cake and everyone thanks me as I put a piece in their hands. They sit around the long tables and Carlos stumbles around and greets everyone, holding on to the benches and the guys' legs.

"Hey, little boy! What are you up to?'

"Hey, what mischief are you up to?"

Everyone laughs.

Luiz is talking with several guys at the table. "They've announced that the Palácio da Alvorada will be inaugurated the end of next month, the 'Palace of Dawn.' A new dawn for Brazil."

Another guy chimes in, "A new dawn for us too. Because now we will move to build the first ministry building. The metal framework is up and it's several stories tall."

Luiz replies, "It's hard to imagine this city will be ready to inaugurate by 1960, even working seven days a week." The guys murmur in agreement. Everyone finishes their cake and says thank you and goodnight. Luiz and Carlos sit at the table as I tidy up.

"Eva, they are building houses in the Cidade Livre, the free city in the Núcleo Bandeirante area. We need a real home, even if it's nothing fancy."

"Luiz, that would be wonderful! How can we make it happen?"

"I'm making inquiries. You keep your ears open too, see if you can find anything out from the camp workers."

"Luiz, I've been waiting to suggest this, but I want to get in touch with Dona Célia, the lady I met on the airplane. She works

137

for the vice president's wife, Dona Maria Thereza. She said she might have work for me."

"That's a good idea. But how will you contact her?"

"She gave me her card with a phone number. I'll go tomorrow to the telephone office and see if I can make the call."

June 10, Tuesday

I'm waiting for the car Dona Célia is sending to pick me up. I'm
going to meet Dona Maria Thereza and if she likes me I may
get some work. The car pulls up and the driver opens the back
door for me. I set Carlos on the seat next to me and the car pulls
into the street. The rainy season is over and it is dry and dusty
and cool. The encampment gets bigger every day and the driver
maneuvers around the many tents and shacks. We ride in silence
for a half an hour before he pulls up to a gate, gets out and opens
it. He pulls in and stops then closes the gate. I see a low white
house with a red tile roof at the end of the lane. He pulls up in
front of the house and opens the car door for me. Dona Célia
comes out on the veranda and greets me.

"Eva, how nice to see you. I'm glad you got in touch with me.
Come in please."

I walk up the steps with Carlos on my hip. Dona Célia grins
at him and curls his little hand around her finger. "Look at you,
how big you are! How old is he now, Eva?"

"Carlos just turned a year old. Thank you, Dona Célia, for
sending the car, and for the opportunity."

"You are welcome, Eva. Come in. Dona Maria Thereza should
be here any minute. Would you like something to drink?"

"Just some water would be nice, thank you."

A few minutes later a beautiful young woman bursts into the
room. She is wearing trousers that are tight-fitting below the knee
but have a bulge around the upper leg, and polished knee-high
boots, and she is tall and thin with large brown eyes and glossy
dark hair. I'm surprised because she looks younger than me.

Dona Célia speaks. "Dona Maria Thereza, this is the lady I
told you about."

Dona Maria Thereza's smile is dazzling. "Hello, thank you for coming. I need help with laundry. Would you be able to do washing for me?"

I have to resist the urge to bow or curtsy, but I just nod. "Yes, Senhora, I would be honored to work for you."

"Well, then, it's settled, thank you. Célia, please organize things. Tchau!" And with that she strides toward the back of the house.

Dona Célia explains that the driver will bring a bundle of clothes to me once a week and return to pick up the washed and ironed clothes a few days later. I can't tell her I have to wash the clothes in the creek. I will need to buy an iron and will have to iron in the cookhouse during the day.

"Perfect, Eva. The driver will take you back to the encampment. Everything else is all right? You're getting along fine?"

I want to ask about getting a house in Núcleo Bandeirante but I'd better wait until I know she is satisfied with my work. "Yes, thank you, Dona Célia. And thank you again for the opportunity."

As the driver stops to open the front gate, I see Dona Maria Thereza galloping away from the house on a beautiful brown horse, leaving a cloud of dust in her wake.

June 30, Monday

The presidential residence, Palácio da Alvorada, is being inaugurated today. It's the first government building in our new capital, and Luiz and his fellow workers are so proud of its beauty and how they worked night and day to get it built so quickly. The city is still dusty roads and shacks for the most part, but Brazilians never give up, and we will get this city ready by 1960, just as President J.K. has said.

It's quite chilly today and I've wrapped Carlos up warmly. Clouds of red dust are everywhere as Luiz and I walk to join other workers in the back of a truck for the trip to the palace. It's a festive atmosphere as we ride with all the guys toward the ceremony.

The truck can't get too close, so we all get out and walk. Luiz hoists Carlos up on his shoulders and Carlos screams with joy and excitement. The streets aren't paved, even near the palace. As we get closer, we can see the majestic, curved columns that seem to rise out of the ground to support the glass walls all around. The huge sky above the high plain is clear blue with just a few puffs of cloud. We can't get close enough to hear the dedication, but we return home with pride and happiness that our president can move into his official residence. The city we are building is truly the dawn of a new age for Brazil.

August 8, Friday

The driver brought me Dona Maria Thereza's washing today, as he does every Friday. The weather is very dry and cold and my hands get chilled doing the washing in the creek, but it makes me proud to be working for the vice president's wife. Keeping the freshly washed clothes clean is a challenge with all the red dust swirling. It's hard to stay warm at night, and I will be glad to leave the tent encampment soon. Dona Maria Thereza's assistant, Dona Célia, has found us a house in the Cidade Livre, where many workers are improvising places to live.

"Hey, son, come say hi to your Papai!" Carlos lurches to the front of the tent as Luiz enters, and Luiz scoops him up in his arms.

"How was work today, Luiz?"

He takes off his jacket and sits on the cot. "It was a bad day today, Eva. One of the metalworkers fell from a high floor of the ministry building scaffolding. He died."

"Oh, that is awful! So sad. That's the second accident this month, isn't it? I know you are being careful, yes?"

"Yes. But the workers need to organize to demand better security for us. He wasn't wearing any safety gear. But it's also a problem that a lot of these guys are from the sticks and are not very well educated. Even if you give them equipment they don't use it."

"These guys come here for a job to make a better life. So sad for his family. I hope he didn't suffer."

"I think he died instantly. But let's talk about happier things. I was just notified today that we can move to our little house in two weeks."

"Oh, Luiz, I will be so glad to have a place to really call home."

"They will charge us rent, but it will be reasonable. We'll

need to find a way to get some furniture. I have a few ideas but be thinking about that too."

"I will love to think about that! I will make our home cozy and nice, I promise you, Luiz."

August 24, Sunday

The Cidade Livre is called a satellite city of Brasília because it's not part of the big airplane that is the main planned part of the capital. So many people have come here to work and the migrants have to live somewhere. The new houses for workers are built out of wood, with several improvised apartments in each building. We open the door to our new home which is tiny with just one bedroom, and the kitchen and living room are the same. There is a pump for water nearby and a bathroom outside, just a shack with a bench and a hole above a pit, but I couldn't be happier.

"Eva, it's not fancy, but it's ours, at least for a while. And the rent isn't bad."

"I love it, Luiz. And the most important thing is our family is together under our own roof."

"Hopefully the roof doesn't leak! Come on, let's see if we can domesticate this little shack." Laughing, he brings our few bundles and boxes of food and supplies inside. Dust coats everything, so I busy myself sweeping and wiping down the cupboards and windowsills. Luiz has arranged a bed for us and we have a small table and two chairs.

It's hard to believe how this satellite city sprang up out of nowhere. The president and the architect had big plans but they didn't really think about how many workers they would need or where they would live. Cidade Livre has a big wide dirt road down the center, and little lanes off that road with shacks for people to live in, and businesses. The electric lines are improvised, rough poles leaning in all directions. Just around the corner from us is a wood building like a ramshackle little barn with a hand-painted sign on the front: "Dentist." There are shacks selling food, hardware needed for building, and cleaning supplies, even a barber shop. So we have all the necessities.

The possibilities for the future seem endless. Brazil is becoming a modern country and the capital we are building here will proclaim that to the world. Where in the Northeast there was no water and no work, here opportunity waits on every corner. To build the city, you must have workers. Workers must live somewhere, so there is more construction. We need food, shelter, and even dentists.

December 18, Friday

It's full summer and the glorious rains are upon us. Our little house is nothing fancy, but we are happy. I'm glad to do laundry with water from the pump, but I don't wash Dona Maria Thereza's clothes with the other women because the garments are so fashionable they would attract attention, envy and possibly larceny, and they also require extra care. It's a labor of love for me and I'm glad to have the income, especially because there is not much work for women.

I always meet the driver a few blocks away from our house to receive the bundle that needs washing and then the next week to deliver the garments I carefully package in paper tied up with string. I'm at the usual place today when the car pulls up and the driver gets out instead of just rolling down the window and handing me the clothes like he usually does.

"Dona Eva, Dona Célia would like to invite you to come to visit next week on Tuesday, the 22nd, if you can have the clothes ready?" He is careful not to say the vice president's wife's name.

This surprises and thrills me. "Of course! I am happy to have it ready. What time?"

"They are inviting you for lunch, and Dona Célia says to bring the little one. I will come to pick you up at 12:30."

"Yes, of course, it will be my pleasure." I wonder how I will dress for the occasion but I don't think I can ask the driver. I'll just have to guess.

"Very good, then." He hands me the bundle and drives away.

December 22, Tuesday

I've dressed up Carlos a bit, combing and smoothing his hair and shining his little shoes. Carlos senses my excitement. I'm wearing the dress I made from Italian viscose that I bought the day I met Luiz in Picuí, and new pumps with heels that are the height of fashion. I hold Carlos's hand and carry the package of fresh laundry with my other arm. We are at the pick-up point early, and it's a beautiful clear day, cooler than usual for summer.

The black car arrives and we sit in the back seat, Carlos fiddling with everything, and keeping my eye on him distracts me from watching out the windows as we are driven to the vice president's home. As we pull into the huge gates at the entrance to the property, I see the residence has been renovated and is somewhat larger than the day I came here to apply for the job as laundress to Dona Maria Thereza, but it's not ostentatious. Carlos and I climb the steps to the veranda and Dona Célia is there to greet us at the front door.

"Welcome, Dona Eva, and Carlos!" I'm impressed that she remembers his name.

We are ushered into the main room, with a glittering silver foil Christmas tree whose multicolored lights are reflected in the gleaming round ornaments suspended from its branches. Carlos wants to run and grab everything and it's a struggle to keep him in tow. There are about twenty people here, and a few of us have brought small children. We are invited to sit around the room and are offered beverages.

After a few minutes there is a hush in the room as Dona Maria Thereza enters. She is the most beautiful woman I have ever seen, her sleek dark hair upswept in a French twist and her deep brown eyes lined with a dark cat's eye, the latest fashion I've seen in the magazines. Her smile is warm and genuine as she looks directly at each person in the room.

"Welcome, and Merry Christmas! We invited you here today to thank you for your service, and to celebrate this festive time of year. Lunch is now served, if you will please follow me."

She leads the way to a large room where a long table is set with fancy china and cutlery. There is murmuring among the guests as no one imagined we were going to be served like fine people, but we are. Staff pull out chairs and unfurl crisp linen napkins on our laps. Everyone is speechless as we are served a consommé, and I give Carlos a toast point to chew on. Then a lettuce salad with a pungent blue-veined cheese and vinaigrette.

The main dish is served, and the chef with his high white toque announces it's beef Wellington, with the meat coming from the vice president's farm in Rio Grande do Sul, the southern state on the border with Argentina and Uruguay. It's the most delicious thing I've ever tasted, though after I take just a few bites Carlos is distracted and wants to get down and run around.

Just then Dona Maria Thereza comes over to me and, grinning, makes clucking noises at Carlos. He is fascinated and giggles. "Dona Eva, may I take Carlos to look at the Christmas tree?"

I am dumbstruck but manage to act normal. "Of course, Dona Maria Thereza. Thank you."

She exits the dining room holding Carlos's hand. "Let's go see the beautiful tree!"

I savor every bite and then dessert, a mango mousse that is so light it melts in my mouth. Coffee is served and then everyone is ushered into the main room to sit around the Christmas tree.

Dona Maria Thereza gives a wrapped gift to each guest, saying something personal to each of us.

"Dona Eva, you have cared so carefully for my clothing. Not even the experts in Europe did as nice a job as you do. I am very grateful." I want to cry but manage to stay calm.

When everyone has received their gift from her hands, we are told to open them. Mine is a beautiful sweater, so soft it doesn't seem real. Then the children are given gifts to open, and those with older children are given similar packages to take home. Carlos rips his apart and it's a stack of colorful picture books.

I ride back to the Cidade Livre in a daze with Carlos's sleepy head on my lap, trying my best to commit every detail to memory, every delicious moment of a day I will never forget.

1960

April 21, Thursday

Today we inaugurate Brasília, hacked out of the scrub of the high plains of central Brazil in just forty months, fulfilling our president J.K.'s promise. The blood and sweat of so many nordestinos who left their homes in northeast Brazil to find jobs, working hours and days on end, made it possible. We are proud to be candangos, the name they call people who made these modern concrete structures rise from the red dirt: Luiz, an electrician, his brother Chico, a carpenter, and so many others; people like me, washing the vice president's wife's clothes in the creek, ironing them in the tent-camp cookhouse until we got our little house in Cidade Livre.

Luiz, Chico, Sónia and I have lived together in our small shack with our kids for the last year, after Sónia traveled from Picuí to join us. The house is small, with a roof that leaks in summer when it rains, and in winter the chill wind coats everything with dust. It's rustic and cramped, but we don't care because we feel like we are living an adventure and everything is possible in the future, just like the capital itself. Sónia and I find ways to make money cooking, baking, and washing clothes.

We dress up in Sunday best and join the surge of people riding in the backs of trucks to the Esplanade of Ministries, the huge open area outside the Palácio do Planalto, the official offices of the president. The sight of the long line of tall ministry buildings rising up from the red dirt gives me goosebumps, and the Congress building with its upturned bowl on top looks like it could lift up and fly away to the enormous sky. The day is sunny, but towering gray clouds are gathering, riding along above us.

We arrive at the big open area where everyone is gathering

below a marble ramp and viewing tower overlooking the crowd where J.K., as we all call President Kubitschek, will conduct the ceremony. The crowd keeps getting bigger, and everyone is smiling and feeling the excitement of this historic day. The inauguration doesn't begin on time, but we don't lose our enthusiasm as we wait. Finally, J.K. and other dignitaries walk up the ramp to the speaking platform in front of the Palace, the swooping curves in front of its glass walls so clean and modern. Our hearts swell with pride as J.K. speaks to our new capital and a bright future for Brazil.

"From this central plateau, this solitude that soon will become the brain of high national decisions, I cast my eyes once again upon the tomorrow of my country and I foresee the dawn with unbreakable faith in her great destiny."

After several speakers and the military band playing the national anthem, the city is inaugurated and the crowd begins to disperse. Everyone will be back at work tomorrow as there is still so much to be done to make the city ready to officially move the capital from Rio to Brasília.

"Eva let's go up on top of the Congress building. I want to see the upturned bowl and look out over the city." Sónia is excited but I'm afraid of heights.

"Sónia, you go ahead with Chico and Luiz. I'll stay down here with the kids." They head off and the kids run around and play, giggling and getting red dust on their nice clean shoes.

Soon enough, our two families are on the way back to our home in the Cidade Livre. We are tired but happy, proud to be part of something bigger than ourselves, part of the limitless future of our great and modern country, with the promise of order and progress, just like it says on the flag.

PART III

1963

August 10, Saturday

Sónia and I laugh and chatter as we make our way back home from the Saturday-morning market, laden with fruit and vegetables fresh from the farms nearby, and beef and sausage to barbecue for lunch today. The sun is barely up but we are wide awake and excited because today is Chico's thirtieth birthday and we will make a special meal and cake to celebrate. We like to get to the market first thing, because the really good stuff goes quickly. It's a neighborly atmosphere where everyone knows each other and banters about the weather and how crops are faring.

"Are you sure you want to make that rolled icing for the cake? It's so much work. Chico will be happy with any of your cakes." Sónia doesn't love baking like I do, so it just seems like extra trouble to her.

"I love the way fondant looks, like it's not real. I love making it. And I'm going to make a lattice on the sides, like woven ribbons. It's fun to play with."

Sónia rolls her eyes. "Only you, Eva, only you." She laughs.

Before long we are back home, where our two houses stand side by side. We have been in Taguatinga for a year now, the satellite city to the west of Brasília. It's half an hour's travel into Brasília itself where I have a real job now, but it's worth it to be buying our own homes. My new job is ironing uniforms for the military officers at the Army barracks, and they send a bus to Taguatinga to pick up workers each morning and take us home at night. Sónia stays home and takes care of the kids. She and Chico now have three kids, with their baby girl Eliane six months old, and she carries the baby while I carry our purchases.

I gratefully drop our shopping baskets on the table in my kitchen, where Sónia and I usually prepare our main meals. On Saturdays and Sundays our families have lunch together, and we usually eat outside on the veranda unless it's cold or raining. Sónia puts the baby down in the improvised bassinet in the corner of my kitchen.

"Let's have a café before we get to work, shall we?" I light the burner on the stove.

"Let me check on Carlos." Sónia peeks in at the door to his room just off the kitchen. "Sound asleep."

"A train could go through his room and he wouldn't wake up." I put the cups and sugar bowl on the table.

Sónia sips her coffee. "Eva, how are your family in Picuí? Any news?"

"I write Papai a letter every month and he writes me back nearly as often. He is still head of the post office, and my stepmother seems to have babies once a year. My brothers and sisters are all fine. Papai always comments on the news from Brasília."

"That's good, I know you miss them."

I sigh. "Yes, I wish I could go see them, but I can't take time off work, and it's so expensive to travel. Maybe next year."

"Chico and Luiz should be home by early- to mid-afternoon, which will give us plenty of time to get everything ready."

"I'm glad they can take the rest of the weekend off. It's great there's still so much construction work, but I didn't think they'd still be working seven days a week in 1963." I finish my coffee.

"Well, then, let's get at it." Sónia clears the table, quickly washing the cups and setting them in the dish rack to dry.

We each grab an apron and tie our hair back in ponytails. From the pantry shelf I pull down the four cake layers I baked yesterday and set the trays on the table. Sónia washes the tomatoes, onions, green peppers and cilantro and begins chopping them for salsa to serve with the grilled meat. We work without talking, our movements like dancers who've been together for years. This too is a happy silence.

By early afternoon everything is ready. The table is set, the meat is ready to grill, and our side dishes are covered with cloths. The cake turned out beautifully and it's waiting in the pantry. Sónia is sitting on one of the chairs on the veranda giving mamar to Eliane. The other kids are all playing down at the soccer field. Cícera is nine years old and she takes her role as the oldest seriously, keeping a close eye on Lorival and Carlos and bossing them around. No doubt they will get dirty playing in the dusty field but Cícera will get them tidied up, and they will sit at their own little table while the adults enjoy the birthday lunch. It's almost two o'clock, so Luiz and Chico should be home any minute now. I sit on the chair next to Sónia and sip a glass of water.

She looks over at me. "Eva, don't you want more kids? I know it was hard when you lost the baby last year, but why don't you try again?"

I sigh and think a minute before speaking. "It was very sad, and I will never forget her. But that's not why I'm not in a hurry to get pregnant again."

"Neither of us wants to have a baby every year, like your stepmother. And I'm really glad to know how to avoid getting pregnant unless I want to. You taught me that."

"Yes. Dona Severina was not just a midwife, she was a wise woman in so many other ways. I will be forever grateful to her for teaching me how to pay attention to my cycles and how to know the signs of the fertile time."

"But why not have another baby? You're a wonderful mother."

"I love babies more than anything in the world. And watching Carlos grow up, I keep wishing I could stop time. But every age is wonderful."

"So why not another, maybe a little girl so you have one of each?"

"I want to be able to chase my dreams, and that means I have to be more independent. I want to start my own real business one day. I've learned a lot selling sweets and salgados, but I have something bigger in mind."

"Well, if anyone can do it, it's you. You work harder than anyone I know. Are you still happy with your job at the military barracks?"

"Oh yes. The supervisor is very demanding, but when he criticizes me I just know he's helping me learn to do better. How well I iron the uniforms reflects on the officers who wear them."

Voices outside mean Luiz and Chico are back home. Sónia unlatches Eliane from the breast and holds her against her shoulder, patting her so she'll burp. I go to the front door and greet them. "How was your day? I hope you're hungry, because we have lots of food that needs to be eaten!"

Luiz laughs. "No worries about that, we'll just take our showers and I'll light the barbecue." Chico heads over to his house, Luiz grabs a towel from the peg by the back door and goes out to the bath house, and after just a bit of splashing around he is buttoning a fresh shirt and folding me in his arms, kissing me.

"I'm so hungry I could eat a whole cow. Let's get this meat grilled."

He starts the fire in the barbecue. "Are the kids down at the soccer field?"

When I nod yes he lets out a piercing whistle to call them home.

After lunch, singing "Happy Birthday" and eating cake and washing up afterwards, I call Cícera to come into the kitchen. "Querida, take these pieces of cake to the neighbor lady and her husband."

"Yes, Auntie." And she is out the front door with a skip in her step. Everyone loves birthday cake so it's a happy chore.

I hang my apron on the peg behind the back door and rejoin everyone on the veranda. Luiz and Chico are drinking cold beer, sitting at the table in earnest discussion.

Luiz's voice is a bit louder than usual. "Listen, we are on the brink of a revolution. Jango is on the right track with workers' reforms and making things more equal for people, but you know, he's a millionaire himself so he doesn't mind if things take a while to improve. But land reform and workers' rights can't wait!" Like everyone, Luiz calls President Goulart by his nickname, "Jango." Jango was vice president to J.K. when Brasília was just beginning to be built, when I washed Jango's wife Dona Maria Thereza's clothes in the creek. It seems so long ago.

Chico jumps in agreement. "Yes, the workers' party is on the brink of a real dawn of equality and justice for Brazil. And it can't come soon enough, with things getting more expensive and the cruzeiro constantly being devalued. And the people who suffer are the workers, not the powerful people in charge."

"This meeting tomorrow is very important. I'm glad we'll be there to show solidarity and help propel the movement forward." Luiz's dark eyes are intent and his mood is somber.

I can't stay quiet. "Luiz, I didn't know you were going to a political meeting tomorrow. I'm really worried about you and Chico being so involved in this."

Luiz turns to look at me, then looks at Chico. He takes a deep breath before speaking. "Querida, the future of Brazil is at stake. The future of the people is at stake. We can't sit idly by. We must put our shoulders to the task, alongside others."

I look down at my hands in my lap, and say nothing more.

August 11, Sunday

Sunday dawns clear and cooler than usual, though it will be very warm by the afternoon. Luiz is up early to go with Chico to the demonstration in Brasília at the Esplanade of Ministries, in the long grassy area outside the Congress building. I prepare fried cheese and scrambled eggs for his breakfast. We sit together at the kitchen table eating and drinking coffee and juice.

"Do you know what time you'll be back home?"

"Not for sure. But probably late in the afternoon, or early evening. Go ahead and have lunch with Sónia and the kids, don't worry about us."

"Let me pack you some sandwiches and fruit, and you'll need water. It will be hot later."

"Thanks, but no need. We can't be carrying a bunch of stuff, our hands will be busy carrying our signs. We'll buy something to drink if we need to."

"Luiz, I'm worried. This is not a good time to be out in the street protesting. It's dangerous."

"Don't worry so much. In a democracy we can express our views in public. It's our right. And we need to work for change. I won't take unnecessary risks, everything will be fine." He pushes back from the table and puts his dishes in the sink.

Chico taps on the door and asks Luiz if he's ready to go. They head out to the street, walking toward the main square to catch the truck into Brasília. I stand outside the gate watching them until they turn the corner in a few blocks and are gone from sight.

Sónia is in the kitchen with the baby when I get back in the house, and we can sit and enjoy coffee together until the kids wake up and ask for breakfast.

"Eva, I know you're worried. But they'll be fine. No one will bother peaceful protesters, it's a common thing these days.

Everyone wants to express their opinion, with salaries frozen and everything we buy getting more expensive. Some good changes need to happen, and soon."

"I don't disagree with the need for change, I just don't want our husbands out there when things are getting so heated up. I want peace and calm, and to be home together on the weekends."

"Why don't you go to church today? It's been months, and I know how important it is to you. You can take Carlos, or leave him here at home. It's nice that there's an evangelical church here in Taguatinga."

"Thanks, Sónia, but I don't think I'll be going to that church anymore."

"Why not? You were raised in the church, with your father a pastor and all."

"I don't feel like I fit there now. They look at me funny, and the sisters whisper behind my back. I cut my hair, and wear short sleeves, and even make-up. I don't have a baby every year so that isn't normal to them. And my husband isn't active in the church, so that causes gossip too."

"That's really too bad. People can be so unkind."

"And going to church just makes me miss my father, and the whole family. I know Papai would be disappointed that I don't go, but he would never understand."

"Have you heard anything from Seu José? I know you write letters to your dad regularly."

"I've been sending him a letter in the mail every month ever since we had a fixed address. In the beginning Papai would write me every month, but I haven't heard anything in a few months. I wish I could take Carlos and go up to Paraíba to visit and see how they are, but I can't leave my new job and traveling is too expensive. Five years since I've seen them seems like a century."

The day passes slowly, and I can't stop worrying about Luiz

and Chico. When they arrive just after dark I throw my arms around Luiz and hold him close.

He kisses me and smooths my hair. "It's okay, querida, everything is okay."

"How did everything go?"

"It's really inspiring to be part of something bigger than ourselves. We need change in Brazil, and marching side by side with our comrades gives me strength and the courage to keep fighting."

"You're sounding more and more radical. I don't like the idea of you fighting in the streets."

"It's just an expression; we need to fight for better living and working conditions in Brazil. I can't sit by and do nothing."

I hold him close and say a silent prayer to God to keep him safe.

September 12, Thursday

I'm up as usual at five in the morning. I get dressed and eat some bread and coffee and pack our lunches. Luiz will be up with the sunrise in an hour, and I make his breakfast and cover it with a cloth and pour hot coffee into the thermos. Carlos will go next door to Sónia and Chico's when he wakes up. There is no fence between our houses so Carlos goes out one kitchen door and into another. Sónia will feed him breakfast and send him off to school with Cícera and Lorival. It would be so much harder for me to have a job without Sónia's help.

I head out the front gate and walk to the main square to catch the bus that carries workers into Brasília, to the Army barracks. When I get to the square, workers are milling about as they wait for the bus to arrive. Some are smoking, some chatting and laughing. The sun is just rising and the pink ipê trees are in full bloom, carpeting the ground around them with fallen blossoms. The blooms only last a few days but they are one thing I love about September. When the bus comes we all file on, and I take a seat toward the back by the window. Today no one sits next to me, so I lean my head on the window and fall asleep.

I doze lightly on the half-hour trip into Brasília, and wake up when the bus turns into the barracks, gathering my lunch and pulling my sweater close as I exit the bus. The workers file in through the gate, showing the guards their identification and entering the compound when they get the nod from the guard. As we enter the laundry, my coworkers greet me. "Good morning! Everything good?"

"Yes, thanks, and you?"

Everyone heads to their respective work areas, in my case long rows of ironing boards. I put my sweater and lunch under my board and tie my hair back in a bun and cover it with a hairnet.

I'm at my workstation and ready for the day before they start bringing me items to iron. I heat up my iron and smooth the fabric of my board, and my container is filled with water to sprinkle on the freshly laundered and starched uniforms. My first batch is a bundle of white shirts that the officers wear under their jackets. I follow the required procedure: collar, shoulders, sleeves, then the rest of the shirt, one after another, hanging them crisp and beautiful on the garment rack until someone comes to roll them away. Next is a bundle of blue-grey shirts worn only by the highest-ranking officers, who wear ties. As the day warms up I feel perspiration on my brow, and quickly look around before I pull a handkerchief out of my cleavage to dry the sweat. The work has a rhythm to it that is soothing somehow, and time is suspended as the hours pass toward lunchtime.

A whistle goes off at noon at a nearby factory, and everyone steps away from their work and goes to sit outside to eat on this beautiful spring day. Some of the workers are murmuring intently to each other. I overhear snippets of conversation.

"There was an uprising this morning by some sergeants, but I hear the generals already have it under control."

"I heard that soldiers parachuted into the area outside of Congress."

"No, really? How can that be?"

An officer walks by and everyone stops talking and pretends they are very interested in their lunches and looking down at their feet. Once he passes, the gossip begins again.

"There were tanks in the Esplanada dos Ministérios! And the airport was shut down."

I know better than to try to engage is this conversation, even if they wanted me to talk with them, but it worries me. It's possible they're exaggerating, but it is just one more sign of dangerous times. Everyone is worried about having enough money to get by, with food and gasoline getting more expensive every day. People are angry, and they are taking to the streets. Now it's lower-ranking members of the Army who are protesting.

The afternoon passes slowly and I keep my ears open for any other news, but everyone in the laundry is very quiet and keeping their heads down. The laundry facility is a huge airplane hangar and the giant fans that circulate air from one end of the building to another keep up their dull roar to help us stay cool. Our supervisor is a captain and he walks up and down the rows with his hands clasped behind his back, looking at everyone's work. I think today he is also looking for any sign that people are talking about the sergeants' skirmish at the airport.

The whistle blows for the end of the workday at six o'clock and everyone organizes their workstations and ironing boards to be ready for tomorrow. People gather their belongings and file out to the bus waiting to take us back to Taguatinga. The sun is setting as we board, but I'm too anxious to rest. When we get off the bus at the main square I rush through the streets to our house, calling out to Luiz as I walk in the front door.

"Luiz! I'm home."

"Hey! Come have a snack with us." He gets up from the table to kiss me as I enter the kitchen. "Are you all right? You look a little upset."

I glance over at Carlos and back at Luiz. "I'm okay. We can talk later."

I kiss Carlos on the head and sit down at the table, pour myself some hot milk and add powdered cocoa to it. I nibble on a piece of cassava cake but I'm not really hungry. Carlos chatters about school and playing soccer with his cousins. I pick up his pajamas and take him out to the bathhouse for a shower. Once he's asleep I close his bedroom door quietly and look at Luiz.

"Have you heard what's going on? I overheard some of the

people at the laundry talking about an uprising at the airport, but I couldn't hear the details. Do you know if it's true?"

"I think it is. Some guys who do deliveries to the apartment buildings we're working on said the roads to the airport were blocked off this morning. And one guy said he heard there was the same kind of trouble in Rio, and that the radio and telephones were shut down until early afternoon."

"Will there be more trouble? This was lower-ranking soldiers? I don't understand how they thought they could succeed."

"Yeah, I heard it was a 'sergeants' revolt,' but the military leaders put them down quickly. The Brasília airport was back to normal by the afternoon. There are forces in the military loyal to President Goulart, even though he's a leftist."

"Luiz, it makes me so anxious. It feels like things are ready to explode. I hope you won't be getting too involved in the protests."

"Let's not worry about that now. We're home, we're safe, and we're together." He pulls me close to him and we kiss, and now I'm the one ready to explode. He makes me giggle, and we fumble our way into the bedroom and melt together on the bed.

December 27, Friday

"Do you need anything at the grocery store?" I stick my head in Sónia's kitchen door.

"Do we have enough flour for the New Year's cake orders?"

"Exactly what I'm going to get. I checked the prices yesterday, and I have just enough to cover what we need."

"Great! We have the weekend to get organized, so that's good. It's so nice you have two weeks off for the Christmas holidays."

"It feels like a vacation, spending time with the kids and just doing normal things. See you in a bit."

I walk out the front gate and toward the main square, pulling my little rolling cart behind me. The sun is already high at ten o'clock, though high billowing clouds mean rain later. I greet the cashier as I enter the shop, and head to the aisle that has staples like flour, rice and sugar. The shelves were well stocked yesterday but today there are only a few bags left—and the price has gone way up. I pull my money out of my pocket and realize it's not enough to buy what we need to make the cakes. My heart sinks as I grab two bags each of sugar and flour and calculate to make sure I'll be able to pay.

Back home I put the bags in the pantry and go over to tell Sónia the bad news.

"Can you believe it? I checked the price yesterday and today the shelves are nearly empty and they jacked up the prices so much I couldn't buy what we need."

"It's crazy how prices keep going up, and then everybody panics and buys as much as they can. It's getting so it's not worth it trying to make money with our side business." She frowns and shakes her head.

1964

January 14, Tuesday

It's Carlos's bedtime and he says his prayers before I tuck him in. "God bless Mamãe, and Papai, and Tia Sónia, and Tio Chico, and my cousins, the animals and birds in the forest, my teachers . . ." He remembers everyone and everything he loves, and we say Amen.

Carlos lies down and puts his head on the pillow, and I cover him with a light blanket. He turns on his side and looks up at me. "Mamãe, the teachers make us pray in school, but it's different from how we pray."

This surprises me. "Mmmm, tell me more."

"Well, they stop us in the middle of class and tell us it's time to pray. All the other kids have these beads and take them out. Why don't we pray with beads?"

"Son, our church is different. Most everyone in Brazil is of the Catholic faith, and they pray with beads called rosaries. I grew up with the faith called Protestant, and it is not common in Brazil. What are the teachers praying about?"

"Everyone prays the Lord is with thee, and Jesus and Mary, and death and sinners. And then they say it over again a lot of times. Then the teachers ask everyone to repeat: 'Lord, please keep Brazil from becoming communist.' What is communist, Mamãe?"

Praying against communism? It takes me a minute to think of how to respond. "Communist is a kind of government, but I don't think kids should be worrying about things like that. And I don't want you to worry that you pray differently. The Bible says there are many gifts but the same spirit, and the same God in all of us. So just bow your head when they pray, and think your own prayer, just like you do at bedtime. Okay?"

He lets out a big sigh and puts his arms up for a hug. I kiss him, stroke his sweet head, and tuck the blanket around him. I sit on the bed and listen until his breathing tells me he is asleep.

March 13, Friday

"Things are looking like they will change, it feels different this time." Luiz looks up from his coffee and his optimism is contagious.

"What is different about today? I didn't hear any whispers at work." It feels good to sit at the kitchen table after a long week. Carlos is sleeping soundly and there's a nice breeze coming in the window, bringing the scent of jasmine.

"President Jango gave a talk at the Center of Brazil rally in Rio today. He laid out all the basic reforms we've been asking for, including land, finances, elections and education."

"But can the president get the Congress to go along?"

"I believe Jango will make these things happen. It makes all the strikes and protests worthwhile. Real change can happen if the people stick together."

"It would be so good to not have to worry so much about money; if Jango can get prices to stabilize and make the kids' schools better, that would be wonderful. I hope you're right and Brazil is finally getting on the right track."

"Do you and Sónia have a lot of orders for Easter? It's just two weeks from now."

"Quite a few, though less than last year since we had to raise our prices. And I've learned the hard way that we have to stock-pile ingredients to know how much to charge. We'll be busy on Good Friday and the day before. But I love making pretty Easter cakes."

Luiz just laughs and shakes his head, reaching over to draw me close and kiss me.

March 29, Easter Sunday

The dream is terrifying and vivid. I know I'm dreaming but there's a sickening reality to it and I want to wake up but I can't. Luiz and I are on the beach together, the sun warm on our bodies, when clouds gather. The sky turns to inky darkness and I can hear distant thunder. I look down to see we are standing on a tiny bit of sand and rising water surrounds us.

I sit bolt upright in bed and gasp for breath. Luiz is sleeping peacefully next to me. My heart is racing as I turn the shower on full blast and let the cold water shock my senses. I push the dream from my mind and get dressed in Sunday clothes.

"Carlos, time to get up! We're going to church today. Come take a shower and get dressed, I've got your Sunday clothes laid out for you."

Carlos stumbles out of bed and rubs his eyes, yawning. "Can I have something to eat first?"

"First get dressed. We're going to have a big lunch later, after we get back from church, but I've got some bread and cheese and juice for you."

Carlos is almost seven and growing fast. He's going to be tall like Luiz, and I have trouble keeping up with his growth spurts when it comes to clothes for special occasions. We are both ready and we walk toward the evangelical church on a side street in town. The Catholic church bells ring to call everyone to mass. Christ is risen! I reach over to Carlos but he doesn't want to be seen with his mom holding his hand.

"Mamãe, why doesn't Papai come to church with us?" He looks up at me as we walk.

"Your father has decided not to participate in organized religion, and I must respect his wishes. When you are older you can decide for yourself. But for now, let's worship together, you and

I." We reach the church and I lift my scarf up from my shoulders to cover my hair. This church is very strict so I've worn long sleeves and pinned my hair back in a bun.

"Good morning, sister. Glory to God on this blessed day." Several deacons are greeting people as they arrive. The church is simple but the ends of the pews have been decorated with fresh white lilies, the kind they call "cup of milk." Carlos and I sit together in one of the back pews.

This day is one of joy, with Christ risen from death after suffering on the cross. The sermon is a dark one, though, focusing on the sins of men and admonishing us to repent our ways. I can feel Carlos squirming next to me, and he's looking around at everything. He looks up at me questioningly when the pastor shouts darkly about fire and brimstone.

I don't know if it's because this church is different than the one in Picuí, or because I am more different now than I realized. After the service I lead Carlos to the fellowship hall, where they are serving coffee and sweets. The church sisters hang back near the walls and look me up and down, not offering words of welcome or any conversation. I don't feel at home here. I decide we won't stay to eat anything, and Carlos looks relieved when we leave the church and walk home.

March 31, Tuesday

I'm on my way to the main square to catch the workers' bus to the Army barracks. It's early, so I'm the first, but in a few minutes people begin arriving, milling about and talking, some smoking. It's time for the bus to pull up to the gathering area but ten minutes pass, and ten more. People's voices begin to rise as they ask each other where the bus could be. After nearly an hour of waiting and wondering, a military truck pulls up across the road. A man wearing civilian clothes gets out and walks toward the group, clapping his hands for attention though no one is talking as we watch him approach. He swaggers a bit and pulls his belt up on his waist, a cigarette hanging from the side of his lips. He tosses the cigarette on the ground.

"Listen up, people. There will be no work today and tomorrow, a special holiday is being given to you. Go home and stay there."

No one says a word as we watch him get in the truck and drive away. People mutter to each other but the crowd disperses and everyone leaves the area. I walk back home, wondering what could be going on. I have a bad feeling about this. I walk in the house as Luiz is putting his breakfast dishes in the sink, and he is startled to see me.

"What is it, querida? Are you ill? What happened? You look like you've seen a ghost."

"The bus didn't come to pick us up. We waited forty-five minutes and a guy drove up in a military truck, but he wasn't in uniform. He told us we have a special holiday for two days and we should go home and stay here."

Luiz snaps his fingers. "That's it! It's the revolution! The time has come, and Chico and I need to do our part." As he says the words, Chico is at the kitchen door.

"Hey, brother . . . Eva, what are you doing home? Are you all right?" Chico looks down at me with concern.

Luiz replies. "The workers' bus never came, then some guy came to tell them they have two days off and to go home. Something big is going to happen."

Chico nods vigorously. "I'm sure you're right. Let's go to the work site and see what's going on."

Luiz grabs his lunch kit, pull me close and kisses me. "Big changes are coming, I can feel it in my bones. We'll be back at the usual time, or earlier, depending on what's happening at the building site." His eyes are shining as he releases me from his embrace.

I make myself a coffee and sit at the kitchen table to think about things, but my reverie is short-lived as Carlos wakes up and is shocked to find me at home.

"Mamãe, why are you here? Is something wrong?" His little brow is furrowed with worry.

"Querido, I have a special two-day holiday. The Army barracks won't be working for two whole days. Come here, give your mom a hug." He leans his head on my shoulder and I squeeze him close. "So get dressed for school and we'll go over to Sónia's together for your breakfast."

Sónia looks at me in surprise as I walk in her kitchen door with Carlos, and opens her mouth to ask a question. I speak before she formulates her thought. "The barracks are closed for two days, we've been given time off."

Sónia looks worried but her face quickly composes in a smile. "Well, then, that's nice! Kids, eat your breakfast quickly so you can get to school on time."

The kids giggle and fool around as they eat, and we give them their lunchboxes and hurry them out the door. Sónia and I watch them disappear down the road, chattering and skipping as they go.

I grab Sónia by the arm and pull her into her kitchen, and we sit at the table. At first we just look at each other.

I break the silence. "I have a bad feeling. Luiz and Chico are excited because they think the revolution is here, after everything that's been going on with strikes and protests and trouble with government finances and the cost of food and gas. We'll have to see what they find out at work."

"When do you think they'll be home?"

"No way to know. They could have a regular workday or come home soon. I only hope they don't get caught up in anything dangerous." I sit quietly and think about whether to tell Sónia about my premonition. I take a deep breath and look at her, watching her expression. "I had a bad dream last night, and the same dream a few days ago. Luiz and I are at the beach, and the sun is shining, and we are so happy. Playing in the waves and laughing. Then I look out to sea and there are dark clouds forming, then rolling closer, and then I look down and we are standing on a little bit of sand, surrounded by water that comes up to cover our feet, then our ankles, and I know we are going to drown. Then I wake up." I can't stop the tears that roll down my cheeks.

Sónia leans over and hugs me, and neither of us speak for several minutes as I sob. She sits back in her chair and looks in my eyes. "I understand, because I believe in dreams too. But they're not always telling us what we think they are."

I try to catch my breath. "But it was one of those dreams that feels so real, not a crazy dream that you laugh about when you wake up."

"I know, querida." She hugs me again and smooths my hair away from my face. "But what else can we do but try to make the best of things?"

"You're right. We have to keep going, just like we always have. And hope for the best."

"Good. Let's have a café and try to enjoy this lazy day we didn't expect. Shall we make a special cake for the kids, since we have all afternoon?"

I wipe my eyes with the backs of my hands and try to smile, hoping it will make me feel better. "Yes, let's make a nice cake. What kind?"

"How about orange and carrot? We have some raisins and we can put flowers on it."

"All right, then, let's get to it!" I push back from the table, reach behind the door and grab my apron, tying the sashes behind my back.

The kids come home from school and we make them a quick lunch, then send them out to play. The hours pass. We call the kids in as the sun gets lower in the sky. Their faces light up as I take the cake out of the pantry and put it on the table, and they sit politely until everyone is served before each of them silently devours their slice of cake. We get them ready for bed, and Sónia sits in the living room with the children and reads them a story, but I am pacing in the kitchen, sick with worry about why Luiz and Chico aren't home yet. It's later than normal for them to arrive home on a workday. We put the kids to bed and Sónia and I sit on the sofa in the living room without talking. Just when I think I can't stand another minute, I hear footsteps, and Luiz and Chico walk in the front door.

"Hey, sorry we're so late. Everything all right?" Luiz sits next to me on the sofa and hugs me, kissing my forehead.

Chico reaches for Sónia and kisses her. "Is there coffee? Anything to eat? We've been in meetings all afternoon."

We gather in the kitchen as Sónia and I warm up rice and beans and fry some beef and slice vegetables for a quick salad. Chico and Luiz get beers from the refrigerator and drink them as they wait for the food. Sónia and I exchange glances as we serve them supper, and we sit at the table waiting for them to tell us what's going on. They eat ravenously, silent until they finish. I make coffee and Sónia gives them each a slice of cake.

"Wow, special cake! This is great." Chico takes a sip of coffee and then attacks the cake. "Delicious!"

Luiz finishes his cake and puts down his fork, taking a breath and looking at me across the table. "So, we got to work, and after some confusion the construction bosses arrived and told us they were closing the building site for a few days, and that we should go home and wait for news."

Chico jumps in. "So the guys who are in the workers' resistance movement with us asked us to go to a meeting to talk about what is going on and what we need to do next."

"We need to defend the Republic. We know something is going to happen soon, probably tonight or tomorrow. And we can't sit idly by, we have to put our shoulders to the struggle, to join the uprising of workers and resist the oppressors." Luiz's excitement is palpable.

Chico reaches over and puts his hand over Sónia's. "We're going to meet with some comrades at a school park in Brasília. We'll be gone all night. We don't know what will happen, but we will be there to help."

I gasp without thinking, then cover my mouth with my hand as they all look at me. "Luiz, Chico, please don't go to Brasília tonight. I know you think it's a good revolution coming, but I'm really scared."

Luiz gets up from his chair and leans over to kiss me. I can't keep from crying. "Please, querida. Don't cry. We will be careful. We'll come home in the morning. Everything will be fine."

Just then I hear a car honking outside. Luiz and Chico kiss us each again, and quickly head out the front door, gone before we can say anything more.

April 1, Wednesday

I wake before dawn as Luiz comes into the bedroom and sits on the bed next to me. I sit up and embrace him fiercely. "I can't believe I slept at all. What happened? Are you all right?"

Luiz leans over and gently kisses me. "Actually nothing happened. We stayed in the park all night, but when we didn't hear any news, we all went home. A false alarm, I guess."

"Do you want something to eat, some café?"

"No thanks. I'm tired. Let's sleep for a while." He gets into bed and curls up behind me, drawing me close. I'm so relieved and the warmth of his body always calms me. We are both asleep in minutes.

We wake up when Carlos comes in and jumps on the bed. "Mamãe! Papai! Wake up. Are you going to work?"

I reach out to hug him close as he lies down on the bed between us. "No, querido, not today. We have to see what the day brings us. I think you kids will be staying home from school today. Let's get something to eat?"

Carlos jumps up and pulls my arm to get me up. I smooth his hair and kiss his cheek. "How about something special for breakfast. Couscous, or tapioca with coconut?"

"Tapioca, tapioca, tapioca with coconut!" Carlos is jumping with excitement.

We are all in the kitchen, and I gather the ingredients on the counter as Luiz turns on the radio. At first there is only static, then a recorded announcement from the office of the president of Brazil. It is not Jango, but a new president, and his manner of speaking is overly fancy and hard to understand.

"Our whole nation has been squeezed by the forces that are now trying to overthrow the democratic regime and in the light of which we have made a peaceful and Christian evolution of our

177

homeland, and upon the legalistic principles that drive all my actions I will act with the utmost energy against the insurgents, so that they will not be deceived by false defenders of democracy that are leading them to a real fight between brothers."

There are a lot of words but they make no sense. There is static, then a voice saying this is Brazil's new president, whose name is Castelo Branco, and the announcement is repeated again. We listen to it three times before Chico comes in the kitchen door.

Chico looks at Carlos. "Little guy, go over to our house and have breakfast with the other kids." Carlos reluctantly heads out the back door.

The recorded announcement comes on the radio again and we listen in silence until Luiz turns it off. We all look at each other.

Luiz speaks first. "There may be a new president, but he isn't in control. The Army generals have taken over the country. The revolution is now in our hands, to resist the military oppressors. I didn't tell you this before, Eva, but we were told that if the military took over, we should go to protest at the Congress and they will provide us with arms. President Jango may have been removed from power, but there are still people in the Army who support him. So Chico and I have to go to Brasília to join the resistance."

Tears stream down my cheeks as I look up at Luiz, sobbing. "Please don't go there. It's going to be very dangerous. Weapons, resistance . . . how can you win when they have all the power? They probably killed President Jango. Please, I'm begging you, stay home and safe, and then just see what happens."

Luiz pulls me close in a lingering embrace. "I know you're scared. We're scared too. But this is our country, and because we love Brazil we have to go. You and Sónia and the kids stay inside."

I sit at the kitchen table and it's like a nightmare, Luiz and Chico speaking quietly with their heads close together, murmuring plans and putting food in a rucksack; and then they are gone, out the front door, and I wonder if we will ever see them again.

Time seems to stand still though the day passes from morning to evening and Sónia and I keep the kids occupied inside the house, reading and playing games. We don't even let them play in the backyard. There is nothing on the radio except the recorded announcement that is broadcast over and over. I pray to myself, *Please, God, keep Luiz and Chico safe. Please let there be peace in Brazil.* I'm on the verge of crying all day.

After dark, Carlos is tucked into bed and sleeping soundly when I hear a car pull up outside. I hold my breath, hoping it's not the police or other authorities with bad news. A sort of shuffling outside, and a knock on the door. Thank God, it's Luiz. He comes in quietly and locks the door behind him, and I throw my arms around him and hug him so hard he gasps for breath.

"It's okay, querida. I'm all right. I know you're worried but everything's okay."

I step back to look at him and make sure there's nothing wrong, searching his eyes and caressing his face. "Do you want some café?"

"No, just a drink of water." We sit at the kitchen table and he quietly tells me the story of his day.

"We got to the Esplanade of Ministries, but our vehicles couldn't even get close because the whole area was cordoned off by the military. There were several tanks rolling back and forth between us and the blocked-off area. We pulled back to the W3 residential zone and stayed at a comrade's apartment. We went up on the roof of his building and had enough cover to not be noticed, but we could see military and even some guys not in uniform patrolling the streets."

"But Luiz, how did you get home? How could you know it was safe to go out on the streets?"

"Well, it really wasn't safe. We had comrades out surveilling what was going on and coming back to the apartment to update us. A couple of them went to the prearranged meeting place outside the capital where they were supposed to be holding arms for us and it was completely deserted, just an empty warehouse."

"I'm sorry, but I'm glad there wasn't a stash of weapons available to you guys. Besides, how could you possibly have prevailed against the force of the military?"

"Well, you're right about that, of course. I didn't say anything to the rest of the guys, but I think there was someone on the inside who betrayed us, maybe sold the weapons and took the money."

He takes a big drink of water and begins his story again. "They say Jango is still alive and that he fled to exile in Uruguay. That's probably where a lot of resistance guys will end up, trying to wait things out."

I lean over and reach up to hold his face between my hands. He turns to me and doesn't look away. "Please, Luiz, I'm begging you. Please don't try to fight against these people. I love you so much, and Carlos and I need you. Please don't do anything to risk your life."

He takes my hands in his. "Querida, the movement is going to lay low for a while, to see if the generals call for new elections and step down. But I can't let this travesty of justice continue if they don't. I need you to understand that I won't tell you what is going on, for your own protection. And please don't ask me."

I look deep in his eyes and nod, unable to speak because of the lump in my throat. Tears don't come because I will respect his passion and commitment and do my best to help us all survive this horrible time.

Luiz rises from his chair and lifts me toward him, and we are kissing like the very first night we spent together, desperate with love mixed with fear and uncertainty for the future, pulling and grasping and aching, and then falling asleep next to each other.

May 15, Friday

I'm definitely pregnant again. I've been sick and vomiting off and on all day for a couple of weeks. Sónia noticed right away, but she didn't say anything. At first I was nervous because of losing the last baby, so I didn't want to make any announcements. It took Luiz a while to catch on, but when he did, he was ecstatic. I'm happy too, but nervous about the future.

Luiz and Chico are back at work as usual, and the kids are going to school every day. Work is a little rough for me with the nausea, but I sip water and nibble on crackers and manage to get through the days. I'm glad it's autumn and things are cooling off, because I don't think I could take the heat right now.

I can't believe Carlos will be seven years old this month. He's a sweet boy and he is doing really well in school, thank goodness. I was worried he might have trouble reading, like me, but he learned really quickly and often has his nose in a book. He is learning English in school and teaches me new words each week while I help him study.

Luiz and Chico come home right after work and they haven't gone out to any workers' movement meetings that I know of. Everyone knows the military is running the country but prices are stabilizing and things are calm so we all just settle into familiar day-to-day rhythms and try to ignore politics. I'm glad things are peaceful and I try not to think about bad things that could happen.

October 4, Sunday

I stick my head in Sónia's kitchen door. "Hey, I'm going to deliver the big cake order to the Sousa family, be back soon."

"Okay, thanks!" she hollers from the back bedroom.

It's a huge sheet cake for a birthday party, and the Sousas live a few blocks away so I have to walk carefully. We've had a lot more orders for cakes and canapés for parties recently, now that things have calmed down and people feel confident celebrating and don't have to worry about prices constantly going up. The generals haven't been all bad when it comes to how things are going in the country.

When I arrive at their house, Senhor Sousa is busy putting up balloons to mark the occasion, and holds the gate to invite me in. "Eva, perfect timing. Let's put the cake on the table here on the veranda."

"Certainly. What festive decorations! Ana Paula must be so excited." I wrote her name on the cake, so I remember it. Carlos proudly supervised me to make sure I got it right. I'm usually fine with writing but I'd hate to mess up a whole cake.

"Yes, ten years old. A big milestone." He smiles and pulls out a chair for me to sit. "Can I get you something to drink? A glass of water?"

"I'm okay, Senhor Sousa. No need to fuss over me." But he insists I sit down while he goes to get the money to pay me.

"Here you go, Eva. You've done a beautiful job as usual. Ana Paula will be thrilled with the pink roses, and she loves chocolate."

"I'll be very glad if she is pleased; thank you." I start to get up but he seems to want to talk with me, so I wait.

"Eva, you know I supervise the kitchen crew for the generals' dining room."

I nod my head. The generals are said to dine on only the finest gourmet dishes prepared by a chef trained in Paris. There is an elite group of sous chefs and Senhor Sousa supervises the lower-level workers, who prep ingredients, wash dishes and serve at table.

"Well, I believe I will have an entry-level position coming open after the holidays. Usually they require an examination to evaluate candidates, but I have enough influence to hire someone who is especially promising." He looks at me over the top of his horn-rimmed glasses. "When is your baby due?"

My heart is beating a little fast but I smile and take a breath. "The baby is supposed to be a Christmas present."

"The timing could be good, then. I would like to have someone who could start in April. That is, of course, if you are interested?" He tilts his head as he asks the question.

"Senhor Sousa, of course I am interested! In fact, it would be a dream come true. I love to cook and I love to learn and I would work very hard to be worthy of your faith in me."

He smiles in a fatherly way. "Eva, you have a wonderful reputation from the laundry. And I have seen ample evidence of your culinary skills. I have no doubt you will work hard and move up in the ranks, learning as you go."

"Oh my goodness, thank you, Senhor Sousa. I don't know what to say." I can feel myself blushing and I wish I wasn't.

"Just say yes, and I will make it happen. For now, just concentrate on your health and that of your baby, and keep me posted. You may consider the position yours, but please don't tell anyone besides your husband."

"Oh yes, Senhor Sousa, I won't say a word to anyone else. Thank you, I am very excited. Thank you!"

"You are very welcome, Eva. We will keep in touch." He opens the gate and waves goodbye as I head back home with a spring in my step I can barely suppress. I can't wait to tell Luiz the good news.

Luiz is on the back veranda when I get home, and I give him a nod toward the bedroom. He raises his eyebrows but follows me, and I close the door behind us.

He grins wickedly at me. "Querida, the middle of the day? Let's go!"

I laugh and shake my head. "I just have to tell you something and we can't tell anybody else. Senhor Sousa is going to hire me for the generals' dining-room staff. I'll start in April when I go back to work after the baby. I'm so excited!"

He looks at me but doesn't smile. "Working for the generals?"

"Yes! It will pay much better than the laundry. I'll start out in the lowest tier of the kitchen crew, but I know I can work my way up quickly. And I'll learn how to make a lot of fancy French dishes. It will be good for us."

He sits down on the bed, but doesn't say anything for a while, then looks up at me. "I'm sorry, querida, I know I should be happy for you. And of course you deserve to be recognized for your skills and hard work. It's just that you know how I feel about the military. They are criminals who have stolen our country."

My excitement is gone now, and I don't want to have a gulf between us. "If you don't want me to accept it, I'll tell Senhor Sousa I've changed my mind. I wouldn't have said yes if I thought you'd object."

He takes my hand. "It's okay, Eva. You go ahead and take the position. It's not your fault what's happening in our country. Hopefully there will be new elections soon. Come here."

He gently pulls me down to sit on his lap, wrapping his arms around me and the baby.

December 24, Thursday

"Eva, sit down and put your feet up. You don't need to be worrying about cooking and you need to keep up your strength because this baby will be here any day now." Sónia has been fussing over me for the last week.

"Don't worry about me, I'll just finish making the sugared fruit centerpiece for the table. It won't take me more than a few minutes."

Sónia shakes her head. "All right, but only a few minutes. Your ankles are puffy and I know the heat bothers you."

"I really hope this baby comes in the next couple of days. The doctors are so impatient, not like Dona Severina. She always let Madrasta go for a week or more after her due date, because God knows best. On Tuesday the doctor offered to break the bag of water around the baby and give me a drug to start labor. He acted like I was a simpleton when I said I'd rather wait."

"Well, things are more modern here. Sometimes we have to change with the times."

"In this case, I think the old ways are better. The doctors act like pregnancy is a disease. I wish I could have the baby at home, but I know it has to be in the hospital."

"It will be fine, Eva, it's not your first child. Once labor starts I bet it goes quickly."

"If God wills."

I can hear the kids shrieking with excitement as they run around playing in the backyard. Luiz and Chico went to pick up the toys from the local shop, and they'll hide them in a closet until the kids are asleep. We'll eat our dinner at midnight and put the kids to bed before setting the gifts out for them to find in the morning. All the cousins can talk about is Papai Noel.

It's almost seven o'clock and nearly dark. The table on the

veranda looks beautiful and I sit in the yard under the guava tree with my feet propped up. I hear Luiz and Chico come through the gate, chatting and laughing.

"Let's have some music!" Luiz brings out the Victrola, putting on some country music with accordion, tingling triangle and thumping zabumba, Luiz Gonzaga singing his classic song about what he left behind in the Northeast because of the drought, and how much he misses his home.

Just before midnight the roast chicken and potatoes, grilled meat, a beautiful salad, rice and beans are brought to the table. A true feast that only happens once a year. Carlos says a prayer for us and everyone digs into the delicious food. After dessert the kids are sleepy and also eager to go to bed so Papai Noel will come and leave presents for them.

I sit while the adults clear the table and do the dishes and Luiz and Chico set the presents out for the kids. Carlos is going to be thrilled with his fire truck, which is just like a real one. Luiz and I sit outside in the yard looking up at the night sky glittering with stars. The moon is high in the sky.

"Look Luiz, the moon is waning, almost the last quarter."

He laughs. "I'm always amazed at how you know the phases of the moon. I never paid attention to that stuff, growing up."

"Papai taught me to look up at the moon, and that if I can hold the round part in my left hand it's waxing, getting bigger, and my right hand, waning, getting smaller."

"One thing is for sure, it's a beautiful sky." He reaches for my hand and we sit together quietly, listening to the night sounds and watching for shooting stars. You can make a wish when you see one, but you can't say what it is or it won't come true.

1965

January 6, Wednesday

Our new son is here and he is healthy, thank goodness. I thought he would be a girl and I had several nice girl names in mind, but because a boy was a surprise we didn't have a name picked out. So he is named after his dad, and we will call him Junior. I'm so glad to be home after five days in the hospital. Sónia is puttering back and forth, organizing baby clothes, bringing more pillows to prop up my back for feeding Junior, and keeping the kids quiet so I can rest.

"Sónia, I don't know what I'd do without you. Thank you so much for everything."

"You'd do the same for me—in fact you did! I'm just so glad everything went well and you are both safe and healthy."

"Thank God. It was kind of lonesome having the baby in a hospital without sisters around me to help. And since Junior was a week late he just got bigger. So the cutting, the forceps, the pulling, the stitches . . . I think it hurts now worse than giving birth."

"Just take it easy, every day will be better. You're a strong woman."

I unlatch Junior from the breast and pat his back to burp him. "I was worried Carlos would be jealous, but he is so excited to be a big brother. It's so sweet."

"Yes, kids aren't always happy to share their parents, especially if they've been the only one for seven years like Carlos." Sónia puts Junior down in his bassinet and closes the shutters to darken the room, and I fall asleep immediately, so glad to be in my own bed.

April 5, Monday

I'm wide awake before dawn getting ready for my first day of work in the kitchen of the Army generals' headquarters, giving mamar to Junior, packing my lunch, eating breakfast. Luiz is helping and Sónia pops her head in the kitchen door to check on things.

"Eva, let me have that baby—don't worry, he'll take a bottle from me, since he won't smell his mom nearby." She laughs and reaches for Junior.

"I'm really nervous, just all butterflies."

Luiz pulls me toward him for a hug. "Just take deep breaths. You are a good worker with lots of skills, and you get along well with everyone. You'll be fine."

Sónia holds Junior up to her shoulder and smiles at me. "Remember what we talked about: when you have a break, go in the bathroom and relax, and express out milk so you can keep your supply up. You'll give Junior mamar first thing when you get home."

"I know, I just have to calm down. If I think of the baby the milk comes in, so I think I'll be okay."

It seems like years since I walked down the dark streets to catch the military workers' bus. Everyone is milling about as usual, and they all greet me and say congratulations on the new baby. I don't sleep during the trip to Brasília because I'm too keyed up thinking about my first day. The bus stops at the barracks where I always used to get off and everyone says goodbye to me and wishes me well in my new job. The bus is nearly empty as the driver continues on to the generals' headquarters, stopping in front with a whoosh of air brakes and opening the door. I thank the driver and wait in line at the sentry gate, where the guard checks for my name on his clipboard.

"Yes, Senhora, you may enter and go to administration, where they will get you registered." He points out the building and I enter the office, where a young sergeant checks my documents and puts them on a machine that takes pictures of them. He fills out several forms with five copies and has me sign each one. After he is satisfied with everything, he has me sit on a chair against the wall and takes my picture with a camera and flash.

He staples a paper to my ID from the laundry. "Your supervisor will give you your identification card when it's ready. Use this for now to enter through security. Follow the signs to the officers' dining room and enter through the kitchen door in the back. Senhor Sousa is expecting you."

I murmur my thanks and find my way to the kitchen. The sun is bright now and men in uniform are bustling about in all directions. I knock on the kitchen door. A lady wearing kitchen garb with a white cap covering her hair opens the door and raises her eyebrows at me.

"Good morning. Senhor Sousa is expecting me?"

She doesn't speak but holds up her hand to indicate that I should wait. Senhor Sousa comes to the door and greets me.

"Eva, welcome! How are you, how is the family? Are you ready for your first day of service in the officers' kitchen?"

"Yes, Senhor Sousa, thank you. I just finished with administration."

"Of course, good. Let me get Altamira to help you with your uniform, something temporary until we get yours. You will start today washing dishes, and we'll see how things go from there."

Altamira gets me sorted out with work clothes and I change in the women's bathroom. She's waiting for me outside the door and helps me put my things in a small locker, then takes me into the kitchen.

"Everyone, meet Eva! Eva, meet . . ." There are ten people and she says each of their names and what they do, but there's no way I will remember. The chef is on the other side of the kitchen and looks up and waves distractedly, absorbed in his work. I smile at everyone and they all say hello and welcome, and then I'm led to the dishwashing station. First pots and pans from what's already been cooked, then it's a blur. I don't have a chance to rest until after the officers' lunch service is concluded and Senhor Sousa tells me I can take a lunch break. I take off my rubber apron and rush to the women's bathroom to pee and express milk. Then there's only time for a few quick bites and gulps of water and I'm back washing all the dishes from lunch. When the day ends I'm exhausted, but happy because there were no complaints about my work. I fall asleep on the bus on the way home.

June 7, Monday

"Good morning, Eva!" Altamira calls out to me as I enter the kitchen. She has really taken me under her wing, helping me navigate the rules and expectations. Senhor Sousa made her responsible for my training and she treats me like a work-daughter; she's demanding but quick to praise things I do right. I washed dishes for the first couple of weeks, then Altamira learned that I know how to use a knife, so moved me to prep. It's amazing how many vegetables are needed every day just for the elite officers.

Today will be my first day working in the dining room. For the last few weeks Altamira kept me in after work to teach me how to serve: always on the right of the person seated, except dessert, which is from the left. How to tell when diners are finished, how to remove the plate and cutlery without making noise or, heaven forbid, dropping anything. How to pour coffee, when to replenish the water glasses, how to balance big trays laden with heavy dishes.

I do some prep work until a couple of hours before lunch, when Altamira signals to me that it's time to set up. The dining room is spacious, with ten tables. Five of us will work lunch today, and we unfurl the crisp white tablecloths and place napkins and cutlery and glassware in exactly the right configuration.

It's five minutes before the doors open, and Altamira pulls me aside for a last reminder. "Aside from serving properly, what is the most important thing?"

"Don't hear anything. Don't see anything."

"Exactly. And if any of these guys look you up and down, remember you are the Queen of England and they are not worthy."

This makes me laugh. "Yes, Dona Altamira. I will remember."

The doors are opened and officers enter in small groups, chatting and laughing. I can tell each officer's rank based on his uniform from my time ironing in the laundry, but I remind myself not to see anything. There are some men in plain clothes who talk in loud voices and I recognize they're speaking English, but I remind myself not to hear anything, and not to notice that they are probably American. I'm nervous, but service goes smoothly. One of the Americans points at me with his thumb and makes a comment that the Brazilian officers laugh at, but I keep my face impassive and carry on with my work.

We get through lunch without any problems, serving dessert and clearing the dishes, then all the officers are gone and we empty ashtrays, roll up the linen for the laundry, and wipe everything down so it's sparkling clean.

Back in the kitchen Senhor Sousa is doing his administrative work. Altamira pulls me beside her and he looks up from his desk. "Senhor Sousa, Eva did a great job. She has real class, this one."

Senhor Sousa smiles broadly. "Very good; thank you, Altamira. Good work, Eva."

The rest of the afternoon goes quickly, with prep work for tomorrow and cleaning, and I feel happy on the bus ride home. It's dark and chilly as I walk home from the square, and I pull my sweater close. When I get home Sónia has me sit on the sofa, props the pillows around me and hands me Junior, who giggles and pulls at my hair. I coo at him and pull him close to mamar, and Sónia brings me tea and food which I eat with my right hand while feeding Carlos with my left breast.

"How did it go? I know you were so nervous about lunch service today."

"Everything went fine, thank goodness. How was your day?"

"Great, the kids played soccer down in the field, did their homework, and they're playing card games in our living room now."

"Aren't Luiz and Chico home from work?"

"Yes, they got home at the usual time but they've gone to pick up our new car! Well, it's a used car, but you know what I mean."

"The Renault Gordini? I know they got a good price, but it's only three years old; is something wrong with it?"

"Chico says the car has a bad reputation because of suspension problems, but it's because of Brazil's bad roads, not the car. And he and Luiz can do all the maintenance and any repairs."

Just then we hear a "beep, beep" as Luiz and Chico pull the car into the driveway between our two houses. All the kids come running and shrieking out of Sónia's living room, and I hold Junior to my shoulder as we all go outside.

It's a really pretty car with four doors, hard to see all the details in the light from the house, but it's a shiny light brown metallic color. Luiz and Chico are laughing.

"Querida, what do you think of our limousine?" Luiz grins at me.

"Pretty darn nice! So when can I drive it?"

Luiz looks at Chico and chuckles. "I should have known she'd want to learn to drive. We may never see this car again."

Sónia chimes in. "Me too! I want to drive this car!"

The kids are swarming around, opening and closing the doors, sitting in the seats, grabbing the steering wheel and pretending to go on a trip. We have a hard time getting them back in the house and settled down to sleep.

July 9, Friday

I moved to salad preparation Monday, so this is the end of my first week in the new position. It's not just a matter of chopping vegetables, often it's a composed salad with vegetables that are cooked so they are still a little crunchy, arranged in colorful swathes on the serving plate, with roses made from tomato peel and little flowers made out of carrots. I love all the details and getting everything exactly right. Chef Orlando is very picky and because he's an artist he can fly off the handle if things aren't the way he wants them. But he hasn't gotten mad at me too often. Whenever he criticizes, I thank him for teaching me.

We throw out the ends of vegetables or ones that are misshapen. I asked Senhor Sousa if I could keep the pieces we would normally throw out, and after a moment of looking at me funny he said yes. I wash out a big empty can each morning and put the odd pieces of vegetables in it, and at the end of the day I have enough to make a big pot of soup.

When I get home everyone is in Sónia's kitchen having an evening snack, with café for adults and hot cocoa for the kids, since it's winter now and chilly. Carlos is holding Junior and gets up from his chair to hand him to me. Luiz pulls out a chair and I sit and give Junior mamar, gratefully sipping the café with hot milk that Sónia puts on the table in front of me and nibbling on cassava cake with my free hand.

"It's so good to sit and rest after a busy week. Thank you, Sónia."

Sónia grins and looks over at Luiz. "You better rest well tonight, because tomorrow Luiz is going to teach us how to drive our car!"

Luiz rolls his eyes and laughs. "My God, what have I done to deserve this?"

Chico piles in: "Yeah, you know what guys yell at women who don't drive well: 'You should be driving a stove!'"

I snort my disapproval. "Yeah, well, we'll show them, won't we, Sónia?"

"Oh yeah." She gives Chico a withering look and puts the dishes in the sink while shushing the kids and sending them to get ready for bed.

July 10, Saturday

Luiz drives the Gordini and I sit in the back, Sónia in the front. It's just a few kilometers to Tagautinga's big soccer field, a huge area of packed dirt where we will learn to drive. We pass a little market that is bustling with people early on a Saturday morning. When we get to the soccer field, Luiz stops the car and explains how everything works: the clutch, the brake, the gear-shift.

"It's like cooking, and the accelerator is salt. You don't want too much salt. You use the brake to adjust the amount of salt."

Sónia goes first. She sits in the driver's seat, puts her hands on the wheel and takes a deep breath.

Luiz gives her the sequence. "Left foot, push the clutch down. Right foot on the brake. Gear is in neutral, move to first. Now put your foot on the gas and slowly let out the clutch."

The car lurches forward and the engine dies. "That's okay, it takes practice. Just try again."

After several tries, Sónia gets the car moving in first gear, and shifts to second. She looks back at me with a big grin. "Hey, not bad, huh?"

Luiz grabs the wheel and yanks it to the right just before she hits the soccer goalpost. "Whoa! You got the clutch figured out, now you need to work on the brake and the steering wheel!"

After a few seconds to recover we all laugh uproariously. I'm laughing so hard I'm afraid I'll pee my pants. "Why can't you teach us somewhere we can drive in a straight line?"

"Because any place in a straight line has traffic and other people you might kill. Any other questions?" Luiz shakes his head and sighs.

Soon Sónia is shifting smoothly, braking and turning like a real pro. I look at her face in the rear-view mirror, full of concentration. "Wow, Sónia, this is great! Let's go on vacation to the beach in Rio, just you and me."

Luiz looks back at me and shakes his head. "Okay, you can go on a nice trip when you both know how to drive. Sónia, it's time to turn the wheel over to smarty-pants."

I take my place behind the wheel and tell my brain to follow the steps. Despite my concentration, I jerk the car around the soccer field for quite some time. I wonder if I will be able to drive after all.

Luiz looks over at me and pats me on the arm. "You can do it, querida. I know you can. But much more of this and my teeth will fall out of my jaw. And I need them to eat with."

I give him an evil look and slam on the brake a little too hard. After a deep breath and a moment to think about what I'm doing, I put the car in gear and take us in lazy circle eights around the soccer field. I stop the car, put it in neutral and pull up the hand brake.

Luiz gives me a thumbs-up. "There you go. I knew you would do it if I made you mad enough." We lean together for a kiss.

1966

January 8, Saturday

I've been back at work for a week after celebrating the Christmas and New Year holidays, and Junior's first birthday. The days of vacation pass too quickly, a blur of happiness and laughter with our two families together. Junior is mostly weaned, only taking mamar at bedtime. He's active and happy, cruising around holding on to furniture or the older kids' hands. Today is special because Sónia and I are going on a road trip for the day, just the two of us, in our cute little bronze Renault Gordini. Luiz and Chico knew better than to argue with us, but they did insist on making us practice changing a tire.

We're heading north on the Belém-Brasília national highway, a paved two-lane road. There are slow-moving trucks we have to pass from time to time, which is nerve-wracking, but the truckers use their turn signals to indicate when it's safe to pass. We wave out the windows and give them a "beep, beep" of thanks, and they beep back. Two women out driving alone is not a typical sight, and some of them lean out the window and whistle or hoot at us. Our destination is Salto do Itiquira, a spectacular waterfall a couple of hours north of Brasília.

When we arrive at the turn-off to the waterfall the road is rougher, so I have to concentrate. I try not to grip the wheel too hard, but I'm relieved when we finally arrive at the dirt area where other cars are parked. We grab our picnic basket and towels and hike up the trail through dense greenery, maneuvering around rocks and helping each other along. I'm glad I wore my rough-walking shoes. We reach the top and the towering cascade is before us, dropping into an emerald-green pool at the bottom.

I put my arm around Sónia's shoulders. "Oh my gosh, I have

never seen anything like this in my life."

Sónia gasps. "Look at that. Come on, let's get settled."

We spread our picnic cloth and put our food hamper and towels down. The other new thing today is wearing bikinis, the latest kind like in Rio. We had a lot of fun sewing them and they're really cute. Still, I feel like I'm walking around in my underwear.

Sónia grabs my arm. "Let's go!"

We run to the edge of the pool, looking up at the waterfall, and dip our toes in.

"Come on, don't be a baby!" Sónia wades in up to her knees, and then pushes forward to the deeper area, submerging her head. She waves at me to come in.

I dip my feet in, then push forward to the deeper area and lie back in the water, gazing up at the rainbow refracted in the sun on the thundering cataract. We don't really know how to swim so we don't go out too far, but we linger in the cool water and marvel at the beauty before us.

We dry off with our towels and attack the picnic packed in our hamper. I've never had such an appetite and we devour our food in silence. A couple of guys come over and try to start a conversation but we just wave them off. We curl up and nap for a little while, covering ourselves with our towels, and too quickly the sun is bending past midday and it's time to get back on the road. We definitely don't want to be driving in the dark. It's a calm trip back, and we pull into the parking area in front of our homes in Taguatinga at sunset, satisfied with ourselves after a beautiful day we will never forget.

April 11, Monday

Chef Orlando has me learning to make main dishes now, and today I will assist him and learn the recipe for roulades de boeuf, rolls of thin beef stuffed with minced pork and braised slowly, with a cream sauce and roast potatoes. First he shows me how to take the big flat beef cuts and pound them so they're really thin. Chef is wiry and dark-haired with a thin mustache on the edge of his upper lip, and his white chef's hat is crisply starched.

"Dona Eva, you don't want them too thin, and they must be uniform in size or they won't be pretty." His movements are delicate and efficient.

I watch carefully but there's no time for me to practice pounding the meat, and Chef directs our attention to the ingredients laid out on the counter in metal bowls. "And what do we call this?" He gestures to the bowls in a sweeping arc.

"Mise en place, which is French for 'put in place.' We want all our ingredients at hand before beginning to cook."

He smiles and nods. "Exactly right, Dona Eva. And now you know why our prep staff are so important."

We proceed from step to step, Chef often just gesturing to the next task without saying anything. We bustle about in the space like dancers, anticipating each other's moves with a common purpose. My favorite part is preparing the cream sauce at the end, using the big whisk and creating a smooth final touch for the dish. It's time now for mains service, as the couvert of olives, bread and paté and salad courses have been served and staff are clearing the tables for the main dish. The servers are not moving as quickly as chef would like and he hisses at them. "Come now, people, these plates will be cold!"

He picks up each warmed plate and puts a beef roll on it before handing it to me. I pour the delicate sauce over the roll, add a serving of potatoes and a sprig of parsley, before putting it on the counter for the servers to pick up and deliver to the officers in the dining room.

There's no time to relax or reflect on our work because the dessert course must be timed perfectly. We are offering a colorful fruit salad, passion fruit mousse and a selection of Italian ice creams. We put the fruit salad and mousse servings on the counter in beautiful crystal bowls, and serve ice cream based on orders.

At the end of the day I'm exhausted but proud and happy. We work alongside the rest of the crew to clean everything until it's pristine and ready for tomorrow. Chef Orlando smiles at me and gives me a thumbs-up, which is worth more to me than money.

It's a cool clear evening as I walk home from the bus stop, my thoughts on various dishes I've seen Chef Orlando prepare and want to learn to cook myself. If I do a really good job and learn as much as I can, I might be put in charge of the kitchen when Chef goes on vacation. He's told me about his home state of Guanabara and the old capital city of Rio, and how much he loves the beach resort north of there called Búzios, which is very chic and popular with the jet set, even the French movie star Brigitte Bardot. But he won't take time off until he has someone he can trust to keep the kitchen well managed while he's away.

I'm torn from my reverie as I walk into the house and find Luiz and Chico pacing back and forth in the kitchen. I look to each of them and wait to hear what's going on.

Luiz runs a hand across his forehead and shakes his head. "The kids are all with Sónia: Chico and I needed to talk. A couple of guys were killed at the job site today."

"Oh no! That's so terrible, what happened?"

Chico looks at Luiz and then at me. "They were digging a deep trench without any protective walls, and it collapsed. They hire anyone to do those kinds of jobs and they don't really know what they're doing, and the job bosses don't care if guys get hurt."

Luiz lets out a deep breath. "Workers are just animals or insects to them. If they lose a few, more will replace them. Workers have no rights or protection. And now there is no one to provide for their families."

I hold my breath a few moments but I have to ask. "Are you planning anything because of this?"

Luiz sets his jaw and I see the anguish in his eyes. "Eva, we have to organize and try to act, people's lives have to mean something. I didn't promise you I wouldn't be trying to achieve change from behind the scenes, I only said I wouldn't tell you what I'm doing. And that remains true. It's better if you don't know."

May 10, Tuesday

Workdays are hectic and don't allow any time for brooding, and when I'm home I concentrate on my happiness and love for my boys and Luiz, and our two families enjoying time together. Luiz and Chico are working on a new site, a smaller project building eight shops for businesses here in Taguatinga. The federal district area is growing so fast that they can pick and choose their construction projects, and they like this job boss because he's more ethical. It's nice for them to be able to work close to home, too. I try not to worry about Luiz being involved with the resistance movement, so I just push it out of my mind. Being busy makes it easier.

Today I'll be making the main dessert, and since Chef Orlando has given me the freedom to make something of my own choosing, I'm going to make pavê. It's made with champagne cookies, layered with chocolate and vanilla cream, with chocolate sprinkles on top. I bought the cookies yesterday evening on the way home because we don't keep any in the kitchen pantry. It's simple but absolutely delicious and everyone I've ever served it to loves it.

Altamira greets me as I enter the kitchen. "Good morning, querida, are you ready for a busy day for a change?" She giggles.

Teresa is the woman who opened the door for me my very first day, and she's a real sourpuss. This morning is no exception. "Good morning, Miss Fancy-pants. What divine things are you dreaming up today?" She laughs humorlessly.

"Good morning to you, Teresa. I'm planning to have a wonderful day and I hope you are too." I smile at her but she just snorts and goes back to chopping vegetables. I tie on my apron and begin organizing things at my end of the preparation area. Chef Orlando finishes up the administrative work at his desk and, after washing his hands, comes over to talk with me about the dessert menu.

"Dona Eva, what are you planning for dessert today? Your carrot orange cake, or lime meringue?"

I smile at him. "Something new for today, Chef. Pavê."

He looks horrified and just blinks at me with his mouth open for a minute. "What? That is a dessert for maids and taxi drivers! Not the top military officers in the country!"

I begin to doubt my choice but smile and persevere. "Chef, just this once. You'll see, it will be delicious. I know it's common but I make it special."

He rolls his eyes and sighs. "All right, Dona Eva, just this once."

As I finish preparing the pavê, Altamira sidles up to me while she dries a large pot. "I hope you know what you're doing, querida."

"We'll just have to see. Teresa is gossiping about me, and she makes sure to talk just loud enough for me to hear."

Altamira puts the pot down, leans forward and pats me on the arm. "That one is just jealous. She's been here for years and is still on prep. You're Chef's favorite and you have great skills."

I manage a smile and we both turn back to our tasks. There are lots of other things to be done before lunch service, so I don't have time to worry. Before I know it the mains are cleared and servings of my pavê are being offered, along with the usual fruit salad and ice creams. I don't hear any commotion in the dining room so at least it's not a disaster. Servers come back for more pavê and I hurry to plate more servings in the glass dessert dishes.

Dessert service is finished and we are beginning prep for tomorrow's menu when the kitchen falls silent. I look up and a tall man with four stars on his shoulders has entered the kitchen and everyone is looking at him.

Chef Orlando speaks. "Yes, General, how can we be of service, Sir?"

His voice is a booming baritone. "Who made that chocolate dessert?"

I am trembling with fear but Chef gestures toward me. "Why it was Dona Eva, Sir. I hope you found it satisfactory?"

"Satisfactory? It was absolutely delicious." He turns toward me. "I wonder if you would be willing to give me the recipe so I can give it to my wife."

I stammer out an answer. "Yes, General, Sir, of course. Thank you, Sir." I suppress the desire to curtsy as heat rises up my neck and I know my face is bright red.

The general smiles. "Excellent, thank you very much."

Chef Orlando smiles and looks at me. "Dona Eva will have that ready for you tomorrow, general."

No one speaks while everyone recovers from the general's visit to the kitchen. Altamira smiles at me. "I thought you were going to faint, Eva. But it's good, your pavê was a success!"

Teresa smirks at me. "Yeah, if I were as scared of stars as you are I wouldn't look up at the sky at night."

Chef is laughing and shaking his head. "Good work, Dona Eva. Well done."

October 3, Monday

Luiz and Chico are in heated discussion as I arrive home.

"Congress electing a president. What a joke. Costa may take power as president, but until we have direct elections the military dictators are fully in charge." Luiz is pacing back and forth in the kitchen. He looks up. "Oh, querida, how was your day?" He reaches to pull me close and kiss me.

"It was fine, busy as usual. But I'm always learning new dishes and that makes me happy."

Chico nods his head toward his house. "Sónia has a snack waiting for you, you don't need to stay here and listen to the two of us rant and rave."

Luiz kisses me again and I head over to Sónia's. The kids are all sitting around the kitchen table having their evening snack; Cícera is twelve now and she's cutting up pieces of cheese for Junior, who is two and thinks he doesn't need any help. It's funny to watch. Junior looks up and sees me and puts his arms out for me to pick him up.

"You're a big boy, but you want your mama to pick you up?" I smile and reach for him. I sit down and put him on my lap and Cícera goes to the stove to get me a cup of hot milk and I spoon powdered cocoa into it. Carlos chatters about his day at school and the soccer game after, until it's time to get ready for bed. Carlos puts on his pajamas and I get Junior ready and we say prayers before I kiss them goodnight and turn off the light. Luis and Chico are still talking animatedly in the living room, but in hushed tones.

Sónia and I sit together on the veranda in silence for a few minutes before she lets out a big sigh. "I really hate it when they get so riled up over politics. It makes them want to take stronger action, and that's dangerous."

"I agree. But what can we do? Luiz doesn't tell me what's going on, and he said he never will because it's better if I don't know."

"I heard on the news that people have been arrested for having weapons."

"It's possible they were framed by the police, isn't it? Where would people buy weapons?"

"Eva, we have no idea what's going on in the underground. There's a real resistance out there, and they're risking their lives. I just hope Chico and Luiz aren't becoming more radical."

1968

June 21, Bloody Friday

When I arrive home from work the adults are all sitting around our kitchen table in heated discussion. Luiz gets up to give me a hug and kiss, and I feel his agitation.

"There is a huge student movement boiling up in Rio. First reports through our comrades say that dozens are dead and wounded in street demonstrations." Luiz pulls out a chair for me to sit.

Chico shakes his head. "They were protesting the murder of a student in March, who the police commander killed with a point-blank shot to the chest. He and the others were fighting the high cost of meals at their university. What a stupid waste."

We sit quietly absorbing the news, then Luiz speaks. "Students are rising up across South America. The revolution is coming, I can feel it."

June 27, Thursday

The kids are all in bed and Luiz and I sit with Sónia and Chico on their back veranda. Everyone is excited but worried at the same time.

"What happened yesterday was unbelievable." Luiz is animated but I feel the weight of his words.

Chico sits forward in his chair. "A hundred thousand people protesting in the streets of Rio. Nothing like this has happened in the modern history of Brazil."

I'm happy that people are rising up but scared of the consequences. "What do you think will happen as a result?"

Luiz replies quickly. "The military will have to call elections. They can't manage this level of discontent."

Sónia sounds hopeful. "So maybe things will change. Maybe they will have to listen to the people."

I wish I saw it differently. "Or maybe they will crack down harder than ever in an attempt to control things so they can stay in power."

We sit together in silence listening to the night sounds. A sliver of waxing moon sits above the western horizon, and I imagine holding her pearly light in my left hand, the crescent cool against my palm.

September 13, Friday

My hands grip the edge of the kitchen sink as the first hint of light begins in the east. I haven't slept at all, waiting all night for the sound of Luiz arriving home. I paced the floors in the living room and kitchen, walked around the back yard, sat on the front veranda. I try not to cry but tears come anyway. My nose is stuffy and my face aches from the congestion of unshed tears.

Luiz doesn't tell me where he is going or what he's doing with the resistance, but he's been increasingly active in the last few months. He's gone out several nights a week but always comes home in time to sleep for a few hours and get ready for work and kiss me before I leave to catch the workers' bus to Brasília. Sometimes he arrives in the early hours of the morning, and I only begin to breathe again when I hear his key in the door and he crawls into bed beside me. But he's never been out all night. The morning has never dawned without him next to me.

My head is pounding and my heart races as I throw together some food for my lunch and get dressed. I have to act normal for the kids and so no one at work will suspect anything is wrong. I repeat a prayer over and over for God to keep Luiz safe, to bring him home to me.

I knock on Sónia's kitchen door and it's early so it takes her a few minutes to get up and come to the door. "Eva, is everything all right?"

I wipe tears from my cheeks. "No, it isn't. Luiz hasn't come home. I have to go to work. The boys are still in bed."

She opens the door and gives me a hug. I try not to cry. "Don't worry Eva, I'll take care of the kids. Luiz will be home soon, he's just gotten delayed. Maybe there was car trouble. Maybe he stayed at someone's house so he wouldn't be in the streets in the middle of the night."

I pull my sweater close and nod in agreement. "Yes, I'm sure everything will be fine." We both know it won't be fine. I turn and put one foot in front of the other on my way to the bus stop.

September 19, Thursday

I'm sick with worry. Luiz hasn't been home in a week. Chico finally told me a few days ago that Luiz had gone to a workers' movement meeting the last night we saw him, but he doesn't have any other information because Sónia convinced him to quit his involvement with the resistance. We're all frightened and waiting for a knock on the door in the middle of the night. I won't let my mind go to the worst things. I have to act normal at work or people will suspect me too.

The streets are dark and so are my thoughts as I trudge home from the military workers' bus stop in the town square. As I'm walking, a man comes out from a side street and walks in parallel with me. I hold my breath and wonder how he might want to harm me and what I will do.

After a few moments, he speaks. "At the next street walk left and wait in the middle of the block. I'll come back around the other way in a few minutes."

My heart is pounding as I follow his directions, then he's next to me, pulling me into the area between two darkened houses. "You have friends who want to help you. You can't tell anyone about our talk. Agreed?"

I stammer out a yes.

"Your husband has been taken to a location in Rio, the São Conrado section. He is being held there but he is still alive. He will be released at midnight next Thursday. From Avenida Niemeyer turn right on Estrada da Gávea. The favela Rocinha will be below you on the right, and on the left there's a car mechanic and a tire shop with a big gate to a private road between them. Park and turn off your lights and watch for him to come out of the gate."

"But driving to Rio? I'm not sure I understand where to go." I can feel myself starting to shake and I can't control it.

"You will have to figure it out. Remember what I said. Rio, São Conrado, Estrada da Gávea. Drive there alone, don't take anyone. You can get there in three days. We have someone on the inside who will let him go at midnight next Thursday. Don't get caught on the trip back. That's all, I have to go. Good luck." He disappears into the shadows.

I wait for a few minutes to slow my breathing and calm down, my mind jumping around in all directions. Luiz is alive! It doesn't matter what it takes, I will go get him in Rio.

I walk into the house and Carlos is working on his homework, with Junior playing on the floor with toy cars. Carlos jumps up from the couch and looks at me. "Mamãe, are you okay?"

I know he senses something. "I'm fine, querido. I need you to take Junior over to Sónia's and ask her and Chico to come here, I need to talk with them."

"Mamãe, I know I'm not supposed to ask questions, but I'm worried. I'm worried about Papai, and I'm worried about you."

I pull him close in a tight hug. "I know, querido. I know. We can't talk about it and you can't talk to anyone about Papai being gone. Please trust me. You are very grown up for eleven years old and I'm very proud of you. I know it's hard. We will get through this and our family will be together."

He reaches for Junior's hand and asks him to bring his toys and go over to Sónia's. I sit at the table with a pencil and paper and write down all the details the man told me before I forget them. A few minutes later Sónia and Chico come in the kitchen door.

"Sit down, I have something to tell you." I fold my arms and take a deep breath and tell them what happened.

Chico absorbs the news quietly for a minute. "Oh, thank God. That is the best news we could hope for. But Eva, it's a long way. I know you are a good driver and you're pretty street smart. But it's really risky."

"I know it is. But what else can I do? I have to go get him. You can't go, I have to go by myself."

Chico puts his hand on my arm. "We can help you plan the trip, I have maps and we can look at where you will stay at night, where the highway police stations are and what to say if they pull you over and ask questions."

Sónia looks worried. "What will you tell them at work? We have to think of something believable but not a lie they can check and get you in trouble."

I take a deep breath. "You're right. I think Chef Orlando will give me the time off, because it's really rare for me to ask."

Sónia's face brightens. "I know! Whenever you tell men you have some female problem, they just want you to shut up so they agree to whatever you ask. You just have to be vague and not say anything that's a lie."

I laugh. "You are so right about that. I hadn't really thought about it before, but any time it's an issue of pregnancy or other female issues, they just say, 'okay, okay, I get the picture, fine.'"

Chico gives a little smile and shakes his head. "Okay, it sounds like that will work. So you go into work tomorrow and tell the Chef you need to be off for two weeks? Because with the drive there and the drive back and who knows what else, you'll need at least that long."

I reach for each of them with one arm and bow my head and hug them tight. "Thank God for you. I don't know what I'd do without you."

September 20, Friday

I put on a peaceful but tired face as I enter the officers' dining-room kitchen. Altamira is tying her apron on and kisses me on both cheeks. "Everything okay, querida? You look exhausted." "I'm okay, Altamira, thanks. I'm a bit tired: the usual woman things, you know."

She looks at me with a sweet smile and squeezes my arm. "Don't worry, I'm sure everything will sort itself out."

"Thanks. Just so you know, I'm going to ask Chef Orlando for some time off. I really need a couple of weeks to rest."

"Of course. You know how I always nag you about never taking time off, so, good!"

We are busy until after lunch service, and Chef Orlando seems preoccupied. I lean around the kitchen office door. "Chef, may I have a minute to speak with you?"

He looks up at me and smiles. "Of course, Eva."

I sit down in the chair next to him. "Chef, I need to take some time off. I need a couple of weeks because . . ."

He holds his hand up. "No need to explain. You never take time off and of course I accept that. So let's say you'll be back at work on, let me look at the calendar . . . October 14th, Monday?"

I'm so relieved he isn't asking questions. "Yes, Chef, exactly. Thank you so much, I don't know how to thank you."

He smiles quietly and looks in my eyes. "You are welcome, Eva. Please take care of yourself, until then. Why don't you take the rest of the day?"

I gather my things and wave goodbye to everyone. "Have a good weekend, everyone."

Everyone waves and wishes me well back.

When I arrive home Chico has driven the car around to the backyard and the trunk and the two back doors are open.

"Chico, didn't you go to work today?"

"I went in this morning and told the foreman I need a few days to do some things. I've already changed the oil and done a tune-up, plus new brake shoes."

Sónia comes out to the yard with a glass of water for Chico. "Eva, how did it go with Chef Orlando?"

"No problem at all, he didn't even want to know why I was taking time off at such short notice. He was really nice." I walk around and look at the car as I imagine driving it all the way to Rio by myself. "Chico, what are you working on in the trunk?"

"I think you need to transport Luiz in the trunk, especially because the guy said not to get caught on the way home. The federal police could pull you over in a highway stop. And honestly, I'm afraid he may be in really bad shape. They could take one look at him and . . ."

Sónia touches me on the arm. "It's a lot to take in, I know. Another thing I thought of is what you will tell the police if they pull you over, about why you are traveling alone to Rio. You want to have a believable reason."

"The regular bus is so slow I had lots of time to think, and I've come up with a cover story. You know how we made our own bikinis to go to Itiquira a couple of years ago? I'm going to go to boutiques in Ipanema and buy several bikinis that we can use as patterns."

"That's actually a really good idea. Especially with 'The Girl From Ipanema' song being so popular."

"Eva, let me show you how this works." Chico has the back of the rear seat folded down toward the front, and he's fashioned a strap that Luiz can pull to close it from inside the trunk. He's also put padding in the trunk to make it more comfortable, though someone tall like Luiz will have to curl up to fit.

"That's really good thinking." I get into the trunk to try it out myself.

Chico frowns a bit. "I think Luiz should stay in the trunk the whole way, just in case. Definitely he shouldn't drive. But this way you two can talk and the air circulation will be better with the trunk open to inside the car."

Sónia waves to me to come into the house, and we get busy making a meal for everyone. After supper is finished and all the kids are tucked in bed we sit down at the table and Chico pulls out a couple of maps.

"So, this map has the area from Brasília to Rio, and this other one is Rio itself. We need to figure out how far you can comfortably drive in one day, and look for likely places to stay overnight at each distance."

We come up with a rough plan, and some ideas where the federal police stations are along the route, and I take notes.

Once the plans are finalized, Chico folds up the maps. "So, you'll leave tomorrow just before sunrise. Keep some money in your purse but most of it in the two hiding places. At night take the rotor under the distributor cover off like I showed you, because no one can steal a car that won't drive. If the fuel level is even near half empty, pull over when you come to a gas station. Keep plenty of gas in the car at all times."

We pack the car, putting a couple of suitcases and rolled-up hammocks in the trunk, things that can conceal Luiz if the federal police stop me on the way back from Rio and make me open the trunk. I pull together the most chic clothing I have and pack it in a small bag; I will need to look the part of a fashionable entrepreneur.

I go into the boys' bedroom to look at them sleeping and kiss them. I feel the weight of the trip I am about to undertake. Carlos wakes up and looks at me when I kiss him. "Mamãe, is everything going to be all right?"

I smooth his hair back from his brow. "Son, I need you to

be strong. I'm going to be gone for a few days but I can't tell you anything about it. Promise me you will be brave and take care of Junior and put on a good face for anyone outside our family. And you can't talk to anyone, okay?"

He nods and hugs me fiercely and I lie down next to him until I hear from his breathing that he's asleep. When I move to my bed it feels huge without Luiz here. I'm grateful I'm so tired that I fall asleep right away.

September 21, Saturday

I'm up more than an hour before sunrise and quickly put food and containers of water into a rucksack. I look in on my sleeping boys and say a prayer to keep them safe, and to bring me home safe with their father. Sónia and Chico are waiting in the darkness by the car.

"Don't you want some café? It will just take a minute and you can take it with you." Sónia is being cheerful but I can hear the fear in her voice.

"Thank you, querida, I'll just get going. I will stop on the road for café."

I hug them both and start the engine, letting it idle for a few minutes like Luiz taught me.

"Go with God, Eva." Chico pats the hood of the car and I back out onto the street, waving as I head south toward the unknown, feeling scared but excited in a mixed-up kind of way. The sound of the engine and the tires humming on the road has a rhythm of its own, and I'm quickly out of the developed area of Taguatinga and on the nearly deserted Highway 251. Soon I hit the main highway and turn right onto the 040, which will take me all the way to the big city of Belo Horizonte, and on to Rio.

The sun is rising on my left, bathing the vast high plains in a golden light with a few puffs of cloud riding along the horizon. A gas station is ahead and I'm ready for the bathroom and some café. I pull in and park in front of the little building, and put some toilet paper in the pocket of my jeans before I go in. I cringe at the filthy backed-up toilet and lack of water to wash my hands, drink a small bitter coffee served to me by the humorless woman behind the counter, fill the Gordini's tank and head south again.

The road is straight and goes on forever as the sun climbs higher in the sky. I have too much time now to think about everything, and I resolve that every time I start worrying I will stop and say to myself: *It will all be okay. I am strong. I can do it.*

It's only nine o'clock when I get to Cristalina, a small town known for its semi-precious gem mines. There's a Saturday-morning market as I pass through the center of town, and I park to take a break and look at the wares. There are tables of raw crystals and geodes, cut stones and jewelry of amethyst, aquamarine, tourmaline and polished green agate and jasper. Then on to the booths of more common things, and I buy a pair of sunglasses with big black frames, gold hoop earrings and a paisley hair scarf. Back at the car I look in the rear-view mirror as I put them on, and laugh because I look very chic. Like a woman who might buy bikinis in Ipanema.

The road out of town is straight and I sing to myself to stay alert, passing the occasional lumbering truck on the long road that dips slowly down on the way to the coast. I'm really hungry since I've only nibbled on some fruit and bread from my rucksack as I pass the sign saying I'm leaving the state of Goiás and entering Minas Gerais. The town of Paracatu is a welcome sight, and I find a small restaurant along the banks of the river, the outside tables surrounded by pink ipê trees in full bloom.

A girl comes to greet me as I sit. "How are you? We have a plate of the day, unless you want something else. It's beef, or we can fry you an egg."

"Beef will be great, thanks. And a Coca-Cola, please."

I can hear the water tumbling over the dam and it calms me as I wait for my food. My head begins to nod but I catch myself before I fall asleep, and I'm wide awake when the girl brings my food. It's a simple plate of overcooked beef that I gnaw on, rice and beans, and a slice each of tomato and onion. The Coca-Cola is cold and sweet. I'm finishing my food when I notice a couple of men sitting smoking at another table, staring at me. Maybe they're just two guys staring at a girl but I start to imagine they are with some secret agency of the military keeping tabs on my movements. I head to my car, resisting the urge to look back and see if they are following me.

I start the car and pretend to adjust the rear-view mirror as I keep my eyes on the restaurant's outdoor seating area. The men haven't moved. I can't afford to waste energy being paranoid, but I have to know what's going on around me at all times. I put the car in gear and head south again, driving a little too fast and constantly checking the road behind me.

The road is relatively straight for a couple of hours, then becomes curving with lots of hills as I get closer to tonight's destination, the town of Três Marias. I'm thankful it's still light when I reach the town, and I pull over on a side street just before the long bridge over the São Francisco River and the huge dam and reservoir below. I find a guesthouse overlooking the river, and pull in to check in at the office.

An older man behind the counter gives me a friendly smile as he squints at me through his glasses. "Good afternoon. May I help you?"

"Yes, Sir, thank you. I need a room for one night."

He looks at the cubbies behind him and pulls out a key attached to a big piece of wood with the room number carved on it. "Would you like to see the suite?"

Suite sounds very grand, and it's a good idea to take a look. "Yes, please."

The room is simple and very clean, and has its own bathroom. "This will be fine, thank you, Sir."

I'm able to park right in front of the room, and after taking a shower I walk back to the main house where they have a small restaurant on the veranda. A lady greets me. "We are almost closing, but I still have some fish stew if you would like."

After I finish the delicious stew I ask how much I owe her, and she just smiles. "Meals are included. We start serving breakfast at seven."

"Thank you, but I'm afraid I'll be leaving really early."

"Let me make you breakfast to take with you, querida. It'll just take me a minute."

She returns with a package wrapped in brown paper. "It's nothing fancy, but you can have a picnic breakfast on the road."

"I really appreciate it. Shall I leave the key in the room tomorrow morning?"

"That will be fine. Safe travels."

September 22, Sunday

It seems my little alarm clock buzzes five minutes after I fall asleep. It's still dark as I head out, crossing the river and getting back on the open road. Less than an hour later there are glimmers of dawn in the sky to my left. The mountain roads are curving and from time to time there are slow-moving trucks traveling together in convoys. I stop for lunch at a small restaurant just outside Belo Horizonte that offers hearty food typical of the region. The city itself is in a valley surrounded by mountains, and I wish I were a tourist here to enjoy the view, but it's still some distance to where I will spend the night.

A couple of hours later I arrive at Barbacena, a mountain town with steep cobbled roads nestled in greenery. A beautiful church with two towers dominates the main square, and I find an inn on a quiet side street. The cool humidity hits me as I step out of the car. I'm pleased to find that this small hotel is also very clean and my room has its own bath. The walls are brick and the furniture chunky dark wood, with simple white coverlets on the two twin beds. I'm so exhausted I eat some bread and cheese left over from my breakfast package, take a shower and fall asleep. It's only 300 kilometers to Rio from here, so I will sleep in tomorrow and have breakfast before I set out on the highway.

September 23, Monday

It feels like a luxury to sleep until the sun wakes me up, but it's still early. I feel well rested but I'm worried about driving into Rio since I've never driven in a really busy city before. I get dressed and take my room key to the dining room, where they have breakfast laid out. There are fresh roses in little vases on every table.

"Good morning, Madame. Would you like café?" A serious young man holds the coffee thermos and turns over my cup and pours when I nod yes.

"May I have some hot milk?"

"Of course, Madame."

I fill a plate with watermelon and mango, sliced cheese and bread, and pour myself some guava juice. It feels good to savor the food and enjoy the moment as though I were on an adventure and I try not to think about the challenges ahead. I sip my coffee with milk and when scary thoughts intrude I repeat to myself that it will all be okay, I am strong, I can do it.

The route out of Barbacena is mountainous but descends easily for a while, then there are more ups and downs. My sporty little friend Gordini hugs the curves, and he's with me all the way as I pass trucks and they beep their horns at me, and he purrs happily as I put him in overdrive and sing at the top of my lungs and we speed together down the straight parts of the road.

Juiz de Fora is a major transit for commerce and it really frazzles my nerves. There are so many huge trucks that I feel like an ant in my small car. I just gun the accelerator or slam on the brakes without thinking about anything. It's a relief to get past that and enter the town of Três Rios, the last place in the state of Minas Gerais. Soon I will enter the state of Guanabara and its capital, Rio de Janeiro, the country's old capital before we built Brasília.

1968

The highway descends rapidly into hairpin turns, and I grip the wheel tightly and concentrate on my driving. I come around the last curve before the highway drops down to Rio and pull over where I can park and take in the vista below. The water of Guanabara Bay is sparkling in the sunlight, with the city's neighborhoods nestled between giant humps of black rock, the turquoise ocean in the distance. It's just like the postcards Dona Francisca showed me as a child, but even more beautiful now that I'm here.

I plan to stay in the neighborhood of Botafogo, because it isn't fancy and expensive like Copacabana and Ipanema, but it's easy to get to those areas from there. Driving into the city I pass gritty industrial areas, the favelas of rickety shacks built up the steep hillsides, and the docks with their huge ships. Once I get to Botafogo I turn right into the side streets, and drive around looking for guesthouses. I settle on one in the middle of a quiet block, a white colonial with blue trim. I find a parking place further up the block and walk up the steps to the veranda and the front reception area. It's a big living room with couches and small tables, and newspapers and books thrown around. Bossa nova music is playing in the background.

"Hey, babe." A fashionably hippie young woman comes out from the office and greets me with a bored smile. She rests her cigarette in the ashtray on the counter and waits for my reply.

"Oh, hello. I need a room for four nights, leaving Friday."

"Single or double?"

Assuming all goes well and I am able to pick up Luiz as planned at midnight on Thursday, we can't leave before Friday, and we'll need a double bed Thursday night. "Double please."

She doesn't bat an eye, though I'm obviously by myself at this point. "Okay, ten cruzeiros a night, paid in advance."

"May I see the room first?"

She takes a key from the hooks behind the counter and hands it to me. "Knock yourself out. Up two flights and then left. The bathroom is at the opposite end of the hall."

The house is old-fashioned and the stairs are narrow, with landings between floors, sunlight filtering through a stained glass window at each. The smell of incense and herbal smoke pervades the first floor, and there's music with jangling guitars and a strong beat, and I can make out the words "all right" and "revolution." The sounds of voices laughing and singing along follow me up the stairs.

The second floor is quieter, though I pass rooms with doors open and people lying on beds reading and chatting. There's a birdcage in front of the window at the end of the hall, with two canaries flitting about. They chirp as I put the key in the door, opening to a room with a window that looks out on the wall of the building next door. I pull down the covers and the sheets are clean and there are two clean towels folded on the bed.

The hippie receptionist is lounging on a couch reading a magazine and smoking a cigarette when I tell her I'll take the room. I give her forty cruzeiros and go to the car to bring up the small bag with my clothes and toiletries. I walk back to the guesthouse beneath the purple arc of jacarandá trees and look up the narrow street to the steep black rock and Christ the Redeemer with his arms outstretched in blessing to the city.

After I settle into the room and freshen up, I'm not tired, but I am starving. It's a nice walk over to Botafogo Bay, with outdoor restaurants lined up along the beach walkway, an undulating black and white design built of many small square stones. There's a fresh breeze down from the mountains and I order grilled shrimp which is smoky and delicious and just perfect with a squeeze of lime.

I'm pretending to be on an adventure to avoid thinking bad thoughts, but a stab of guilt hits me as I think of Luiz and what he must be going through. I put down my shrimp skewer and start to cry, when Luiz himself appears across the table from me as vivid as life.

"Is something wrong with your shrimp?" He gives me that smile like he's keeping a secret and I feel a wave of desire and sadness, aching with how much I miss him.

"The shrimp is delicious. I feel bad to be enjoying it without you." The tears stream down my cheeks.

"I'm waiting for you, querida. Be strong. I want you to enjoy the good moments in this terrible time."

My thoughts are broken by the waiter, who steps over to my table with a concerned face. "Madame, is everything all right? Is there a problem with your food?"

I wipe the tears from my cheeks with the backs of my hands. "No, everything is really good. Please excuse me."

"No need to apologize, Madame."

He appears a few moments later with a glass of water. "For you, Madame, to help you feel more calm."

He is so earnest I feel I must take a sip, and as I expect it's water with a great deal of sugar added. I smile to myself as I appreciate the gesture. All Brazilians know that if you're upset you drink a glass of water with sugar and you will feel better. So I dutifully drink it down and hand him back the glass with a big smile. "Thank you very much. I feel better already."

After I finish eating, I gaze at Sugarloaf Mountain across the bay, the lights along the promenade reflected in the water. The walk back to the guesthouse is peaceful and I remember what Dona Francisca said when I told her I wanted to see Rio: *Perhaps you will, child, perhaps you will.*

September 24, Tuesday

I descend the steps of the guesthouse in Botafogo and walk to where the Gordini is parked, carrying the rotor in my hand. The car sits undisturbed where I parked it last night, dusted with purple jacarandá blossoms that look pretty but make a real mess. I raise and latch the hood after cleaning it off, unclip the distributor cover, reinstall the rotor and I'm ready to go. Like Chico said, they can't steal a car that won't run.

It's a lovely cool morning and I can smell the ocean from the nearby bay, a bit of a dirty smell that surprises me. I review my map to make sure I know which way I'm going, first to São Conrado to get some idea of where that section of Rio is, and then back to Ipanema to do my cover story shopping at the boutiques.

Leaving the quieter side streets of Botafogo, I'm back on the main road and immediately enter a tunnel, turning on my lights and gritting my teeth as buses whiz by me. My little car will be crushed if I don't drive aggressively. Out in the sunshine again, then another tunnel, and emerging into the light Copacabana is in front of me and I turn right on the beachfront avenue. I can hear the waves and feel the salty breeze through my open window. The beaches are teeming with people and there are sounds of drums and singing as I pass the many bars along the street, people already partying at this hour on a Tuesday morning. At the end of Copacabana I come around Arpoador Beach and now it's Ipanema with its huge expanse of sand and the avenue lined with palm trees. The road transitions seamlessly to Leblon, and soon I'm on Avenida Niemeyer, an elevated road hacked from the rock above crashing waves below. It's an odd sensation of flying above the ocean, negotiating the curves until I see the massive granite Pedra da Gávea looming in the distance, and the exclusive neighborhood of São Conrado sparkling in the sun. I don't want to think about being here in darkness Thursday night, and I set my mind to the task of learning my way around, without attracting attention.

The road curves sharply to the right, skirting around the steep, densely wooded slope climbing up until it meets the Estrada da Gávea, where I turn right, and soon there are hairpin turns and then the road smooths out again and I am looking for the entrance road on the left that was described to me by the furtive man in the darkness of Taguatinga last week. It seems years ago now. I'm looking for a huge gate on my left between a car mechanic's shop and a place selling tires.

It surprises me how quickly I see exactly what I'm looking for, and my blood runs cold at the sight of two guys in plain clothes standing outside the huge gate smoking. I jerk my head to focus on the road and commit the place to memory so I can find it Thursday night. The favela Rocinha is just below me and it's amazing how ingenious people are to build shanty houses hanging off the cliff, one on top of another.

Soon I'm into switchbacks with the road up against the black rock, gripping the wheel and sweating. I wonder if it's best to stay on this road, or maybe I should turn around and go back the way I came. The decision is made for me as there's no place to turn around. The road straightens out and I pass the entrance to the Botanic Garden, and the horseracing track of the Jockey Club is below on the right. The big lagoon, Lagoa de Freitas, is shining below and I know Ipanema is on the other side so I take some turns and end up on the quieter back roads of the fancy neighborhood. I drive up and down streets to get an idea of the place; most of the boutiques are on the street just behind the beachfront road. I find a place to park and head toward the beach, walking along the black and white mosaic sidewalk and marveling at the aquamarine ocean and waves crashing on the sand. People are sunbathing but I don't see anyone swimming.

I sit at a bistro table and order an espresso from a kiosk, trying to slow my breathing and willing the sea breeze to calm my nerves.

I ask the waiter a question. "I don't see anyone swimming, why is that?"

"Madame, it is a very dangerous current and the water is very cold." He clears my cup and saucer and I nod a thank you.

I sling my purse over my shoulder, though most of my money is in my bra and panties, and the car key is in the pocket of my jeans. Rio is famous for its clever pickpockets and petty criminals who will yank a gold chain off your neck if it catches their eye. I'm quickly developing a big city sensibility and heightened awareness of what's going on around me. I stop in front of the first boutique I come to and take a deep breath, mentally disguising myself in a cloak of wealth and privilege as I open the door.

"Hey babe." Clearly this is the greeting these days. The shop girl is wearing bejeweled flat sandals, loose striped pants with a metal link belt around her hips, and a flowy white shirt tied up under her breasts, which are unencumbered.

"Good morning. I'd like to browse a bit, and in particular I'm looking for bikinis."

"No problem, querida. Just let me know what you like."

The racks are sparse, and there is only one of each item, which puzzles me. I pick up a couple of bikinis and she glides forward to help me. "I'm not sure if these are my size?"

A husky little laugh of amusement. "Oh, querida, we have all normal sizes available. Just point to what you want and I'll bring them to you in the fitting room. Do you mind if I make some suggestions?"

"No, of course not."

She pulls aside the dressing room curtain and I enter. "Would you like an espresso, a soft drink, beer or wine?"

I want to laugh out loud but just smile and murmur no thank you.

Soon she returns with several items and crisply pulls the curtain closed. "Try these and we'll take it from there."

I take off my clothes and I'm putting on my first bikini when she pops her head in. "Oh querida, see these?" She points to a tissue dispenser on the wall. "Put those in the bikini bottoms to try them on." She winks.

Okay, crotch sanitation, got it. I put on the bikini bottom as directed and she walks right in while I'm standing there topless, like it's the most normal thing in the world. "Here, let's see if you like this." She helps me put the bikini top on and pulls back the curtain with a flourish. "Let's go to the big mirror, so you can get the full picture."

I feel awkward but pretend it's really old hat and step up on to the little elevated stage in front of the three-way mirror. "Oh, babe, you were made for this! It looks absolutely divine." She gently nudges me to turn this way and that as I gaze at myself.

Several more bikinis and it's clear she's just warming up, as she appears at the curtain with several frocks. "I know you said bikinis, but try these on just for fun? They said they were calling your name. By the way, I'm Isabella, and you are?"

I don't want to give her my real name. "Isabella. Pretty name. I'm Ana." I take the frocks and put on the first one, a lime-green strapless.

Isabella pulls me out of the dressing room to view the dress in the mirror. "Oh, I hope it falls down! Lovely!"

I can't believe she said that. "You hope it falls down?"

Husky laugh again. "That's what we call a dress with no straps: 'I hope it falls down.'"

I have to laugh too. After an hour in the shop trying on one thing after another, I choose two bikinis. As I exit the fitting room I notice a bunch of clothes tossed on the floor in a back corner. "Isabella, what are those clothes on the floor?"

She sniffs. "Oh those, they're last season's fashion. We just get rid of them because nobody wants them."

"Do you mind if I look?"

"Knock yourself out. If you see anything you want I'll give you a good price." She looks askance at me but I don't care. Rummaging through everything, I find several bikinis and a sundress and add them to my purchases. She sells them to me for next to nothing but acts like I'm taking out the trash after her valiant effort at selling me the latest. I pay in cash with a big smile and leave with my hot-pink shopping bag.

September 26, Thursday

The moment I've been preparing for is almost here and after a couple of days of pretending to be a fashion plate and a tourist it's gotten harder and harder to distract myself. I park in front of a busy restaurant in Leblon so I can time my arrival outside the gate in São Conrado at midnight. I don't want to get there too early because it's dark and right next to the favela. I check my watch and it's 11:20, so I had better get going to leave time for anything unexpected. I start the engine and put the Gordini in gear, pulling out into traffic and driving south toward Avenida Niemeyer. As I round the final curve, the lights of São Conrado extend from the beach up the hillsides, and I turn to drive up the Pedra da Gávea road. The street is nearly deserted with the businesses closed, and I park in the block past the gated entrance, which now has no guards, turning the car around to face back in the direction I came. My heart is hammering in my chest and I take deep breaths. It's ten minutes until midnight. I can't stand sitting anymore and the gate is deep in shadow so I get out of the car and walk closer, hiding in the trees across the road, where I have a better view.

The minutes crawl by and there is no traffic. Then the gate creaks open slowly and mechanically and I hold my breath. No one appears for minute upon minute, until I see a stumbling figure coming down the road to the gate, looking right and left, then tentatively stepping on to the sidewalk. It's so dark I can't see the man well, but I know it has to be Luiz so I step into the street and the figure moves toward me haltingly and I rush forward and stop a few steps from the person. The man is hunched over and seems older and I begin to doubt it's him.

He looks up. A gasp and a little sob. "Eva, oh my God, is that you?"

I throw my arms around him and can't believe how thin he is. "Yes. It's me. Let's go."

He feels fragile as I help him into the passenger seat, and I rush around to turn on the engine and stick it into first gear to get the hell away from here. I'm driving too fast around the curves and constantly checking the rear-view mirror because the devil himself could be following us. As we descend to the populated area I slow down and head back on Avenida Niemeyer.

"Eva, you're something." His voice is scratchy and his hand is trembling as he pats me on the thigh.

"I love you." I don't say anything more because I don't want to cry and I have to navigate the road above the ocean until we get to Leblon. Once we are on the avenue along the beach at Ipanema, I pull the car over and park. The bars are busy and there are people walking on the promenade.

Now I cry. "Oh, thank God I got you. Thank God. Let's go sit on the beach."

We stop at the edge of the sand and I take off my chic new sandals and Luiz is wearing a pair of flip-flops that I take as he removes them. The waves are crashing on the shore and people at the bars are singing and laughing and we sit in silence holding hands.

"Eva, I . . ."

"We will have lots of time to talk. You're safe. We're together. Shhhhh."

We lie back on the sand and look up at the stars, the Southern Cross bright against the white swathe of the Milky Way. An hour later we get back in the car and I drive to the guesthouse in Botafogo. He walks slowly and has to stop and rest every few steps as we climb the stairs to our room. The canaries wake up and begin chirping and warbling and waving their wings as I put the key in the door. Luiz sits on the bed.

"Querido, let's take a shower." I reach for his hand and pick up the clean towels. Luiz follows me to the bathroom. I unbutton his shirt and slip it off, and his pants just fall around his feet. I turn on the water and adjust the temperature and he steps under the water, groaning.

"Oh my God, Luiz!" His back is covered in angry red scabs and healing linear scars.

"That part was easiest." I gently soap him all over, appalled at how much muscle he has lost. He sits on the toilet seat as I towel him dry, and stops me when I begin to wash his clothes. "I will never wear those again."

"That's all right, I'll get you some new clothes tomorrow." I wrap the towel around his waist and secure it, walking with him back to the room. We lie down on the bed together, I put my arms around him from behind and feel his heart racing. It takes a long time until he calms down and I hear from his breathing that he is sleeping.

September 27, Friday

It's already hot when we wake up just after dawn. Luiz sits up on the bed and I arrange the two pillows behind his back. He stares into infinity, his eyes unfocused and his face expressionless. When it's time for breakfast I go down to the dining area alone, eating quickly then taking food and café up to him.

"Thank you." He hunches over to eat, his arms circling the food in his lap, trembling.

"Will you be okay here while I go buy you some clothes?"

He looks up at me and nods. On the way out I let the receptionist know I need to pay for two more nights, which isn't a problem. Luiz is in no condition to travel and I hope he'll be stronger in a couple of days. I pull out of my parking spot and head to the commercial center, which will have a variety of clothes at good prices. Central Rio is already busy with men in business suits and women in smart dresses bustling on the sidewalks. It's hard to find a place to park but I manage, and I find everything I need in just a couple of shops.

When I get back to the room Luiz is still sitting in the same position, staring. His eyes flicker and for a second he doesn't seem to recognize me, but then he gives me a thin smile.

"I've got clothes for you. Let's get dressed and go for a walk, we can have lunch by the beach." I take the clothes out of their wrapping, removing price tags and laying them out on the bed, then I help him get dressed. "Let's see how these sneakers fit. Hey, perfect."

"How are the boys? Are they okay?" There are tears in his eyes. It's like he's coming back to the reality of our life together.

I reach over and hold him close. "They're just fine, Luiz. We can be so proud of them. Carlos looks after Junior, and of course they are always with Sónia and Chico and their cousins."

"What did you tell them about what happened?"

"Carlos knows I promised to bring Papai home and not to tell anyone outside our family. He keeps Junior happy by playing with him, and everyone understands I'm on a shopping trip to Rio."

"A shopping trip. That's a good one." He looks at me and brushes my hair away from my face.

"Well, that's the best I could do. And I did buy bikinis, and making them to sell in Brasília is actually a good idea, Sónia says. Chef didn't even ask the reason when I asked for time off."

"Okay, let's go have lunch." He rises slowly from the bed and we make our way to the restaurants along Botafogo Beach.

September 28, Saturday

Luiz seems a little better today as we eat lunch at an outdoor table on the Copacabana promenade, though he still hunches over his food and eats his rice and beans quickly. The waves aren't as wild today, and there are people swimming and surfing.

I squeeze lime on my grilled shrimp. "Don't you want anything besides rice and beans?"

He looks up at me. "No, this is fine. Thank you, querida."

I look around to be sure there is no one within earshot of our table. "Luiz, who do you think it was that got you released? Does your resistance group have connections on the inside?"

"We never had links within the government. I have no idea who it could have been. Couldn't it be a connection through someone you know?"

I laugh at the absurdity of this. "I'm a cook, and before that I worked in the laundry. Of course I don't have any connections."

Luiz stares into the distance and sighs. "It's a mystery, and I guess we'll never know. But it's a loose end that bothers me."

"I know, me too. But all we can do is move forward. We have no idea who the guy in the alley was, or who directed him to help us. I feel pretty safe here in the big city walking around and eating in restaurants, but the drive home to Brasília is a different story. The guy was very clear about us not getting caught by the authorities on the way home."

His eyes shift from the distant ocean to mine, and he nods. "Okay."

"So, Chico and I talked about the drive back. And the risk of federal police highway stations, especially if they are doing a blitz and stopping everyone. Chico fitted out the trunk and you can ride with the back seat down so we can talk and you have more air circulation. He made a strap you can use to close it if we get pulled over."

"Okay, I understand."

"I hate to be so paranoid . . ."

He gives a bitter little laugh. "No, paranoia is the right attitude."

September 29, Sunday

We're on the road leaving Rio just after dawn, and soon we are at the switchbacks just before Petrópolis. As soon as we get to the summit and the road straightens out, I pass the convoy of heavy trucks that had slowed us to a crawl. The truck drivers beep and wave, and I wave back.

"Whoa, Madame, you are some driver! You must have had a very good teacher."

"You think so, do you?" I'm glad to hear Luiz cracking jokes again.

We stop at small gas stations to fuel up and use the bathroom, getting a café or mineral water and eating some of the food I packed for the trip. We make it to the outskirts of Belo Horizonte and find a nameless town off the main road, where I knock on someone's door.

"Good evening. Does anyone here rent rooms for the night?"

The lady points to a house across the way and I knock on the door, and rent a room for two cruzeiros. The room is bare but has hooks on the walls where we hang our hammocks. When I ask about the bathroom the lady points out back. The shower facility is an oil drum full of water and an empty olive oil can to pour it.

"No one would look for us here, that's for sure." I look at Luiz and he shakes his head. We eat a few things from our food stash and settle down for the night, sleeping well because we're exhausted.

September 30, Monday

It's almost noon and we're making good time. I'm starting to breathe easier since we've passed several federal highway stations and most of them have been deserted. Luiz seems calmer by the day.

"I think we can make a good distance today, stay overnight and then get home to Taguatinga tomorrow night." I look back at Luiz, reclining against the seat.

"I wish you'd let me help with the driving, we could travel all night and be home in the morning."

I'm actually considering this when I see a federal highway station up ahead, and this time there are several cars pulled over to the side and a uniformed cop standing in the middle of the highway.

"Oh my God, Luiz. It's a blitz. Hide!" I hear the back seat slam shut.

I calm my breathing and put on a big smile as the cop waves me over to the side.

"License and registration." No nonsense from this guy.

"Of course, Officer." I reach into my purse and hand him the documents. He scrutinizes them, unsmiling.

"What is the reason for your travel?"

I put on my best smile. "I made a trip to Rio to buy bikinis that I can copy and sell to ladies in Brasília. Just a little more income to buy my kids Christmas presents."

He grunts. "Open the trunk and step out of the car."

I wonder if he thinks I've stolen something, maybe my story isn't a good one. I pop the trunk and it clicks open slightly. I let my sundress ride up my legs as I turn to get up. I'm sure he's looking at my cleavage behind those aviator sunglasses. I walk to the back of the Gordini and he's about to fully open the trunk. I think the hammocks and suitcases and bundles of stuff will cover Luiz but I'm not willing to take a chance.

"Officer, like I said, Christmas is coming . . . I'm just trying to make a little extra money to buy my kids gifts. Could I make a donation to the officers' fund for the holidays?" I reach into my cleavage and bring out a twenty-cruzeiro note. I hold my breath.

He looks at me and grits his teeth. An eternity passes before he speaks. "Yeah, gimme that and get the hell out of here." He slams the trunk shut. I drive as calmly as I can until we're a ways down the road.

Luiz opens the back seat. "Damn, Eva, you scared the hell out of me. Do you think I really need to keep hiding in the trunk? It just makes me look more suspicious."

"Chico and I talked a lot about it. We don't know if it was a rogue officer who let you go or if they have an alert out for you. The guy in the alley told me they had someone on the inside and not to talk with anyone, and he specifically said not to get caught. Once we get back to Brasília, you and Chico can quietly use your contacts to try and figure out what is going on."

"Yes, that makes sense I suppose. Like I said, paranoia is the right attitude."

We drive in silence to the next gas station, and the next, and finally stop for the night at a no-name town off the highway, where we get a room for the night in a run-down hotel.

October 1, Tuesday

The rest of the trip is uneventful and we make it home in the early afternoon. I pull the car into the backyard between the two houses and Sónia comes running out, sobbing and throwing her arms around me. "Oh thank God you're safe! And Luiz . . ."

Luiz gets out of the back seat and Sónia is speechless when she sees him, tears streaming down her face. "Oh, Luiz."

He reaches for her and hugs her. "I know, I look terrible."

Luiz sits at the kitchen table as Sónia prepares café, and I look in on Junior, who's napping peacefully but must sense my presence, because he wakes up. "Mamãe!" I hug him and kiss him and when he sees Luiz he runs to him and jumps into his lap. Luiz holds him for a long time, tears pooling in his eyes.

We unload the car and I hear the kids arriving from school. Carlos sees the car and rushes into the house, crushing me in a hug and then going to Luiz, who's resting in the bedroom.

"Papai?" At eleven years old, Carlos notices things that Junior, at almost four, doesn't. Luiz reaches for Carlos and they sit on the bed for a long time holding each other, both crying.

Sónia and I try to act normal, pulling together a supper with what's available and making the kids do their homework before they go out to play, though Carlos wants to keep Luiz and me in his sights. Just after sunset Chico gets home from work.

"Luiz, Eva, thank God you're home!" He rushes into the kitchen and embraces us. He sits down at the table and tries to smile. "We can talk later tonight."

After supper and with all the kids tucked in bed, Chico gestures to us to go to the backyard, and sets up four chairs under the trees. We all sit and Chico speaks first. "They could be listening. We can't talk about anything inside. Agreed?"

We all murmur agreement and he continues. "Luiz, I won't

ask you to talk about what happened until you're ready. But when you are, we'll develop a plan to figure out next steps."

Luiz clears his throat and a moment passes. "I'm ready to begin. There are things I don't know how to say out loud, and those will come later."

We wait and I hear him swallow hard. "They grabbed me on the street on my way home from a meeting. Eva, I didn't tell you and Chico what I was doing. I wanted to protect you. But I knew from my comrades what the military was doing, and yes, I was resisting."

I can't help but look around as though someone could be watching us. "It's okay, Luiz, we don't need to look back at what might have been."

After a pause Luiz continues. "They handcuffed me and put a black bag over my head and shackles on my ankles. I was shoved into a truck with other people, both men and women. I didn't know where they were taking us until I heard sounds like an airport. We were put on a plane, a military transport with a metal floor. It seemed like forever but I guess it was a couple of hours, then we landed somewhere."

His voice catches. "They stripped me naked and hung me by my knees on a parrot perch, a bar with my wrists and ankles tied and my head hanging down. When they took off my black hood I saw that it was an auditorium in a Quonset hut like here in the general barracks, and there were maybe a hundred officers sitting in chairs like it was a concert or something. And a guy came up on the stage and demonstrated various torture methods so they could learn."

I can't wrap my mind around this. "They demonstrated methods?"

"Eva, they demonstrated torture methods. They used methods on me for the officers to see and learn."

I feel I am going to throw up and we are all sobbing quietly, but Luiz does not cry. "I was there for several days. The only way I got through it was by saying, 'Just one minute, I can stand another minute,' and after that minute I could stand the next."

We wait silently for him to go on. "After several days, I don't know how many, but many, they put me in a car and took me somewhere else. That's where I figured out where I was, because in the times with my hood off, when they took me to a bathroom or fed me, I could see I was in an old mansion and the back of it was built into that black rock, like the hills in Rio."

Chico leans over and hugs his brother. "And now you're home. That's enough for today. There are no words any of us can say. We will talk in the days to come. We love you."

It's just me and Luiz sitting in the warm night air. "Look, a waxing moon." I reach over for Luiz's hand and we sit there for a long time, saying nothing.

October 14, Monday

My first day back at work. It seems like years since I entered this kitchen. I am a different person but I have to act like I'm the same. I mentally put on a mask with a smile as I stash my things in my locker and change into my work uniform.

Altamira is already busy with prep but she gives me a big hug and kisses me. "Querida, we have missed you. The kitchen isn't the same without you."

Teresa looks over at me with her usual sneer. "Oh, hello, Eva, how was your vacation?"

"Some day I will take a vacation. But I'm fine, thank you, Teresa." A silly person like Teresa can't get a rise out of me.

Chef Orlando comes out of his office. "Welcome back, we missed you!"

"I missed you all too, and it's good to be back." It's partially true.

I throw myself into the rhythm of work and the day passes quickly with no time to dwell on my worries. We are cleaning up from service and beginning prep for tomorrow when the major who is chief of operations for the entire complex, including the dining service for the officers, enters the kitchen. We all stand at attention even though we are civilians.

He goes to Chef's office and looks in at the doorway. The major is dark-haired and as handsome as a movie star in his crisp uniform. He closes the office door and the major and Chef have a brief conversation.

The door opens and the major says over his shoulder, "I'll expect that budget a week from today. Please address the over-spend and have proposals for improvement."

As he heads toward the door he looks over at me briefly, and I wonder if some of us will be let go to cut the budget. I need this job now that Luiz isn't working. My blood boils with anger at what they did to Luiz but I can't betray those feelings.

When I arrive home the boys are over at Sónia's and Luiz is in our darkened bedroom, with the lights off and a pillow over his head.

I sit down next to him on the bed as softly as I can and speak quietly. "Querido, another one of those headaches?"

He grunts a yes. I go to the kitchen and get ice and a cloth and put it on his neck, and give him aspirin. "I'm going to make you a café, my father always says it helps a bad headache."

He manages a few sips and he seems a little better in a couple of hours.

"I know a headache is coming when I see sparks of light." He rolls over and groans.

"I know, querido, and noise and light make it worse. I'll keep it dark and quiet and it will pass."

In a few hours Luiz is feeling a bit better, sitting up on the bed. I kiss him on the cheek and adjust the pillows. "Querido, I think it would be good to see a doctor. You're getting these headaches every few days."

"You can't trust doctors. The last doctor I saw was there to check me and see if those guys could continue the electric shocks. To make sure I wasn't almost dead. He told them I could handle more without dying. No doctors. Never."

His vehemence takes my breath away. "All right, querido. No doctors."

These moments when he gives me glimpses of what happened are rare, but they are like a knife to my soul. Sometimes I don't know how we are going on day to day, pretending things are normal. But we do it for the children, and because there's nothing else we can do.

December 14, Saturday

Sónia and I are getting ready for Christmas, putting up our artificial trees and lights, making gifts and buying toys for the kids. We've got several orders for cakes for the holidays. It's late and everyone is in bed.

Sónia laughs. "It sure seems like there aren't enough hours in the day."

"It's true. But we'll get everything done."

"No doubt about it. How is Luiz doing the last few days?"

"He has headaches a couple of times a week. He sometimes gets work at the hardware store installing lighting for people. Every little bit helps."

"That's good."

I lower my voice to a whisper. "He had a terrible headache last night, after we heard about the A1-5 law that passed Congress yesterday. He says it makes repression and torture legal in Brazil."

Sónia whispers back. "It's shameful. I don't know what will become of our country."

Things just seem to keep getting worse, and I just nod because there's nothing else to say.

Sónia speaks again, at a normal volume. "Eva, any more word on whether they will let people go at your work?"

"Everything seems normal as far as the kitchen goes. I hope they wouldn't give us a dismissal notice right before Christmas. We just have next week, then the kitchen is closed until the New Year."

December 31, Tuesday

"Happy New Year, querida." Luiz reaches over to kiss me. We're sitting under the trees as neighbors shoot off fireworks in greeting to 1969.

"I love you, Luiz. Happy New Year."

We sit quietly and the humid summer breeze caresses us as the waxing moon disappears below the horizon.

Luiz clear his throat. "I need to tell you about my thinking on everything that happened."

This is a surprise on a festive night. "Yes. We really haven't talked much about it since that first night back from Rio."

"Chico and I put out feelers to all our contacts, and no one has any idea who might have helped me escape. Could it have been someone at the generals' quarters?"

"That seems so unlikely."

"Unlikely but still possible. Just keep thinking and noticing, okay?"

"Okay."

"And I want you to know what I'm planning to do."

I swallow hard. "Okay."

"I'm laying low for the time being and not doing anything active with the resistance. But I wrote down everything I can remember about being kidnapped. I keep it in a secure place. Promise me that no matter what happens, you will keep that document safe. Some day our country will want to know the truth."

"I promise. But where is the secure place?"

"You're sitting on it. I dug a hole and the document is in a metal box under a layer of tile and several inches of dirt. It's my hope that we'll dig it up together one day. But if not, you know where it is."

1970

June 7, Sunday

"Oi in the house!" Our neighbor Joana announces her arrival.

"Hey, Joana, I'm back here." I greet her from the veranda, and she walks through the house like someone who feels at home. She's already part of the family though we've only known her for a year, since her family bought the house across the street.

"I brought you the tea-towels and bikini bottoms. I just need some more fabric to get going on the next batch." She gives me an energetic smile. Joana is just twenty years old but she's a force to be reckoned with.

"We did really well at the market yesterday, you're quite a saleswoman and your English is really good. It's great that we have so many tourists these days, with plenty of money."

"The market at the television tower on the Esplanade of Ministries is a fantastic place to sell your bikinis and other stuff. It's great to make things that require so few materials, just our time and effort, and that give us a such a good profit margin."

I grin at her and shake my head. "You're learning a lot studying business. It's so good to have you as a partner. I learn a lot from you."

"There are things you learn in school, but it doesn't matter how good you are with finances if you don't make products people want."

"We should make a trip to Rio together in August, to check out the boutiques in Ipanema and Leblon, buy some samples and get a jump on the styles for next season."

"That sounds fantastic, let's plan for when I have a break from university. But Eva, are you sure it isn't too much for you to do all this work, on top of your job at the generals' dining room?"

"I love cooking, and I love creating and sewing. So none of it feels like work to me. And the extra income helps a lot, since Luiz can't work that much because of the headaches."

"Maybe I can start doing more. Like, why not let me start doing the bikini tops? I know they're harder to sew, but I'm sure I'll get the hang of it. I'd like to take some of the burden from you. You had such faith in me when you gave me the sewing machine."

"I saw your talent. You have good hands and I knew you would learn quickly. And motivation is more important than experience."

"You sound like one of my business school professors." We laugh.

"And what about you, Joana? You can't let our little side business distract you from your schoolwork, you need to get good grades and graduate and get a real job."

"A real job? Here in Brazil? We never talk politics, but you know Brazil is a mess. They say the United States is the land of opportunity, and I believe it. The money I make from this little side business, as you call it, will make my dream of living in America possible."

"How is your other side business going? How many students are you teaching Portuguese?"

"Just two Americans right now, which is about right since I don't have a lot of extra time."

"You know, I'd really like to learn more English, and Carlos is unhappy with the English instruction at school. He's thirteen and a bit impatient. He says the teachers don't know much more than he does."

"Well, I'm sure he's right. Let's practice English together, then. I'll bring my sewing machine over next Sunday and we can chat while we work."

"Whatever happened to the day of rest?" Sónia walks in the kitchen door and shakes her head at the stack of finished items on my kitchen table.

I laugh. "Haven't you heard that idle hands are the devil's workshop?"

Sónia rolls her eyes. "Well, it's time for a lunch break. Joana, querida, you're joining us aren't you?"

I get up from the table. "Let's go eat lunch."

September 1, Tuesday

"Hello, I'm home!" Luiz and the boys are in the kitchen fixing the evening snack. I put down my things on the table by the front door and look through the mail that came today.

"Oh my God." One of the items sends a chill through me.

Luiz stops what he's doing and looks up. "What is it, querida?"

I hold up the envelope so he can see it. "Return to sender, no such person at this address. This is the last letter I sent to my father, a month ago."

Luiz looks puzzled. "I know you haven't heard from him, or anyone else in the family, for years. But you've still been faithfully sending him letters every month."

"Luiz, I have to go to Picuí. I always told you they might as well be living on Mars, since my father quit writing to me a few years ago. I have to see once and for all what's going on."

"When will you go?"

"I'll see what Chef says tomorrow. I'd like to take the boys but they would lose too much time from school."

Carlos and Junior just look at me, puzzled. They know I'm upset, but I've always told them happy things about my family, except for my mom's death. If I'm able to sort things out I can take them to visit Paraíba later.

September 8, Tuesday

The flight from Brasília to Recife was uneventful, and much less exciting the second time on an airplane. No buses for me this time: I rented a car at the airport so I can travel freely. I have no idea what I will find. I'm almost to João Pessoa, the capital of Paraíba, on the coast a couple of hours north of Recife. I'll stay in the city tonight and drive to Picuí tomorrow, which will no doubt take several hours, and the roads may be in bad condition.

Driving up the highway parallel to the coast, I come over a hill and the arc of the beachfront city of João Pessoa is before me. The water is bright turquoise and there's a breeze coming off the ocean. I'll splurge and stay in a beachfront hotel tonight. Soon I find a modest-looking place just across from the sand, and park in front.

The young man at reception beams at me. "Welcome, Madame, may I help you?"

"Yes, thank you. I need a room for one night."

"Let's see . . . I have one with a lovely ocean view."

"That sounds perfect." I complete the registration and settle into my room on the fourth floor, marveling at the vista. After a quick shower I put on a sundress and stop at reception.

"Is there a restaurant that serves typical Nordestino food nearby?"

He laughs. "No, Madame, I'm afraid not. Places like that are only found in the interior. João Pessoa is quite cosmopolitan. I am happy to make a recommendation if you like."

"Thank you, that's very kind. But I think I will just go for a walk on the promenade and find a place along the way."

"Of course, Madame. It's a lovely evening."

"One other question: do you have any idea how long it will take me to drive to Picuí tomorrow?"

The idea of going to Picuí flummoxes him, and he stammers. "Well, uh, I'm not sure. That is quite a ways."

"No problem, I just thought you might have some idea."

"I'm afraid I don't. I've lived here all my life and I've never been to the interior."

I give him a smile. "Thank you very much for your help."

My hotel is at the south end of Avenida Cabo Branco, which curves along the tranquil bay lined with coconut palms. There is a soft breeze off the ocean as I walk to the end of the promenade, then I return to a restaurant that caught my eye. It's a place for tourists but the décor is rustic, with chunky dark wood furniture and red checked tablecloths.

The waiter brings bread and butter. "Would you like to see the menu, Madame?"

"What fish do you have for grilling this evening?"

"We have a very nice grouper, we can grill a portion for you."

"Yes, that will be fine. It comes with salad and fried potatoes?"

"Yes, Madame. Something to drink?"

"Mineral water please, no ice."

After a delicious meal I walk back to the hotel and sleep peacefully.

September 9, Wednesday

The light wakes me and I remember how early the sun rises close to the equator. I drive west out of the city, and it isn't long before the landscape changes to scrub brush and the road is bumpier. The gas stations are few and far between and I stop and fill up at each one to make sure I don't get caught in the middle of nowhere without fuel. Hours later, and after several adventures navigating stretches of severe potholes, I climb the hill into Picuí.

I'm sure I couldn't find my family home on a map even if I had one, so I follow my nose, and as I get closer memories flood back. The town square, the big Catholic church and the dusty roads, most still unpaved. Everything looks smaller to me now, even the sky. I turn right, left, right, without thinking, and there it is. The house where I grew up.

I park across the street and go up to the gate, and it has a doorbell now, which I push. A minute passes and a woman comes to the door, then out to the gate.

"Yes, may I help you?" She is middle-aged and dressed simply, and I see three small children peering out the front door.

"Senhora, I grew up in this house but I have lived in Brasília for more than ten years. I'm hoping to find my family, because my letters have gone unanswered and recently one was returned." I hope she will help me with just this bit of information.

She gives me a sad smile. "I'm so sorry to hear that. We bought the house a few months ago. The woman that sold it to us gave me her address, if you would like it."

My heart is pounding. "Yes, I would appreciate that."

She goes into the house and returns with a piece of paper with an address written on it. She explains how to find it. I get back in the car and drive to the other side of town. The small house is connected to others with no front courtyards, their doors opening directly on to an unpaved street. I take a deep breath and knock on the door.

"Yeah, just a minute, I'm coming!" A voice calls from inside. A teenage girl opens the door and looks me up and down. "Yeah?"

Like a punch to the gut, I admit to myself in this moment that my father is gone. So I ask for my stepmother, Madrasta. "Hello, I am looking for Dona Amara. Does she live here?" I have never said her name out loud before.

"Who wants to know?" The girl eyes me suspiciously from the barely open door.

"My name is Eva. She married my father when I was young."

"Just a minute." The door closes.

I look up and down the dusty street as I wait. Finally the girl opens the door. "Yeah, come in."

The house is cramped, its rooms too small for the large pieces of furniture. A television show is a low hum in the background. The young girl beckons to me to enter the living room. Seated on the couch in front of the television is a middle-aged woman, her flowered house dress tight against her curves.

The woman on the couch speaks without taking her eyes off the television. "Well, look what the wind blew in." She doesn't offer me a seat and at first I don't realize it is Madrasta, because she looks so old.

It takes me a moment to recover. "Amara? I've come a long way and that's all you have to say to me?"

She finally looks at me. "No, that isn't all I have to say. Not that you care what I have to say."

"May I sit, please?"

"Sure, sit."

I pull over a chair from the dining table. "Please tell me about my father."

"Your father? He's gone. He left me here with a bunch of kids and a post office pension."

My blood is boiling and I want to slap her or worse, but instead I get up and turn off the TV. "I'm sorry to inconvenience you, but I need you to tell me the whole story, starting from the beginning."

"Well, let's see . . . Once upon a time there was a girl who couldn't read or write . . ."

"Amara, stop it. Can we please just have a normal conversation? What happened to my father?"

"A few years after you left, your father he had a stroke. He couldn't walk, or speak, or anything, and I had to take care of him. Then he got an infection and died two years ago. End of story."

I am raging inside but keep my composure. "I wrote letters every month. I got letters back from my father for a few years, and then I heard nothing back even though I kept writing. What did you do with my letters?"

She gives me a bored look. "I never read them, if that's what you're wondering. I kept them all in a box. You're welcome to have them."

"Please tell me where my father is buried, and please tell me where my sisters and brothers are, and if they are here in Picuí, how I can find them." I won't give her the satisfaction of seeing me break down completely. I never did when I was little, even when she beat me.

"Your father is in the church cemetery with your mother, where he always wanted to be. I was just a convenience."

I feel pity now, no urge to cry. "It makes me so sad that you feel that way, Amara. You had many children with him. Where are they all now?"

"Well, your favorite, Miriam, ran away and I haven't seen her in years. Good riddance, if you ask me. The rest of my children all live here in Picuí, like most of your actual brothers and sisters."

My heart aches. "All of my father's children are my brothers and sisters. I never saw any difference. I love them all."

She calls to the teenager to bring an address book with their addresses, which I write down in a journal I brought with me. The girl gives me the box with my letters at Amara's direction.

I am ready to leave. "Amara, I am very sorry for the loss of your husband, José, and everything you went through caring for him after his stroke. I hope you have a happy life from now on."

She says nothing but looks in my eyes for the first time, and I feel her deep well of bitterness and regret.

I rise from my chair and put my journal on top of the box of letters. "Amara, I forgive you. I forgive you for everything. And I wish you God's love and the peace that passes all understanding."

Weeping, I drive to the evangelical church with its small cemetery. Mamãe and Papai's headstones are next to each other, and I stay there for a long time saying a prayer for them. They are together and at peace.

I find a guesthouse on the outskirts of town that's clean but charmless, surrounded by featureless houses and beige hills in every direction. I take my things to the room and open the box. All the letters are unopened. I sit on the bed staring at nothing until I rouse myself to get out and try to find my brothers and sisters. I show the girl at reception Daniel's address and she explains how to get there.

As I drive I remember how close we were as children, with me the oldest and Daniel just a year younger. It has been twelve years, a lifetime, since I last saw my family. I park the car and compare the address listed with the modest yellow house surrounded by a wall with magenta bougainvillea tumbling over the top. My watch shows four o'clock, so Daniel may not be home. I take a deep breath and ring the bell by the front gate.

A pretty, petite woman comes out the front door and stands on the veranda. "Yes, may I help you?"

"Hello, my name is Eva. I'm looking for Daniel, my brother."

She hurries down the steps and opens the gate. "Oh my goodness! I have heard so much about you. I'm Rita, Daniel's wife, please come in." She smiles and leads me inside.

"Daniel should be home within the hour. May I get you some café or tea?" She pulls out a chair for me to sit at the kitchen table.

We are just finishing our tea when I hear a man's voice. "Querida, I'm home."

He walks in the kitchen and stops in his tracks. Those blue eyes captivate me, and he's so like Papai I am speechless for a moment.

"Eva, is it you? Oh my God, I can't believe it!" I jump up from my chair and we hug, both of us crying. He holds me at arm's length and looks at my face, then hugs me again. Rita is staring in amazement.

Daniel wipes his face and we sit without speaking for several minutes.

"I've thought about you so much, wondering if you were all right, but Amara said she never heard anything from you and that something must have happened." There's a catch in his voice.

"I'm fine, Daniel. Just too busy working and raising my two boys. Carlos is thirteen and Luiz Junior is almost six. Do you have kids?"

He smiles at Rita. "Yes, we have twin girls, they're eight years old."

"I've been writing letters every month and Papai sent letters to me for the first few years. Then nothing. And then a couple of weeks ago one of my letters was returned. I should have come before, but . . ."

"I understand. I am so glad you're safe and well, and that you have come to see us. We have so much to catch up on. How long can you stay?"

"Just a few days. I work as a sous chef for the military officers' dining room and can't be gone long. What work do you do?"

"I'm a teacher in the same elementary school we attended. I love educating children, especially kids with learning differences."

I laugh. "Like me?"

He reaches over to give me a hug. "Yes, just like you. Smart and determined, full of spirit. My sweet big sister. We have so much to talk about."

There's a commotion as the girls arrive home, one with a violin case and the other a clarinet. "Papai, Mamãe! We want to go down the street to play soccer with the other kids . . ." They stop in the kitchen doorway and go quiet as they see a strange woman sitting at the table.

"Eva, these are your nieces, Márcia and Patrícia. Girls, this is your Aunt Eva, she's visiting us from Brasília." Daniel reaches for them and holds one with each arm.

Both girls stare at me shyly and Márcia looks up at her dad. "Papai, she looks like a movie star."

Everyone laughs and begins to chatter as Rita prepares a snack for us. Rita looks at Daniel. "Let's have a dinner tomorrow, see if everyone can come." And we begin planning what will no doubt be a big gathering.

September 10, Thursday

Rita and I have been busy all day shopping, cooking and having so much fun that I feel like we've known each other for ages. Family are bringing food also, but I get carried away preparing the Nordestino dishes like carne de sol that I haven't cooked or eaten in so long. Picuí is home to the best dried meats and because it's spring there are ample fresh vegetables to choose from. We will serve the food buffet-style on the veranda because there are so many of us.

Before we know it people start arriving. Ana, Paulo, Samuel, João, Deborah, Mordecai and their families. It's beautiful confusion, with everyone talking, laughing, hugging and kissing, and lots of kids running around. Food is served and we all sit eating and chattering at the same time, trying to catch up on everything.

Ana hugs me and won't let go. "Eva, Amara told us she had heard nothing from you. She said you were gone to the 'land of the forgotten' down in Brasília. I can't believe she hid your letters all these years, and never even opened them to read to Papai."

I wipe away tears. "But would Papai have understood them if she read them to him? She makes it sound like he wasn't functioning at all."

Ana shakes her head and exhales a big breath. "He couldn't talk or move but he understood everything. He was a prisoner in his body. Even if he couldn't speak, when I sat with him I knew he understood everything. I can't explain it, I just knew."

"I believe you, Ana. I feel bad I wasn't here. It breaks my heart."

"You did the right thing. And Amara could have contacted you any time. She just . . ."

I hug her and we don't say anything for a long time. "Ana,

262

we have to forgive her. She never knew any better, and she is a victim of her own bitterness."

We wipe our tears and join the tumult, kids running around and going crazy over the desserts. Then everyone sits eating the sweets in silence, the silence of happiness and joy in being together.

September 15, Tuesday

It's good to be back home in Taguatinga for my birthday, and it's my last day off before returning to work tomorrow. I've made my favorite orange and carrot cake with cream cheese icing. The kids have done their homework and they're playing soccer down in the field and I can hear their laughter and happy shouts in the distance, bringing back memories of my childhood when play-time was precious because there was always so much work to do around the house. But I have no regrets because it made me the woman I am today. The warmth of reconnecting with my brothers and sisters is tinged with sadness about Papai being gone.

Sónia sweeps in, her arms loaded with things for dinner. "Wow, that cake looks delicious. It seems a shame you have to make your own cake, but since no one can make a cake better than you, we just have to let you do it."

We laugh and I step back to admire my work. "I can't explain it, but when I'm cooking or baking or sewing, my mind becomes calm and all I see is what I'm working on. It makes me happy."

"That's a gift, Eva. And speaking of gifts, I imagine seeing your brothers and sisters after all these years was a nice birthday present."

"Yes, the best in years. They really wanted me to stay to celebrate but I had to get back for work."

"Well, now you can keep in touch. You have their addresses and they have yours."

"Yes. I wish telephone lines weren't so expensive. Can you imagine if you could just call and talk to someone any time you felt like it?"

Sónia sighs. "I wonder if it costs so much in other countries. I bet it doesn't."

"Maybe not. I just wish Picuí wasn't so far away."

"Eva, you're amazing, driving from João Pessoa to Picuí and back, and the trip last year to Rio. You're a regular world traveler."

I make a face. "I think to be a world traveler you have to go to another country."

"Picuí is another country, if you ask me." We laugh. "Eva, I'm so sorry about your father. I have no words, just I'm sorry."

We hug. "I know he is at peace, after a lot of suffering. Although I should have been there to take care of him."

"Eva, you couldn't. You would have, but you couldn't. Don't forget that Amara never let you know, never sent you a letter, kept your letters hidden . . ."

I don't want to start crying, so I take a deep breath. "The only other thing that makes me sad is not seeing Miriam. Today is her birthday too. I'm sending out a prayer for her."

"Nobody has any idea where she is?"

"No. She ran away when she was sixteen. Today she turns twenty-four, and I'm thirty-three. How can that be? Time moves so quickly. When you're young it seems like time crawls by."

"Amara really said good riddance about Miriam?"

"It was a sad situation, and I only put all the pieces of the puzzle together as I got older. Miriam's skin is dark and everyone pretended she was born early, but she was a full-term baby. Papai became depressed when she was born, but of course he knew all along Amara was already pregnant when he married her."

"You were Miriam's big sister and her mom too."

"I adore Miriam. She's so smart, and spunky, and beautiful. Maybe some day we'll be together again."

1971

January 14, Thursday

I've just arrived home from work and Luiz pulls me outside to talk in the backyard. "They've released the National Liberty Action prisoners!" He's bubbling over with excitement.

"What does it mean?" I'm confused by events, especially because they're usually not reported accurately on the television news, which is controlled by the dictatorship.

"This is huge. A group of their members kidnapped the Swiss ambassador in December and demanded the release of their comrades in prison. And they won! Seventy political prisoners were flown to exile in Chile, and now they're telling journalists how they were tortured by Brazil's military. Not just men, women too."

I shudder to think about this, and I don't know where Luiz is getting all this information. "Luiz, are you at risk? Are you getting involved in the resistance again?"

"Eva, you are involved in the resistance. You rescued me from the torturers in Rio and hid me in the car and brought me home. You're my angel of resistance." He hugs me close and I can feel his heartbeat.

January 16, Saturday

"Querida, I'll be home later tonight. Don't wait on me for supper."

I stand stock-still in the kitchen looking out the window. I can't breathe and only whisper: "Luiz, please don't do this. Please stay home."

He comes up behind me and enfolds me in his arms, kissing me on the neck, and time stands still for a moment as he whispers back: "Querida, I have to do this. Our country is at stake. We can't let the atrocities continue without a fight."

I'm walking around the house in a daze, sick with worry, when Joana opens the front door. "Hey, Eva, I'm ready to cut out more bikinis. Shall we work in the kitchen or out on the veranda?"

It's a relief to have a distraction, and we set to work lining up the fabric, pinning on the patterns and cutting out the pieces.

"We made some good money today at the market. Everybody wants a new bikini for the summer." Joana sits down to take a break.

"Yes, it's great. How's your travel fund going?"

"Actually, I need to update you. I've got a really good amount of money saved and I plan to go to the US when I finish college in May."

"Wow, that was fast! But how exciting. All your hard work is paying off." I give her a little hug. "So tell me all about your trip. Will you go to New York? Miami?"

Joana gives me a sly smile. "Actually, my destination is somewhere you've never heard of. North Carolina, in the south of the US."

This surprises me. "No, I haven't. Is it a city? Where is it? Why there?"

Joana laughs. "Remember I told you about David, who I tutored in Portuguese? That's where he's from. North Carolina is a state between Florida and New York, on the coast, and it's where his university is. He just finished his year studying here in Brazil and went back last week."

"It sounds pretty serious. Are you in love?"

Joana giggles. "I guess you could say that. He's a great person and we have so much fun together. I want to be with him."

"Well, you have my very best wishes. You deserve love and happiness. So let's make a lot of money between now and May!" We laugh and get back to work.

January 26, Tuesday

Walking home from the military workers' bus stop in the town square, the sky is dark and moonless. It's a hot and humid summer night and I'll be glad to get home and put on a light dress. My mind is busy with the things that need to be done for the kids, for the bikini business, and tomorrow at work. I've got lists to keep track of everything.

My thoughts stop cold as I realize a man is walking in parallel without talking to me. He breaks the silence. "Take the first left."

I know what to do from the last time, and it's the same voice. I duck into the first side street and slip between two darkened buildings. My heart is hammering as I wait for him in the shadows.

Suddenly he's next to me. "Same rules as before. You can't tell anyone about this, except give this message to your husband. Agreed?"

"Yes." My voice trembles.

"Your husband has to stop. Things are getting worse. It's normal operating procedure now to disappear people. That is what will happen if he doesn't quit."

I take a deep breath. "Don't you think I've tried? He's passionate about the cause and won't give up."

"Look, someone on the inside in Rio let your husband go and you got lucky when no one came after him. But next time we won't be able to help you. I told you, things are getting worse."

"I appreciate your help more than I can say. Who do I have to thank?"

"Oh no you don't. You know I can't tell you that. Curiosity kills the cat. Go home and tell him. Stop."

My throat aches and I can only whisper. "Okay, thank you. Thank you."

He begins to walk away but stops and looks back over his shoulder. "Maybe some day, when this is over, you will know more. Lay low but don't forget. Keep it in your memory for the day of justice. It has to come."

I wait as he melts into the darkness, gulping deep breaths to calm down. Lightning flares in the distance and I hear thunder. I rush to get home.

As I walk into the house Luiz is leaning over the kitchen table helping the boys with their homework. He looks up with a smile but his expression changes once he sees me. "Mamãe is home! Okay, guys, let's finish up and get ready for bed." Luiz helps them organize things and I say a prayer with the boys before giving them goodnight kisses.

Once they're sleeping I look at Luiz and point to the backyard. The air is crackling with the smell of rain. We stand outside in the darkness.

"Eva, what is it? Did something happen at work?"

I let out a deep breath. "Luiz, I'm sick. I'm sick of worrying. And I got a warning tonight, a message to give to you." I tell him every detail, and I try not to, but I'm crying.

He is silent for a long time. "This has to be someone from inside the military. Saying 'operating procedure' is very military."

"Stop! Like he said, you have to stop! Stop trying to guess. Who cares where the warning came from? Was he wrong about Rio?"

Luiz becomes very quiet. "No, he wasn't wrong. But he's also right that things are getting worse. We can't let our voices be silenced."

I become quiet too. "Luiz, what do you love more? Your family? Me? Or Brazil, after all she has done to you."

Lightning turns the sky to daylight with a crack of thunder. We dash inside as the rain begins to pelt down. I remember my dream: Luiz and I on a small bit of sand with the ocean rising around us.

February 23, Shrove Tuesday

This week is Carnaval so I'm off until Thursday, the day after Ash Wednesday. I've been busy sewing bikinis and completing cake orders for the holiday. I'm exhausted by the time the boys are in bed. The threat to Luiz is a ghost hiding in the back of the closet waiting to jump out when I least expect it. Somehow I think if I keep the worry in the front of my mind it won't get me, but I can never relax. I can never let my guard down.

"Mamãe, Mamãe!" Junior runs into the kitchen, excited to tell me something.

"Shhhh, querido. Papai is resting, he has one of his head-aches."

Junior gives me a guilty look and whispers. "Can I go with the big kids to see the people getting ready for the parade? I'm six years old!"

He's so earnest that I agree. "You tell Carlos he needs to hold your hand the whole time, all right?"

Junior nods vigorously and sprints out the door. I prepare a café and take it to Luiz in the darkened bedroom with some aspirin and a glass of water. "Here, querido, this will help a bit."

He turns over slowly and squints at me. "I don't know, I'm so nauseous."

"I'll leave it by the bed. I'll just be out here in the kitchen if you need me."

Later in the afternoon I'm surprised to see him come out of the bedroom, dressed to go out. "Oh, you must be feeling better?"

He kisses me on the back of the neck. "Yes, your treatment helped. I'll be back later tonight."

I turn to look up at him. "Will you tell me where you're going?"

He puts a finger to his lips and raises his eyebrows. "Just out for a drive."

I get up from the table and hug him fiercely. "I love you so much. Please be careful."

After he leaves I sit at the table for a long time, staring at nothing.

I'm still wide awake and sitting in the kitchen after the boys are in bed, and at midnight I hear the car drive up, and Luiz is home safe, and we make desperate love then lie together front to back, sleeping peacefully until long past dawn.

March 14, Sunday

The first light of dawn seeps in my bedroom window. Luiz went out Friday morning and hasn't come home. He told me he'd be back in time for dinner. It's silly, I know, but somehow I think if I act normal then everything will go back, time will re-spool and all the horrible things will go away, and if I don't act normal it's bad luck. I repeat silent prayers for his safe return home. I feel ready to snap, like the blood vessels in my neck are about to explode.

Carlos and Junior get up early and join me in the kitchen. They don't say anything but I can feel their anguish. I make them tapioca with coconut as a special treat for breakfast but they just pick at it. I put the dishes in the sink and the boys sit at the table without moving.

"Why don't you guys go play with your cousins?" I try to make my voice bright.

Carlos looks up from the table. "Mãe, I want to be here when Papai comes home."

I hug him. "I'll come get you immediately. Go ahead, I'll stay here."

I busy myself ferociously cleaning the kitchen, putting all the furniture on the veranda and scrubbing the floor. I take down the curtains and put them in the sink to wash, and wash the windows inside and out. I take everything out of the refrigerator and defrost the freezer, empty and re-stock all the cabinets, lining up the cans and jars in perfect order.

I dust everything in the living room and take the pillows from the sofa outside on to the front veranda to shake them. When I go to step back into the house I notice there's something on the welcome mat, and I lean over to see what it is. At first I'm not certain, but then my blood runs cold. It is a wedding ring. I feel everything going black and my vision narrowing, and I hold on to the door jamb to steady myself, sliding down to sit on the mat.

I take deep breaths and run through explanations in my mind. Then I pick the ring up and examine it. Inside is etched "Eva". It's Luiz's wedding ring. Mine has "Luiz" inscribed inside. A howl comes from somewhere I don't recognize, along with an ocean of tears.

Chico comes running out his front door. "Eva, what is it?"

I hand him the ring, speaking between sobs. "Luiz's wedding ring. I found it on the front doormat. Now there's no doubt."

Chico's voice is trembling. "Oh my God, Eva."

"This time I'm going to report him missing. I know they won't do anything to help me but I want it on the record. The boys know Luiz hasn't been home for two days and soon I will tell them he's officially missing. But I won't tell them about the ring." I let out a deep breath. I can't tell Chico about the shadowy figure's warning in January, because I promised to keep it between me and Luiz.

"We can't lose hope, Eva. I agree with your plan. Is there anyone besides the police who might be able to help?"

I shake my head, but he's given me an idea.

March 15, Monday

"Chef, I need to speak with you if you have a moment." I've put my head in his office door.

He looks up from his work. "Of course, Eva. Come in."

"May I close the door?" He nods and gestures for me to sit in the chair next to his desk.

"Luiz is missing. He went out Friday morning and hasn't come home." My words fall like a heavy weight and it takes him a moment to respond.

"Oh dear, Dona Eva, I'm very sorry to hear that. How can I help you?"

"I just need a couple of days off to report him missing to the authorities."

He looks like he wants to say something but just nods. "All right, take as much time as you need. Don't worry about today, we'll get by. Good luck."

The municipal bus back to Taguatinga takes way too much time and a couple of transfers. The Civil Police office is next to the town square and I go up to the front desk, where a female officer sits behind a wall of glass and takes a long time to stop chatting with her coworkers and turn to look at me.

"Yes?" She looks bored.

"I'd like to report a missing person."

She takes a paper from a stack and gives it to me on a clipboard. "Fill this out and bring it back to me."

I sit on a bench against the wall and fill out the form, which is complicated but I take deep breaths and get it done. I'm grateful that my handwriting looks pretty, not childish like when I was young. I put the clipboard on the counter.

The female officer is studying her fingernails and looks up at me. "Have a seat and an officer will call you."

275

The bench is hard but I don't want to make a scene, pacing or acting impatient. The clock on the wall has a second hand that jerks as it marks the slow passing of time. I've waited more than an hour when an officer opens a side door and calls my name.

"Eva Lima?"

I get up and follow him into the back office, where he points to a chair next to his desk.

"You say your husband is missing." It's a statement, not a question.

"Yes, Sir. He left Friday morning and hasn't come home."

He gives me a condescending smile. "Well, it's only Monday. Men have their little things on the side, and three days isn't a very long a time."

My blood is boiling but I keep a flat face. "Luiz isn't like that."

He laughs. "No offense, Senhora, but all men are like that."

I just sit and stare at him, battling to show no emotion though I want to scream and punch him in the nose.

He sighs and rolls his eyes ever so slightly. "Senhora, do you have any reason to believe he has been harmed? Was he into drugs? Did he gamble? Did he owe money?"

I know he wouldn't care if any of this were true. But I can't tell him anything about Luiz and the resistance. "No, Sir. Like I said, Luiz isn't like that."

He stands up, indicating it's time for me to leave.

I get up from the chair. "What will happen next?"

"I'll file the report."

"And then?"

He is losing his patience with me. "I said, I'll file the report."

"Can I get a copy?"

Now he does roll his eyes. "Come by the station in a week, I'll have a copy of the report at the front desk." He gestures to the door.

"Thank you, Officer." I walk several blocks before I kick at nothing and curse as loud as I can.

March 16, Tuesday

I didn't go to work again today. I feel numb. I don't cry, because there are not enough tears in this world. I have no illusions about the situation. I have to get through this, keep my kids safe, and keep moving. Keep working to support our family. But I don't want to think about a future without Luiz, so I have to focus on this minute, this hour, this day.

I filled Sónia and Chico in on the visit to the Civil Police, and we talked about what we should say to my boys and their kids. Luiz's disappearance is on the record, so we just need to be careful about what the kids might say to their friends. Our two families have supper together as though it were a normal evening, or as normal as we can make it with Luiz's chair empty.

My boys get ready for bed and I take them to sit outside. The sky is clear and the moon is waning but still bright as it dips below the horizon. They look at me with wide eyes.

"My sons, you know your Papai hasn't been home for a few days."

Carlos looks at me. "Papai has been gone since Friday. Four days."

"That's right, Carlos. Four days. The first thing I need to say is that Papai loves us, he loves you, and he would never leave us unless something happened."

Junior starts to cry and I pull him over to sit on my lap, and he looks up at me. "Mamãe, what happened? Is Papai going to be okay?"

"I have reported your Papai missing to the Civil Police. And I will do everything I can to find him."

Carlos coughs to stop crying. "Mamãe, Junior was too little to remember, but I know Papai was missing a couple of years ago and you left for a few days and then you came home with him."

I take a deep breath. "Yes, Carlos, I did. And I can't tell you what happened then. Some day, but not now."

"Mamãe, go get him again! Go find him! I know you can, Mamãe," Carlos implores me.

We sit together crying. "Boys, I will do everything in my power to find Papai. But we all have to be strong. And it's important for you to know what to say when people ask about it."

"What do we say?" Carlos wipes his eyes with the heel of his hand.

"You can say that your Papai is missing. That it has been reported to the police. That your family is doing everything we can to find him."

"What if they ask other questions?" Carlos is becoming agitated.

"Just keep repeating the same thing. And if they ask for more, you don't know. Okay?"

Carlos nods his head.

"Junior? Tell me what you will say?"

"That Papai is missing and the police will find him."

"Yes, Junior. That's right."

We go inside and both boys lie down on Carlos's bed and Carlos hugs his little brother. I stay there until I know they're asleep.

March 19, Friday

I park the Gordini on the street and look again at the paper with the address for Dona Célia in the Parkway Mansion sector. The house is quite plain, with a high wall and a sculptural iron gate. I ring the bell.

I'm taking a risk just showing up, but I can't call her on the telephone. I don't have a phone at home and if I use the public phone office there will be a record, besides the fact that the government may be listening to our conversations. I will never forget Dona Célia's kindness when I met her on the flight from Recife to Brasília, when Carlos was a baby and I had no idea what I was doing and I just wanted to be with Luiz. She was executive assistant to Dona Maria Thereza Goulart, the wife of the vice president, and gave me the job of washing her clothes. And Jango (everybody called João Goulart Jango) was later president until the military took him down in the coup d'état of 1964, and we have had the dictators ever since.

Dona Célia might not be home, she might not agree to see me, she might even be disappeared. But I have to take a chance because I don't know where else to turn.

A few minutes pass and a woman descends the steps to the front gate, a puzzled look on her face. "Yes, may I help you?"

"Yes, Senhora. I would like to speak with Dona Célia if she is available."

The woman leans forward to get a closer look at me. "Is she expecting you?"

"No, Senhora."

"What is your name?

"Eva Lima. I worked for her washing clothes for Dona Maria Thereza, many years ago. I would be most grateful if she has a few moments to speak with me."

She looks skeptical. "Wait here, let me see."

Several minutes pass and my heart is pounding. This is crazy, I shouldn't have come. I'm just about to get in the Gordini and drive away when I hear a metallic sound and the gate swings inward. I go up the steps to the veranda and Dona Célia opens the front door.

"Querida, oh my goodness! How many years has it been? Please come in." She comes forward, kisses me on both cheeks and gives me a little hug.

I enter the foyer, with its sweeping staircase to the upper floor and walls lined with colorful oil paintings. The house is far grander than it appears from the street.

Now that I'm here I'm not sure what to do. Dona Célia puts her arm around my shoulder. "Querida, why don't we go outside. Everything is in full bloom with our lovely rain recently."

She shows me to the back veranda, and the beauty of the garden below takes my breath away. Ghostly palmettos silvery in the full sunlight lead to a winding walk past manicured plantings of burgundy and chartreuse.

I feel silly commenting on the garden when I have come to ask a favor, but I can't help myself. "This is so beautiful! I have never seen anything like this."

The laugh of tinkling glass, like the first day I met her. "It is something, isn't it? The garden was designed for me by Roberto Burle Marx, the landscape architect for Niemeyer's projects. He's a genius."

We walk past a shallow pond with large lily pads and there is a sitting area with chairs and a small table. "Please have a seat. Marta is bringing us a cool drink."

After the drinks are served she leans forward. "How can I help you, Eva?"

"Dona Célia, you have been so kind to me, and helped me so

much when I first came to Brasília. I can never repay you for your kindness, and I feel badly coming to ask your advice. But I really don't know where else to turn."

She pats me on the hand. "You are most welcome, and please don't worry. I am happy to see you and I will help you in any way I can. First, tell me what you've been up to with work, and your family."

I update Dona Célia on my work and side businesses, and that I have two sons now. Then I take a deep breath and tell her everything about what's happened with Luiz, including the shadowy figure who told me how to rescue Luiz in Rio and then warned me a few weeks ago. That Luiz made a detailed record of his torture in Rio and that I have it safely hidden. Luiz's wedding ring on the doorstep. That I reported him missing to the authorities. That it's been only six days but I am certain I will never see him again.

We sit in silence as she absorbs what I've told her. "Eva, I'm so sorry. I wish I didn't think you were right, but sadly, I think you are. You have reported it and there is a record. That's very important."

I wipe my tears with the backs of my hands, exhaling a big breath. "What can I do? Is there anything else? I know Luiz is gone. I know it."

Dona Célia gives me a long hug until I stop crying. "I don't think there's anything a single person can do right now to get Brazil back to normal. Torture and human rights violations are now enshrined in the law. The government has exiled so many, some you know about, like the musicians Gilberto Gil and Caetano Veloso, who are living in London, and many others who aren't so famous living around the world."

"Are Dona Maria Thereza and President Jango all right?"

"Yes, I hear from them through intermediaries from time to

time. They have a ranch in Uruguay on the border with Brazil. He is raising cattle and says he will never get involved in politics again. He tried to help return Brazil to democracy for the first couple of years but he gave up on that in 1966."

"Dona Maria Thereza was so kind, I always felt she truly cared about people."

"She had a lot of ideas about how to help the poor. Like a basic basket of goods that a family of four could live on for a month, instead of just giving people money. Ways to better educate children. She was a wonderful first lady for Brazil, she had so much potential."

"Dona Célia, are you in danger? It seems your association with the former government would be a problem for the generals."

"I stay out of their way. I have administrative skills and help foreign embassies with social and cultural events. I don't say or do anything political. But I also know they may have bugs in the house, devices to listen in on my conversations."

"That's why we're sitting outside, isn't it? We do the same thing at home. How sad that it's come to this. So, you don't feel you need to leave Brazil?"

"No, I have too many ties here, this house and my apartment in Recife, which is where I'm from originally. And when I say I don't do anything political, that is just for now. When things begin to improve, and they will, I plan to run for the Senate."

"I would vote for you! We need more women in powerful positions. I hope things improve soon."

"The government has lost its hold on the people. Economic conditions are getting worse, and that is the kiss of death for them. When you see them increasing repression, it's because they don't have popular support and it's the only way for them to stay in power."

"Dona Célia, if you were in my situation, what would you do?"

She sits back in her chair and looks at me intently. "I would go to the United States. Work there and make money in dollars and plan to return when Brazil stops being insane. It would be good for your boys, too. They'd speak English quickly. And Carlos is almost fourteen, which means he may start getting involved with the resistance before long. His anger about losing his father will burn strong."

I sit quietly for a moment considering what she's said. "I hadn't thought of that at all. Wow."

"Well, think about it. You're a sous chef, you are a successful seamstress and businesswoman, all skills that are useful anywhere in the world."

"I've been learning English by helping my sons study for school. And I have a friend who is living in the states now, maybe she could help. But it's such a huge step, so far away. It scares me."

"Querida, you made the journey to Brasília with a baby in your arms. Did that scare you?"

I laugh. "Oh yes, it did. But I was determined."

"Well, this thing is scary. And you will do it. And when the next thing is scary, you can look back on how much you have done even though you were scared, and forge ahead. As they say, faith in God and your foot on the accelerator!"

We laugh together, and I feel at peace.

I reach for her hand. "Dona Célia, I thank God for placing you in my life. I thank you for everything. Even though the idea of going to the States just came into my head, I think I will do it. I hope we can keep in touch."

She squeezes my hand and leans forward to give me a hug. "We will. We absolutely will."

August 20, Friday

So many days I wake up happy and then I remember I'm not. I remember my husband is gone and I'm alone. I'm sad and angry at the same time: angry at the dictators, but also angry with Luiz for not stopping his work with the resistance when he was warned. I lie in bed and cry for a while, then take a deep breath and force myself to get up. I wash my face and put on a mask of calmness to present to my boys and the people I work with.

The workday is busy as usual. I'm still learning every day from Chef Orlando, and we are constantly improving our lunch menus. I pretend to myself that we are in Paris, serving people sitting at bistro tables on a sidewalk terrace outside our restaurant. If I think about serving the military officers I imagine going out in the dining room and stuffing food down their throats until they suffocate on cream sauce.

After lunch service is over and prep is well on the way for tomorrow's menu, I go to Chef Orlando's office and put my head in the door. "Chef, do you have a moment?"

"Of course, Dona Eva. Please come in." He pulls out the chair for me and closes the door.

"Chef, I would like to take some time off. I want to take the boys to America to visit a friend. I need some time away."

"Of course, I understand. When would you like to go? And for how long?" He smiles at me like an uncle or father.

I'm relieved that he's taking it so well. But I'm nervous to say how long. "Well, actually I'd like to take all my vacation, I have almost ninety days."

"The usual rule is thirty, but I am able to make an exception. I can't imagine how hard it's been for you since . . ." His voice trails off, and I know he doesn't want to say out loud that my husband is gone.

"Chef, thank you. Yes, it's been impossibly hard. I need to take the boys and get away for a while. A change of scenery."

"I understand, Dona Eva. When do you want to begin your time off?"

"The first of October, if possible. I need some time to get passports and put things in order."

He reaches for my hand and takes it in both of his. "That will be fine, Dona Eva. I am here for you if I can help in any way. Your sous-chef position will be here for you when you return."

When I arrive home, Carlos looks up from the kitchen table, where he is helping Junior with his homework. "Mamãe! I have a snack ready for you. Junior and I already ate."

He's so grown up and responsible, for fourteen. "Thank you, querido. I want to talk with you boys about something."

They look up at me, worried and hopeful all at once. "It's not about Papai. But I do have an important plan and I will tell you first, then I will let Tia Sónia and Tio Chico know."

I sit at the table and they look at me with wide eyes. "My queridos, we are going to visit America. I've been corresponding with Joana, and we are going to visit her in a place called North Carolina. We'll be gone for three months. It will be an adventure."

I was afraid they would react badly, but they begin a chant, laughing and jumping up and down. "USA, USA!"

I have to shush them. "Calm down, boys. I haven't told Tio Chico and Tia Sónia, so let's keep it down right now, okay?"

They look like they want to jump out of their chairs but they nod vigorously.

"So, please get ready and go to bed, and I will go talk with Sónia and Chico."

Carlos has bedtime well underway when I go next door and ask Sónia and Chico to talk outside. The sky is completely dark.

We sit under the trees.

"I've asked Chef Orlando for time off, and he has agreed. I'll use all my vacation days, three months. I'm taking the boys to the United States."

It takes them a moment to absorb this. Sónia speaks first. "I think it's wonderful for you to take time off. And a complete change of scenery is a good idea."

Chico's voice cracks. "I think we all know Luiz won't be coming back. You've done everything you can to register his disappearance without putting yourself in danger. Luiz would want you to do this."

I start to cry. "I have to do this. The thing I need you both to understand is that even though Chef is holding my position open, I'm hoping things will work out in America and I can stay there until Brazil is a democracy again. Until they acknowledge that people disappeared. And I'm sure more people will disappear before that happens."

"If you aren't going to come back in three months, what about the house? What about your job?" Sónia's voice rises a bit.

"I'll let Chef know if I'm not coming back. As for the house, if you can keep it in good repair while I'm gone, and rent it to someone reliable, I will appreciate it so much."

Chico leans over to hug me. "Of course, Eva. Of course we will."

"One more thing. I haven't told the boys that I plan for us to stay if we can. They think we're just visiting."

Sónia gives me a hug. "Understood."

September 19, Sunday

It's a big job organizing things to travel, planning which clothes to take, deciding what things to pack away for storage. It will be autumn in America and the weather will be getting cold in the winter; it could even snow. I'm glad to have all the activity to keep my mind occupied. Yesterday after the boys went to bed I dug up the metal box Luiz had buried in the backyard, and now I'm sitting down to read the record he made me promise to preserve. I will take it with me to America to keep it safe.

After just a few pages I have to take a break and go outside, gulping the night air as tears dry on my face. It's a new moon and the sky is completely dark, the Southern Cross constellation bright against the Milky Way. I hadn't planned to read everything but I can't stop myself, and I couldn't sleep now anyway.

Luiz's account documents everything in minute detail: names if he heard them, descriptions of people and places, and voices if his head was covered with a hood. His disbelief that night in São Conrado when they told him to walk down the road to the gate and he found me waiting for him. His determination to not let them get away with it, even if it meant losing his life.

People's lives mean nothing to the dictators. Power is the only thing they care about, and they will do anything to keep it. They rationalize the things they do by telling themselves they are patriotic, that they are saving the country from communism and making the economy good for business. They build dams and power plants with money given to them by Tio Sam, and half of it goes into their pockets.

They created a system of dealing with political prisoners that has become an institution. Classrooms for teaching torture, with an audience of a hundred military officers taking notes. Suspending the supposed communist naked from a bar, the parrot perch, and carefully attaching electrodes to various parts of the body to discover which is most sensitive. Pouring water down the throat of the example prisoner until he almost drowns. Stuffing their victim into a cage that's too small and keeping him awake for days until he hallucinates. They are endlessly inventive.

They are assisted by doctors who check the victims if they lose consciousness and give the go-ahead to continue if it won't result in death. They are schooled in their techniques by shadowy guys in mirrored aviator sunglasses, who look bored and chain-smoke cigarettes.

If you don't give up your comrades they keep going until you do. If you don't give up the locations where you meet with your comrades, they keep going until you do. And if you don't break, they won't bother with you anymore and they will move on to the next victim. And you are disappeared.

PART IV

1971

October 4, Monday

Junior and Carlos are so excited they can barely contain themselves, and even our flight in the middle of the night can't dampen their energy. They each doze for a bit but at different times, and I don't get much sleep. The boys have been talking for weeks about our trip on an airplane, going to the beach and seeing the ocean for the first time and eating hamburgers; the possibilities are endless to them.

I just want to get past passport control and out of the Miami airport without the authorities suspecting that I've come here to stay long past the three months it says on my visa, escaping into the wilds of the United States and finding work, school for the boys, learning to speak proper English and earning a lot of dollars before I even think of returning to Brazil.

Of course I couldn't tell the kids about my plan, because they might tell their friends, and their friends might tell their parents, and their parents might know where I work, and Chef Orlando thinks I'm just taking all my weeks of vacation. After several years in the kitchen cooking for the generals, working my way up from dishwasher to general assistant to prep to salad and dessert and then sous chef, no one would suspect I would leave it all behind for a chance to live in America.

I've dressed the boys nicely and I'm wearing my most stylish clothes, my paisley headband and gold hoop earrings, and a nice dress. Before landing, I go into the bathroom and re-do my eyeliner and lipstick. After they finish breakfast, Carlos takes Junior into the bathroom to wash his face and wet and comb his hair. I've filled out the landing card and have our passports organized in my chic handbag. Looking the part is half the battle. I don't want the immigration officer thinking I've come to the US to wash people's clothes, even if maybe I have.

The plane lands with a couple of bounces and we descend the metal steps to the tarmac, then we're hit by a blast of cold air as we enter the airport. We wait in a long line to have our passports checked. When we get up to the front and the officer gestures to me to come forward, Junior is keyed up, that odd mix of too tired and restless. I mentally cross my fingers.

"Ma'am, what is the purpose of your travel to the US?"

I've practiced this, so I give him a big smile. "Vacation with my sons." I beam down at them.

Junior starts jumping up and down. "Beach! Hamburger!" He's practiced those words but I don't want him using them now.

"Shhhh, querido." I pull him closer to me and resist the urge to yank him by his shirt collar.

When I turn to look at the officer he smiles and stamps our passports. "Welcome to the US. Enjoy your stay."

"Thank you, Sir." I put our passports in my handbag and we proceed to baggage claim and out through customs. I stop at a currency exchange to get dollars. I feel like I can't breathe until we step outside the airport, where the warm humid air feels liquid on my skin. We get a taxi to Miami Beach, where Joana says it's cheap and safe. We'll stay until tomorrow and find how to get a bus to North Carolina.

I manage to make the taxi driver understand we want to go to a hotel in Miami Beach, and he slows in front of a huge fancy building on the beachfront but I shake my head and make a sign with my fingers for smaller. He understands and continues driving north until we come to a row of small hotels. I pay him, and the boys carry our two suitcases along the sidewalk as I wonder which hotel to try. They are funny old curved boxes with 1930s lettering on the front, coral pink and aqua, tangerine orange, blue and white. There are old people sitting on the verandas.

I pick a hotel at random and we step into the reception area. An older lady sits behind the counter smoking a cigarette, her dyed hair shellacked into a bouffant. "Yes, sweetie?"

"One night please."

She stubs out the burning cigarette in the ashtray and pulls down a key. I pay for the night and once in the room we immediately lie down on the beds and fall asleep. It's late afternoon when Junior wakes me up, pulling on my arm and asking to go touch the ocean. We change into our swimsuits and cross the street to the expanse of sand. The boys splash and play and we sit on the beach watching the waves until the sun goes down.

After showering and getting dressed I take the boys to a restaurant for sandwiches and a coke. There's a new lady on duty at hotel reception and I manage with gestures and writing on scrap paper to get directions to the bus station. The boys are excited about the next part of our journey but we all sleep well until the sun wakes us up.

October 5, Tuesday

American hotels don't provide breakfast so we walk to the bus station, a red and white building with a sign that says "Trailways." It smells like an ashtray and there are newspapers, ticket stubs and cigarette butts on the floor.

The man at the ticket counter looks disgusted with me when he can't understand what I want, so I write down "North Carolina" on the scrap paper I now carry with me. When he reads what I have written he rolls his eyes and says something I don't understand and I pay for three tickets that say "Atlanta." It's an hour until departure so I buy some horrible things from a vending machine, and the boys are hungry so they eat the salty orange bits and gulp the Coke, but I just can't. I buy some comic books and a map of the eastern United States from the newsstand.

Carlos hears the announcement before I do, and I make us stop for a bathroom break before we get on the bus. It's a relief to get aboard, but the bus is dingy and sad. It's disappointing that we can't see the ocean from the big highway as the bus speeds north. It takes hours to get to the top of Florida, a city called Jacksonville, where the bus heads west and then north again. The driver stops every couple of hours for breaks, but the food is awful. I buy greasy hamburgers and French fries during the dinner stop and we sit at a counter to eat them. There's a covered glass pedestal with a cake and a fly buzzing around trapped inside. I force myself to eat because I'm getting dizzy from hunger. The boys' appetites are unaffected and they wolf down their food and make noise with their drinking straws when only ice is left. I indulge them with ice cream cones.

I know from the map that Atlanta is not in North Carolina, and it's late and dark when we arrive at the big bus station with a long thin dog lit up in neon on the front. I want to find a hotel for the night but when we step outside the streets are deserted and all the shops are closed, and there may be hotels nearby but I don't want to walk in the dark with two kids lugging suitcases. The ticket counter is closed but a schedule on the wall shows a bus leaving tomorrow morning for Raleigh, the capital city of North Carolina and not far from Chapel Hill, where Joana is, on the map.

"Boys, we will have to stay here tonight. It's too dangerous to go out in the streets, and I don't know where we'd be going. So we just have to make the best of it."

Carlos looks at Junior and then at me. "But how will we sleep?"

It's a good question. "We just have to sleep sitting up. We can do it for one night."

Junior can't get comfortable and starts whimpering. "Mamãe, it's not good for sleeping!"

I want to whimper too but pull him over on my lap and he rests his head on my shoulder. At almost seven years old he's too big to sleep on my lap but he dozes fitfully. Voices telling me this is all a mistake are hissing in my ear, so I repeat to myself: *It will all be okay, I am strong, I can do it.* Over and over again.

October 6, Wednesday

The station stays open all night and a couple of buses arrive in the wee hours and people clean and mop the floors, working around us. I'm grateful when the morning comes and I show the guy the map and he sells us tickets to Chapel Hill.

We sleep on and off the first part of the trip, waking up when we get to Charlotte, the first big city in North Carolina. The sun is slanting toward evening when the bus drops us in Chapel Hill. I call Joana from the public telephone. She's expecting us but the exact day wasn't certain. She sounds excited and says for us to wait just a few minutes and she'll drive over to pick us up.

A few minutes later a white-over-yellow Volkswagen bus pulls up and Joana jumps out and comes running to us. "I can't believe it! You made it!"

We kiss and hug and the boys are jumping up and down with excitement as we load the suitcases into the back of the van. It's getting dark but I can see this is a pretty town with lots of trees. Joana drives us a short distance and pulls into a dirt driveway in front of a light blue clapboard house with peeling white trim and a sagging front porch. We are greeted in the living room by a pretty woman with long dark hair and a shy little boy about Junior's age hiding behind her legs.

Joana introduces us to her housemates. "Lupe, this is Eva, and Junior and Carlos. This is Lupe and her son, Juan."

Everyone nods and smiles, and Joana switches to English. "Everyone needs to learn English, so we will try not to speak Spanish or Portuguese, okay?"

Junior and Carlos chime in. "Yes, we speak English."

Joana smiles and shows us to our room, switching back to Portuguese. "Okay, we'll speak just a little so this part is clear."

I nod and look at the little room, which has three twin beds and a white-curtained window. "How long can we stay here?"

Joana smiles. "You live here! Your new home is on Oak Street in Carrboro, the town right next to Chapel Hill. Lupe and Juan have one bedroom and I have another. We share the two bathrooms, kitchen and living room. I'm either working or with David, so I'm not here a lot."

I'm worried about money. "Is it expensive?"

Joana laughs. "Not at all, it's one hundred a month plus the utilities. You don't have to worry about it until you get a job and start making dollars."

Carlos interrupts. "Mamãe, are we going to stay here in the US? I thought we were on vacation."

I pull him close. "We'll talk about it tonight. I had to get us here safely and we'll only stay if everything works out."

Joana looks at Carlos and Junior. "The schools are nearby and you can walk there. Once you're settled, your mom will get you enrolled. I think you'll really like it."

"Joana, how will I find a job? I don't really speak English."

She smiles. "Jobs are easy here if you're willing to work. I clean houses, but I heard about a job at a restaurant you can probably get. It's a janitor's job, cleaning the bathrooms and taking out the trash. Once you speak more English I'm sure you can find a job cooking. Maybe not sous chef, but cooking."

"Thank you for everything, Joana. I couldn't do this without your help."

"Of course, we're family so we have to stick together." She looks over at Carlos and Junior, who have each staked their claim to a bed. "Come on, let's fix something to eat."

After supper the boys get ready for bed and we say prayers. The first thing we ask every night is for God to watch over Luiz, Papai. And we thank God that we are safe and together, and remember all our family.

I hold them both close. "My sons, we are going to do our best to make things work so we can stay here. I need you to understand that Chico and Sónia will always know where we are, and if Papai comes home, or if the police have any news for us, they will let us know immediately. If Papai comes home we will go back to Brazil right away." We cry together for a while then sleep peacefully.

October 31, Sunday

It's our first American holiday tonight, Halloween. Kids dress up in costumes and go house to house asking for candy, and we are ready. We have carved a face into a pumpkin and lit a candle inside, and I put it on the front porch as night descends. I look up at the dark sky that is so unfamiliar I know we are on the other side of the world.

The boys have practiced saying "Trick or treat!" and now that it's dark Carlos is taking Juan and Junior around the nearby streets while Lupe and I stay home to give out candy, sipping tea and chatting between knocks on the door. Neither of us speak much English yet so our conversation is a mix of English with Portuguese and Spanish combined, which we laughingly call Portañol.

"Lupe, why North Carolina?"

She laughs. "It's funny, I never heard of it when I left Mexico. I'm from Monterrey, not far from Texas. So I go there first. My cousin got work here and my son and I been here two years."

"Do you miss Monterrey?"

Lupe shakes her head. "No, it's a big ugly city, not pretty with trees like North Carolina. And there is no good work for me there."

"It's nice that Juan and Junior walk to school together. It's good to have a friend in a new place."

"Es verdad. And Juan is glad to have a new amigo."

Junior is in the first grade and Carlos has started high school. They have to work hard to catch up since classes started in September, on top of learning English. I'm amazed at how well they're doing, making new friends and adapting to American customs.

The second week we were here, I started a job at Burger Shack on Franklin Street, just a short walk from our house. It's not really a restaurant because all they sell are hamburgers and fries, and everything they cook is frozen or pre-made. People take their food in paper bags and sit at plastic tables or they eat in their cars. I keep all areas clean, from the dining tables to the bathrooms, and make sure the trash is taken out regularly. I don't really like the food but it seems popular because the store is always busy.

The day after we arrived, I sent letters to Sónia and Dona Célia with our address and phone number. We have a phone at home but it's too expensive to call Brazil. It's important to have a telephone in America for jobs and schools. We can manage without a car, but not without a phone.

1972

February 7, Monday

Work has become a boring but predictable routine and I have enough money to pay the rent and get the boys what they need, even save a few dollars. My English is improving because I spend time every day practicing, learning new words and helping the boys do their homework. I carry a small notebook with me to write down things to look up or remember. Some of the guys in the kitchen have been here for years and still only speak Spanish, but I'm determined to learn English.

It's a blustery day and I'm wearing my jacket under my big apron since I'm always taking out trash and have to sweep the parking lot. The boys are always hoping for snow but they were disappointed we didn't have what Americans call a white Christmas. Cold weather like this is not my favorite but spring will be here soon. I'm imagining flowers in bloom and warm breezes when all of a sudden there's a huge commotion and people running, being chased by guys in dark jackets with holstered guns on their hips.

I take off my apron, stuff it in the trash bag and walk calmly over to a lady who's parked on the street eating her food. I knock on the passenger door and give her a pleading look when she turns toward me. She doesn't object as I open the passenger door and sit down.

She is blonde and well dressed and doesn't act like she's scared. "Are you being chased by them? Do you know who they are?"

I nod. "Immigration."

She starts the car and pulls out onto Franklin Street. "Let's get the hell out of here."

I just nod and try not to look around, but I see one of the guys from the kitchen with his arms handcuffed behind him being pushed back toward the burger place by one of the immigration officers.

She looks over at me. "Where are you from?"

"Carrboro."

"No, I mean, where are you *from*?" She raises her eyebrows.

"I'm from Brazil. I have two sons who go to school here. I can't leave them."

She's a nice lady, she looks sad for me. "Well, you got away this time." She pulls over to the curb on the university campus and turns off the engine. She reaches in her purse and hands me a twenty-dollar bill.

"Ma'am, you don't have to give money. I thank you very much for help me."

She smiles. "Go ahead, please take it. And I suggest you don't go back to work at that place. Good luck."

My heart is in my throat as I get out of the car and I walk around the campus to catch my breath and calm down. All I can think about is what could have happened if they had picked me up and found out I don't have papers.

Lupe looks up as I walk into the house. "Pobrecita, you are upset, qué pasó?"

I begin to sob and haltingly tell her the story. She hugs me and murmurs that things will be okay and brings me a glass of water.

"Thank you." I wipe my face and blow my nose.

Lupe looks concerned. "You are right, La Migra is danger. My friend got pick up and deportada back to Mexico. They took her kids, they in a inmigración place in El Paso. She have to pay lawyers to get them back. Muy triste. But you are okay, don't go back the Burger Shack."

I shake my head no. What would happen to Junior and Carlos

if I'm deported? It's just too awful to think about. I have to find work that won't catch the immigration authorities' attention. After the boys are in bed I call Joana, she's over at David's apartment. He answers the phone and hands it to her.

"Joana? I have to tell you what happened today."

When I finish the story she's silent for a minute. "Eva, you can do odd jobs for a while. I can use your help since I have more houses to clean. And we can buy the stuff to make cakes, we can get that business going by word of mouth. We might even make bikinis again, what do you think?"

"I think those are great ideas. I'm not going back to Burger Shack. I can't take the risk. And I'm lucky to have a partner who studied business."

"Okay, then. I'll be back in the morning and we'll make some plans."

1975

March 10, Monday

I jump up to help Joana when she arrives with grocery bags. After we put away the groceries we sit down to review the calendar. I'm surprised at the numbers when we total them up. "We have so many orders for Easter. And we charge enough per cake to make a nice profit."

Joana shakes her head, smiling. "There's nothing like scarcity to make people want something, and the numbers we produce are limited. We're doing well, but there's something I want to talk to you about."

"Okay, what is it?"

"The health department is cracking down on food that isn't prepared in a safe environment."

This makes me mad. "What do you mean? I have the highest standards for cleanliness!"

Joana nods. "I know, Eva. That's not the question. The authorities require a very controlled environment, and we don't have that. You're supposed to only cook in restaurant conditions. And your cakes are so popular they will investigate, sooner or later. They've shut a lot of home operations down."

"So what do you think we should do?"

"Let's finish the orders for Easter. Then I think you should get a real restaurant job worthy of your skills."

I sigh. "Of course. But where can I get that? I'm not going back to Burger Shack."

She gives me a sly smile. "I just heard about something that's a perfect fit for you. I think you'll have to start out like you did in the officers' dining room, but I bet you can move up."

"What is it? Where?"

"You know that abandoned building where Chapel Hill becomes Carrboro, at the end of West Franklin Street?"

I'm confused. "Yeah, what about it?"

"There's a chef named Nora Wells who bought the building and she's going to make it into a restaurant."

I make a face. "Great, an abandoned building. The perfect place for me to be a sous chef in America!"

Joana shakes her head. "Okay, very funny. So listen. I heard about this from David, he knows the guy doing the building renovation. The restaurant will be called Chez Alice."

"Yes, 'Home of Alice.' Who's Alice?"

"Who cares? Focus! Nora Wells has a completely new vision for food in America. She wants to do something she calls farm-to-table, with local meats and produce. She will create menus using only the freshest ingredients in season."

"What's new about that? Poor people without refrigerators have been doing that forever in Brazil."

"That may be. But here in America it's a new idea."

I think for a minute. "I guess you're right. Burger Shack isn't exactly fresh stuff. Frozen and all the same, day after day."

"Exactly." Joana draws a little map with an X marking the restaurant. "They're taking applications for workers starting next week."

March 17, Monday

The pink redbud and tulip magnolias are in full bloom and the sun is warm on my face as I walk the few blocks to Chez Alice. When I get to the main street I turn toward Chapel Hill, and there's a sign outside the building that says they're hiring. I step into the main room, where workers are installing flooring and a man stands behind the bar.

"Hello, are you here to apply for a job?" He gives me a welcoming smile.

"Yes, please."

"What position?"

I'm not sure what to say. "I'm an experienced cook."

"Line cook? Where have you worked?"

I'm not sure what line cook means. "I was sous chef in a military dining room in Brazil."

He doesn't make a face but he wants to. "Do you have any formal training?"

"No, I guess not."

He holds out an application form. "We have an opening for dishwasher. Fill this out please."

My heart stops momentarily. "Can I take the form and bring it back later?"

He points to a bar stool. "We want it filled out here. Need to make sure people can read and write in English."

I hate being watched when I struggle with reading but there's no escape. I wonder if he's watching me as I try to write but I don't dare look up to see. My heart is pounding as I work to make sense of what's written on the page and fill in the blanks. I'm sure he wonders why I'm taking forever, but I slowly complete the form with my prettiest lettering and hand it back to him. He smiles and nods and says they will be in touch. I breathe a sigh of relief as I leave the restaurant.

April 21, Monday

It's my first day at Chez Alice, and we'll have a few days of training before we open for dinner later this week. Nora is at the front door to greet everyone as we arrive, and she invites us to sit in the dining room. The place is cozy and peaceful, with round tables and booths around the walls, and an outdoor patio with rustic wooden tables.

The training is to start at ten o'clock and Nora glares at a couple of people who walk in a few minutes late, glancing over at the manager, who will no doubt make note of who didn't arrive on time. Nora is a pretty, petite woman who seems to have enough energy for someone twice her size. She claps her hands to let everyone know it's time to start.

"Welcome, everyone! We are so excited to have our whole team here, and can't wait to open on Friday. Today we want to share our vision, not just for Chez Alice, but for food." She waits a moment for us to absorb the enormity of what she's saying.

Nora continues. "Food in America is an industry, designed to make profits for giant corporations. Small farmers are an endangered species. Vegetables are hybridized for the longest shelf life so they can be transported and stored without spoiling, but these new varieties have no flavor. Restaurant menus are designed to serve what's popular, and, quite frankly, what's expected. We are going to serve what's best and in season, letting the bounty of local farmers direct our choices."

She continues with details about menu development and lists the products and the farms that will supply them. Then she introduces the manager, Guy, who leads us into the kitchen to explain Chez Alice's procedures and how each of us must keep to the Chez Alice standard. We're then invited to look around for a few minutes before we begin drills to make sure things will run smoothly on opening night. I laugh to myself, thinking that it wasn't this regimented when I cooked for the military.

I'm the only dishwasher but there's a guy who's a general kitchen helper who drills with me. He will work dishwashing if I'm off, and when I take breaks during busy times. He takes me through an entire set of dishes and pots. "So, Eva, everything has to be perfect. It has to sparkle. Anything less than that has to go back and get washed again."

I'll be responsible for assuring the proper water temperature, for controlling the cleanliness of everything before food touches it. Before opening, I will polish glasses and cutlery, though others will pitch in to help.

When we've gone through our drills for a couple of hours, Guy claps for our attention. "We are all responsible for the quality of Chez Alice and the experience of our diners. I don't care if your job is dishwashing, if you see something that doesn't look right, speak up. Any questions?"

It's past lunchtime and we're invited back to the dining room, where spinach and onion tart and a lettuce salad dressed with vinaigrette are served, along with sparkling water and coffee. I can't believe how delicious these simple dishes are. I want to soak up everything there is to know about this kind of cuisine, and I'm already a convert to the food religion Nora preaches.

May 29, Thursday

"Hurry up, Junior, it's time to leave! We can't be late for your brother's graduation." I'm getting impatient.

Junior rushes out of the bathroom buttoning his shirt. Carlos, Junior and I jump into Joana and David's waiting VW van and head over to Chapel Hill High School. I adjust Carlos's tie and he puts on his cap and gown and enters the auditorium. Soon they let in family and friends and we find a place to sit together. The graduates are all seated in the front rows. The ceremony begins with the pledge of allegiance and the school choir leads the singing of the national anthem. There are speeches and then students go up on the stage in alphabetical order. I'm bursting with pride and watch through tears as Carlos approaches the stage.

The principal calls his name, Carlos José Alves Lima Neto, though he mispronounces most of it. José is Ho-say like Spanish, not Joe-zay; Lima he pronounces like the beans; and Neto, which means grandson, is Neat-o, not Net-oh. Carlos's middle names are my father's names: José Alves. Correct pronunciation is too much to expect so Joana and I just look at each other and laugh.

After the ceremony we go back to Joana and David's house, where we have a celebration ready with a banner saying "Happy Graduation Carlos" and another banner, "Happy Birthday," since he turned eighteen three days ago. Lupe and her son Juan arrive and we sit outside while David barbecues burgers and hot dogs.

"Lupe, how is your apartment? It's great to have your own place, isn't it?" I sit next to her and we sip iced tea.

"I love it. And I know you're happy to have the whole house now, so the boys each have their own bedroom."

Junior and Juan obviously miss each other and they're deep in competition with a Rubik's cube. "No, I got it, I got it! Aw, darn it." Junior loses his turn and hands it to Juan.

Lupe beams at Carlos. "Congratulations, mister graduate! We are so proud of you. What will you be doing for the summer?"

Carlos gives a shy smile. "I have a job at the Varsity Theatre which is full time for the summer, then I start college at State: North Carolina State University."

Lupe hands a small gift box to Carlos to unwrap. It's a mechanical pencil set. "Thank you, Miss Lupe. This is so nice."

Lupe gives Carlos a hug. "Since you want to be an architect I think you need a pencil."

Carlos opens Joana and David's gift, a North Carolina State University necktie with little wolves on it, their team mascot. "Thank you guys, this is great."

My oldest son is going to college in America. I fight back tears as I think how proud Luiz would be. I feel Luiz's presence, a big sad hole where he should be, but also a happy glow of pride in our boy's hard work and accomplishments.

July 10, Thursday

Chez Alice is already a success, and Nora has gained a lot of attention with her new concept in food. There have been articles in the newspapers, radio interviews and even a segment on the local TV news. I couldn't love my job more. I take every opportunity to eavesdrop on Nora and the sous chefs, and make note of the many dishes in my little notebook.

It's almost midnight, the end of the shift, and everyone has cleaned their stations and prepared for tomorrow's business. Some of the line cooks are hanging around the back door passing around a joint, and the pungent smell of marijuana smoke wafts into the kitchen. It's part of the culture here and seems harmless, it just doesn't interest me.

I've finished my work and clocked out and I'm trimming and chopping the ugly vegetable stubs to take home for soup, just like I did in the officers' kitchen in Brazil.

"What are you doing?" Nora's sharp voice splits the air.

I look up at her and stammer a little bit. "Oh, I'm sorry, Nora, Guy told me I could keep the vegetable ends that are put in the compost. I thought it was okay, I'm sorry."

Her face is serious but she makes a waving motion. "No, that's not what I meant. Where did you learn knife work?"

I let out my breath in relief. "Oh, I worked cooking in Brazil, but I started learning back when I was a kid."

She leans forward and looks at me as if for the first time. "Where did you work? What sort of food did you cook?"

"I worked my way up in the officers' dining-room kitchen in Brazil's capital. When I left Brazil I was sous chef. Chef Orlando taught me, he was trained in France."

"Mmmm. Well, carry on. I hate waste, so eating is better than compost."

I finish chopping and clean the station, putting the vegetables in a container that I then put in my bag. As I gather my things to leave, Guy calls me over to the bar. "Eva, Nora wants to try you on prep. Come in a little early tomorrow so you can get oriented."

My chest wants to burst with excitement. "Yes, Guy, absolutely. Thank you so much!"

"It's a trial, so we'll have to see how you do before we make any permanent changes."

I want to skip like a kid as I walk home, the fireflies dancing and the crickets singing in the darkness.

August 25, Monday

"Junior, time to get up! Your breakfast is on the table. Today is our day to go through your clothes and see what you need to be ready for school."

Junior stumbles into the living room rubbing sleep from his eyes. "Mom, does it have to be today?"

"Yes it does. It's my only day off and I want to have a week to get things organized, since school starts next Monday. And we have dinner with Lupe and Juan at Joana and David's tonight. I want you to take all your clothes out of the drawers and the closet and put them here in the living room."

He grumbles a bit but complies, and we begin sorting out things to give away and things that still fit. When we've put everything in different piles Junior sits down next to me.

"Mom, I want to change my name."

This is a shock but I resist the urge to react. "Tell me more."

"I don't want to be called Junior anymore. It sounds like a baby and kids sometimes make fun of me."

I sit and absorb this for a moment. "I see. Have you decided what you want to be called?"

"Kai. Rhymes with sky. Spelled K-A-I."

"Kai? That sounds nice."

He lets out a deep breath, because I'm sure he thought I'd be upset. "Mom, my name is Luiz Carlos Caetano Lima Junior. Caetano sounds like Kai-tano. So Kai."

I give him a hug. "That's a lovely name, and very unique. And since you're ten years old I think you're old enough to choose you own nickname. Do you think Kai sounds more American? There are American kids called Junior, aren't there?"

He looks up at me. "I don't know any kids named Junior. Kai sounds more cool. Junior is not cool."

"All right, then! Let's finish organizing these clothes, Kai."

1979

June 11, Monday

I'm nervous as a cat and say a silent prayer just before I serve my audition menu to Nora and the two sous chefs at Chez Alice. I worked my way up from dishwasher when I began in 1975, to prep and then line cook. I now have the opportunity to be promoted to sous chef, but Nora does things differently than other restaurant chef-owners. And she can, because Chez Alice is now one of the top restaurants in America and you have to book months ahead for a reservation. To move up I had to develop my own menu with the freshest local ingredients, and I'm about to serve. Two prep staff helped me cook all day, because Chez Alice is closed on Mondays.

I asked the prep staff, who are my friends, to stay and help me serve. We set down the appetizer plates in front of our diners simultaneously, and I announce the dish.

"Beet carpaccio with a fig-infused vinaigrette." The plates are beautiful, with wafer-thin slices of golden, burgundy, and white and pink candy-striped beets. I turn to withdraw to the kitchen but Nora calls me back.

"Eva, tell me about the dish." She's still eating it, so that's a good sign.

"I salt-roasted the beets to sweeten them and take out some earthiness, but kept them crisp. Sliced fine with the mandoline, and quick-pickled with the vinaigrette."

She finishes a bite. "Where'd you get the fig-infused vinegar?"

"I made it at home last summer. Then extra-virgin olive oil, minced shallots and a bit of Dijon mustard to emulsify."

One of the sous chefs has almost finished his plate. "It's very good, Eva. Just crunchy enough but not raw."

"Thank you; and the main will be served in just a moment." I head back to the kitchen.

We plate the fish stew, served over fluffy basmati rice in a big flat bowl, garnished with a perfect sprig of cilantro. I set the dish before Nora as my colleagues serve the others. "This is my variation on Brazil's moqueca de peixe, fish stew. Grouper cheeks in a tomato and coconut broth."

They all breathe in the aroma and begin eating with the big soup spoons I've set at each place. I withdraw to the kitchen and pray. After a few minutes I peek through the porthole windows in the swinging doors and all three of them are eating in silence. A happy sign to my eyes. I step through to be ready to answer questions.

Nora looks up. "This is absolutely delicious. Why grouper cheeks?"

I take a breath and answer. "Because it's a part of the fish that's normally discarded, but I asked our fishmonger if he could bring me the heads this morning instead of throwing them away. We call the fish 'garoupa' in Brazil. The bochechas, the cheeks, are luscious and meaty but only poor people in Brazil eat them."

Nora thinks about this for a minute. "I hate waste. That is brilliant. And the rest of the ingredients?"

"Moqueca normally uses dendê, or palm oil. But that is impossible to find and not very healthy, so I used olive oil. Onion, red and green bell pepper, fresh chopped tomatoes. Cumin and just enough coconut milk to give the fragrance."

The three of them are nodding and they eat every bite. I take their empty plates away and return with dessert: my cocadas, that I have been making and selling since I was young, two on each plate with a fan of sliced strawberry and a nasturtium flower.

"Cocada, Brazilian coconut sweet. Please enjoy."

I withdraw and hug my prep colleagues. They wish me well and step outside to smoke a joint before they head to the

Rathskeller, a local hangout, for some lasagna. I lean out the doorway.

"Thanks, guys."

"Good luck, Eva. I think you killed it. Come by the Rat later if you can. We'll buy you a beer."

I laugh. "I'm the one owing beers! I won't be by tonight but we'll catch up later."

I steel myself and walk back into the dining room. There are no cocadas left on the plates.

Nora sits back in her chair. "Very nice, Eva. I have a few more questions. Did you use condensed milk in the cocadas? Canned coconut milk in the fish stew?"

I'm thrilled with this question. "Nora, coconuts are exotic and not local, but I was able to source fresh ones. I shredded the meat for the cocadas and used the liquid for the moqueca. The cocada is made with only coconut, water and sugar. I refuse to use anything but cane sugar."

Nora nods, a bit surprised. "Well, then. Very good use of ingredients. My favorite cake is coconut, made from scratch just like you did. It's too labor-intensive and expensive to sell in the restaurant but these cocadas echo that, and in a smaller package. Bravo."

I take the plates away and begin cleaning up the kitchen. I know they are talking about me but I have done my best. I'm exhausted, and if it doesn't work out and I have to still cook on the line that's okay.

My thoughts are interrupted as one of the sous chefs pops his head in. "Hey, Eva, could we have some espressos? We're all going to enjoy a dessert wine, and hope you will join us."

I nod in agreement. "Thanks, espressos coming right up."

I serve the espressos and Nora pours us all a sweet wine made from local grapes.

Nora raises her glass. "Santé!"

I reply, "Saúde," and we all clink glasses.

The sweet wine is delicious. I'm a bit dizzy because I haven't eaten, but I'll dig into leftovers at home later. When everyone is finished, Nora speaks. "Eva, we are very pleased to offer you promotion to sous chef." They all applaud.

Happy tears sneak out of my eyes. "Oh, thank you, I am so grateful. This is a dream come true."

Nora gives an ironic laugh. "Maybe so, but believe me when I tell you it will be a nightmare at times."

Everyone laughs. The guys shake my hands and leave and it's just me and Nora.

She puts the cups on a tray, carries them into the kitchen and puts on an apron. "Come on, lady, this kitchen isn't going to clean itself!"

"Nora, you don't have to help me. I'll clean this place up in a flash."

She's already puttering around cleaning. "Well, the two of us will clean it in half a flash."

We clean everything quickly, and as I'm finishing up Nora leans back against the service counter and looks at me. "Eva, you must have an incredible story. I'd love to hear some of it whenever you feel like sharing it with me."

I take my apron off and put it in the laundry bag. "It's a long story, Nora. But no more or less than anyone else in this world."

"You have two sons. You are from Brazil. You have been at Chez Alice since the beginning. I realize that's about all I know about you."

I look down at the floor. "Well, let's see. I'm married. My oldest son is in school at NC State. My youngest is in middle school."

She waits for a while. "And if I can ask, what does your husband do?"

It feels like a giant leap to say some things out loud. "My husband was in the resistance in Brazil. He has been missing since 1971. That's why I left." I realize I just spoke about Luiz in the past tense. "I'm sorry, Nora, I'm very tired and I need to go home."

She looks at me and nods. "Of course, Eva. I'm so sorry. I shouldn't have pushed you to talk to me."

"It's okay, you didn't push me. I just never talk about it, so it's strange. Maybe sometime later we will talk again. For now, please know how happy I am to be sous chef. Thank you for everything."

Walking home I'm exhausted yet full of the glow of success. It's hard to wrap my mind around being sous chef in one of the most sought-after restaurants in America. My journey from Dona Francisca teaching me about cooking as a child in Picuí to all I learned from Chef Orlando runs through my mind like movie clips.

I never talk about Luiz. Speaking out loud about him to Nora makes me realize what I hold in my mind but don't think about. I still imagine that Luiz is in exile in Argentina but protects me by not being in touch; that one day Chico and Sónia will call me and tell me that he has miraculously appeared on the doorstep after all these years. Tears stream down my cheeks as I walk.

December 12, Wednesday

I have a day off to help with the Christmas bake sale at Kai's school, raising money for the sports team and the choir. Kai is the kicker for his middle-school football team. American football is a sport I will never understand, with all the bashing and bumping. At least there are penalties for roughing the kicker.

I make my version of cupcakes at home, but people at the bake sale whisper that I'm the sous chef at Chez Alice. I just smile and say nothing, and sell out quickly. I'm out of there in thirty minutes.

I pull up in the driveway, lug my empty containers up on to the porch and check the mailbox. There's a letter from Sónia and Chico, an electric bill, and a business envelope postmarked Brazil with no return address. I leave the containers on the porch, open the front door with trembling hands, sit on the sofa and carefully open the envelope.

> Dear Eva,
> Please forgive this anonymous letter. I mention Loide Aero, cold creek water and books for babies so you will know who I am. I write because there are people gathering information about the tortured and disappeared. The record you have is crucial to this effort. Please make copies of the documents and send them in confidence to the Archbishop of São Paulo at the following address . . .
> They passed a law this year giving amnesty to everyone involved in torturing and murdering Brazilians. They may not be punished in the justice system for their crimes, but the record of what they did will bring the truth forward, so that this can never happen again in our country.
> All my love,
> Your friend and supporter

This is from Célia. I met her for the first time on the Loide Aero flight to Brasília when Carlos was just a baby, I washed the vice president's wife's clothes in the cold creek water, and Dona Maria Thereza gave Carlos children's books for Christmas. I will make copies of Luiz's documentation and send them to the commission.

1981

March 15, Saturday

It's almost midnight and Nora calls to me from the dining room. "Eva, leave the side work. Give it a rest."

I finish polishing wine glasses and grab a slice of sweet potato tart and a coffee and join Nora at the bar. "Everybody loves sweet potato pie, so the tart is genius."

"Genius was your braised oxtails with watercress. It sold out early, so next time plan for more."

I grin at her. "It's a classic Brazilian combination. Maybe we should put it in Portuguese on the menu, rabada com agrião."

She gives me a face. "Now you're pushing it." We laugh.

After all the staff say their goodbyes we sit quietly together making notes. I put down my pen and look over at Nora. "I never told you anything more about me after the night of my audition. You are very kind to be so patient."

Nora looks at me. "You don't have to tell me about things that cause you pain."

I look down at my hands. "I want to tell you more. I have had to accept that my husband, Luiz, is gone, which I knew but hadn't mentally accepted back then. He made a record of his kidnapping and torture. He escaped the first time but was disappeared a couple of years later. I sent copies of his handwritten record to a group in Brazil that are secretly documenting everything."

Nora sits quietly, absorbing what I told her. "Eva, I'm so sorry. You are keeping his memory alive by making sure the record is preserved. Bravo."

Nora's not a hugger but she gives me a hug. "Eva, is there anything I can do for you?"

I sit back and wink at her. "Yeah, actually. Tell me why the

1979

hell the restaurant is called Chez Alice."

Nora laughs. "Well, good move on changing the subject. Okay, since you just shared what you did, I will tell you. But it's a secret, so don't tell anyone else. Okay?"

"My lips are sealed."

"So, I was tripping on acid, LSD, way back years ago. And *Alice in Wonderland* floated into my mind. *Eat me, drink me.* I remembered it later and thought, wow, that's what I'll name my restaurant. Back when everybody thought I was crazy to think I could have a restaurant. *Eat me.*"

We laugh uproariously and then sit quietly together and finish our coffees and Nora and I hug and go our separate ways out the back door.

April 26, Monday

Carlos and Kai are cleaning up after supper, and I've asked our family to meet to talk about our future plans. Monday is my day off and the only evening we get to spend together. They dry the dishes and put them away and sit with me in the living room.

"Guys, first I want to tell you about what's happening in Brazil behind the scenes; about people like your Papai who were disappeared. Your father made a detailed record of everything that happened to him in 1971 when he was taken to Rio and I went to get him. Do you remember that time?"

Carlos nods and Kai furrows his brow. "Mom, I kind of remember but I was little. Carlos told me about it."

I didn't realize they talked about it, but of course they did, maybe still do. "Yes, I didn't give you many details because it is so disturbing that I wasn't able to talk or even think about it. I received a letter a couple of years ago saying I should send a special commission a copy of his record. So I did, and I just heard back last week that the commission, called *Brazil Never Again*, will be listing Luiz as disappeared."

Carlos reaches over and hugs Kai close to him. "Mom, we know that Papai is dead."

This shocks me although it shouldn't. "Carlos, Kai, I love you so much. And your Papai loved you more than anything in this world."

We're all crying. Carlos wipes his tears and looks at me. "Mom, will the people who did this to Papai be punished?"

I hate to say this. "Brazil's Congress passed a law two years ago giving amnesty to all the people involved. So they won't face justice in the courts, but by giving the commission Papai's record we hold them accountable. They are accountable before God."

Kai looks at me. "What's going to happen?"

I take a breath before speaking. "I think it's time to go back to Brazil. There are signs that the military is losing its hold on power. And I want to be there to help change happen. I promised your father."

Carlos seems relieved. "Mom, I wanted to tell you about my plans, so I'm glad we're talking about this now. I don't think Kai knows this yet, but we are illegal here in the US. I was able to go to school but when I graduate next month working as an architect will be a problem. I know my papers are forged. The school doesn't check those things but an architecture firm will. So I want to go back to Brazil to look for a job."

Kai is upset. "No, Carlos, I want you to be here with us!"

I lean over to Kai and say clearly what I know will be hard for him. "Kai, I want you and I to go back to Brazil too. To Paraíba, the capital city of João Pessoa, on the coast. The state where I was born and grew up."

Now Kai is really upset. He jumps up and starts shouting. "I don't want to go to Brazil! I want to stay here with my friends. I have two more years and I'll graduate from high school, just like Carlos did!"

"Querido, I understand and I'm so sorry. Please let me explain more what I have in mind for us."

Kai reluctantly sits down with his arms crossed, refusing to look at me and trying not to cry.

"Kai, Carlos knows that we don't have valid documents. I bought fake social security cards for us and all these years I've lived in fear that we'll be found out and deported. Especially that I would be deported and you guys would be left here by yourselves."

Kai looks worried. "Do you think immigration will raid Chez Alice?"

Carlos hugs him again. "Mom works in a top restaurant, they're not like a chicken factory with lots of illegals."

"Guys, the other part is this. My dream is to open my own place. I've saved a lot of dollars and they will go a long way in Brazil because they have hyperinflation: the money there is worth less and less every day. I plan a really unique restaurant on the beach in João Pessoa, a combination of Nora's fresh local ingredients and the typical food of Brazil's Northeast."

Kai looks at me. "What will happen to me?"

I move to the sofa and give him a hug, even though he's sixteen and usually doesn't let me. "I know it's hard leaving your friends in the middle of high school. But the high school in João Pessoa is one of the oldest and best in all of Brazil, the Lyceu Paraibano."

Carlos is thinking about all of this. "Kai, I plan to go to São Paulo, which has world-class architecture firms. I've saved money from my part-time jobs and I'll find a place to live, and with my education here I should be able to find a good position. I know São Paulo is the opposite end of Brazil from where you and Mom will be, but I'll fly up often."

Kai looks skeptical but he's beginning to come around. "Mom, when will we move?"

Now we're getting down to plans, a good sign. "Well, I'm thinking September. And for now this is just between us, because I won't tell Nora until a month before, the required notice for sous chefs."

Carlos gives me a hug. "Mom, I know your restaurant will be amazing. Just like you."

May 16, Saturday

Nora greets me as I tie on my apron. "Hey, Eva, congratulations on Carlos's college graduation. How was the party last night?"
"It was great. We did pulled pork sandwiches and of course I made a couple of huge cakes."

I begin setting up my station and notice we have a new guy working prep. I look questioningly at Nora and she introduces me. "Eva, meet Michael, he's joining our team on prep. Last night was his first night."

He turns to me. "Hey, nice to meet you."

I stop in my tracks because his blue eyes grab hold and won't let go. A nicely trimmed reddish-gold beard and a knockout smile. I recover after a bit too long. "Nice to meet you too."

I'm flustered and it makes me mad because it's so silly. The guy is probably ten years younger than me and I'm not in the market. I concentrate on ignoring him and getting ready for opening. We were fully booked as of six months ago with all the university graduations in the area, and Chez Alice is the hottest restaurant in North Carolina. I'm grateful for the frantic pace and the night flies by. We finish all the cleaning and side work for tomorrow then everyone gathers their things to leave.

"We're going out for a drink, Eva, come along?" Michael looks at me with those damned blue eyes.

"Oh, well, I really need to get home. But thanks. Maybe another time."

"Just fifteen minutes? My treat if you join us." He smiles at me and I wonder how he does that; when he talks to me it's like I'm the only person in the world.

"Well . . ."

"There, that's settled." He holds the kitchen door open for me. We are walking up Franklin Street, moving between pools of light and dark along the sidewalk. The rest of the group is up ahead and it's just us walking together, which feels awkward.

The breeze feels cool to me and I pull my sweater closer. "Are you working tomorrow?"

"I'm off tomorrow, but back again on Tuesday."

"Oh. I work tomorrow." I don't know what to say and it's killing me.

We slip into a Mexican restaurant. "What'll it be?" He orders drinks and I try to find someplace to put my eyes that isn't him.

"You have a charming accent, where are you from originally?" He sips his Corona from the bottle.

"I don't have an accent, you have an accent. Brazil."

"You're right, everybody has an accent. I love Brazil."

"Really? Why?" I mentally cringe because I sound aloof.

"I love the music, the culture. I'm a musician."

This is interesting. "What do you play? What kind of music?"

"Guitar. I guess you'd say popular music, but I'm very eclectic. I like to mix things up." That smile again.

There's an awkward silence and I stare at myself in the mirror behind the bar.

He talks to my reflection in the mirror. "What do you do for fun?"

"Fun?"

"Yes, you know: the things people do when they're not working." He laughs and turns those eyes on me again.

"Cooking is fun to me, it doesn't feel like working."

He smiles quietly. "I know you're good at it or you wouldn't be sous chef at Chez Alice. I trained at culinary school but I was thrilled to get an entry-level position because I really believe in Nora's farm-to-table vision. Hopefully I can work my way up."

I turn and smile at him. "That's what I did. I started out as dishwasher. I was sous chef in Brazil but it was old-fashioned

French cooking, the heavy stuff with lots of cream."

"Really? Why did you start as dishwasher with all that experience?"

I laugh at myself. "Because my English wasn't good enough to explain. I started with the original crew. It's been fantastic, I've learned so much."

He leans a tiny bit closer. "Please tell me more about you."

I understand this is code for finding out if I'm in a relationship. I feel like I'm in quicksand but I also know that fighting it just makes you sink. "I'm married. I have two sons. My oldest just graduated from NC State. My youngest is in high school."

He leaves a long silence, saying nothing. It occurs to me he wouldn't have approached me if I wore a wedding ring. "I'm married, but my husband was in the resistance to the dictatorship in Brazil and he got disappeared in 1971. That's why I came to the US."

My eyes fill with tears but they don't fall. I look down and wipe my face with my hand.

"Eva, I'm so sorry. I shouldn't be so pushy. Please forgive me."

I take a quick breath and look at him. "No, it's okay. I'm trying to get used to saying it out loud. I used to pretend he was in exile in Argentina and he'd be back, but I know better."

There is silence again but it's a comfortable one.

I put my empty Corona bottle on the bar. "I'd better get going."

He helps me put on my sweater. "Yeah, let's get out of here." He waves at the rest of the crew across the bar and we're back on Franklin Street.

"Well, it's nice to meet you, Michael." I put my hand out for a handshake like Americans do, but it goes wrong when he covers my hand with his two warm hands and I feel an electric current up my arm. Oh God, help me.

"Do you have a car parked at Alice?"

"No, I live just a few blocks away in Carrboro. I walk to work."

"May I walk you home?"

I just nod and we walk in silence. He looks up at the sky. "The moon is about to set. It's almost full."

I look up. "A waxing moon."

"Sounds like you know your moon phases."

"If you imagine the moon in your hand, with the curved part against your palm, the waxing moon is in your right hand. But to me the moon is backwards."

He turns his gaze from the moon to me. "Why backwards?"

"Because it's the opposite in the Southern Hemisphere. The waxing moon is in my left hand, in Brazil."

We arrive at my house. "Here I am. Thank you for the Corona and the conversation."

"Eva, maybe the moon changed my magnetic field or something. I don't want to be disrespectful, and you can tell me to go to hell. But let's go to my place."

It's like when you're walking on the beach and the ocean is calm and a huge wave comes out of nowhere and knocks you over and pulls you out to sea. I steady myself and take a deep breath. "I'll just be a minute."

May 17, Sunday

The early morning sun filters through the window and sets his skin and hair aglow. I trace the muscles of his chest and arms with a sense of wonder in the golden bubble we inhabit, this bed an island of happiness and contentment. Michael folds me in his arms and before and after cease to exist.

His shirt is thrown over the back of the chair next to the bed and I put it on. "I'm starving. What's there to eat?"

"That looks much better on you than it does on me." He pulls me over to him and nuzzles his face between my breasts.

I bury my nose in his neck and breathe in. "I want your smell. In Northeast Brazil we say, 'Me da um cheiro,' which kind of means, 'Give me a smell.' Like this." I nuzzle his neck again.

We work together in his kitchen without talking, sipping coffee as we make an omelette and squeeze oranges for juice. I hum a bossa nova tune.

"I love that song but I can't remember what it is."

"The lyrics are beautiful; something like, 'I was so sad and then you happened.'" A happy tear slides down my cheek. Michael wraps me in a hug and we kiss.

We sit at the table outdoors eating breakfast in the dappled sunlight, to the music of birdsong and the breeze rustling through the trees, this magical Sunday in May.

May 25, Monday

"Kai, Carlos, Michael is here!" My sons come out of their rooms and wait in the living room as I open the door for Michael, who's carrying two large pizzas. He hands me the pizzas boxes.

"Michael, I'd like you to meet my sons, Carlos and Kai. Guys, this is Michael."

Both boys look very serious and shake Michael's hand, murmuring, "Nice to meet you."

I gesture toward the kitchen. "Let's eat before it gets cold."

We all sit and pizza is served, and after an initial silence conversation begins.

Michael looks at Carlos. "Your mom tells me you work at the Varsity Theatre. Is it all work or do you get to see movies?"

Carlos puts down his pizza slice. "Mostly it's work. I can see movies for free when I'm not working. But they pretty much keep us busy."

Kai narrows his eyes a bit, perceptible only to me. "So you work with my mom at Chez Alice?"

"That's right. She's a sous chef and I'm on prep, but I hope to follow in her footsteps and move up."

Things loosen up a bit and the conversation flows naturally. Carlos and Kai get up to do the dishes, but Michael waves them away. "Hey, I got this. Not much to clean up, anyway."

Kai is itching to go be with his friends. "Mom, can I go shoot hoops with the guys?"

"Sure. Be home by ten, okay?"

Carlos excuses himself and goes into his room.

We clean up the dishes and Michael gives me a hug. "Did I pass muster?"

I laugh. "Of course. The boys are very protective of me but Carlos told me he trusts my judgment." We both laugh.

"Role reversal, for sure." Michael chuckles. "Will they be okay if we go over to my place?"

"No problem at all. Carlos will keep track of Kai."

We head out the front door and walk to Michael's house in Chapel Hill, just a few blocks away.

"You switched careers to music and you're working toward being a chef. You said you studied another area in college, what was it?"

"Engineering. A really bad fit. I did okay in school and got a bachelor's degree, but I could never work in the field. I need to do things that are creative. Singing, songwriting, playing guitar, cooking, even some painting."

"Painting? Tell me about it."

"I do abstract stuff, very colorful. What the spirit moves me to paint."

He puts his arm around my shoulders and we walk together in peaceful silence.

June 14, Sunday

I've asked Nora to talk with me privately, so we sit at the bar after everyone has left for the night.

"Nora, I'm a professional and would never do anything to compromise my work. So there's something I need to tell you."

She gives me a mischievous look. "You and Michael?"

I'm stunned but I try not to lose my cool. "Um, yes, Michael and I are in a relationship. It's only been a month, but I wanted to make sure it isn't a problem."

Nora laughs. "Oh hell no, as long as you both do your work, why would it be a problem? It happens all the time, the heat in the kitchen and all that. I'm happy for you."

I let out a sigh of relief. "Oh gosh, thanks for understanding. The second thing is we want to go over to the beach for a couple of days next month, if we can have the same days off."

"Sure, just let me know."

"Nora, thank you. For everything."

July 17, Friday

Michael parks his beat-up Toyota Corolla and we take our stuff into the beach cottage. It's early afternoon and hot, but the breeze off the ocean is fresh.

He holds the cottage door open for me. "Let's take a nap until it cools off, then we can go get some funky seafood for dinner."

When we wake up the sun is slanting toward evening and we walk over to a bright blue shack that sells fried shrimp and flounder and we eat outside at a picnic table.

"Why do they call them hushpuppies?" The little round fried breads are always served with seafood in the southern US.

Michael laughs. "I guess they fed them to dogs to keep them quiet, but I'm not sure."

The breaded, fried shrimp are delicious, served with a cold cabbage slaw. We drink sweet iced tea with lemon in the true Carolina tradition. After dinner we go back to the cottage for Michael's guitar and a blanket, and stroll down to the beach to watch as the sun sets and the full moon rises, its luminous glow reflected in the water.

"It looks so huge at the horizon. Mystical." He begins playing and humming a tune.

"That's nice, what song is it?"

He stops playing. "I'm not sure, I haven't finished writing it yet."

I want to keep this moment forever, and I take a picture in my mind so I'll never forget. "I'm so happy, Michael."

He puts his arm around me. "So explain the backwards moon thing to me again. When it's full it's the same everywhere, I guess."

I get up and use my toe to draw the number nine in the sand in front of him. "So, what do you see?"

"Nine."

"Okay come over here and look from this direction. What do you see?"

"Six."

"Exactly. It's all in your perspective. It's a six or a nine depending on what side you're on. Just like which side of the earth you're on to see the moon."

We sit gazing at the water, the rhythm of the waves in time with our hearts, and a tiny shadow indents the edge of the moon.

"Eva, look, the eclipse is beginning." We sit there for more than two hours, watching the moon become less than half her full self and progressing until the shadow subsides. We walk back to the cottage and fall asleep to the sound of the ocean.

August 17, Monday

Carlos, Kai and I sit in the living room waiting for Michael to arrive. Carlos's bags are packed and waiting next to the front door.

"I wish I could go with you, Carlos." Kai's voice cracks.

"Mom, are you still determined to go back to Brazil next month?" Carlos looks to me for a response.

"Yes, querido. And please don't say anything to Michael; I will tell him soon but I haven't yet."

Kai looks puzzled. "Mom, is Michael going to come with us to Brazil?"

I think for a moment before answering his question. "Michael and I have only known each other for three months. He has a well-established life here."

Carlos gives me a serious look. "Mom, you love him. I can tell. You've been alone for ten years. Don't worry about what people think."

I smile. "I only care about what you guys think. I'm glad you approve. Life makes a lot of twists and turns, so who knows?"

Our conversation ends when Michael pulls into the driveway. Carlos puts his suitcases in the trunk and we all pile into the car for the trip to the airport. After seeing Carlos off at the gate and watching his plane take off, we stop at Italian Pizzeria in Chapel Hill and take a large pie home for a late lunch.

Kai and Michael finish putting away the dishes and I give Kai a hug. "Are you okay? It's so hard for us to say goodbye to Carlos."

He puts on a brave smile. "I'll be okay. I'm gonna go shoot some hoops with the guys."

"Will you be okay if I'm not here tonight?"

He scoffs. "Please, Mom. I'm gonna watch TV and eat the leftover pizza. I'm sixteen years old, Mom."

"Okay, if you're sure. If you need me I'll be at Michael's, you have the phone number."

"Yeah, Mom. Have fun and I'll see you tomorrow."

Michael and I open a bottle of wine at his place and sit on the sofa while he plays his guitar and sings. American jazz standards, folk songs, Beatles ballads. His mellow tenor is simple, with no vibrato, and it pulls me in every time, a perfect counterpoint to his artistry on the strings.

When he takes a break I get the courage to tell him about my plans. "Michael, I need to talk to you about something."

He raises his eyebrows. "Oh?"

"I've been making plans to go back to Brazil for some time. Only Kai and Carlos know about it. I haven't told Nora. I wanted to tell you first."

He puts his guitar to the side and moves closer to me but doesn't say anything.

"I didn't tell you sooner because it felt like I would be pushing you into being serious about me. We've only known each other for three months."

"It's not a push, it's a pull. Like gravity. Like the moon."

"Michael, I do love you. But I can't expect you to abandon your life and dreams here in the US. It would be too quick."

He looks serious. "Eva, you're forty-three years old. I'm thirty-six. We're not kids. When you know something is good, you have to go for it. But I'm the one feeling like I'm pushing now. First, tell me about your plans."

I take a breath. "I've always dreamed of having my own restaurant. Originally I planned to specialize in the traditional food of the Northeast of Brazil, which would be revolutionary in itself because it's considered poor people's food and never served in fine restaurants. But cooking at Alice has broadened my vision. So it will be a mix of the traditional and fresh local ingredients in season."

"Does your restaurant have a name?"

"Jah-shee, spelled *J-a-x-i,* accent on the second syllable. It's the word for moon in the indigenous language Guarani."

"Very cool name. Where in Brazil?"

"A city on the coast, João Pessoa, the capital of the state of Paraíba, where I grew up. It's a beautiful place on a shallow bay, seven degrees below the equator. Very green with lots of palm trees."

Michael is very quiet. "So, when will you and Kai leave?"

This is hard. "The end of September. I'll give Nora notice next week. I have to sell a lot of stuff, because Kai and I are going to travel light."

Michael puts his hand on my cheek and looks deeply at me with his bottomless blue eyes. "Can I come visit?"

I start to cry. "Of course, I want you to! Just give me time to get settled and get the restaurant open."

"Do you have enough money for such a big investment?"

I laugh. "The cruzeiro is worth almost nothing and the dollar is strong. I've been saving all these years, so this is the right time. Also, I made a promise to help bring to light the abuses people like my husband Luiz suffered under the military, and the time is right for that too."

Michael is very quiet and we go to bed early, curled up together, each wrapped in our own thoughts.

September 28, Monday

Champagne corks are popping and the Alice team is enjoying a spread of appetizers as they wish me well in my new adventure. Kai is here for the celebration and has a mocktail of juice and club soda made especially for him. Joana and David, Lupe and Juan are all here.

Nora clinks her glass with a fork and everyone quiets down. "Let's raise a glass to Eva as she begins her new adventure. We wish you only the best for Jaxí, or as I like to think of it, Chez Alice South!"

"Here, here! Hooray! Bon voyage!" Everyone hollers at once. "Speech, speech!"

I raise my glass and look around at everyone. "Thank you all, I will miss you so much. Nora, I learned so much from you. About cooking, about the business of food, about life. All of you are special to me, and I will never forget you. Please come visit Brazil, you will love it."

September 30, Wednesday

Michael puts our suitcases in his trunk and we head to the airport. We are all very quiet, each lost in our thoughts. He parks the car and he and Kai carry our three bags into the terminal and check them and we go to our departure gate, stopping at a restaurant to sit and wait since we're very early.

Michael breaks the silence. "You'll send me your address and phone number as soon as you have one?"

"Yes, absolutely."

Kai gets up and puts his knapsack over his shoulder. "I'm going over to the gate so you guys have some time to talk." He reaches out and shakes Michael's hand.

Michael gets up and gives Kai a shake-half hug. "Good luck, man. Take good care of your mom for me, okay?"

Kai just nods and leaves us alone together.

Michael's voice is thick with emotion. "I'm not letting you go, Eva. Keep me in your heart, where I belong."

I don't want to cry but it's a struggle. "Michael, you know I will. We'll keep in touch. I'll keep you updated on how things are going."

We sit in silence for a while then walk to the gate and hold each other close for a long embrace. Then he turns and I watch until he's gone at the end of the concourse.

PART V

1981

October 21, Wednesday

Coconut palms bend in the breeze along Cabo Branco beach, the turquoise water of the bay stretching to the horizon where puffs of cloud ride above. I am filled with gratitude at our fortune in finding a beachfront building with restaurant space on the ground floor and this apartment three stories above. We're renting for now but I have designs on buying it once Jaxi is established and profitable.

"Mom, what's that other apartment behind the kitchen?" Kai is exploring our new home.

"That space is for a housekeeper, so she has her own bedroom and bath."

"Mom, we're not going to have a housekeeper, are we?"

I give him a sheepish smile. "It's the norm here in Brazil, querido. And I'll need someone to help out because I'll be busy with the business. And it would be considered odd if we didn't employ someone when we have the means."

He looks shocked. "Mom, that's just weird! I remember when you cleaned other people's houses in the States."

I have to admit it's ironic. "You're right, of course. But when in Rome . . ."

He shifts his focus. "This place is huge, Mom. Four bedrooms.

Which room is mine?"

"Let's go look together and you decide. I'd like the bedroom with its own bath, then you choose your bedroom, then a guest room for when Carlos visits, and an office for me."

"Sounds good. Now all we need is some furniture, but I'm glad to be home and not in a hotel."

November 16, Monday

Workers are bustling around in the restaurant space and I'm surprised how quickly the renovation is progressing. They've gutted everything and are putting in the walls, to be followed by the terracotta tile floor. The kitchen was a horror and I had them tear it out down to the skeleton; I'll put in new appliances and some unexpected features like a wood-fired brick oven.

One of my first priorities is hiring a manager, someone like Guy at Chez Alice, who knows the business and can manage the kitchen workers and wait staff, keep track of inventory, do the front-end role of welcoming guests and making sure everything is humming along as it should. It's an almost impossible job and requires knowledge, people skills and a calm temperament. I've already interviewed several people who turned out not to be qualified. So I'm a little weary and skeptical when the next candidate ambles in. He looks kind of shy and unassuming, so I don't have high hopes.

"Hello, I'm Eva. Are you here for the manager position?"

A crooked smile. "Anderson Moreira. Pleased to meet you."

I gesture to a little metal table with two chairs that are the only places to sit amid the construction. "Please have a seat, Seu Anderson."

He looks nervous and adjusts his tie as he sits down. He looks around at the space, interested. That's a good sign. It's also a good sign that he wore a suit and tie on a hot day. I look at his application form and note that he has quite a bit of experience. "Please tell me about your background and why you are interested in this position."

He clears his throat. "I am from João Pessoa. I started out in restaurants here and once I became an expert in Brazilian barbecue I went to Europe. I managed churrascarias in France and

Portugal. But I wanted to come back to Brazil to be close to my family. And I've heard about what you plan for Jaxi, and I'd like to be part of it. I think I would do a very good job for you."

I realize he's humble, not unqualified. "I would like to open in March, which is a very tough goal. My vision is a mix of fresh local ingredients and traditional food of Northeast Brazil. How could you help me with that?"

His face is serious. "If you'll be doing traditional dried meat dishes I think the best sources are in Picuí, in the interior. I have contacts with famers in the area because I grew up here. I can recommend public relations people who are very good. You won't be disappointed if you hire me." He takes a big breath.

I have a good feeling about this guy. "Seu Anderson, I learned from Nora Wells, of Chez Alice in North Carolina in the US. She began what's called the farm-to-table movement. She treated all of us as a team, and that's my vision for Jaxi."

He nods his head. "I read about Nora Wells. It would be exciting to be part of your vision. And I always wanted to be part of a real team."

I stand up and extend my hand. "Seu Anderson, this has been a very nice conversation. I'll be checking your references but I expect I will be in touch. Don't take a job anywhere else without letting me know, please?"

He looks like he will burst into tears. "Dona Eva, it would be an honor. Thank you for considering me for this important position at Jaxi."

November 30, Monday

It's early afternoon as I drive toward Búzios, a beach village north of Rio that's a major destination for the jet set. The flight south was uneventful and I'm brimming with anticipation at the thought of meeting an artist in the village Arraial do Cabo, just south of Búzios. There's water on both sides of the road: on the right, the ocean, with its booming waves, and on the left, calm salt pans. I find her studio without difficulty, but I'm surprised that it looks like a car mechanic's shack. I park and clap my hands to announce my arrival.

"Oi in the house!"

A compact woman with a tight Afro and piercing gaze wipes her hands on her paint-spattered denim apron and comes toward me. "You must be Eva."

I smile and nod. "Yes, and you are Maya? I am so excited to meet you."

Her look remains serious. "I was surprised when the owner of the new gallery in João Pessoa called to arrange a meeting for us. Most of my commissions are in Europe. Here it's usually tourists who want some art to match the color of the sofa." She snorts in derision.

"No, Dona Maya, I want folkloric pieces for my new restaurant, Jaxi."

"Jaxi? Are you a moon worshipper?"

I shouldn't be surprised that she knows indigenous language. "I guess maybe I am. I would love to see your work, if I may?"

She takes me into the studio, where various pieces are in progress. Brightly painted dark wood carvings representing folk traditions, a procession following a costumed ox, women worshipping the mermaid goddess Yemanjá who rides on aqua waves. These are powerful naïve works depicting the Northeast of Brazil.

"Well then, Eva, tell me what you have in mind."

We sit at a work table and I show her the layout of the restaurant and the two long walls of the main dining room, where I would display her work exclusively. After calculating measurements and some brainstorming, we arrive at twelve pieces, on one side folk traditions and the other animals and plants.

She sits back and looks at me. "One more thing, let me show you some photos." She opens an album with pictures of her commissions in Europe, some of them huge carved doors. This is the pièce de resistance I hadn't thought of. After the foyer and host stand, there is a double doorway, and I'll put these doors there, with the theme of the moon in all her phases. We agree on price and delivery time, and Maya will oversee the installation.

"Maya, I am thrilled. Your work is just what I needed to bring Jaxi to life. Thank you."

She smiles broadly and extends her hand. "It's a deal."

As I get up to leave I turn to ask her a question. "I'm going to stay overnight in Búzios, but I've never been there before. Can you recommend a nice inn? Not touristy."

She nods. "Dois Tucanos. Very nice and calm. From the main road take the first left toward the beach, it's on a bluff above the ocean."

"Great, thank you so much!" I wave to her as I drive away.

Pousada Dois Tucanos is a curvaceous stucco structure with a painted, carved wooden sign on the front of two toucan birds just like the name, and I recognize it's Maya's work. The young lady at reception offers me a room with a balcony view of the sea.

I take the key. "Thank you. Are there any nice restaurants open nearby? I'm a chef and really interested in innovative cuisine."

She smiles and shakes her head. "The best restaurant is right here, but it's only open on the weekends. One of the inn's owners is a retired chef, so he doesn't cook full time. He does a lot of interesting dishes."

"I see you have a bar, when is it open? I'd love to talk with the chef if he's around."

"The bar's really open any time. Why don't you settle in and come back for a drink? I'll let him know."

My room is beautiful and clean, with colorful artistic touches and a copper sink in the bathroom. I take a quick shower and change to a kaftan, then go down to the bar and order a glass of wine from the receptionist, who seems to work all aspects of the inn.

As I sit at a rustic table outside, light filters through the lattice covered with fragrant jasmine. I close my eyes and listen to the waves crashing on the beach below.

"Hello, Madame, Elisabete said you wanted to talk with me? She says you're a chef?"

I turn and smile at the gentleman and nearly faint when I see that lithe physique, the thin mustache on the upper lip, that unmistakable style. "Oh my God in heaven! Chef Orlando!"

It takes him a moment. "Eva? Is it you? Did you come here to find me?"

I jump up and we hug and laugh and look at each other. "No, Chef, it's pure luck. An angel must be guiding me."

He sits across from me and Elisabete brings him a glass of wine. "How long have you been back in Brazil? Where are you living?"

"I've been back for a couple of months. I'm opening a restaurant in João Pessoa, hopefully in March. When did you leave the generals' quarters?"

"Two years ago. My partner and I opened this inn last year."

"Chef, I remember you always loved Búzios. I'm only sorry I can't stay to enjoy your restaurant."

"I'll do better than that, querida. You must join us for dinner in the private residence. I'll even let you help with prep." We laugh and finish our glasses.

An hour later Orlando opens the door to the penthouse. "Come in, querida. Eva, this is Nelson."

The man is tall and movie-star handsome, with a neatly trimmed silver beard. He extends his hand. "Welcome."

When I hear his voice a key fits in the lock of my memory and I realize with a shock it's the major who was the administrative manager of the generals' quarters. "Major?"

There's a brief silence and then they both laugh. "Yes, it's me." Nelson smiles and gestures over to some bar stools at the kitchen counter.

Orlando hands me a chopping board and a knife, and I wash my hands at the sink. Orlando and Nelson are like an old married couple, loving and comfortable. We catch up on news about the generals' quarters and people we knew in common, and I bubble over telling them about the plans for Jaxi. Orlando bustles around the kitchen and I do prep as he hands things to me.

After a delicious dinner we sit on their veranda with glasses of port; candles burn in hurricane lanterns with the peaceful rhythm of the waves in the background.

Nelson breaks the silence. "Eva, we need to tell you some other things. I always wondered if we'd see you again, because there is something I want you to know."

This sounds very serious. "Yes, Nelson. Please go on."

"Orlando and I have been together for many years, but we had to hide our love. After the coup d'état in 1964 I became increasingly upset with the extrajudicial abuses of military leadership. One day I saw your husband's name come up on a list of people to be targeted. I tracked what happened and surreptitiously arranged his release from the torture house in Rio. And we sent someone to tell you."

I am stunned but this makes perfect sense. "Oh my God. I remember Luiz thought someone in the military had warned us, something the guy in the alley said about 'operating procedure.'"

He smiles grimly. "There wasn't much we could do in those days. And when your husband continued with the resistance, I knew there would be no second chance. That was when we gave you the next warning. I'm so sorry, Eva. I wish I could have done more." His voice breaks.

I feel a sense of calm. "Nelson, God put you and Orlando in my life. The only thing I feel is gratitude. Luiz made a detailed record of his kidnapping and torture and I sent it to the *Brazil Never Again* commission. He will be listed as one of the disappeared in their final report."

Orlando looks over at Nelson and I feel the love between them. "When they passed the amnesty law in 1979, Nelson and I decided we would retire and come here to Búzios, where people are artistic and open-minded. For the first time in our life together we can stop looking behind us and worrying about being discovered. And I think Brazil is getting better, I think there will be elections soon. The dictators are losing their hold on power."

We sit quietly together for some time. I feel the pieces of the puzzle of my life falling into place. "Orlando, Nelson, thank you so much. For everything. I will call you when I know a definite opening date, and I hope you can be there."

Orlando laughs and hugs me. "Querida, you know we will! And let us know in plenty of time even if the date isn't certain, because I want to tell all our friends. I know Jaxi is going to be fabulous."

Nelson pulls me toward him for an embrace and we're both in tears. We don't say anything more, just nod and look at each other.

December 4, Friday

"Senhor Kai, you best get going or no time for breakfast!" Cirlene has the broad accent of someone from the interior, and though she's only been with us as housekeeper for a week she's definitely taken charge. Her references were excellent, the only criticism being that she could be bossy. She has little formal education but you'd make a mistake if you thought that meant she wasn't smart.

Kai comes ambling out of his bedroom and sits to eat the eggs Cirlene has prepared to his liking. I'm drinking my second cup of coffee at the counter and making a list of things to do today.

"Querido, how has school been this week? Is it getting any easier?"

Kai sips his juice. "Well, my Portuguese is terrible. I talk like a five-year-old, can't get the genders or verbs right. But kids aren't mean about it."

I understand the feeling. "That's normal. It's all in the back of your brain somewhere, and you sound like a Brazilian except for the mistakes."

He sighs. "I didn't expect school here to be harder than the States. But it really is."

I smile as he puts his dishes in the sink and pulls his knapsack over his shoulder. "Bye Mom. Bye Dona Cirlene." He gives me a kiss on the cheek and he's out the door.

Cirlene puts a hand on her hip. "Dona Eva, what special things can I do for you today? This place needs lots of cleaning but that will take weeks. I think a family of pigs lived here before."

I laugh out loud at the image. "Would you make the beef filet roast for dinner?"

"Certainly. Are you sure you want me to take the weekends off? Nobody else does that, Dona Eva."

"Five days a week is plenty, Dona Cirlene. Thank you for a

352

great first week and I'll see you on Sunday night."

I take the elevator to the ground floor and things are already busy in the restaurant space. "Good morning, Seu Anderson!"

He gives me a wide grin. "Good morning, Dona Eva. Would you like a coffee?" The bar is now built and an espresso machine was a priority.

"Thanks, but I better take it easy on the caffeine. I'm jumpy enough about the installation of the appliances. How do you think it's going?"

He shakes his head. "They weren't very happy with me yesterday when I made them pull the cooktop out and do it again. Hopefully now they'll do things right the first time. Lazy people work harder because they have to do everything twice."

"Well, thank you for staying on top of it. What about applications for prep and dishwasher?"

"A few might work. Once I narrow them down we'll set a time for you to talk with them. Are you sure you want to hire people with no experience?"

"I'd rather give an opportunity to somebody who wants to learn and is a good team player than someone who thinks they know everything."

He nods. "Okay, got it. I have some menu designs for you to review. And we need to make the final choice on dining chairs and the pendant lights for above the tables."

We spend the day making these decisions, and Anderson gives me really good advice. We're already talking about seasonal menus and coming up with preliminary ideas, though we can't test recipes until the kitchen is complete. The day flies by and it's almost seven o'clock when we close the restaurant and I head upstairs.

Kai is studying at the kitchen counter when I come in the door. "Hey, querido, how was school?"

"Pretty good, Mom. Are you ready for dinner? I'm starving."

"Querido you don't have to wait for me. I lose track of time."

"It's okay, I had a snack." He pulls out the tray with beef and roast potatoes, and gets the salad out of the refrigerator. It's all perfectly prepared.

After dinner we sit on the sofa and look out at the palms swaying in the ocean breeze. Stars glimmer in a dark sky.

"Mom? Can I ask you a question, and don't get upset, okay?"

I wonder what is coming. "Yes, Kai, what is it?"

"Mom, did you send a letter to Michael with our address? Because I was there when you promised you would."

"Yes, I did."

"Have you heard anything? Has he written you a letter back?"

I have tried not to think about it. "No, not yet. I'm sure he's busy."

Kai looks bothered by this. "Well, at least he could write a letter. That doesn't take that long."

December 21, Monday

Things are beginning to shape up now that the kitchen is fully functional. Décor can wait until closer to our planned opening, but we can now get to work on recipe development. Anderson has made a trip to Picuí to see some meat suppliers, and he went by my brother Daniel's to tell him more about the restaurant. I sent a quick note by mail but want to make sure my family knows, since it's been more than a decade again since I've seen them.

I haven't had time to do any decorating for Christmas, but I had Kai set up an artificial tree and ornaments so we can be a little festive. The enormity of opening in March is looming, and there aren't enough hours in the day. I've hired two prep people who work weekdays to help me test recipes, and Anderson has worked as a line cook so he pitches in when my hands get too full. I really need people with sous chef experience, but everyone who's applied has exaggerated their skills. I'm contemplating bringing Cirlene down to work. I can't think about it too much or I'm awash with anxiety. Prayers are all I can do.

Anderson's voice pierces my thoughts. "Dona Eva, there's a guy here who says he wants to apply for the sous chef position. I told him to fill out an application but he said he wants to talk with the chef first. I think he's a bit cheeky, but since we're desperate for staff I told him I'd check."

I sigh and turn off the flame under the sauté pan and wash my hands. "Might as well talk to him, I suppose."

It's three o'clock already and I still have things I need to do. What a waste of time when I least need it. I retie my ponytail and look around the dining room but I don't see anyone, and I figure that the guy gave up and left. Or, more likely, he's out front smoking a cigarette. I look at Anderson and he throws his hands up; he doesn't know where the guy went either. I'm losing my patience but I go out the front doors to check.

"Hey, babe, will work for food." I whip my head around to see who it is although I'd know that voice anywhere. I just can't believe it's Michael. I'm frozen for a minute and then nearly knock him over, hugging him and crying. "Oh my God, what . . . how . . . when? You know!"

He holds my face between his hands and kisses me. "We've got all the time in the world for me to explain."

I'm crying, but with happiness. "I had given up. When you didn't write me back, I thought you must have a new girlfriend."

"I came as fast as I could. Selling everything I owned took longer than I expected."

"Don't you have a backpack or something? What about your guitar?"

"It's upstairs in your apartment. Kai isn't home from school yet but the guard dog masquerading as a housekeeper finally took my stuff inside."

Now I can't stop laughing. Anderson peeks out the front door, no doubt thinking I've lost my mind. "Come on in, meet Anderson. Anderson, this is Michael. Let's show Michael around Jaxi."

December 22, Tuesday

It's three o'clock in the morning and Michael and I sit out on the balcony listening to the waves and eating a snack. The stars glitter in the inky sky and palm fronds rustle in the breeze off the ocean.

"Michael, I'm so glad you're here. I wish we could just spend time together but there's so much to think about right now with the opening of Jaxi."

He reaches over and squeezes my hand. "I'm here for you, babe. I'm here for Jaxi. We'll get it all figured out. Just being with you is enough, no matter what we do."

We sit in happy silence for a while then go back to bed to sleep until dawn.

Michael wakes up when the bright sun invades the bedroom window. "Eva, it's late, how long did we sleep?"

I turn on my side and smile at him. "What time do you think it is?"

He looks out the window. "Around ten o'clock?"

I laugh. "It's five. The sun is up and fierce early here near the equator. Then sunset is a little after five. There's daylight for twelve hours all year long but they didn't coordinate the solar time with the clock very well. It takes some getting used to."

We get up and make coffee, Cirlene gives me the look to sit while she makes breakfast for us, and I obey. Kai will be up soon but Michael and I are already on the way down in the elevator, armed with a list of tasks. The ever faithful Anderson arrives just after six and we sit to plan the day. It turns out Anderson speaks quite a bit of English, which is a huge help. The day passes quickly but much is accomplished.

Back in the apartment we shower and pop open a couple of beers. Michael gets out his guitar and tunes it, then begins to sing for me. That mellow tenor, no vibrato, quiet and irresistible, beautiful phrasing. I can never get enough of it. He plays a couple of jazz standards, then a bossa nova tune he hasn't played for me before.

I shake my head in wonder. "Your voice makes me melt. I think I fell in love with you before I heard you sing, but the music sealed the deal."

He looks at me shyly. "I'm not really a singer, not fancy enough. Brazil inspires me, samba and bossa nova inspire me. You inspire me, my muse."

1982

March 31, Wednesday

The debut of Jaxi is finally here, and I'm nervous as a cat. We're fully booked and fully staffed. Michael and I are doing one last walk-through from the point of view of the customer. Freshly showered and crisply attired, we descend the elevator and stand in front of Jaxi. I take a breath and open the front door. To my right is the host stand, with its display of fresh vegetables just like Nora did at Chez Alice, and an arrangement of bird-of-paradise flowers. To my left, a life-sized paired of yoked oxen, painted electric blue. And in the center, Maya's gorgeous carved doors with green and aqua phases of the moon entangled in lush vines.

Anderson opens the doors and the dining room is before me, the bar to my left. The tables are simple wood covered with crisp white tablecloths, perfectly set with dishes, cutlery and sparkling goblets. The chairs are comfortable rattan club chairs because I want people to enjoy the meal and not feel rushed. Wicker pendant lights hang above each table. Along both walls are Maya's brightly painted carved wood pieces. It looks perfect and I'm happy.

Now to the kitchen, and everything is ready to go. We're offering a varied menu of shrimp risotto, grouper cheek moqueca, carne de sol with caramelized onions, and a braise of cupim, the hump of the zebu cow, finished in the wood-fired oven.

Vegetables include colorful beet carpaccio, cassava root done various ways, and tostones, Puerto Rican plantain fritters. Winter squash with okra, and tiny emerald eggplants called jiló.

For dessert, a fig sorbet, persimmon mousse, orange carrot cake, good old simple chocolate pavê, and of course chocolate truffles, called brigadeiros.

After some last-minute shuffling in the kitchen, Anderson puts his head in to let me know it's time for lift-off. I nod to him and take a deep breath. "Okay, team, let's get this done!" It's frantic and crazy for two hours but things run as smoothly as I could have hoped for on opening night.

Just after nine o'clock Michael nods toward the dining room. "Go take a victory lap and greet your guests. The VIPs had reservations for eight o'clock so they should be enjoying a coffee."

I enter the space and recognize Orlando and Nelson toward the front, and Senator Célia at a nearby table. Sónia and Chico are here from Brasília, my brother Daniel and Rita from Picuí. I don't recognize most of the faces but Anderson tells me they're local politicians and business people. When Orlando sees me he and Nelson stand up and applaud, and in a slow wave the rest of the people in the room join them. Anderson brings me an armload of floral bouquets.

The room goes quiet and all eyes are on me. I take a deep breath and manage not to cry. "Thank you so much for making Jaxi's first night a success. I'm grateful to everyone who made it all possible: my mentor Chef Orlando, Senator Célia, manager Anderson Moreira, the whole team, and especially Michael Parker."

Michael is standing by the kitchen doors and bows his head to me. I circulate among the tables and have a brief conversation with so many people that my head is spinning. It's a wonderful feeling and I'm exhausted. After hugs with family and promises to spend time together soon, the restaurant empties and we begin clean-up and side work for tomorrow.

Anderson is grinning ear to ear, though he looks tired. "Parabéns, Dona Eva. Congratulations."

I give him a hug. "Thank you, Seu Anderson. For everything."

Michael is smiling. "So, two seatings tonight, and I think we're ready for three tomorrow. There were a few glitches in the kitchen but I think we covered our tails okay."

Anderson lowers his voice conspiratorially. "There were two restaurant reporters here tonight. They think I don't know who they are, but I watched them out of the corner of my eye. They were loving everything."

Michael pops a champagne cork and the whole crew is served a coupe of bubbly. I raise my glass in tribute. "To every single one of you, the best team Jaxi could dream of. Thank you from the bottom of my heart. And get some sleep tonight, because tomorrow will be another busy day." I glow with happiness as we toast. Jaxi is off to a good start.

September 21, Monday

The restaurant is closed today so we are testing some spring recipes. Shrimp moqueca, the spicy Bahian stew. Collard greens with cumin, mustard seed and wilted onions, very different from the usual collards with bacon. Sorbet of jabuticaba, the Brazilian grape tree.

Jaxi has no available weekend reservations through the new year. The main newspapers in Rio and São Paulo have done pictorial features, and I was invited on a women's TV show to talk about the farm-to-table movement and demonstrate a recipe; I did a vegetable risotto.

Michael and I are bustling around the kitchen making recipe notes as we go, when Anderson pops in. "Dona Eva, there's a woman here asking to talk with you. I told her we don't have any open positions, but she said she's not here about a job."

Yet another distraction, but I try to keep an open door to people in the community, so I wash my hands and go through the carved moon doors to the host area. The light is fairly dim in the foyer so I open the front door and invite her outside. "I could use some fresh air, and it's a lovely day. How can I help you?"

She is a beautiful woman in her mid-thirties, her hair with loose, silky, dark curls wearing simple but fashionable clothes. She gives me a shy smile. "Dona Eva?"

There is something familiar about her but I can't put my finger on it. "Yes? And you are?"

"I saw you on TV and I came up from Maceió to see you."

That's way south of Recife, quite a journey. "Well, that's a long way to travel." I wait for her to tell me her name and why she came.

"You don't recognize me, do you?"

It hits me like a giant wave. "Miriam? My sister, Miriam? Oh my God!"

We are hugging and crying. I keep stepping back to look at her in amazement, and then we hug again.

"All these years! I'm so sorry I didn't recognize you at first. You were only eleven when I left Picuí. All this time I hoped I'd find you. Please, come in."

We're laughing and wiping our tears as we walk in the dining room. Anderson looks at me questioningly. "Seu Anderson, this is my sister Miriam. I haven't seen her in more than twenty years."

I pull out a chair for Miriam to sit and excuse myself for a moment. Michael looks at me as I enter the kitchen. "Michael, you won't believe this. Remember I told you about my sister Miriam, who my stepmother told me ran away from home as a teenager? She saw me on that TV show and came all the way from Maceió to see me."

Michael shakes his head in wonder. "Wow, that is amazing. You need to spend time with her, I'll keep on with the show here. Don't worry."

I introduce Miriam to Michael, give him a kiss and nod my thanks to Anderson, and Miriam and I go up to the apartment. I put cups of espresso on the coffee table for us. I can't take my eyes off her. "Tell me about you? Do you have kids? What do you do in Maceió?"

She sighs. "My daughter, Bruna, is five. It's just Bruna and me, her father left us when she was two years old. I work doing various things to pay the rent: cleaning, I've been a restaurant hostess and washed dishes, and some sewing, which you taught me."

"You were almost twelve when I left Picuí. I couldn't get back until 1968. I sent letters for years but the letters I got back from Papai stopped after a few years. Amara was putting my letters in a box after Papai had a stroke, she never opened them or read them to him. She didn't bother to contact me, not even when Papai died. And she told me you ran away as a teenager."

Miriam shakes her head. "Amara may have given birth to me, but you were my real mother. You always protected me from her. When you left, and then José had a stroke, she unleashed her true feelings toward me. I figured out that José was not my father, though he was always kind to me. But Amara resented me, because she wouldn't have had to marry José if she wasn't pregnant with me. And then I was dark, not like the blue and green eyes in your family."

"So how did you get by, when you ran away? How old were you?" My heart aches as I imagine what she must have gone through.

"Well, I went to Recife for a while, I was sixteen. I got a job as a maid for a couple of years, but I never went back to school. I met Bruna's father and moved with him to Maceió, because he worked as a merchant seaman. He treated me pretty well, and he wasn't home much. But he was unhappy about having a child, and, well, you can imagine the rest."

"Oh, Miriam, I'm so sad things have been difficult for you. But you are a survivor. Do you have to stay in Maceió? Could you move here to João Pessoa?"

Her voice catches. "I don't have any money, Eva. Not enough to rent an apartment and all. I'll work toward that goal, though, because I'd love to be back in Paraíba."

I move next to her on the sofa and give her a hug. "Miriam, there are a couple of small apartments for rent in this building. Go get Bruna and I'll arrange for you to live in one. You've worked as a hostess and you can help me out by doing that. After that we'll figure out what you want to learn, and I'll teach you."

She pulls me into a fierce embrace. "Oh, Eva, it would be a dream come true. I can never repay you but I will spend my life trying."

1983

June 10, Friday

"Carlos! My sweet son, it's so good to see you!" He's tall and handsome and so like his father, I look at him in wonder.

Carlos gives me a hug. "Mãe, I miss you too. I'm so glad to be here for Kai's high-school graduation."

"The ceremony is tonight, but the big celebration is on Monday, with family coming from Picuí and Brasília. We'll have a big dinner in the restaurant."

"How's Michael?"

"He's fine; down in the kitchen making sure everything is on track for tonight's service. We won't be back up here until late tonight, but you don't have to wait up for us, we can talk tomorrow."

"That's fine, Mom. I'll take a nap. Cirlene made sure I have everything I need in the guest room."

"Is everything good at work?"

"Absolutely. My apprenticeship with Lina Bo Bardi doesn't pay as much as other firms would, but she has a unique vision of 'architecture for everyone.' And women architects are rare. She's a strong woman, like my mom." He smiles and hugs me again.

"Make yourself at home, son. I'm just going to jump in the shower and head down to get ready for tonight."

"Mom?"

I turn to look at Carlos.

"I'm so proud of you, Mom."

June 13, Monday

The dining room is full, the tables are lined up in a big rectangle so everyone can see each other, and Kai has the seat of honor at the head next to Carlos, Michael and me. Family from Picuí, Orlando and Nelson, Senator Célia, Sónia and Chico and Eliane, Anderson and his family and most of the restaurant staff are here. I invited Cirlene but she went to visit her mom in the interior.

I rise for a toast. "Welcome to all our loved ones, as we celebrate Kai's graduation from Lyceu Paraibano. We are so glad you are all here. This is a happy day. To Kai!"

There's much clinking of glasses and shouts of "Speech, speech!"

Kai rises to speak. "Thank you to everyone for being here. I am grateful to so many people, but special thanks to my brother Carlos, to Michael, and most of all to my amazing Mom. She inspires me to do great things." Everyone smiles and shouts "Parabéns!"

Michael stands to invite everyone to enjoy the food. His Portuguese is getting better every day. "Everyone please make yourself at home, the buffet-style food is served."

My heart bursts with pride and happiness.

September 19, Monday

Miriam comes into my kitchen office with a bounce in her step. "You wanted to see me, Eva?"

Her effervescent energy always brings me joy. "Yes, have a seat. How is everything? How is Bruna's school?"

"She loves it. We're so happy to be here. Every day when I wake up I thank God."

"I do too, Miriam. I wanted to talk to you about our plans for a new, casual restaurant. You know the building behind this one, that sits on the road behind us?"

"Yes, I do. I know it's falling apart and it doesn't have a roof." She looks skeptical.

I give her a mischievous look. "Falling apart is a good thing, you know why?"

She looks puzzled. "Not really."

"Because we bought it for almost nothing. We're going to renovate it and it will be kind of a snack bar, but with high-quality food. And we'll feature live acoustic music, nothing loud or jangly. For sipping a drink and listening, not dancing and getting rowdy." I laugh.

Miriam nods. "That's a great idea! What will you call it?"

"Meia-Lua. Since it's a sister bistro to Jaxi."

"'Half a Moon'! I like that."

I lean forward in my chair. "Here's the important thing. I want you to be the manager."

She giggle-shrieks just like she did as a child. "A manager! I'm only just learning to be a line cook. I don't think I'm ready."

I pat her on the arm. "You're smart, you have common sense, you're honest and you work hard. You'll be my right arm at Meia-Lua. I know you can do it. Besides, it's going to take us six months to be ready to open. The seating will be covered but outdoors, so

367

really we only have to do kitchen construction. But there are a couple of other pieces to the puzzle, and if you don't want to do it after I tell you about them, that's absolutely fine."

She looks at me with rapt attention. "I want to do it, Eva. I just don't want to disappoint you."

I shake my head. "You won't disappoint me. Here is the first thing. Kai has decided he wants to work in the family business. I'd rather he went to college, but I told him we'd do a trial run. He understands he has to start out as dishwasher and work his way up. But my goal is for him to have some responsibility at Meia-Lua."

She nods. "Of course, that's fine, great in fact. Kai is a good kid."

"Here's the second thing. I'm going to build out Meia-Lua as a full kitchen, and we will run a new operation for feeding the hungry out of it. The Catholic church just north of here on the beach will handle distribution. We just have to prepare the food."

Miriam has tears in her eyes. "Oh Eva, this is God's work and it will be an honor. I will do my very best, I promise you."

I give her a big hug. "I know you will, querida. I know you will."

1984

January 26, Thursday

"The people are rising up across Brazil, and I want to stand with them." I have a hard time containing my passion.

Michael looks concerned. "I understand, but what are the chances that things could go wrong? That the military will take violent action?"

"The movement is too big, and it's gaining strength every day. If they harm anyone it will just fan the flames, and I think they know it. The military dictatorship can't keep putting off the inevitable, continuing to appoint presidents through Congress instead of letting us vote."

Michael nods. "I understand. But I'd like to go with you, if that's all right?"

"Of course it is!" And we walk toward the main square, with others in the street heading the same direction. Thousands of people are gathered and there are several speakers. The chant goes up, the multitude speaking with one voice.

"Direct elections now! Direct elections now!"

The demonstration is peaceful and Michael and I hold hands as we walk home together.

March 25, Sunday

"Can you believe it will be two years since Jaxi opened?" I lean my head on Michael's shoulder. "And Meia-Lua opens in a couple of weeks."

"It is unbelievable. It doesn't feel like two years have passed." We are sitting on the beach across the street from Jaxi and it's past midnight. There's a sliver of moon starting to peek above the ocean.

Michael points to the horizon. "Look, the moon is in my right hand. The waning crescent."

We sit quietly for a few minutes, then Michael takes my hand. "Eva, will you marry me? I made a life commitment a long time ago, so a certificate won't change that. But if you're not ready, it's okay."

I pull him toward me for a fierce kiss. "I should have been the one to ask you. I hate to talk about the legal stuff, but now that Luiz is officially declared . . . And it's unlikely you'll have a problem with immigration, but it would be good to make sure. I love you and want to spend the rest of my life with you. So yes, let's get married." We kiss and lie back on the sand.

He wraps me in his arms. "One more thing. Let's keep it simple. I know the Brazilians will want to put on a party, and I've seen how celebrations just get bigger and bigger. And all the politicians would compete to give us the biggest gift. I'll only tell my mom and dad and sisters in the States. This is for us, not anyone else."

"We need two witnesses, what do you think about Kai and Carlos? It will take us a few weeks to gather all the documents, and we can plan for when Carlos can come up from São Paulo."

"Eva, that's perfect. I wouldn't want anyone else."

We sit together watching the moon climb higher in the sky.

I feel a glow of wonder and gratitude that life has brought me to this place, with Michael.

"Shall we go in? It's getting late." He holds out his hand to me.

"I'll just stay here a few more minutes, okay?"

"Of course, my love." He kisses me on the forehead and I'm alone on the beach.

I look up at the luminous slice of moon suspended above the water, the echoes of her light in the waves lapping at the sand. "Luiz, I know you're out there. Gone from this earth but always with me. I love Michael, Luiz. You would like him. I think you would approve, and I know you would want me to be happy. Please give me a sign."

Just seconds later a fiery meteor streaks across the sky and falls below the horizon. Tears stream down my face, happiness and peace and sweet sadness all jumbled up.

"Thank you, Luiz. Thank you. I love you."

April 2, Monday

We are up early so Michael can drive me and Kai to Recife to get our flight to São Paulo. It's a rainy day as we drive south to the airport, the view of the ocean obscured by clouds. I hold the package tightly in my lap, lost in my thoughts.

Michael breaks the silence. "Carlos will pick you up at the airport?"

"Yes, he's taking a few days off. It will be good to see him." I look at Kai in the back seat, who is very quiet.

"That's good, Eva. I wish I could go with you but I'll stay here and keep things humming at Jaxi and make sure we're ready to open Meia-Lua."

"Thank you, querido."

Everything goes smoothly and the flight leaves on time, touching down at Guarulhos Airport a little bit early. Kai and I only have carry-on bags so we go straight to the main concourse to meet Carlos.

"It's so good to see you guys." Carlos hugs us both at once. He drives us across the city to his apartment, and we sit in his living room in silence, all of us staring at the package on the coffee table.

Kai looks at Carlos. "I haven't looked at the papers, have you?"

Carlos shakes his head. "No, Mãe said I could when I was older but I've decided not to. I don't need details on what Papai went through, it haunts me enough already."

I look at Kai. "I won't be keeping any copies once we give them to the commission. They have thousands of pages of documents like this, and their report will be published next year. So many people suffered, and the book on the report, *Brazil Never Again*, will be a document for posterity."

We have a quiet dinner, and afterward we sit together remembering Luiz, their Papai.

"The most important things for you to remember about your Papai are how much he loved us, and how much he loved Brazil. He gave his life fighting for what he believed was right. When we have direct elections and Brazil is a democracy again, and I think that will happen soon, remember that your Papai was one of the people who made that possible."

April 3, Tuesday

We take a taxi to the Catholic Archdiocese of São Paulo, which heads up the *Brazil Never Again* commission. It's in a nondescript office building but security is tight and we have to go through several checks before entering.

I step up to the reception desk, flanked by Carlos and Kai. "My sons and I have brought documents for the commission handwritten by my husband, a torture victim who later disappeared. I mailed photocopies from the US in 1979, but we want the originals to remain with the commission."

The receptionist looks at us kindly. "Yes, Senhora, please have a seat and someone will be with you shortly."

In just a moment a man comes forward and shakes our hands. "I am Brother João. Please, let's go back to the conference room."

We sit and I place the package of documents on the table. "My sons and I have brought you these documents. My husband survived torture once but then disappeared in 1971. Before his disappearance he wrote down all the details of his imprisonment in Rio three years before. He asked me to make sure this record came into the right hands."

Brother João bows his head slightly. "Senhora Lima, we will commit his record and his bravery to the country's memory."

"And there is one more thing." I reach into my pocket and bring out Luiz's wedding ring. "This was left on my front doorstep two days after his final disappearance. Please put it with the artifacts relating to the atrocities."

He bows his head. "We will add these precious documents to the archival record, and his wedding ring to the artifacts. May God keep you safe and bring peace to you all."

There's nothing more to say, and I walk out into the bright sunshine with my sons. The three of us hug, but there are no tears, just pride in their father and his courage.

April 16, Monday

Meia-Lua opened to great applause last week, and Miriam, Kai, Michael, Anderson and I are meeting to go over everything and plan for this week. We expect to be very busy in both restaurants, so the one day we're closed is crucial for planning.

The movement demanding direct elections has reached fever pitch, with demonstrations in various cities across Brazil every few days. Today's protest in São Paulo is expected to be the biggest of all. We have a small television on in the Jaxi office to watch events unfold.

Kai looks up from the TV coverage. "Mamãe, when we talked on the phone last week Carlos told me he plans to be there."

"I'm glad. It's a historic moment and his father would be proud of him for being part of it."

On the Globo TV network a reporter stands against a backdrop of so many people it's hard to imagine how many there are. "The demonstration is peaceful, and now this massive group is moving from Praça da Sé in the city's center to the Anhangabaú Valley, because the downtown square is too small to contain them. The crowd is estimated at 1.5 million people."

We all gaze at the television in silence. Michael speaks first. "There is no way the government can hold out against this overwhelming support for direct elections."

I feel chills up my spine. "This is the largest demonstration in the history of Brazil. Change is coming, and it has to be soon."

May 18, Friday

"Eva, do you want to make any changes to the Meia-Lua small-plates menu for this weekend?" Miriam and Kai stick their head in my office door at Jaxi, where Michael and I are finalizing the menu for this evening.

I look at Michael. "Your thoughts?"

"We have a lot of delicious apples, and the apple tart isn't moving that fast in this dining room, so let's make apple hand pies, American style. I bet they'll be a hit."

Miriam claps her hands. "Sounds good, you make them and we'll sell them." She and Kai head back across the alley to Meia-Lua.

Anderson pops his head in. "Another one, Dona Eva, Seu Michael."

Michael groans. "Oh no, who is it from now? I thought we were keeping our marriage quiet, but the gifts just keep coming."

Anderson hands me the envelope that came with the delivery, and I open it. "State Tourism Board."

Anderson laughs and goes back to work.

I put the box on top of the stack to go upstairs. "Querido, the law requires the civil office to publish pending marriages. I didn't think people followed marriages so closely, but obviously I was wrong. Of course people expect at least a reception, but I'll say in the thank-you notes that we have kept it just to family."

Michael shakes his head and laughs.

May 21, Monday

Our marriage ceremony at the civil office is moving, though brief and simple. My sons sign as witnesses and we all go out to lunch afterward at a beachfront restaurant. After we get back to the apartment Carlos and Kai head out for a drive to the beaches north of the city. I gave Cirlene a three-day weekend so Michael and I are alone. He pops a champagne cork and we toast our official union.

"So, I don't have a physical wedding gift for you, but I wrote you a song. It's called 'The Moonlight In Your Eyes'."

I sit back as he tunes his guitar and wish this precious moment would never end.

The moonlight in your eyes
Pulling me out to sea
That's how you happened to me . . .

The mellow calm of his voice and the feeling behind the words envelop me and I'm transported somewhere beyond time and space. He puts his guitar to the side and I stand and wrap him in my arms, kissing his neck as he nuzzles his face between my breasts. The flames engulf us and we don't make it back to the bedroom.

Lying on the floor as I come to my senses, I notice a champagne glass on the rug and it strikes me funny. "This marriage thing is messy."

We lie together on the damp rug laughing, and then in peaceful silence.

"Michael?"

"Yes?"

"I love you."

June 26, Tuesday

The television reporter does a sound test with her camera crew and I take a deep breath as they check the lighting. We're seated at one of the tables in Jaxi. She looks at me as if to say, are you ready? I nod.

She speaks to the camera behind me. "We're here with Eva Lima Parker, chef-owner of Jaxi in João Pessoa, one of the most celebrated and innovative restaurants in Brazil. Chef Eva is going public with the experience of losing her husband, Luiz Lima, in 1971, when he disappeared. Chef Eva, why are you coming forward now?"

"Renata, my family is just one among so many who suffered at the hands of the dictators, but because I have a voice I think it's my duty to use it. The country is moving toward democracy, and I hope direct elections will happen soon. But it's too easy to forget the painful period that ruined so many lives. In fact, there are some who now deny that the torture and kidnappings ever happened."

"Could you tell us about your late husband, Luiz Lima—what happened?"

"Luiz was active in the workers' movement when I first met him in 1956, and he became more passionate while working to build the new capital, Brasília. He fought for workers, the poor, land reform, and for the right of everyone to live in peace and dignity. He was imprisoned by the military in 1968, and withstood unspeakable torture before being released. He was never the same, suffering migraine headaches and flashbacks that made him unable to work."

"I'm so sorry, Chef Eva. That must have been so difficult for your family."

"Yes, it was. But the most cruel thing is his disappearance. Luiz left the house one morning in 1971 and never returned. I reported him missing to the authorities, but nothing was ever done. Two days after he disappeared I found his wedding ring on our front doorstep. The message was clear."

"That is unspeakably cruel. What do you want our viewers to take away from your words?"

"Never forget. The amnesty law passed in 1979 means none of the perpetrators will pay for their crimes, but one day they will stand before God. I've given documents handwritten by Luiz to the *Brazil Never Again* commission, telling what happened to him in 1968. Their report will be published next year. That is my message: *never again*. We must keep the memory alive, and put a democratically elected government in place. The military dictators are illegitimately in power and they must leave. We must have direct elections now."

Renata looks up at the camera behind me again. "A powerful message from Chef Eva Lima Parker, who came forward to tell the story of her first husband's disappearance in 1971. Thank you, Chef Eva."

The filming ends and Renata gives me a hug. "I'll be in touch to let you know when your interview will air. Thank you for your courage."

"Thank you for amplifying my voice."

The crew packs up and leaves, and Michael, who has been watching in the back, comes forward and wraps me in his arms. "Eva, Eva. Well done."

I have fulfilled my promise to Luiz, and he can rest in peace.

1985

September 30, Monday

Sónia and Chico are visiting from Brasília, and Sónia and I are sitting by the swimming pool with a cool drink, looking out at the vast ocean from the bluff above Cabo Branco.

"I love the new house, and the view of the bay is spectacular."

"Yes, we love it. I never imagined having a house this big, but now we have room for family to visit. And Carlos is going to design a new wing for Michael's music studio."

"Carlos is a successful architect and Kai is in culinary school—and our three are doing well with their careers and families. We couldn't have imagined it when they were little."

"Thank God they are all happy."

"Eva, your accomplishments are amazing. I always knew you would be a success, because you have such tenacity and a creative mind. But you have gone beyond anything I could have imagined."

"I am grateful for it all. God has been good to me."

We sit in silence for a few minutes. "When will Michael be home?"

"Late night. He's recording at Odeon in Rio, with some great Brazilian musicians. I'm so happy for him."

Chico joins us by the swimming pool. "Eva, this place is beautiful. Luiz would be so proud of everything you've accomplished, and of your fight to keep the memory of those we lost alive."

I gaze out at the turquoise ocean. "Since *Brazil Never Again* was published in July there's been increased interest. But forgetting is the easy thing, and people don't want to remember. It's too horrible."

Chico lets out a breath. "Well, at least the dictatorship is ended, with President Sarney in power, even though he wasn't directly elected. Direct elections must come next."

The sun dips behind the bluffs and the moon rises over the bay.

"There's your moon, Eva." Sónia gives me a hug.

"Let's get something to eat." We putter around the kitchen chatting and talking and putting food out on the counter. It's good to have unhurried time, and it brings back memories of all we've been through together. I am struck by how my life has unfolded, and I'm filled with gratitude.

It's almost nine o'clock when I hear the gate open and Michael drives up to the house. I rush down to meet him, and we wrap ourselves in an embrace. We sit by the pool, the moonlight reflected in the water.

"I love you so much, Michael."

"I love you too, my Eva."

"Do you know why I tell you I love you all the time?"

He take my hand and kisses it. "Because you love me?"

"Because I know how precious love is, how precious you are to me, and I know how quickly life can change. I always hold my love for you close in my heart."

"As do I. I express my love in my music. The recording sessions went really well, and I'm thrilled with 'The Moonlight In Your Eyes'."

I squeeze his hand. "Look at her: she's almost full but waning. I feel I could reach out and touch her."

"That old backwards moon."

"She's just where she's supposed to be. The moon is perfect as long as I'm with you."

GLOSSARY

AI-5: A military decree in 1968 that suspended Brazil's constitutional protections and authorized the president to force the legislature to recess; widely regarded as institutionalizing torture during the dictatorship.

Aeromoça: Stewardess, flight attendant.

Alpargatas: Simple, flat shoes with a rubber sole.

Baiana: A woman from Bahia, a state in the Northeast of Brazil.

Baião de Dois: Typical dish of Northeast Brazil, a casserole made with rice and black eyed peas, often with sausage or dried meat added.

Blitz: Term used in Brazil to describe a police operation where blockades are set up to stop all drivers.

Bloody Friday: A student demonstration in front of the US Embassy in Rio de Janeiro on June 21, 1968, where 28 died and hundreds were injured.

Café: Coffee

Cafezinho: Small black coffee or espresso, served in demitasse cups.

Campina Grande: The second largest municipality in the Northeast state of Paraíba, in the interior.

Candango: A person who worked on the construction of Brasília.

Capon: A rooster that is caponized, or neutered at a young age and fed to become fat, typically roasted in the oven.

Cajú: Cashew. The cashew tree has bulbous fruits ending in the cashew nut. The fruit is used to make juice.

Canjica: A creamy porridge made of hominy with milk, sugar and cinnamon. Served during Festa Junina.

Carnaval: Carnival, celebrated the five days ending in Ash Wednesday, which marks the beginning of Lent.

Carne de charque: Thin strips of beef salted and dried in the sun.

Carne de sol: Heavily salted beef dried in the sun to preserve it.

Cassava: Root vegetable, also called manioc or yuca. Used to make tapioca.

Churrascaria: A Brazilian barbeque restaurant.

Cidade Livre: The Free City, a tax-free area created to house workers during the building of Brasília.

Ceará: A state in the Northeast of Brazil.

Cocada: A chewy, rustic sweet made with coconut.

Cruzeiro: Brazilian currency from 1942 to the 1990s, sometimes with slightly different names.

Dona: A title of respect used before a woman's first name.

Esplanada dos Ministérios: Tall rectangular buildings lined up along a grassy plain in the center of Brasília, representing all of the government agencies, or ministries.

Favela: A shantytown of improvised homes, often built precariously on steep hillsides.

Feijoada: The iconic Brazilian dish, a stew of black beans, pork and beef. The name comes from the Portuguese word for beans, feijão. Typically served on Saturdays with rice, slices of orange and braised collard greens.

Festa Junina: June Festival, also known as the Feast of Saint John, celebrates the birth of John the Baptist and other saints. They occur in the southern hemisphere's midwinter, having been introduced by the Portuguese in colonial times. Typically practiced in rural areas, especially in the Northeast of Brazil.

Forró: A couples dance typical of the Northeast of Brazil, also refers to the music featuring accordion, triangle and zabumba drum.

Fortaleza: Coastal capital of the state of Ceará, in the Northeast of Brazil.

Goiás: A state in the interior of Brazil.

Jabuticaba: Brazilian grape tree.

Jango: Nickname of João Goulart, vice president under president Juscelino Kubitschek and later president of Brazil.

Jaxi: The word for moon in the indigenous Guarani language of Brazil.

João Pessoa: Coastal capital city of the Northeast state of Paraíba.

Juazeiro do Norte: A city in the interior of Ceará, a state in the Northeast of Brazil.

Lina Bo Bardi: An Italian born Brazilian modernist architect. She promoted the social and cultural potential of architecture, notably in her design of the São Paulo Museum of Art.

Maceió: The coastal capital city of Alagoas, a Northeast state of Brazil.

Madrasta: Stepmother

Mamãe: Mom

Mamar: Breast feed, can be a verb or a noun.

Maracujá: Passion fruit. It is reputed to help anxiety and insomnia.

Mercadinho: Grocery store.

Natal: A coastal city in the Northeast of Brazil, capital of the state of Rio Grande do Norte.

Nordestino: Someone from the Northeast of Brazil, male form. Female form is Nordestina.

Oscar Niemeyer: Modernist architect instrumental in the design of civic buildings for the new capital of Brasília. Noted for bold forms and curves and the use of reinforced concrete.

Paçoca: A traditional Brazilian sweet made of ground peanuts, sugar and a bit of salt.

Palácio da Alvorada: The official residence of the president of Brazil in the capital, Brasília. A modernist building designed by the architect Oscar Niemeyer. Literal translation in English is Palace of Dawn.

Palácio do Planalto: The official workplace of the president of Brazil, a modernist building designed by the architect Oscar Niemeyer. Literal translation in English is Palace of the High Plains.

Papai: Dad

Papai Noel: Father Christmas, Santa Claus.

Parabéns: Congratulations

Paraíba: A state in the Northeast of Brazil. Ponta do Seixas, in the southern part of the capital city of João Pessoa, is the easternmost point of the North and South American continents.

Picuí: A town in the interior of the state of Paraíba.

Praça: Town square, plaza.

Querida: Darling, honey. Female form. Male is querido.

Recife: A coastal city in the Northeast of Brazil, capital of the state of Pernambuco.

Renault Gordini: A sporty four door sedan sold in Brazil in the 1960s; a modified version of the Renault Dauphine sold in France.

Rio Grande do Sul: Brazil's southernmost state, bordering Uruguay and Argentina.

Roberto Burle Marx: Modernist landscape architect who designed the public gardens and many urban spaces in the new capital of Brasília. Noted for large swathes of plants with blooms of the same color, curving walkways and water features.

Salgados: Deep fried savory snacks, often with chicken or meat filling.

Saúde: Health. When raising a glass it means "to your health!"

Senhora: A title of respect for a lady, Mrs., Ma'am.

Sertão: Outback or back country, hinterlands. In Brazil it refers to an area that includes part of the Northeast states of Alagoas, Bahia, Pernambuco, Paraíba, Rio Grande do Norte, Ceará, Maranhão, Piauí, Sergipe, and Minas Gerais.

Seu: A title of respect used before a man's first name.

Tagautinga: A satellite city of the capital Brasília.

Tapioca: A sort of crepe or pancake made from granulated cassava root. Can be sweet or savory, with coconut, cheese or other ingredients.

Tio, Tia: Uncle, aunt.

Veranda: A covered terrace.

Yam: Large white root vegetable used to make mash or soup. Different from yam in the US, which is a sweet potato.

Zabumba: A bass drum historically made of wood and animal hides.

ACKNOWLEDGEMENTS

I owe a debt of gratitude to everyone who supported me in writing my first work of fiction.

My dear friend since the first day we met at Duke, my soul sister, Vicki Scott: thank you for reading everything I write. You will always be my Ideal Reader.

Huge thanks to my friend Cristina Lima, for the gift of *Brasil: Nunca Mais* (Brazil Never Again), the report of the commission on institutionalized torture during the dictatorship.

Thanks to my reader panel for your brilliant insights and suggestions: Annemie Tieman, Bryony Mortimer, Cassiopeia Frank, Chris Everett, Clare Marwood, John Meredith, Liz Healey, Peter Whitaker, Philip Marwood, Ruth Wilkinson and Susan O'Dell.

Thank you to my teacher, mentor and editor, Martin Ouvry, my guide to the ways of fiction. Martin provides encouragement, perfectly blended with ideas for improvement. He teaches me how to fish; he never gives me a fish.

My son Jackson de Oliveira, whose business and marketing acumen, tech and moral support help me immensely.

Jasiel de Oliveira, my husband and partner in everything: thank you for all the years of contributing more than fifty percent to our day to day, and for listening to me read the entire novel to you and helping me keep it authentic. It might all have been possible without you but no way it would have been as much fun.

My dear mother-in-law, Judite de Oliveira: Eva's life is one you never lived, but your work ethic, sense of humor, culinary skill and stories of the early days in Paraíba and Brasília were my inspiration.